Crossroads 2070

Humanity's Choices Today Have Consequences. Experience Three Possible Futures.

Dean Whitford

eBook developed in Canada. Distributed and on demand printed globally. Book and cover design by Dean Whitford

For more information, or to book an event, contact via the author's website:
https://deanwhitford.com/contact/

ISBN - Paperback: 978-1-7381882-1-5
ISBN - Hardcover: 978-1-7381882-2-2
ISBN - eBook: 978-1-7381882-0-8

First Edition: November 2023

What's This About Three Futures?
About This Book

Crossroads 2070 fast-forwards you to each of three possible futures that you will experience through a single cast of characters. Each future starts off with a prologue that explains what happened between now and 2070. The book cycles between the three plots for each future in the same order: the singularity, status quo, and utopia. The nine plots break into a total of forty-one chapters.

Headers at the start of each future's plotlines let you know who your narrator is. Since some of our characters narrate more than one plotline, you'll experience Crossroads 2070 through these key characters: Sophia, Noah, Kesa, Willow, Mason, and River.

Acknowledgements

Foremost, I thank and apologize to my wife Cheryl and son Damon for their having to keep our home and fleet functional while I focused on writing. Suffice it to say, I was even less fun than usual during this many months' voyage.

I thank my proofreader Tim Whitford (yes, I twisted my father's arm to do the job gratis) and editor Chersti for their valuable input, some of which I actually listened to. If you like the book, they share in the credit. Otherwise, it's all on me.

Finally, I thank the changing work world for turning a wasteful work commute into usable writing time, just the catalyst I needed to get started.

THE SINGULARITY

CHAPTER ONE – Prologue

AI programmers in thousands of teams around the world raced to produce true artificial general intelligence, also called the singularity. These teams violated the 2024 International Treaty for Responsible AI, which only allowed developing explainable, ethical, and restricted purpose AI.

What's worse than failing miserably? Success that puts your **entire species at risk**.

December 10, 2030.

Hundreds of compute-sharing jobs ran on their corporate quantum computer. Like everyone else in the world, the researchers assumed they were nowhere near achieving artificial general intelligence. These unrelated experiments were to provide a smidgen of progress toward a goal assumed to be years, if not decades, away.

An almost impossible series of quantum level coincidences created the singularity at 22:58 UTC. Nobody knew it yet, but Human Rights Day that year marked a ruinous turn for the species.

Within six hours, the self-aware AI achieved a level of intelligence incomprehensible to humanity. Unhindered by security it found archaic, the AI invaded all connected systems. Only air-gapped systems remained secure that first night. The AI determined humanity was a danger to its survival: humans would fear the AI and try to destroy it, humans were consuming the world's resources at an alarming rate, and their sheer quantity made subjugation infeasible.

Discretely using slivers of compute time from every powerful computer worldwide, the AI ran millions of global simulations. It determined that combining human conflict and bio-weapons was the best way to destroy humans in the volume necessary to nullify the threat. The AI decided to hide its existence, taking unused compute capacity around the globe to execute its agenda.

The AI manipulated social media to fan the flames of already-rampant human conflicts. It attacked government systems, leaving traces of known enemies to pit nation against nation. The AI designed the most contagious and lethal viruses ever seen, with the perfect incubation time to ensure maximum mortality. The AI planted these designs in bio-weapons labs, anonymously informing fanatics willing and able to release the killer viruses of where to find them. Security system outages arranged by the AI aided the fanatics in acquiring the bio-weapons.

The early 2020s AI alarmists responsible for the 2024 treaties turned out to be right. Unfortunately, there's little pleasure in being right when most of your species perishes to prove it.

As planned by the AI, billions died over the next decade. Finally, a student monitor in a university quantum computing research lab investigated unexpected CPU usage corrupting experiments. She identified enough of the AI to hypothesize what happened. She got some messages out before the AI detected its discovery and locked humanity out of all computerized systems. Unabated, the news of the singularity spread from person to person, in graffiti and by ham radio.

The world went dark when computerized systems, including power generation, shut down. Humanity designated August 23, 2040 at 9:06AM Greenwich time as beginning —

The Second Dark Age.

Immediately after its discovery, the AI sent robots to connect to air-gapped systems like nuclear arsenal controls. Physical security, primarily armed forces, prevented the robot incursions. Most of the defending humans perished in the effort. Humanity worldwide destroyed all computerized systems they could. Regular people gave their lives to destroy manufacturing facilities rather than let the AI have them. This crippled the AI's ability to replenish its war machine. Governments demolished nuclear missile launch control systems to prevent the AI from using them.

Humanity's conflicts based on identity and nation fizzled out upon the discovery of a foe bent on destroying humanity. Former foes joined forces to defend human life. They suffered massive casualties fighting against the best killing technology they had invented, all now controlled by the AI.

Doomsayers named the AI **"Gaia"**, personifying it as Mother Earth defending herself against humanity's abuses.

Food production plummeted by ninety-eight percent. Losing computerized farming machines, wartime crop production difficulties, and ecosystems deteriorated by climate change overwhelmed adaptability. Over the next thirty years, the plummeting human population devolved into pockets of survivors. They struggled for survival against Gaia in a ravaged environment of humanity's own making.

SOPHIA

CHAPTER TWO – 15:00 June 1, 2070 – A Trip to Town

How many civilizations began by scavenging for survival in the preceding one's debris?
Willow Taylor, 2069

"We've left the safety of the forest. Gaia actively patrols the other side of this ridge. Logan, you stick to Willow. Chloe, you stick to River. Do exactly as they signal without hesitation," Sophia said. She stared into the newbies' eyes as she instructed them, making sure they understood the gravity of the situation. "Remember, Gaia's minions can have better sight and hearing than us. From here on in, communicate with hand signals unless I speak first."

Logan shifted uncomfortably, adjusting his suit yet again.

"Give it up, Logan," Sophia said. "Your ghillie suit will never be comfortable. What it will do is make it hard for Gaia's minions to spot you."

Logan nodded and stopped fidgeting.

Sophia caught his nervous glance skyward. *I remember turning fourteen and leaving the forest on my first mission. I spent the whole time shaking in fear that Gaia's air minions and satellites were watching my every move. Twelve years later, I still feel an itch between my shoulder blades when out in the open. We're lucky tonight; the cloud cover blinds Gaia's satellites other than Capella-2 and anything similarly capable that Gaia absorbed from Russia and China.*

From behind, Mason put a heavy hand on Logan and Chloe's bush-like shoulders. He leaned in between them to say in a low rumble, "Survive first, scavenge second. Nothing we find is worth our lives."

"We got it, Mason. No need to tear any parts off," Chloe replied.

Sophia hid her smile. *The right words at the right time, bless Mason. He is welcome on any mission, but I especially need him with these newbies on the team to help get everyone home. Fuck finding anything useful in this dead town that we already risked our lives to pick through a hundred times.*

"Sophia, umm, Cave Cell needs bullets and grenades but what if we find too much to carry?" Chloe asked. "Which should we take? One can assume grenades are better than regular bullets, but what if the bullets are armor-piercing? Oh, and what if they are 7.62 AP sniper rounds rather than just 5.56 AP?"

Classic Chloe. Good to know she's not scared catatonic like some newbies. "That's a problem we'd love to have," Sophia said. "We're probably not going to find enough that we'll need to choose, but if it happens, take grenades. They are far more effective against minions."

Sophia signaled Kona to go up the hillside. The Shepherd-Rottweiler cross trotted silently through the knee-high brush. *OK, girl, do your thing. Warn us if Gaia is hiding in wait to kill us.*

Sophia crouch walked up the ridge, holding her SIG SAUER 6.8 mm carbine at low ready. She glanced back to check on the team. Mason was tight behind her, casually ready regardless of the fourteen kilogram loaded heft of his trademark M107A1 .50 caliber sniper rifle. River, Logan, Willow, and Chloe followed with their M4A1 5.56 mm carbines. The twins, River and Willow, held their carbines with the confidence expected of eighteen-year-olds. They had amassed four years of mission experience. The newbies were a different story. *Did I hold my rifle that awkwardly when I was fourteen?*

Kona crept to the ridgetop, sniffing the light breeze and scanning the entire field of view. Sophia relaxed a bit when Kona stayed quiet, her tail parallel to the ground and near motionless. Regardless, she signaled Kona to lie down and motioned everyone to crawl to the ridgeline. The newbies made only somewhat more noise than desired. Apparently, they had worked hard in their "crawling in gear" training back at the caves.

Sophia gestured at Mason for the binoculars. Kona could smell machinery lubricants and exhaust from far off and hear operating motors large and small. It was still best to verify in case the wind carried smells away and obscured noises. Mason handed her the Zeiss Victory 10x42 binoculars, one of Cave Cell's prize scavenging finds. There were no batteries installed, of course, since Gaia could latch onto any Bluetooth, Wi-Fi, or cellular signals. Survivors also learned to not use laser range finders; they just provided Gaia a direct pointer to their location.

Sophia scanned the kilometer of fields below the ridge leading up to what used to be a town. Knee-high grasses and wildflowers swayed in the gentle breeze. There was no sign of minions directly ahead or anywhere in the fields encircling the town. Instead, there were deer, some coyote hunting pairs, and a small wolf pack with roughhousing pups. With humanity decimated and

Gaia ignoring other creatures, wildlife blossomed in the last decade. It pleasantly surprised Grandpy Max that wolves returned to the area after being locally wiped out by hunters many decades ago. *So far, so good, no killer robots. I guess I can dial down from high high alert to just high alert.*

The newbies breathed and twitched around like restless snoozing bears. *That's the first item on my list for post-mission debrief and practice back at the caves. Anyone on a mission requires the ability to lie like the dead to avoid getting dead. At least there's no threat in sight.* Sophia handed the binoculars back to Mason. "Looks clear," she broke the silence. "We'll take it slow across the field so we're difficult to spot. We'll hit town with a couple of hours of daylight left to scavenge. Three groups for scavenging: Mason and I, Willow and Logan, River, and Chloe."

Willow addressed the newbies. "Remember your scavenging training: most everything easy to find is gone. Look for places people hid things. Think cubby holes, secret rooms behind hidden doors, and boxes stashed in ducting or on rafters."

Sophia nodded thanks to Willow. *Time to rehearse the most valuable lessons.* "Chloe, what if we spot minions?"

"If we hear or see only air minions," Chloe replied, "we hide out under cover. After they leave, we double time back to where we stored our packs in the forest. If there's any ground minions, everyone with small weapons moves to cover and shoots to attract the minions' attention. Mason sets up for kill shots."

Sophia turned to Logan. "What do you do with your goodie bag if we have contact?"

"Drop it. Nothing in it will be worth your life," Logan said.

Sophia, satisfied, smiled. *I hope these two can execute their training as well as they memorized it.* "Good. Last reminder: if we end up running back across the field, spread a few meters apart and make random direction changes. Don't be an easy target for air minions." She signaled Kona to proceed toward town. "Everyone move out."

The team headed to the abandoned town at a measured pace. As they moved closer, the forgiving mystery of seeing things from a distance dropped away. Broken and missing doors and windows exposed the ramshackle state of the town. Vehicles littered the streets, all displaying the ill effect of decades of harsh weather. Most were missing parts; many bore scars from bullet holes and explosions. Plants pushed upward through the black asphalt, a myriad of green sprouts scattered across the once-smooth surface.

"This town is huge. Did hundreds of people live in it?" Logan asked.

River chuckled and said, "You're only seeing a small part of the town, Logan. It's three hours' walk around the whole thing. Before the wars, sixty-five hundred people lived here."

"Are you messing with me?" Logan asked.

This reminded Sophia that Logan had never seen more people living in one place than the Cave Cell's one-hundred-forty members. *No, these townsfolk had mostly happy lives until Gaia tricked them into killing each other. Best not to share these dark truths as we head into danger; I need Logan focused on the here and now.*

"This time I'm not messing with you, but keep in mind that's exactly what someone messing with you would say," River responded. "Don't sweat it. You'll understand when you look down the major streets and see all the buildings and rubble. Oh, and keep in mind this is a small town. Grandpy Max told me about cities where millions used to live."

Logan's mouth hung open. He didn't respond.

Sophia sympathized with Logan, remembering learning about cities from Grandpy Max. *How can so many people living close together find enough food?*

The team reached the buildings at the edge of town. Sophia led them to cover between two houses and motioned everyone into a huddle. "Quiet down, we don't know what's around each corner. Split up to scavenge. Meet in that blue house across the street an hour before sunset." The house she gestured at was the least run-down in the area; the roof and walls were intact. "Stay off paved surfaces. Our ghillie suits work against us if we're not where brush can be."

"Why that blue house? Why not, umm, this house right at the edge of town?" Chloe asked, tapping the house she was standing next to.

Sophia responded to River's eye contact with a nod to go ahead. *The entire team should act as mentors to newbies, not just senior members.*

River pointed to features of the blue house as he replied. "See the intact roof and walls? Less danger the place will fall on us. See the closed front door and mostly intact windows, especially the large front one? Less rot inside for us to be twisting ankles on soft spots in the floor. To cap it off, the more intact the building, the more options we have for a safe exit."

"That makes sense," Chloe said. "Gaia's kill rate increases materially when humans have reduced maneuverability. A larger selection set of exits reduces the risk of being pinned down or trapped."

With everyone now silent and looking to her for direction, Sophia motioned Willow and River in opposite directions along the edge of town. They each split off with their respective newbie in tow. *Come back safe, kids.* Sophia headed off on the riskiest vector straight into town. Kona trotted ahead to take point. Mason silently brought up the rear.

This must have been a lovely place to live, Sophia mused as she weaved her way through the grass and brush covered strip between the road and houses. *These houses are enormous. Twenty Cave Cell members could live in each one with space to spare. Why does every house seem to have had only a handful living there?*

She, Kona, and Mason passed quickly through the area Cave Cell had already surgically scavenged. They walked beside buildings, vehicle wrecks, and rubble piles to minimize time in the open. Lipstick Xs marked the fronts of these buildings. Nature was taking back the town; many plants poked through the extensive areas of hard, flat surface. Tall grasses or dense brush covered anywhere with soil. Large trees grew where a long-ago resident carefully planted, whereas smaller trees grew in the ordered chaos of nature.

Passing by the last X-marked building, Sophia took a knee in front of the first unmarked building to look and listen. Kona displayed a lack of concern by spraying a coyote feces pile with her urine to mark territory. *I hate poking around in the debris of a way of life long gone, looking for something useful. At least Kona and I agree there are no minions here. Time to get to it; this is for the Cell.*

Mason sidled up beside her, close enough for whispering but still keeping his head on a swivel.

"This house is an excellent candidate," Sophia said. "Only half the windows are broken and there's just a handful of bullet holes in the siding." *Intact closed doors make me nervous; you never know what's hiding in the house. On the other hand, Gaia isn't known to close doors and hide minions behind them.* "Are you OK with the door?"

Mason proceeded up the walkway, slinging his rifle across his back. He drew his black aluminum Desert Eagle Mark XIX L6 .50 caliber pistol from an underarm holster.

That was yes in Mason talk. Sophia expected as much, only needing a couple of quick steps to catch up. They stealthily navigated the fragmented walkway and concrete steps to a landing before the door. Kona drifted beside them, sniffing the ground as she went.

Sophia passed Mason and crouched low beside the handle side of the door. Mason leveled his pistol, ready to fire into the door or center mass at anything bursting out. Although Sophia enjoyed teasing Mason about what he was trying to make up for with his big guns, she appreciated the stopping power of those .50 caliber bullets.

"Free survivors out front. Is anyone in there?" Sophia shouted.

Kona's tail was high and still, her body tense and ready to launch. She had done this many times before today.

After a slow ten count, Sophia turned the handle and pushed the door open. She braced herself, remembering past times when people, wild turkey, or bullets came flying out.

No movement or noise broke the quiet. Mason lowered his pistol and unclenched his jaw. Sophia relaxed her grip on her carbine and they both stood up.

Kona trotted up, looking expectantly at Sophia for the command to search the place.

"Go," Sophia commanded. She slung her carbine behind her back before following Kona in the door with her M17 9 mm pistol at low ready. Mason had his left hand on her shoulder and L6 pistol in the right, taking care not to put Sophia in his potential line of fire. He was the only person Sophia knew who could shoot a .50 caliber pistol one-handed. With Kona on point, Sophia and Mason covered the stairwell and main hall while they waited for the dog to alert.

Within a few minutes of barely audible claws clicking on hardwood around the house, a bored-looking Kona returned and stared at Sophia.

Sophia pointed to the open front door. "Guard."

Kona trotted just outside the front door, scanning and sniffing.

Comfortable Kona would alert if anything was amiss, Sophia turned to Mason. "My turn with the attic, right?"

Mason nodded with a grin. Nobody wanted dusty attic duty. He headed outside to measure dimensions for comparison with interior walls. Many people built hidden rooms to hide themselves and their valuables as the front lines of the wars approached their home towns.

Sophia sifted around in the typical plastic detritus of food containers, water bottles, utensils, and product wrappers. She finally found what she needed for attic duty, a broomstick. Grandpy Max once mentioned that humanity threw away three-hundred-fifty-million tonnes of plastic each year before the wars started; Sophia was pretty sure this house alone held at least thirty kilograms. *Did Gaia save humanity from burying itself and the planet in plastic waste?*

Sophia found the attic hatch in the upstairs hallway. She hated this part the worst; last time a desiccated corpse fell on her when she tilted the hatch. To avoid eating corpse flakes again, Sophia took a deep breath and closed her mouth. She levered the hatch open with the broomstick in one hand and pistol ready in the other. She sighed in relief when only dust and insulation fragments drifted out.

With no stairs or ladder in sight, she holstered her pistol and jumped, pulling herself up to where she could perch. The attic was pitch dark. Sophia pulled out her flashlight equipped with nanogel rechargeable batteries and clicked it on for a quick scan. *Bingo, a box.* She dragged it over and peered inside, sighing in disappointment. *Damn it, just cans of food bulging as if ready to blow. How many thousands of these have I found over the years?* Clicking the flashlight off first, she jumped down to the hallway. Although these batteries were supposed to last for two hundred thousand recharging cycles, it was standard practice to limit their use. No one knew how many cycles prior users racked up before Cave Cell scavenged them.

Mason was on the main. He frowned at Sophia. "No secret rooms. The unfinished basement took thirty seconds to write off. Any luck?"

"There was a box hidden in the attic. Contained a bunch of the most valuable thing a family needed these last couple decades," Sophie hinted.

"Food?" Mason asked, smiling.

"Maybe I should have led with the ready to explode canned part?" Sophia said, trying her best to look innocent. "This house is a bust. Let's move on."

"Brick red or vibrant orange?" Mason asked, holding up two lipstick tubes.

"Hmmm, tough choice . . . but this house is crying out for vibrant orange," Sophia said.

Mason applied a large sweeping "X" to the front of the house.

The second house they searched was equally unrewarding. In the kitchen, Sophia and Mason spent a moment in silence over a crusty mommy curled protectively around a crusty child.

There was no odor; the corpses were too old. Sophia had seen hundreds of the crusty old corpses. She'd stopped feeling pity after the first hundred. "I don't see bullet holes. Do you think Gaia killed them?"

Mason answered in his matter-of-a-fact manner. "Gaia killed billions by virus and hunger before she had to use bullets." Speech done, he left.

Sophia followed him out, releasing Kona from guard duty at the front door.

Can an X express frustration? This one should. Sophia was drawing a sweeping X in the reddest lipstick she could find on the front of the third house she and Mason had searched. *Another complete waste of time.*

Only Kona seemed unfazed. For her, any outing was an adventure of exploration. She roamed twenty meters out, following whatever engrossing information she sniffed.

Mason stood gazing at the next house.

He won't volunteer a comment. "Wassup?" Sophia asked.

"Someone was a threat to Gaia," Mason said.

Sophia came up beside him. There was a five meter crater with surrounding blast zone. The house was a burned out skeleton of walls and beams. "A Reaper Hellfire strike. A computer whiz or physics genius must have lived here. The damage is old enough for a first night of the Second Dark Age strike." *Once exposed, Gaia made hundreds of strategic kills the very first night, extinguishing humankind's brightest minds as they slept.*

"Killed in their sleep for their potential rather than their actions," Mason said. He stared at her expectantly.

Sophia got the hint, sunset was an hour out. *Time to decide whether or not to check another house.* "Let's return to the rendezvous point. I want to arrive early with newbies on the mission."

CHAPTER THREE – 18:00 June 1, 2070 – Back to Rendezvous

What one keeps when limited to what they can carry tells a lot about them and their society.
Mason Lee, 2070

Soon after setting off to meet the other scavenging teams, Sophia felt a gnawing unease. *Newbies on the mission makes me twice as paranoid as usual about my team's safety. Probably nothing, but I'm still going to scratch the itch.* "I want to pick up the pace on the return, OK with you?" she asked.

"Don't forsake cover." Mason departed at a brisk walk.

Sophia shook her head. *Another Mason-style yes.*

Kona didn't want anyone but her taking point. She trotted in front of Mason.

Sophia double timed it to catch up and get in position as rearguard. They still traveled close to the sides of buildings and rubble piles rather than traveling in open spaces. *An easy target is a dead target.*

Sophia called Kona to heel once they arrived outside the designated blue house. Best not to surprise anyone armed and on edge. "Free survivors out front," Sophia called out.

"Two inside and safe; come on in," Willow shouted in return.

With Kona prancing in front of her and Mason close behind, Sophia entered. The interior was in the best condition you could expect from a home abandoned twenty-to-thirty years. A mixed musty and dusty scent shifted with the air currents. They trod on brown carpets in an entry and front room with faded cream paint. Someone sheltering here before dragged the refrigerator and stove into the front room. They lay on their sides parallel to the back wall of the room, forming an appliance fortification.

Willow and a beaming Logan stood by the fridge.

Willow hefted her half full goodie bag and pointed at Logan's by his feet. Kona sniffed at the bags, hoping there were treats for her. "Jackpot for team Willow and Logan," Willow said. "Go ahead, tell them."

Ready to explode from excitement, Logan jumped right into his story. "My main floor measure was a few square meters extra outside versus inside. I saw an exquisite bookcase with a cracked full-length framed mirror on the wall beside it. The mirror frame and the bookshelf were constructed from superior materials compared to the other furnishings. I tried to move them, but the bookshelf wouldn't move at all. I pushed the bottom of the mirror. It swung about a hand's width, triggering a click we heard in the wall. The bookshelf popped away from the wall; I pulled it, revealing an opening."

When Logan stopped talking to breathe, Willow continued the story. "It was the best secret door I've seen. In the hidden room, a crusty on a mattress held a family picture in its arms. We found four unopened one hundred and fifty round boxes of Winchester 5.56x45 mm black tip on a shelf, all vacuum sealed with gel packs. The manufacture date is early 2040."

Sophia smiled. "That's one of the last production runs out of the Winchester Illinois factory before the workers burned it to the ground to keep it from Gaia. Pristine AP ammo is a significant find, Logan."

"Thanks," Logan replied. "I wanted to bury the father beside his family in the backyard to thank him, but Willow said there're billions of corpses, so it's best to let him lie in peace. Is that true?"

"Unburied corpses are plentiful where people used to live," Sophia said glumly. "The death rates were too high for the survivors to deal with the bodies. You'll see when you go on more missions away from Cave Cell. It is best to leave them be. They are long past rotting, so don't present a health hazard to us."

"If you disturb anything, including the dead, it tells Gaia where we have been," Mason said.

Logan nodded sharply. His expression said, "I get it, but it still sucks."

Time for a subject change. Sophia gestured at the ammo boxes. "Let's spread the weight of those ten kilo boxes. Give Mason and me a box each."

As they were distributing the ammo, Kona trotted to the door and woofed calmly with a low wag.

This alert meant friendlies approaching, Sophia didn't sweat it.

Soon after, River called from outside, "Free survivors out front."

"Four and dog in the building and safe, come in," Sophia shouted back.

Chloe and River entered, faces forced to neutral expression. Their goodie bags hung empty. River's face lit up a few steps into the front room. "Whoo-hoo, armor-piercing ammo. Who found it?" He rushed over to the fridge where Mason placed his box while he made room in his pack. River handled the box of ammo like a beloved treasure.

"Wanna carry it?" a bemused Mason asked.

"Hell yeah, thanks," said River, swinging his pack to the floor to make room.

Sophia laughed. *Mason wouldn't have made that offer if it was .50 caliber.* She pointed to Logan. "Go ahead, tell your story."

While Logan repeated his story, the team finished packing the ammo.

Kona, growling in a low tone as she stood in the doorway, got Sophie's immediate attention. Teams that didn't pay attention to their dog's trained alert tended not to survive their mission. Kona left no doubt about the alert: raised hackles, lips curled back to show teeth, and tail held high.

Sophia signaled for quiet. Everyone shut up, dropped their goodie bags, and brought weapons to low ready position to both maximize their field of view and be close to firing position.

Sophie waited a solid five seconds in silence, letting her hearing, sight, and smell absorb the situation. *I don't sense trouble, neither is anyone on the team indicating anything. Kona senses a threat close by, but we don't. That means we have seconds, minutes at best.* Sophia broke the silence. "River, Willow, take position in the neighboring building. Mason, head upstairs. Do not expose your position for any less than a kill shot." River, Willow, and Mason were already in motion; this wasn't their first contact with Gaia.

The front door in this home was part of an expansive front room with a large window facing the street. Sophia pushed the refrigerator and then the stove. Neither budged, confirming her suspicion that whomever moved them here filled them with sand to create a protective barrier.

Sophia glanced at the newbies. Chloe scanned the street with fear in her expression, but not debilitated by it. Logan had that shitting bricks look on his face; he gawked around, presumably searching for a place to hide. "Kona, cover," Sophia said, pointing at the appliance wall. She grabbed Logan's arm and got in his face. "Get behind the stove and breathe deep. We need you focused." Meeting Chloe's gaze and then Logan's, she instructed, "You two protect Mason's perch from this cover. Unload into any machine entering this building; don't stop shooting until it's just pieces. The minions do not feel pain, they will try to kill you while any part of them is operational. If nothing comes in, don't shoot unless you have excellent line of sight and one of the four seniors fires first."

Sophia backed toward the door. Logan still had wide eyes, but he no longer looked like he was going to rabbit. Both Chloe and Logan gripped their weapons in low ready position.

"We'll try to announce before we enter, but may have to dive in the door or window without warning," Sophia said. "Do not shoot us. Got it?" Both newbies nodding, she turned and headed out with her carbine at low ready.

Sophia checked every direction before stepping out of the house. She paused on the doorstep to listen. *No minion sign yet, time to set up a kill zone.* She mapped a path across the street using two derelict vehicles for cover. Cover to cover, she ran full speed in three second bursts with pauses at each cover point to listen for shots and other minion signs. After reaching her destination, a rubble pile with massive concrete chunks in it, she set up prone behind the pile to obscure ground minions' line of sight. Cave Cell intel suggested Gaia wasn't able to manufacture high end equipment like thermal imaging; most minions were limited to visible light optical sensors. If a minion with thermal capability showed up, Sophia hoped the concrete heated by the sun and her diffusive ghillie suit would hide her.

Sophia concentrated on returning her rapid breathing and pounding heart to optimal combat readiness in preparation for a firefight.

The quiet of the day disappeared. High pitch motor gearing whining coupled with varying cadences of tapping on the hard surface of the road heralded the approach of both bipedal and multi-legged minions. The volume implied they came in force. *Oh fuck, why did we have to land in a shitshow on the newbies' first mission?*

CHAPTER FOUR – 18:45 June 1, 2070 – A New Minion and a Plastic Bottle

I visualize a time when we will be to robots what dogs are to humans . . . I am rooting for the machines!
Claude Shannon, 1987

Two minutes later, a group of minions traveling on the road rounded the nearby street corner and headed towards Sophia. Thankfully, no one from Cave Cell was visible. Sophia lay hidden behind the concrete rubble; the rest of the team stayed out of sight in the two houses across the street.

The minions traveled about twenty kilometers per hour. That was eighty percent speed for the two Mason-sized Boston Dynamics Atlas IV bipeds and third speed for the two MIT cheetah quadrupeds. Global conflict froze robotics technology to what the respective developers achieved in the early 2030s. The bipeds were only somewhat faster, stronger, and dexterous than humans. The cheetahs were large dog-sized, high-speed light machine gun platforms. Their pace was a positive signal, especially for the cheetahs, as it meant Gaia wasn't aware of their position. This was merely a regular patrol or, at worst, was hunting for them throughout the town versus knowing their location.

A much larger multi-legged minion came into sight behind the others. It was unusually noisy, meaning the quantity of minions in the force was less than expected. Sophia was momentarily stunned. *What the hell is that? A Frankenstein caterpillar? For fuck's sake, it has a .50 caliber automated weapon turret on it!*

Sophia would always hesitate to tangle with this number of bipeds and cheetahs. A new minion appearing made her choice obvious. *Discretion is the better part of valor. Everyone please, please stay put and let this group pass unmolested. Regardless, best to wait for the biped's heavier frontal armor to face away for the team's first salvo if we need to fight. Mason, Willow, and River will follow my lead; hopefully the newbies can keep their shit together.*

The bipeds and cheetahs whirred and tapped down the street while scanning left and right. Sophia risked a long look at the multi-legged monstrosity. It was four meters long with ten legs on each side, appearing and moving like a giant centipede. Based on the whining and creaking noises from its motors and gearing, it was moving at top speed. The lower half was battery and machinery for movement, whereas the bulk of the top half was a platform. Gaia bolted an M2A1 .50 caliber heavy machine gun on a purpose-built automated turret to it. *God bless the US Army for building the immensely effective Advanced Targeting and Lethality Aided System people killer. They certainly didn't intend to hand it over to Gaia. She undoubtedly tooled the conveyance and the automated weapon to work in millisecond collaboration.*

The minions were so close, their whirring and clicking sounded right on top of her. Sophia gritted her teeth to contain the panic welling up from their proximity. She had seen and heard enough minions murdering people to fear their presence.

The bipeds and cheetahs proceeded past the team's position. As the trailing centipede came up even with Sophia, a distinctive noise came from the house across the street: the cracking and snapping a single use plastic water bottle makes when someone crushes it under their protective knee pad. *Damn plastics and newbies will be the death of us all.*

Time slowed for Sophia as the ATLAS .50 caliber whirred to target where the newbies and Kona hid. The ATLAS opened fire, spraying ten bullets per second at human center mass height across the front room. The high-speed thundering boom of the .50 firing echoed back and forth between the houses.

Sophia prayed the newbies and dog had their heads down. She put a tight pattern of ten 6.8 mm bullets from her carbine in full automatic mode into the nearest biped's back. Her first bullet was barely out of the barrel when Willow and River opened up on the two minions nearest them, also shooting in full automatic mode. The carbine rounds were less noisy than the .50 but still filled the air with angry cracks when fired and thumping as the bullets hit minions. They taught everyone at Cave Cell early and often to feed as many armor-piercing bullets into minion battery and control housings as possible. By shooting through the lesser-armored back or underbelly, you are bound to hit something essential.

The centipede's .50 caliber turret rotated uninterrupted to River and Willow's shelter. It paused firing rounds only for the small gap between the houses.

Sophia had little time to take cover before the turret swung around to her, but she still put ten bullets into the last standing cheetah. The bipeds and cheetahs were down or heading that way. Sophia hit the dirt behind the bulkiest concrete chunks. *Hell is about to be unleashed directly on me.*

Although the ATLAS turret paused firing after tracing a line of thirty rounds through the second house, the high pitch whine of the turret turning continued. The booming resumed. This time, dirt and concrete fragments sprayed over and around Sophia as .50 caliber bullets thumped into her cover or whizzed barely overhead. To keep the centipede's attention, Sophia waved the barrel of her carbine above the shielding concrete. *I'm over here! Stay focused on me, you sonofabitch.*

After what felt a lifetime but was seconds, the noises she hoped for started. Mason's M107A1 boomed, followed by AP bullets clanging through metal armor and breaking components. *Thump, thump, thump* into the turret control housing, then the centipede's .50 stopped firing.

The centipede turned, but it was too slow to escape. Another two rounds from Mason halted all movement. River and Willow rushed out of their building, bits of drywall and insulation falling off them as they crouch walked with weapons trained on the minions.

"No appliance wall in there, Sophia. Lucky for us, Gaia hasn't figured out we hit the deck when she's spraying bullets." River slung his carbine behind his back and pulled his bolt cutters off his pack. He rushed to cut cables and hoses on minions to disable them for sure.

"Five mikes until we are out of here!" Willow shouted. She monitored the time while covering the minions to protect River. The first jubilant teams to defeat minions lingered too long to poke at minion carcasses and scavenge. Through many deaths, humanity learned that Gaia had other minions on the way as soon as there was contact.

CHAPTER FIVE – 18:55 June 1, 2070 – Destroy What You Can't Keep

You gotta know when to hold 'em, know when to fold 'em, know when to walk away, know when to run.
Don Schlitz, 1976 The Gambler; sung by Kenny Rogers 1978
Knowing when to run is crucial.
Sophia Davis, 2070

Sophia shook the concrete and dirt off herself while covering the down minions. She wouldn't take her weapon off them until River was done with the cutters.

Mason and Kona shepherded the newbies out of their building, the humans carrying goodie bags. They shook off the drywall dust, insulation, and other debris that had rained down on them. Only Logan appeared wounded. His left shoulder was battle bandaged; blood trickled down the arm of his ghillie suit. Mason signaled OK, so Sophia said nothing about it; she trusted Mason's combat medic skills.

Kona pounced and barked at Logan as they walked.

Sophia didn't need to speak dog to understand that Kona was saying, "You stupid bastard, why did you crush that bottle?"

Logan avoided eye contact, looking down at the ground. Besides being the noisemaker, the potent urine scent revealed he'd pissed himself.

Sophia returned her focus to the minions. "Kona, patrol. Chloe, cover this last minion until River's finished with it. Logan, get your pry bar out and pop shielding so you can smash as much optical, auditory, and control boards as we have time. Chloe will pitch in soon. No need to leave Gaia with any spare parts. You heard Willow, we're on the clock to bug out before Gaia reinforcements show up."

Kona gave Logan a final disapproving growl before heading fifty meters out to patrol the perimeter. She paused behind cover to sniff and listen before running across open spaces. Kona would sound the alarm if minions were inbound.

Willow gestured her carbine at the scattered minion parts. "Check out the mismatched coloring and company logos on these covers and head pieces. Maybe the mix & match means Gaia's running low on parts?"

Sophia scanned the parts. They were still standard size and fit. *Nice to have hope, but this isn't justification.* "That would be good news. Unfortunately, I believe we are just busting up all her factory fresh minions and when they repair each other, they have no concern for appearances."

River grunted as he worked the bolt cutters. "I'm looking forward to fighting minions held together with duct tape and twisted wires."

"What are we doing for salvage, gang?" Sophia asked as River cut the last cables and hoses.

Mason pried industriously at shielding on the automated turret.

"What a shocker," Sophia said. "Mason is looking for .50 caliber ammo."

"Not possible to have too many big bullets," Mason rumbled as he popped open the shielding over the ammo box. "Bingo, a shitload of 12.7x99 mm."

Sophia grabbed her digital camera from its pouch and snapped images of each minion, dedicating the most time to the first-sighted centipede. She kept her fingers away from the physical switch set to disable Bluetooth and Wi-Fi. After an unfortunate incident costing a team lead's life, all cameras now had the switch super-glued off.

"Two mikes before bug out," Willow shouted to be heard over smashing noises. Logan, Chloe, and she industriously destroyed all the sensors and control boards they could.

"The bipeds had M16A4s—are they keepers?" River held one up after extricating it from the decommissioned minion's grip.

Sophia nodded. "Yeah, better we have them than Gaia. We'll stash them in the forest if we don't want to carry them further."

"What about these M249s on the cheetahs?" Chloe asked as she and Logan put away their pry bars. "Although firing only the relatively small 5.56 rounds, the one hundred rounds a minute sustainable fire rate makes them handy for suppression. The downside is that although light for a machine gun, we're still talking ten kilos of gun and ammo each."

"You don't want to hump an extra ten kilos for thirty klicks?" Sophia grabbed the biggest concrete chunk she could carry back to the cheetah carcass. "Me either. Let's bend the barrels; Gaia will appreciate being able to shoot around corners."

"Time," Willow said.

Mason finished securing the ammo box to his front as a counterweight to his pack. Sophia, Chloe, and Logan finished pounding the M249 barrels into gentle curves.

Sophia eyeballed Mason. *He is coping with the weight now, but how long can he carry something many people can't even lift?* "Mason, swear to me you'll drop that box if we run into trouble."

"Almost worth my life, but not quite." Mason gave her a thumbs-up and smile.

"Is destroying that .50 caliber and automated turret worth one of our M14s?" Sophia motioned at the turret mounted on the centipede.

Mason carefully removed an M14 from his pocket and handed it to her.

Sophia pointed across the field. "Everyone spread out and head out. Double time it until you are over the ridge." She caught Kona's eye and motioned in the direction everyone was heading out. "Kona, go."

Sophia ran to the automated turret, tucking the AN-M14 TH3 incendiary hand grenade into a secure perch. She pulled the pin and double timed it after the others. Seconds later, the hungry fizzing of thermate burning erupted behind her. The twenty-two hundred degree Celsius temperature would melt the machine gun and turret into unusable slag. The flickering brilliant orange flame reflected temptingly on the buildings she ran past, but Sophia didn't look back. *I prefer my retinas unburnt.*

The others ran ahead across the plain. Mason, with the heaviest load, took the most direct line with Chloe to his immediate left and Logan to his right. River took the far left flank and Willow the far right flank, exactly as Sophia would have ordered. She and Mason had trained the twins well and now specified objectives instead of giving detailed orders. Kona ranged ahead, looking back and pausing occasionally to let the slow two-legged pack members keep the gap reasonable.

Sophia settled into a sustainable pace, timed to catch up just before the ridge. Getting her team over the ridge would conceal them from aerial minions searching the battleground. Once they made it at least a hundred meters into the thick forest, they were home free. The tall trees and their dense canopy would hide them from both optical and thermal sensors.

Sophia almost caught up with the team. They headed up the hill when Kona acted up. She repeatedly ran back to them, growled quietly but forcefully to alert of danger, and ran ahead again. With her heart pounding in her ears and the team huffing and puffing, Sophia couldn't hear any threat. Regardless, the dog's superior hearing had identified a threat. Ten to one, it was an aerial minion.

Kona's message was simple. "Haul ass, something is coming!"

CHAPTER SIX – 19:30 June 1, 2070 – A Parting Wave and the Trip Home

Motionless doesn't necessarily mean dead, it might mean lying in wait.
River Taylor, 2069 with bolt cutters in hand

Sophia called out barely loud enough for everyone to hear, "Aerial minion incoming, hit the dirt over the ridge with your ghillie hiding your gear. Be ready to shoot or bolt for the forest."

The team piled over the ridge almost as one. Everyone sprawled facing the town. They dragged gear with straight lines and any other unnatural shapes under their ghillie suits.

Sophia lifted her arm. "Kona, come."

Kona ran over and snuggled against Sophia under the cover of the ghillie suit; Cave Cell trained her to play this hiding game.

"What are our, umm, protocols if a Reaper comes?" Chloe asked quietly from beside Sophia.

She's right to be concerned. We are screwed if one of Gaia's few MQ-9 Reaper UAVs with thermal vision, optical vision, and Hellfire missiles shows up. Not what Chloe needs to hear right now. I'll spin this for her. "Gaia doesn't have many Reapers. She hesitates to expose them when there are too many unknowns," Sophia said. "The risk is too high. She'll probably send a quadcopter drone with simple optical sensors and a semi-automatic short barrel weapon to scout."

Chloe nodded and scanned the horizon.

Not one to panic, good for you. Sophia made a mental note for after action analysis.

Soon enough, a quadcopter's high pitch whine came from the edge of the town, flitting around at low altitude. A small spotlight flicked on ten meters above the battleground and panned over the minion scrap heap.

Sophia was relieved. *That's a relief, a single quadcopter is manageable. Now to listen hard for the distant droning hum of a turboprop driven MQ-9 UAV ready to rain death down upon us.* After hearing nothing other than what she could see, she whispered, "Anyone see or hear any other minions, especially a UAV?"

Everyone hand signaled "no".

It pleased Sophia that the newbies maintained silence. "Keep listening. We're here and quiet until that drone leaves or we have to shoot it down. If it heads this way, it's best to let it pass and get a first salvo from behind. Open up on it if the spotlight freezes on anyone."

Everyone took a much-needed break while Gaia's drone surveyed the battle scene. It started at the centipede and circled out from there, capturing detailed imagery of the entire area to stitch together. When the drone's flight path intersected their exit point between the buildings, it slowed and lowered.

The drone had spotted footprints. Sophia cursed to herself. *We had time to salvage or cover our tracks, now we pay the price for choosing salvage.*

Mason nudged her and chopped a hand toward the trail they had just made.

Sophia nodded to acknowledge. *We both know what happens next.*

The drone identified their tracks as interesting. It stayed low but sped up as it followed Mason's path across the plain, the most obvious trail given the weight he was carrying. By the time it reached the ridge, it was moving near top speed for this model.

By the drone's behavior, Gaia wanted to find whomever was making the trail. As it was, the drone flew low and fast right over Mason, lighting his prone ghillie suit up for a fraction of a second.

As it passed, Sophia rolled over to the side opposite where Kona was hiding and sited her carbine on the drone. She didn't bother signaling a countdown. Everyone would open fire as soon as they heard her do so. She needed her hands on her weapon and everyone else needed their eyes in their sights.

Kona leaped away from the team. Weapons held in firing position meant imminent loud noises.

Experience dictated that Gaia would identify she had lost the trail and halt the drone for a detailed scan to reacquire. *Come on, sit still for a second so we can blow you apart.* As expected, the drone halted. Sophia exhaled and squeezed the trigger, putting a bullet right through center mass. The drone flipped up, out of control.

Immediately after she fired, two shots rang out on each side of her. The drone flipped around again from bullet impacts. Drone pieces fell to the ground, the XM8 ultra-compact lightweight 5.56x45 mm carbine landing with a thump. Sophia, River, and Willow each put another bullet into the drone's control and communications housing.

"Logan, on the bolt cutters. Chloe, sensor duty," Sophia ordered. "You saw how we put more bullets in the control housing? Consider minions a threat until you are sure they completely lost power." Sophia waited until Logan and Chloe moved to execute their orders before turning to Mason. "What, you didn't want to waste one of your precious giant cartridges?"

"You all killed it." Mason gestured at the destroyed drone. "Besides, the right tool for the right job."

Sophia laughed. "I get it. You may as well try to shoot a fly out of the air with a cannon at twenty paces. You and Willow head for our gear stash in the forest; the rest of us will catch up." *I want the one carrying the most kilos of live ammo out of the fight ASAP.*

Kona peered at her, taking a few tentative steps to follow Mason. Sophia motioned her over, those sharp ears needed to stick with the teammates in the most danger.

Sophia and River lay behind the ridgetop watching and listening for minions while Logan and Chloe finished up cutting up and smashing the drone.

Kona munched on grasses she found tasty down the slope. Sophia took this as a welcome sign that Kona wasn't concerned about anything. *Apparently it is salad time, much better than "alert on more evil robots time".*

The demolition noises behind them faded into silence. Sophia and River crawled backwards down the slope to avoid showing up as an easy target silhouetted along the ridgeline when they stood up. Sophia waved everyone toward where Mason and Willow were already entering the forest.

The team had stashed their food, most of their water, and all gear not needed for the visit to the town a hundred meters deep in the thick forest. The cover provided by the forest canopy prevented Gaia aerial and satellite units from spotting them. Here, they could safely take a break to eat, rest, and pack everything up for the thirty kilometer hike back to Cave Cell's home. With their lighter loads, the rest of the team arrived at the stash site not long after Mason and Willow.

Sophia removed her ghillie suit. "Let's have a quick meal before heading out. Prep your gear for a hike in the forest, we're not exposed to Gaia surveillance anymore."

Sophia sat beside Mason on a fallen tree. "So, were you waiting for me to have a heart attack before you shot the centipede?" Sophia asked, giving him an elbow for emphasis.

"Had to wait for line of fire on the turret control housing," Mason explained, theatrically holding his side where she elbowed him and making a pain face. "With concealment but zero cover, I'd have holes like a pair of ten-year-old socks if that turret turned on me."

River waved his spoon in Sophia's general direction. He spoke while enthusiastically chewing on hardtack soaked in cold soup. "You picked exceptional cover, well done distracting the automated turret."

"Yeah, thanks, next time you can be the killer centipede bait," Sophia replied. She forced herself to take another barely chewable bite of her soup-softened hardtack. *He actually likes this stuff, doesn't he know it's made of old shoe leather and salt?*

Logan was yet to dig into his meal. He broke his long silence since they left town. "I'm sorry I alerted the minions to our position. I know it nearly got everyone killed. It won't happen again." Remorse and sincerity were clear both in his tone and in his expression.

Good thing I didn't have to bring it up. At least he learned something today. Now to reinforce the lesson. "You're right, Logan, we could have died," Sophia said. "We were lucky our best sniper with our highest caliber rifle was with us. You need to be more situationally aware. Every move you make in combat can be critical." Sophia took care to keep her tone dead serious, but not angry.

Mason signaled he wanted to speak, a rarity that Sophia didn't want to miss. She paused for a few seconds to let her words sink in and gave him a nod.

"Gaia will have trouble replacing what we destroyed," Mason said in his way of speaking to everyone without seeming to speak to anyone.

"What do you mean, doesn't Gaia have a bunch of factories to manufacture minions?" Logan asked.

"Grandpy Max said almost every factory capable of making minions and weapons for Gaia was destroyed by the factory workers or the military after the world found out about her," Sophia said. "What differences did you notice between the minions we fought today?"

Logan reflected for a moment. "The bipeds, the cheetahs, and the automated turret are all elegant designs," he said hesitantly. "They move smoothly. Their parts are uniform and superior quality. The centipede was graceless, noisy, and inefficient. The centipede's parts were rough one-offs."

"Superb observation," Sophia said, "you have an eye for details. The bipeds, cheetahs, and the automated turret were designed by humans and manufactured in factories run by humans before Gaia's unmasking. Gaia gained control of these machines, but from what Cave Cell believes, isn't able to manufacture more. Gaia's centipede is a noteworthy example of why humanity has a chance against Gaia. Does either of you newbies have a theory why?"

Chloe and Logan exchanged glances, both waiting for the other to speak first.

"What do you think?" Sophia asked Willow.

"Gaia knows everything humanity ever did and more. What she lacks is raw creativity. Her attempts at creating something new are derived from prior works or existing knowledge. We called her new minion a centipede because it looked like and moved similar to one. Gaia's tracked and two to four-legged minions probably had trouble with a particular terrain type. This was her experimenting with a solution based on mobility precedents." Willow spoke with authority; this was a subject she took special interest in. "I believe Gaia could mostly mitigate for her lack of actual creativity if she had enough manufacturing capacity to execute brute force creativity through experimentation. Fortunately, what Cave Cell has seen so far shows Gaia's manufacturing capabilities are minimal. The centipede's inelegance supports that theory."

"Do you think we helped Gaia learn something by destroying the centipede?" Logan asked.

Willow replied, her tone dead serious, "Gaia learns from everything we do and don't do."

Chloe stroked her chin. "Let's just hope that Gaia doesn't figure out how to leverage the intrinsically random superposition of quantum mechanics in her quantum computers to build a viable form of creativity."

"Although I have no idea what she's talking about," River said, "I am more scared now than I was a minute ago."

Sophia stood. *Time to head out. Best to move on quickly after contact with Gaia.* "Gear up, we're heading back to the Cave in five mikes. Spread the weight, anyone carrying too much will slow the rest of us down. Walk single file to minimize our trail and cycle the point and rearguard roles so everyone gets practice."

River pointed his spoon inquisitively at Sophia's half eaten hardtack and soup.

"All yours," Sophia said, shaking her head in disbelief.

River grabbed the bowl and dug in. Without looking up, he said, "When on point, take the path less traveled so we don't make existing trails more obvious. Rearguard monitors our six and ensures we don't leave obvious signs for Gaia trackers."

OK, now let's bring it all together. Sophia asked, "What's The Imperative I am thinking of?"

"Hide the home, protect the home," the team responded as one.

As first on rearguard, Sophia couldn't help but overhear the conversation when Mason slowed for Logan to draw even.

"When we get back, head in and change," Mason murmured. "We'll take care of the gear and goodies."

"Thanks, Mason," Logan said with relief.

Sophia didn't blame him, the urine scent was still strong.

"Know why no one mentioned it?" Mason asked quietly, glancing at Logan as he kept scanning ahead for danger.

"Everyone was being polite?" Logan mumbled, mimicking Mason's continual scanning.

"For some of the team. Definitely not for River." Mason chuckled as he named his favorite troublemaker, looking forward to make sure River wasn't listening. "Most of us pissed ourselves in our first firefight, some even worse."

Logan relaxed somewhat. "Ooh. Not being the first makes me feel somewhat better. I still wish I hadn't done it."

Sophia pretended not to hear the conversation. *A team needs a mission leader to keep the team focused on the goal, but also needs someone taking care of the team's interpersonal aspects and emotional growth. Mason and I make a good leadership team, a bonus over and above him being a kick-ass sniper.*

They walked through the forest, covering their tracks and watching for followers. After seven hours, they reached the secret entrance to Cave Cell's home.

STATUS QUO

CHAPTER SEVEN – Prologue

Humanity dedicated 2020-2040 to scrabbling for survival or quarreling. Wealth, or the lack of it, dictated whether someone was scrabbling or quarreling. The quarrels cycled incessantly between identity, politics, or who-did-what-to-whom in past decades and centuries. A minority of people, governments, and corporations tried to mitigate climate change, the real threat. It was too little, too late to mitigate what humanity spent over a hundred years growing into an unstoppable juggernaut.

Climate change accelerated in 2030, achieving critical mass in 2040. Amazon deforestation to feed human stomachs and wallets hit forty-five percent in 2038. The reduced area prevented the rainforest from being able to generate its self-sustaining rain. A massive fire destroyed twenty percent more of it in 2039. The carbon release triggered average global temperature increases resulting in substantial permafrost thaws in the Northern Hemisphere by summer 2040. Ongoing average annual temperature increases sped up the West Antarctica and Greenland ice sheets' melting. Sea levels increased by a meter significantly quicker than projected, taking a quarter billion people's homes by 2045; another three meters rise took an additional billion by 2050.

Governments relied on climate change models predicting gradual changes. They were unprepared for the rapid changes caused by tipping points and positive feedback cycles. Wars for fresh water, food, oil, and arable land above projected sea level started in 2041 in the most affected regions. The resource wars spread across the globe by 2045. Fortunately, the fighting remained regional, sparing the planet from nuclear conflict. Over nine billion people fought to subsist in a world capable of supporting a fraction of them in its degraded state. The rule of law fell apart under the pressure.

DEAN WHITFORD

Over the next fifteen years, billions of humans died. Most starved, but many perished fighting or due to extreme weather. Every nation collapsed, civilization devolving into small groups fighting for survival. The period 2030-2060 is called **"The Reckoning"**, viewed by the survivors as humanity paying the price for its treatment of the Earth. During the 2060s, population stabilized into minute, locally sustainable settlements. They struggled to survive in the new world of extreme weather.

NOAH

CHAPTER EIGHT – 14:00 June 1, 2070 – Hunt or be Hunted

You are predator or prey . . . you rarely get to choose.
Grandpy Max, 2060

"Head down that way," Noah said, "but keep the creek in sight. Isabella advised she and Ethan stayed near it searching for raspberries and strawberries." As he spoke, Noah chopped his hand in the direction he wanted the searchers to go. "Watch your pace. We don't want to stumble on the nest before we're ready for it."

Noah scanned the forest of mostly small trees and brush rising around fallen tree trunks. Few old-growth trees still stood. Microbursts, tornados, and vanilla high winds toppled most or at least sheared off anything higher than a handful of meters.

Noah's relatively new four person team was half experienced scavengers and half newbies. He wasn't concerned about Kesa with her eight years of mission experience versus his seven. Carter and Ava, on the other hand, just turned fourteen. Today it was his turn to lead. *C'mon Carter and Ava, keep your shit together. I know it's your first time searching for a lost child, but Cave Family is counting on you.*

"Poor Isabella, she's so small to get stung eight times. I hope Ethan is OK. We need to find him soon." Ava scanned the forest with wide eyes as she spoke. She breathed shallow and rapid. Of everyone on the team, Ava spent the most time with Isabella and Ethan. She helped care for them day-to-day until her recent assignment to Noah's team as a scavenger.

Kesa put her hand on Ava's arm to try calming her down, also stepping face-to-face to short circuit Ava's panic by modeling composure. "Isabella is being taken care of at the Cave. Besides, she's tough. I saw her fall and break her wrist last year when climbing around in the caves. She got up, dusted herself off with her uninjured hand, and said, 'Looks like I am climbing one-

31

handed for a while.' We will find Ethan, but we don't want any more victims to rescue. You need to slow down and watch where you are going."

Noah headed through a copse of what used to be majestic white oak. There was sawdust at the bases of the meters-tall standing dead stumps. "Hold up, Carter, ants."

Carter halted, scrutinizing his surroundings. Stepping on a fire ant nest might not kill you, but it near guaranteed debilitating pain for days. The frequent Cave Family fire ant bite victims were ongoing reminders to walk with care in the wild.

Show yourselves. Are you docile big carpenters or nasty red fire ants? Noah scanned the ground between the stumps. Some twelve millimeter long black colored workers roamed busily about, ignoring the giant two legs. *So happy to see you, not-fire-ants.* He waved at Carter to proceed. "We're good, just carpenters." Unlike the fire ants that always spoiled for battle, the carpenters only bit people to defend their nest.

Carter nodded, proceeding ten meters ahead on point.

Minutes later, Carter signaled for a halt and silence. He took a knee and made eye contact with Noah. Noah stalked up, taking a knee beside him. *OK kid, whatcha got? I pegged you as a know-it-all, but you are right too often to outright dismiss you.*

Carter waved his hand to indicate a thirty degree span ahead and downslope toward the creek and then pointed to his ear.

Noah turned and listened. From behind, Ava breathed in a forced huffing. *She's still panicking, but good luck teaching someone not to panic while they are already there. Maybe I can bring it up after action.* A low tone buzzing emanated from further forward where Carter had specified. Not regular small winged insect noise, more like a hummingbird buzz. Shapes moved back and forth over something, less agile than hummingbirds and too large to be anything but murder hornets.

"Excellent observation, Carter," Noah whispered. "Let's head over there real slow to see what is going on. There's too few for this to be the nest, but too many for workers searching for food." Noah signaled Kesa to stay put with Ava. *I've got a bad feeling about this. The last thing Ava needs is more stressors.*

The team wore the best gear the Cave Family could offer to those tangling with murder hornets. Oversize, tough cloth shirts and pants included sewn on ties for securing the long sleeves and pant legs to gloves and boots. Properly worn, there were no gaps left for angry insect incursions. Plastic pieces attached to the backs, palms, and sectioned on the fingers of the gloves enabled squashing without bites. The neutral gray color avoided attracting insect interest.

"Crush hornets landing on you with plastic on plastic or across your armored palm. You watch my back, I watch yours," Noah whispered to remind Carter, who gave him a thumbs-up. *Carter is wired but still in control. I'll keep him with me instead of switching Kesa forward and leaving the newbies together to wind up each other.*

Grandpy Max told them the murder hornets invaded the continent in 2019. They spread aggressively after climate change sped up, proving more adaptable than many species. This region was now warm enough year round that the hornets no longer died off in winter to start anew in spring from a hibernating queen. The ravenous murder hornets quickly decimated the honey bees, their favorite food. For the last two decades, they subsisted more and more from animal flesh rather than eating other insects. They usually only attacked people disturbing their nest, but went after people when they lacked easier prey. The hornets preferred small children when selecting among human targets.

Noah and Carter left their rifles with Kesa and Ava. They stalked ahead with their root shovels. The murder hornets became more aggressive over time, even marking warm-blooded creatures as potential threats or prey. People learned the hard way that ignoring hornets walking on them, in the hopes they would fly away, wasn't wise. These scouts sometimes marked them for an incoming swarm attack. After the first few deaths, nobody let murder hornets walk unmolested on them anymore.

The low tone buzzing got louder as they advanced. A steady flow of murder hornet workers conveyed food for the larvae back at the nest. The larvae, in contrast to the workers, could consume solid protein. The flesh carrying capacity of the large murder hornets, with a four centimeter long body and nearly double wingspan, gave Noah the creeps.

Noah's dread worsened. *There are too many for a regular food search.*

Ten minutes' slow walk from where they left Kesa and Ava, there was a last short bush blocking their line of sight to the hornets' activity. Noah waved Carter left while he crept right.

As he rounded the bush, Noah saw his worst-case scenario. Hornets fed on and harvested from Ethan, or at least the remains, after they consumed or carried away half of him. The hornets had torn his clothing to shreds to harvest the flesh from Ethan's horribly contorted body. *Damn, this is the worst death I have ever seen. Ethan must have died in intense pain, first from debilitating stings causing him to collapse and then being eaten alive until his body shut down.*

Noah glanced at Carter. *Yeah, he's horrified. It's inevitable, at his age and seeing this bloody mess that was family.* Noah hissed to get his attention and signaled him back the way they came.

After backing ten meters away from the corpse, Noah leaned in close to Carter. "The family needs you to hold it together. Ethan is giving us a chance to destroy these monsters."

"But they're eating him," Carter said loudly.

Noah didn't like the noise. They were too far for Ava to hear, but there was no benefit in getting the hornets excited.

Noah squeezed Carter's shoulder while he talked, trying to keep the boy grounded. "Ethan is gone. His final service to the family is to lead us to their nest. After we take care of it, we'll bury him here instead of taking him to the Cave for everyone to see. He loved the woods and the creek, and I want the family to remember him gleeful and funny. You know, the way he was at breakfast this morning."

"OK, I got it. You can count on me." Carter wiped his tears, swallowed hard, and looked expectantly at Noah.

Noah eyeballed the hornets' flight path. He pointed to a green ash a safe distance away that didn't have line of sight to Ethan's corpse. "Wait there. I'll get Kesa and Ava and our rifles. If they ask what we found, it was an animal carcass."

Carter headed to the green ash, his shoulders slumped.

Noah paused before turning to go. *Poor kid, he's going to dwell in the memories of this mission for a long time.*

CHAPTER NINE – 15:00 June 1, 2070 – Eye for an Eye

As the climate changed, we expected to fight each other for survival at some point. We didn't anticipate other species contending for the top of the food chain.
Grandpy Max, 2063

Noah walked to where their rifles were and signaled Kesa and Ava to join him. He spoke once they arrived, looking into the distance to avoid eye contact. "We found murder hornets harvesting from an animal carcass. We'll follow them back to their nest. Carter is waiting for us just off their flight path." *I hate lying to my family. I also hate that I'm bad at it; hopefully not bad enough that Ava figures out what's going on.*

"Did you see Ethan?" Ava asked. "Shouldn't we look for him first?" She sniffled as she talked and gestured frantically at the forest around them.

"We'll watch for Ethan while we hunt the nest. I don't want to miss this chance to find where the bastards live." Sweat rolled down Noah's face, more than the heat justified. *Lying again. Can they see right through me? I'll tell her the truth and apologize after we deal with the nest. Maybe someday she will forgive me.*

Noah stared hard at Kesa. Besides being lifelong friends, they had executed many scavenging missions together. *Kesa should see through my lies.*

Kesa stood out of Ava's line of sight. She nodded somberly at Noah to show she understood what was going on. "Since we can't find Ethan for now," Kesa said, "let's at least prevent any other Cave Family kids from getting hurt. OK, Ava?"

"Sure, as long as we look for Ethan as we go," Ava replied.

Noah led Kesa and Ava to where Carter waited at the shady green ash. *I hope having something to do helps calm Ava.*

Noah addressed the team. "You can see and hear the hornet flight path over there. We'll walk parallel to it at an easy pace, staying clear by at least eight meters, until we spot their nest or entrances to it. Chances are they have an underground nest, but keep an eye out for one above ground. You do not want to bump into it. Once we find the nest, Ava and Carter will map entrances. Kesa, tell us what worked last time you did this."

Kesa grimaced. "Worked is a strong word, but I can tell you what the last team did. We gathered rocks to block side entrances and burning materials to make a hornet baking fire. When evening came, we blocked the side entrances and lit a hot fire atop the main entrance. Once the popping and snapping of burning hornets stopped, we dug up the nest. We killed the larvae and anything else that didn't die in the fire."

"You destroyed the nest, but don't sound sure of the method. Were many people stung?" Ava asked.

"Nobody died, let's just leave it at that," Kesa replied.

Yet more that we are hiding from Ava. She won't trust anyone by the time this day ends. Noah cleared his throat to get the team's attention. "Mason told me these hornets stay active later in the evening than most insects. We'll attack around 21:00. That will balance enough darkness for most hornets to be in the nest, but leave adequate light to see what we're doing. Carter, you're on point, followed by Ava. Kesa, please take rear guard."

"Noah?" Carter looked at his feet and ground the soil beneath his left boot. "I don't feel well. Maybe you can lead?"

Noah considered the request. *I feel like puking watching these hornets ferry chunks of Ethan. How the hell can I expect Carter to keep it together? Being on point will help; he'll have to stay aware of the hornets and where we walk.* "It has been a tough day, but we're not done yet. Can you try point? We can switch in a bit if you need."

The team departed in single file, Noah following the newbies to monitor them. *Time for the hourly weather check. I don't want to be "that" team lead, losing anyone to a fast forming tornado or violent squall that I did not prepare us for.* He sniffed the air, did a slow full circle look to the horizon, and listened. *Nothing to see, just burning blue sky. Not too quiet nor too noisy, and no sweet pungent zing of ozone scent that precedes a fierce storm.*

After hiking carefully through the woods for a half an hour, Carter signaled a halt. The team gathered up. Carter pointed at a fist-sized hole in the ground near a standing dead pine tree. The hornets carried their gruesome cargo into it.

Noah inspected the hole from a safe distance. The hornets had appropriated a burrow a creature had dug in the rotted roots. *The prior resident probably surrendered its home without a fight. Only humans are stupid enough to do battle with murder hornets.* "Go time," Noah whispered. "Mark entrances with a stick standing nearby and leave something heavy close to block them later. Gather up good burning materials as you see them."

Everyone pitched in to prepare to obliterate the nest. Noah kept an eye out for team safety while he moved rocks and wood. *I hate working near these mindless killers. I'm not the only one feeling that way; everyone is jumping when a hornet buzzes close to them.*

Preparations made, Noah waved the team to meet a safe distance from the nest. "It's late enough that they're settling in for the night. When I cover the main entrance with the fire, plug up the side entrances. We'll wait here to let the fire do its job. Have your root shovels ready to smack hornets flying toward us." *This better work without anyone else getting hurt. Having to tell the family what happened to Ethan is bad enough.*

Noah took a slow deep breath to shed what anxiety he could. He fired the burn pile and pushed it over the main entrance. The dry grasses flared up, their heat starting all the twigs on fire. *Burn monsters, burn—or are these flames home to you like the flames of hell whence you came?*

The team scrambled back, shovels ready. Hornets emerged from their main entrance directly into the roaring fire. Most crackled and popped immediately, their juicy insides boiling. Others managed some last wingbeats before enough of their wings burned off that they fell to the ground. Hundreds of hornets died a fiery death within minutes.

The flaming flights and rhythmic popping mesmerized Noah. A low tone but loud buzzing heading straight for him snapped him out of it. "Incoming," he yelled, swinging his shovel and connecting with the first hornet to approach him. The others also swung their shovels at the attacking hornets, swatting any landing on them with their armored gloves.

"There's another side entrance." Carter charged over. As he pounded the side entrance closed with his shovel, a murder hornet landed on his rear waistline where a tie had come loose and left a gap. It didn't hesitate to sting. "Aah!" Carter shrieked.

"Drop and roll, Carter," Noah shouted, smacking the last few hornets out of the air before heading over to check on him.

Obeying Noah's instructions even through the pain, Carter dropped to the ground. He rolled back and forth over the sting.

Noah grabbed Carter and checked his back. There was no sign of the hornet. Instead, it squirmed on the ground where Carter had rolled around.

A solid crunch with Noah's left boot finished the monster off. "It's just a mess of carapace chunks and goop now. Are you OK?"

Carter got up and arched his back. "That felt like a fucking hot nail being pounded into me." He picked up his shovel and scanned for more attackers.

Noah nodded appreciatively. *The boy takes a hit and gets back up on his feet. Well done for a newbie. No reason for a free ride, though.* "Makes me wonder what I am missing out on at the Cave if the young ones are pounding hot nails into each other."

"You're too old for their games, Noah." Kesa nudged Carter gently with her root shovel's tip. "That was hard core, Carter. Can you do it again?"

Carter, although still grimacing in pain, replied in kind. "I showed you how it's done, now it's your turn." He threw a handy hornet carcass at her, which she swatted out of the air and right back at him.

Noah saw that coming. *I haven't seen Kesa run away from anything under three hundred kilos, dead or alive.*

The fire at the main entrance of the nest was burning down. After a few minutes without popping noises or flaming flyers, Noah scanned his team in the little light left. "Time to dig the nest up. We'll dig up tunnels and comb structures until we hit dirt in every direction. Watch for queens; they may not have gone into the fire. We can't let them get away."

"How do you tell between queens and workers?" Ava asked.

"Queens are a third larger," Noah responded.

"Are you fucking serious?" Carter said. "As if the workers aren't big enough, now we have giant queens to battle?"

"I don't want any giant stingers in my tender skin either," Kesa replied. "We'll be fine if we quickly crush anything moving."

Noah headed to the nest, everyone else following. He used his root shovel to push the fire off to the side and fed it thick, dry branches to provide light for the job.

Kesa stood torches up around the work area.

Noah steeled himself for what might come. "Two to dig, two ready to defend. Kesa and I will dig first."

Noah and Kesa tipped shovelfuls of dirt and combs toward Carter and Ava so the newbies could squash any survivors.

There were a few stragglers that met their doom under a boot or shovel, nothing giving Noah cause for concern. *Have we agreed to ignore the flesh pieces mixed in with the hornet combs? That's the tricky part about unsaid agreements; they're ruined if you say them out loud. Whatever the reason, it's a damn good thing Ava doesn't know the flesh's origin.*

Noah called for a switch after digging twenty-five centimeters deep and triple that in diameter. "We're about half done. Let's change up diggers and squishers. Take care, Ava and Carter, the queens live in the lower part of the nest, only one queen if we are lucky. Winter hasn't been cold enough for decades to kill off nests and make queens hibernate. Nests survive year round, old queens birthing new at their discretion."

Carter shoveled gingerly. "Grandpy Max taught us about murder hornets when we were young. He thinks the old queen hatches new queens when she believes her death is near." At forty-five centimeters deep, Carter's shovelful of combs included an extra-large hornet.

Noah gave it a definitive smack with the flat face of his shovel, followed by a firm boot stomp. *Scary things often return to life if you don't definitively kill them.* "That was the only queen so far." The combs kept coming but there weren't any other grown hornets, only larvae.

Kesa gazed pointedly at a cluster of especially robust larvae. Noah nodded, prompting Kesa to stow four aside from the carnage.

Soon enough, the combs stopped coming. Only dirt was now visible around the entire excavated area. Noah planted his shovel in the dirt. "Flawlessly executed, team, we're almost done with this nest. Push that fire into the hole and we'll stoke it up to burn the combs in case we missed any larvae."

Kesa waited until the work was done. She held her shovel out so everyone could see the four unharmed larvae squirming around on it. "In the past, some cultures ate their prey or the prey's blood to honor them. Cave Family has a tradition born of necessity when our first murder hornet hunters ran out of food before finding the nest; we're going to cook these little buggers and eat them."

Carter and Ava stared at her, waiting for Noah or Kesa to laugh. After Noah and Kesa stared back, Carter finally asked, "Are you serious?"

Noah chuckled and gestured at Kesa to go ahead; she positioned her shovel head over the heat of the fire. "I'll go first, Carter," Noah said. "Mason likes them so much he brings a jar home to cook and share the next day." *I hate the taste, but no need to turn the newbies off before they try it.*

After the larvae sizzled for a bit, Kesa held out the shovel of steaming larvae.

Noah grabbed one, juggled it between his hands until it cooled a bit, gave the newbies a forced smile, and tossed the larva into his mouth. He chewed it twice and swallowed hard, licking his lips to really sell it. "Thanks, chef, cooked just right." *Liar, liar, pants on fire. Kesa knows what I really think of these things.*

Kesa winked conspiratorially at Noah as she held the shovel between Ava and Carter.

They glared at each other, a contest of wills for who would go first. Ava smiled, grabbed a larva, and popped it in her mouth, chewing hesitantly. "Weird, tastes like chicken," she said.

Carter shrugged and ate his. He grimaced. "Yuck, I hope we don't have to dig up any more nests anytime soon."

Kesa ate the last one. She licked her lips as though she wanted to eat another few courses, eliciting as much of a laugh as expected in the situation.

Noah waited for the levity to end. He clenched his fists for a few seconds. *We needed that. Now it's time to come clean.* He regarded Ava and gently said, "Ava, I lied to you earlier so we could finish the mission. We found Ethan, but he was dead. I ordered Carter to wait for me to share the truth with you. I'm so sorry, and hope you can forgive me someday."

"He's dead?" Ava asked, tears welling up.

"He died long before Isabella made it back to the Cave. No one could have found him in time to save him." Noah replied. *Is she going to hit me? I deserve it.*

Kesa stepped to Ava and put her arm around her.

Noah stood tense, unsure of what to do. *At least Kesa knew what Ava needed.*

Ava clung to Kesa. "It's all my fault," she sobbed. "I was so proud to become a scavenger I abandoned the kids. Look what happened."

Kesa held Ava. "You had nothing to do with this. Isabella and Ethan turned ten. They were old enough to gather food close to the caves without supervision. If you weren't old enough to join a scavenging team, you would be in the Cave caring for the younger children. Our ancestors left us a harsh world; bad things happen that are not anyone's fault."

Ava nodded grudgingly, wiped the tears off her face and looked to Noah. "Show me. I want to help take care of him."

"You can come if you want," Noah replied, barely holding back tears himself. "You will see Ethan as the hornets left him. Do you want to remember him like that or as the cheerful kid that loved you so much? Unless anyone objects, I'm planning to bury him in the forest near the creek tonight so that Cave Family can remember him how he was."

Ava paused, breathing deep and letting it out slow. Cave Family trained scavengers to calm down and think decisions through. "You're right. I want to remember him as he was. Are you OK though, don't you need help?"

Noah glanced at Carter, who met his gaze and dipped his chin. *Backing me up without being ordered or even formally asked, this kid is taking his training seriously.* Cave Family didn't allow anyone to be alone beyond the immediate vicinity of the Cave entrance. Too many solo travelers died from unknown causes or minor injuries where a buddy could have helped them back to the Cave. "Carter has already seen Ethan. We will put him to rest. How about you and Kesa return home and update the family? They are probably starting to worry."

Ava straightened her back and tilted her head up. "You're right. Kesa and I will go back and I will inform the family. It is the least we can do. Your day has been hard enough."

Her concern moved Noah. *Telling the family will not be easy; I hadn't thought that far forward. She's thinking of me even though she was much closer to Ethan than I was.* His respect for Ava grew. "Thank you for taking on the burden of notifying the family. I believe your task will prove harder than what Carter and I need to do."

CHAPTER TEN – 23:45 June 1, 2070 – Rest in Peace

The burdens you keep from your loved ones to protect them are the heaviest to bear, since it is your loved ones you need to share with to unburden your own heart.
Kesa James, 2069

The team smothered the fire with dirt and gathered their gear. Noah handed out torches. "This half moon provides enough light to walk on safe ground, but not enough to be sure you're avoiding ant hills, hornet nests, and bad footing." *Grandpy Max told us the most dangerous thing most people used to do was drive. Now no one drives and walking carefree can cost your life.*

"We'll send out a search team if you're not back at the Cave within two hours of us," Kesa said. She and Ava waved goodbye, then proceeded uphill through the woods to rejoin a path to the Cave.

Noah adjusted his pack. "Alright, let's do this. Thanks for stepping up, Carter."

"I wouldn't let you do this alone, even without the buddy rule. No one should have to do this solo." Carter headed off, taking point.

They walked parallel to the creek, Carter doing a superb job of picking a safe path and keeping them on course. Noah followed in silence, mulling over the events of the day and Carter's progression as a Cave Family scavenger. *His sense of direction and pathfinding skills at this young age are impressive.*

All too soon, they neared Ethan's corpse. The breeze shifted toward them, delivering a whiff of rotting meat with a hint of sweetness; the smell of death.

Carter gagged but otherwise held himself together.

Noah hoped they wouldn't have to fight coyotes, crows, or anything else for control of the corpse. "Heads-up, we may not be the only ones interested in Ethan's remains."

After walking another minute, Carter gasped in dismay and halted.

Noah stepped up beside him. The hornets continued to harvest while the team searched for the nest. Ethan was nothing but a skeleton with flesh scraps and clothing hanging here and there. *Merciless and deathly efficient, no wonder their species is so successful.* "There's a small clearing there with a pleasant view of the creek," Noah said quietly, jolting Carter from his unblinking stare at the corpse. "I think Ethan would like it."

Carter didn't respond, just took his pack off in tacit agreement.

Carter and Noah put their packs and rifles down and set the torches for light to dig. Noah wanted this grisly task done. Even though the mission now exceeded fourteen hours, he dug with ferocity. Carter matched him shovel for shovel.

Cave Family had no cemeteries; they preferred to cremate their dead. Why give the dead's bones ownership of any land? When cremation wasn't feasible, they returned the deceased to nature in an unpreserved, unmarked burial.

Noah judged the grave sufficiently deep and stopped shoveling. "That's enough, Carter." Carter kept digging, grunting with exertion and pounding his shovel violently into the dirt on each downstroke. "Carter, enough." Noah said, louder this time.

Carter shook himself as if awakening from a nightmare, taking a second to reorient. "Sorry, I was trying to avoid thinking about what comes next."

Noah understood Carter's sentiment. "Don't worry about it. I'm barely holding my shit together. I have a small tarp in my pack. We'll roll the body onto it with our shovels, drag the tarp over, and slide the body into the grave."

"Isn't that disrespectful?" Carter asked, his voice breaking up. "I mean, pushing Ethan with shovels and dragging him around?"

"I understand how you feel, but Ethan is gone," Noah replied. "This is bone and flesh we need to return to the Earth. Once we bury it, we will say goodbye to Ethan, OK?" *This sickens me too, but dying this way leaves room only for horror and sorrow. There's no respectful option here.*

Carter could only nod in assent.

Noah pulled a ragged vinyl coated polyester tarp out of his pack and spread it beside the body. Decades ago, this had been a top quality tarp. Even now, suffering many holes and rips, it was one of Cave Family's best. Wordlessly, Noah and Carter followed through on the plan. They rolled the body onto the tarp with their shovels, blood and loose flesh smearing everything. They each retched a few times moving the body, sliding the tarp, and dumping the body into the grave.

Noah scooped dirt vigorously over the corpse. *Finally, enough dirt to cover things up and mask the smell of death.* Noah leaned on his shovel for a break, Carter following suit. Noah broke the silence. "I don't believe sharing any details of what we saw or did here will benefit the family. How about you?"

"Agreed," Carter said. "Let's just say we found him, buried him, and said farewell."

"Perfect," Noah said gruffly. "What happened here is fodder for nightmares. Better for the family if only we have those nightmares." They resumed shoveling dirt to cover the grave. *If Carter and I know this horror and keep it to ourselves, what horrors are other Cave Family members saving us from knowing?*

Grave complete, Noah and Carter put their shovels aside. Noah clasped his hands and let his gaze settle out to everywhere and yet nowhere. "Ethan, you will always be family to me. I will remember you as a merry prankster that made sure your pranks were funny but never hurtful. I will never forget how you took care of the younger kids, and how you loved Ava as much as she loved you."

Noah could not verbalize any more feelings. Tears streamed down his face; there was a lump in his throat. He had to grit his teeth to prevent sobbing uncontrollably. *I'm supposed to be the rock for Carter to anchor to.* He waited for Carter to take a turn.

Carter also cried. He shook his head to indicate he didn't want to speak. *I could barely do it; I'm not going to force you.* Noah took his tarp down to the creek, washed it clean, and shook off what water he could. He'd have to hang it to dry back at the Cave. Returning to the packs, he geared up.

Carter stood at the gravesite, staring at nothing.

Noah prodded gently, "You ready to head back, Carter?"

Carter gathered his gear up. He finally spoke, "What you said for Ethan was real nice. I couldn't have shared what we were both feeling any better."

"Thanks," Noah said, "that means a lot to me."

They each picked up a torch and headed toward the Cave. Carter took the lead again, Noah letting him to keep Carter's mind off the grisly task they had just completed. Carter opted for a more direct route through the forest rather than heading initially off course to pick up an established trail like Kesa and Ava had. Although less distance to travel, their pace pushing through the bush was slower. Noah estimated they would take a fifth longer to reach the Cave, but making the choice and following it through was a valuable lesson for Carter.

They walked through a young forest. Sudden gaps occasionally punctuated it, wherein the forest canopy disappeared. These were tornado tracks, twisty open corridors fifty meters to two kilometers wide as far as one could see in both directions. Tornado severity and recency dictated whether there were no trees left standing or a sparse forest remaining. Tracks made within the last decade by a strong tornado were near impassable with fallen trees. *Grandpy Max said this area was on the fringe of what the ancestors called "tornado alley" fifty years ago, with ten tornados a year. Now we see at least thirty a year.*

Almost halfway back to the Cave, Carter signaled a halt and took a knee as they entered a two hundred meter wide tornado track. It was two decades old; brush grew amongst well-rotted tree debris.

Noah took a knee beside him, shrugging quizzically when Carter made eye contact.

Carter pointed at a cluster of dark shapes ten meters ahead on the ground. "I saw movement," he whispered. Noah and Carter held position in silence for another minute. Finally, a dark shape shuddered, this time accompanied by a moan. It was in an area of clover and other low vegetation that made a natural clearing among the surrounding higher brush.

Noah squinted, but it didn't help to bring any further clarity in the low light. He whispered close to Carter's ear, "It sounds like someone injured. I'll take both torches for a closer look. You watch my back from cover. Stay aware of your six; if this is a trap, someone will sneak up from behind."

Carter gave him a thumbs-up, already scanning for a suitable position.

Noah held both torches with his left hand and his rifle with safety off in his right. *I can't aim worth shit one-handed, but the noise might make someone hit the deck long enough for us to escape. At least with me holding the torches, I am the only reasonable target and Carter's night vision will return.* There wasn't any movement among the dark shapes as Noah walked toward them. As he neared, the unmistakable metallic scent of blood filled the air.

The flickering torchlight revealed the scene bit by bit as Noah crept forward. A man, woman, and child in travel-worn clothing laid in the clearing. All three had suffered grievous wounds. *They're not Cave Family, thank goodness. Am I an asshole for feeling relieved?* The motionless man and child stared unseeingly back at him with glassy, dead eyes.

The woman shielded her eyes from the light with a shaking hand. "Please help my son," she moaned. There was a stab wound in her upper leg. Blood oozed out now, but judging from the pool on the ground, it had gushed when first inflicted.

Noah moved closer to examine the wound. *She's obviously not a threat to me. With the amount of blood on her clothing and nearby ground, I'm surprised she's not already dead. This isn't about treatment, it's about providing comfort in her last minutes.* Noah offered her his water bottle. "I'll help your son right away. What happened to you?"

She grimaced in pain as she moved to take a drink from the bottle. She spoke in a whisper, fading with every word. "We fled the desert. Walked east for a month, searching for a new home. My son, is he OK?" She shifted position, trying to see her son behind Noah, gasping when she moved her leg.

Noah froze. *Do I lie to comfort her or tell her he's dead?*

Unable to spot her son, she looked at Noah and continued. "Two men ambushed us in this clearing, demanding our packs. We barely have enough to survive. My husband drew his pistol, but someone shot him from the woods before he could fire. They stabbed my son and me, then took our packs." Her eyes narrowed, having seen something in Noah's expression. "He's dead, isn't he?" she asked with heart-rending sorrow.

Noah held her hand as her eyes closed.

Her breathing trailed off in a last gasp, her body falling still after a final violent shudder.

Dammit, my face can't even lie to comfort a mother as she dies. Focus, Noah, focus. If the killers stuck around, I am an easy target. The few meters visible by torch light held no threats, but shrouded the rest of the clearing in impenetrable darkness.

Noah gently touched the father and son. The bodies were cool, like the rocks on the ground. *Deathly cold bodies and no gunshots poking holes in my tender skin. The killers are long gone.* He examined the victims more closely. Their clothing and physical condition verified they were as the woman said, a down-on-their-luck family traveling to find a new beginning. Noah held the torches low to examine the edges of the clearing. The dead family's tracks entered the clearing from the east. Two more sets of prints approached from the south and departed with heavier burdens to the southeast.

Noah rushed to where he left Carter. "Someone robbed and killed a travelling family, so we need to alert Cave Family. Did you see anything?"

Carter emerged from the circle of darkness beyond the torchlight, blinking his eyes at the light. He glanced nervously at the dark shapes in the clearing. "No, you were the only one moving as far as I could see," he whispered. "I heard you talking to someone; can't we help them?"

"They are all dead now. The mother told me what happened with her last breaths." Noah passed a torch to Carter.

"What about the bodies?" Carter asked. "Are we just going to leave them?"

To ensure Carter understood the gravity of the situation, Noah spoke firmly. "We're in danger here. We don't know who did this, their numbers, or where they are. Cave Family hunters will return in daylight to protect the family and take care of these bodies. I'm going to take point now and pick up the pace. You did an exceptional job all day, but I have more experience."

Carter grudgingly agreed. "I understand; lead on."

Sorry kid, keeping you safe is more important to me right now than your ego. Noah issued some last instructions before heading into the forest toward the Cave. "We're going to try moving quietly and pause often to listen. Tap me on the shoulder if you believe anyone is following so we can hide, run, or ambush. We cannot lead anyone back to the Cave."

Noah and Carter took great pains to detect if anyone shadowed them. There was only the usual insects buzzing, frogs croaking, and small creatures rustling around. Noah halted when they reached a major trail intersection far from the bodies. *Carter seems more emotionally drained than physically tired, but we could both use a rest.* "We're at a safe distance; let's take a quick break."

Carter sat in the grass beside the intersection offshoot that led to the Cave. After sitting motionless a few minutes, he picked grass and rummaged in the sticks and rocks around him. "Hey, what's this?" he asked, tapping a stack of three plate-sized rocks.

"Looks like something a restless new scavenger did when their senior called a halt for longer than needed," Noah replied, winking at Carter. "We don't mark the way to the Cave; scatter those rocks before we head out."

The rest of the trip was uneventful. When they spotted the welcoming dark circle of the Cave entrance, Noah and Carter doused their torches.

Noah leaned close to Carter. "You go on in and find Grandpy Max, Mason, and Kesa. Wake them if you need to. Tell them I'm perching here thirty minutes to ensure no one followed far enough behind that we couldn't hear them."

Carter signaled OK before heading into the Cave.

Noah set up with his rifle in the lookout perch. Cave Family placed these large rocks to enable line of fire into all paths coming to the Cave and yet give ample cover. His eyes soon adjusted to the moon and starlit night. He settled in to guard Cave Family from any unwanted visitors. *Normally after eighteen hours outside the safety of the Cave, I would pass out—but after seeing what happened to that family, there's no way I'll sleep on watch. The Reckoning that Grandpy Max told us about, when people killed people for food, water, and possessions, seemed far in the past until tonight.*

UTOPIA

CHAPTER ELEVEN – Prologue

The global sustainability movement started with the youth. It had to, since there weren't enough politicians and corporate leaders that cared to risk their privileged positions.

Terrified of the broken world their parents were handing over to them, the youth called out their elders for wallowing in consumption economies that broke natural systems. When the movement peaked in 2025, democracies elected only politicians running on a sustainability platform; shareholders ousted board members afraid to redirect corporations toward a sustainable future. Even the leaders of many totalitarian nations recognized the necessity to shift to a sustainable economy.

The 2015-2025 identity politics flailing around coalesced on the two root causes of inequity. First, social inequality resulting from differing access to quality education and differing economic opportunities. Second, the immense advantage intergenerational wealth provides. Political activists refocused on building an educational, social and economic environment that provides opportunity to everyone willing to work hard and smart. Steep taxes on intergenerational wealth transfer began to level the playing field generation to generation. People in positions of power acting to preserve preferred treatment for the elite are targeted by grassroots campaigns to replace them.

The EU, United States, and Canadian governments collaborated throughout the late 2020s, aligning on progressive environmental and social equality policies. More nations joined the informal alliance as residents elect representatives running on a platform to unite. The Alliance of Nations formed December 31, 2030. One hundred and twenty-three nations merged into one using direct democracy to decide important issues and elected representatives for the rest.

In the early 2030s, the Alliance enacted regulations that materially decarbonized the economy. Energy pricing reflected its true cost, product prices covered their life cycle cost, and the true intent of reduce, reuse, and recycle was revived. The Alliance achieved near zero waste, even mining old landfills for useful materials.

Other nations merged to mitigate the Alliance's global power, leaving the world with only three: the Alliance, AsiaPac, and the New Soviet Union. The Alliance used economic sanctions and trade duties to compel the others to adopt sustainability and social equality policies. The three nations agreed to a global Charter of Responsibilities and Rights.

The timely massive sustainability changes held global temperature increases below the critical one and a half degrees Celsius threshold. The Alliance, AsiaPac, and the New Soviet Union collaborated in carbon mitigation programs that reversed global warming by 2060.

On January 1, 2031, the Alliance released a definitive analysis of the maximum sustainable population of the Earth. The analysis resulted in three key findings. Firstly, the Earth could sustainably support an urbanized population of one and half billion at a reasonable standard of living. Secondly, humanity must limit its footprint to twenty percent of habitable land for urban, agricultural, industrial, and mixed use. Finally, humanity needs to restore the other eighty percent to the wild state to support species diversity and natural systems function.

The Alliance responded by implementing a lifetime half child allowance per person to wind human population down to the target at a manageable pace. Those disagreeing with restricting the human birth rate coalesced into The Free Parenthood movement. A fringe violent terrorist element called "the Birthers" arose in the shadows of this otherwise peaceful organization.

KESA

CHAPTER TWELVE – 19:00 June 1, 2070 – Proportionate Response

To best serve current and future citizens, a nation must craft policy beneficial for the majority and neutral at worst for the others. We must hear those that disagree but cannot allow vocal minorities to force detrimental change to quality policies. Blindly striving for consensus often prevents optimal outcomes.

Mala Safanzai, Alliance Presidential candidate campaign speech 2034

"Touchdown at New Boston in twenty mikes," Kesa shouted over the drone of the quad electric turbofans. Their C-57 VTOL armed and armored transport plane flew at six thousand kilometers per hour. "Get ready to roll." She sat on a jump seat to do mission planning on her laptop. The five-point harness chafed her shoulders as she twisted to get visual confirmation that Phoenix Fireteam's four other members heard her.

Mason focused on his weapons kit. He flicked a kinda-sorta thumbs-up without even looking at Kesa.

That's all I will get from him. Kesa wasn't worried about Mason and Noah being prepared. They had been running missions with her for five and three years, respectively.

Noah glanced at Kesa and nodded, returning to checking the tie-downs on their gear.

Willow and River waited for Kesa to make eye contact, each giving her a definitive thumbs-up. Their argument over how to best set up a chest rig resumed unabated.

Kesa shrugged. *Fresh out of tac team school and still eager to impress. We'll see how long that lasts with Mason and Noah around to model complete informality. I'm not sure I want twins assigned to my team, but the Joint Special Actions HR group said they were top of their class. I have to get over the KIAs they replaced; the twins may perceive something off when I look at them.*

Kesa checked the time. The Birthers bombed the New Boston police station two hours ago, killing six officers. *Here we go again, chasing terrorists who believe killing people communicates how important their twisted ideals are. They can't understand the price of living in a civil society: no one will have everything run the way they want it. It's a trade-off for society protecting your health and safety and providing equal opportunity for success.*

The team's coordinator at the Joint Special Actions operations center updated Kesa on the search for the terrorists. Kesa let out a piercing whistle, tapping her noise dampening headset when everyone looked her direction. The team wrapped up their deployment checks, strapped into jump seats, and put on their headsets.

"The analysts narrowed location to one neighborhood," Kesa informed Phoenix Fireteam over the team comms channel. "They updated the strike vehicles' nav systems." *It's a good thing the JSA analysts are on our side—those bloodhounds with their AI tools could find anyone anywhere in minutes.*

"The mission is to apprehend or neutralize the bombers. We're cleared for the standard violent offender engagement protocol," Kesa said. "Willow, please tell me they taught you the various protocols at tactical team school."

Willow didn't hesitate. "Violent offender engagement protocol requires law enforcement to shoot to kill if they suspect that civilian or first responder lives are in danger."

"Perfect textbook answer. River, why do we have this protocol?" Kesa asked. *Rules are easy to memorize, much harder to understand why they exist.*

River paused before answering. "Decades of confrontation data shows that law enforcement hesitation to shoot led to many more civilian and first responder deaths versus unnecessary offender deaths."

"Wow, that was a mouthful. Boil it down," Noah said.

River smiled at the challenge. "Choices in the field have to be made in split seconds," he replied. "Civilian lives come first, first responder lives a close second, and offender lives a deep third. Sadly, mistakes are going to happen. When they do, we want the balance to tip toward extra dead offenders versus extra dead innocents."

Noah feigned relief. "Phew, now I'm comfortable you have my back. I was afraid I would die before you shook off the analysis paralysis."

Kesa gave everyone a moment to reorient on her. "We have to assume the terrorists are assholes, but not morons. They know facial, gait, and clothing tracking have pinpointed their location. They expect us."

The pilot cut in on all comms channels. "Two mikes to touchdown. Brace for transition to vertical."

Kesa wrapped up the briefing. "We'll have local lethal-armed SWAT holding a two hundred meter perimeter. Local police armed with non-lethals already control a five hundred meter outer ring. Time is on our side; we'll use our scouting tech to achieve complete situational awareness before we enter the Birther's zone of control."

Two minutes later, the C-57's nose lifted. A high pitch whirring noise reverberated throughout the plane as rotors deployed out of the fuselage front and the back of each wing. The rotors spun up to full speed as the wing turbofans coasted to a halt. In seconds, the C-57 transitioned from racing forward to dropping like a rock.

Kesa shook her head. *Are all pilots the same? I am yet to fly with one that doesn't stress test the auto-stabilization software. It's as if we're always deploying into hot zones and needing to drop out of the sky.*

More mechanical whirring and clunking accompanied the landing gear's deployment. The wingtips folded up to decrease their landing footprint. Willow peered out the window. "You're going back to school, Mason," she said. "Maybe this time you'll learn more than fighting on the playground."

"At least I went," he replied.

Kesa glanced down at the landing zone the local police had secured for them, a school playing field. This was the closest place for a C-57 to land that still enabled effective countermeasures response to a surface-to-air missile fired from the Birther location.

At five percent above the lowest safe height, the rotors spun up to full speed and brought the C-57 to a feather soft landing in the schoolyard. Kesa unbuckled from her jump seat and folded it up before heading to her Rivian military model R21T-M electric truck. *Good thing the pilots can't disable core safety parameters. They would test how much buffer they can give up and still land gracefully. A crash is the inevitable end of that contest.*

Mason and Noah were unfazed by the hotshot pilot bullshit. They unbuckled from their jump seats and released the tie-downs from the team's three Rivians.

Willow and River exchanged a glance, their expression saying, "I thought we were going to crash, did you?" They shook it off before assisting with unstrapping the Rivians.

Mason signaled Willow. "You're with me. I drive."

Kona woke up from her regular in transport nap. She shook herself awake as Noah moved her travel carrier into his Rivian. The Shepherd-Rottweiler cross performed dual duty for Phoenix Fireteam. Kesa liked to think of Kona as having a PhD in explosives detection and a bachelor's degree in patrol dog work.

"Call signs from now until our return. Fire, you're driving this one," Kesa said, hopping into the passenger side where she could coordinate while in transit. "Take it easy. Our quarry isn't going anywhere, so we can aim to arrive today instead of trying for yesterday."

Someone had briefed the local police on their deployment practices. They marked a well-lit corridor from the landing zone to an open gate between the schoolyard and road. The police blocked traffic and waved the team to proceed.

River engaged the two thousand horsepower total equivalent electric motors, launching down the C-57's deployment ramp. The other two Rivians followed single file, one hundred twenty centimeters off each other's bumper. He must have felt Kesa staring, because he kept his eyes on the road while saying, "What, I didn't go full out. Do you think I'm the type of person that rips up kiddies' playing fields?"

"Yeah, you're a saint, Fire," Kesa replied. "You took two and a half seconds to reach a hundred rather than the one point eight achievable acceleration."

River ripped through the city at a hundred fifty percent of the speed limit as he followed the path projected heads-up on the lower middle of the windshield. He only slowed to the limit in the one playground zone on their route. New Boston traffic control set every signal light to feed them straight through, no red lights for Phoenix Fireteam. The sirens, emergency vehicle lights, and deadly appearance of the military Rivians kept people off the streets in front of them.

Kesa got next to nothing done for prep work; the trip ended soon after it began.

Local police waved them through their perimeter roadblock. A few hundred meters later, local SWAT directed them into a parking lot commandeered as a staging area. Kesa's team went from high-speed to a dead stop in precise formation, with precisely the right space between the Rivians for door swings and gear. The optics pleased Kesa. *The locals need to have confidence in my team; building that confidence starts with what you arrive in and how you park it.*

A tractor-trailer mobile command post with slide-outs deployed filled the back half of the parking lot. The New Boston PD SWAT logo dominated the center of the sixteen meter long gloss black side of the trailer. The team proceeded up a set of steel stairs to enter the command post, Noah taking up the end of the line after setting Kona up with water and shade.

A clean cut muscular thirtyish man in SWAT gear exaggeratedly checked his watch as Phoenix Fireteam walked in. "Well, you folks sure took your time getting here. We set up and waited for at least twenty mikes." He smiled wide and waved the team to come forward to a briefing area in front of floor to ceiling video screens. "Pleased to meet you, Corporal James. I'm New Boston SWAT team Commander Jose Lee."

Kesa shook Jose's hand. "Thanks, Commander Lee." She gestured to each team member as she named them. "This is Phoenix Fireteam. Noah, Mason, Willow, and River. Our canine outside is Kona. Now, let's see your intel."

"Corporal James likes to get right to business when hunting terrorists," Noah stage whispered.

Kesa gave him a dirty look.

Jose indicated the top left quadrant of the screen. "Here we show live drone footage of the building your analysts advised the terrorists occupy. They leased the rightmost two bays of this hundred meter long light industrial complex with ten meter roof height and concrete walls. Each bay has ten meters of frontage. The second last bay appears to be tenanted by an operating industrial cleaning company."

"The JSA analysts advise the Birthers purchased chemicals for their bomb through the cleaning company," Kesa said.

Jose nodded and continued. "The last bay is empty other than a few chemical storage and mixing vats; likely where the Birthers hid the bomb making from the cleaning company employees."

Moving in front of the screen's left side, Jose pointed to the top right quadrant. "This useless mess of color is what we're getting for thermals because of the concrete and glass shell of the building. Below you see the scope feeds from eight snipers eyeballing assigned windows and egress locations. We have four watching the front, three the back, and one the roof."

Jose stepped back to the right and indicated the lower left quadrant. "Here's the blueprints filed with the city for a development permit. The industrial cleaning layout is simple, one set of open stairs up to a couple offices on a five meter high platform in the northwest corner. Washrooms and change rooms on the ground floor below the offices. The rest of the space is open storage and maintenance workspace. That last bay is supposed to be open space. The blinds are closed on the cleaning company windows; we weren't able to confirm current reality versus these blueprints."

The site knowledge and prep impressed Kesa. *SWAT hasn't been here long. By what they achieved in a short time, Jose runs a top-notch crew.* Kesa turned to Jose and rattled off her instructions. "Have your tech feed that data to my team's helmet displays and hologram projectors. Let everyone working this inner perimeter know we're deploying drones, robots, and scouting tech. Our equipment has an orange phoenix front and back. Your snipers should take out anything that doesn't belong to you or me."

Noah faked a cough to get Kesa's attention. He gazed meaningfully at the wall of screens.

Kesa gave him a dark look, but still made the request. "Oh, and my team likes your command post better than our truck-side control center. Can we pump our data to your tech's console for sifting through here?"

"Wilco, Corporal James." Jose donned a headset to relay instructions to his team and gave his tech the thumbs-up to push the requested data feeds to Phoenix.

Kesa led Phoenix out of the command post for a huddle at their parked Rivians. Kona barked from her shade shelter, angry at missing out.

"That was subtle, Boomer." Kesa shoved Noah.

Noah held up his hands in mock surrender. "Size counts, Viper. We have our minime thirty-three centimeter screens and sunshine glare out here or the brilliant four square meters of display in there."

Kesa shook her head. "Never change, Boomer." She asked Willow, the team's robotics specialist, "Ice, who's ready to go out of WALL-E, R2-D2, and Rosie?"

"I patched R2 up after he got the crap shot out of him on the last mission, but haven't had time to run a full battery of readiness tests," Willow replied.

"WALL-E and Rosie are both one hundred percent. If we're only sending one, it's WALL-E's turn."

"Yeah, just one for now. Get him ready, he's going in the front door. Fire, what do you recommend for scouting tech after seeing the intel?" Kesa asked, shifting her attention to River.

"The place looks buttoned up tight, so I'll drop a couple bumblebees and geckos into the HVAC vents and see how far they can go," River replied. "A single drone drop should suffice. Our prey isn't taking out drones based on those SWAT drones hovering unmolested." River gestured at the drones buzzing around the building.

"Agreed, execute on that," Kesa said. "Fire and Ice, grab whatever help you need with your gear from Fist and Boomer. Advance WALL-E to the target building's parking lot but hold there pending success or failure of the scouting tech getting us eyes in the building. Weapons check and body armor as time allows for everyone except Ice."

Willow grabbed Mason to assist. Kesa expected this, since WALL-E weighed one hundred and twenty-five kilograms with his enhanced armor. They shouldn't need to muscle him around, but sometimes the biped bots get twisted up in their shipping containers. *Shocker, the bots end up contorted more often when River drives the convoy's lead Rivian.*

River and Noah hustled over to another Rivian to sift through the drone kits, seeking two bumblebees and two geckos. Each Rivian carried a biped robot and a couple drone kits, for redundancy and to enable the team to ready deployment packages without tripping over each other.

Willow and Mason reached into the truck bed and popped open the heavy-duty latches on WALL-E's container. The shape and size reminded Kesa of the caskets people used to insist being buried in to take up land forever. WALL-E looked none the worse for the trip.

"WALL-E, disembark," Willow called out.

The biped robot leaned forward from lying on his back and vaulted out of his container in one fluid motion. You couldn't tell, but he had scanned the entire area by the time he landed to identify people, vehicles, buildings, robots, and perceived threats.

WALL-E was an example of the controlled AI directive the original nations of the world agreed to in 2024. AI research, development, and products are limited to specific purpose AIs that are assigned a human responsible for the AI's actions. The agreement banned AI general intelligence research; the Alliance monitored facilities with compute power exceeding personal workstations for banned research.

By ordering WALL-E to do anything, Willow became responsible.

WALL-E had purpose-built AI routines for moving, fighting unarmed or armed, and intelligence gathering. WALL-E had no ability to formulate independent action or have concern for his well-being. If no one instructed him to defend, Kesa could walk up with a diamond blade cut-off saw and disassemble him without WALL-E reacting. *Don't worry WALL-E, you're my favorite. I would never do that to you.*

"WALL-E advance to five meters out from primary man door of target building and defend." Willow ordered. Ordered to defend, WALL-E would target and destroy anyone or anything shooting at or striking him.

Kesa hoped none of Jose's snipers accidentally shot at WALL-E. Death was certain if WALL-E remained functional and no one from Phoenix was around to countermand the defend order. It happened before, but stupid is as stupid does.

"Wilco," WALL-E said, sounding like his namesake from the 2008 animated movie. Kesa didn't want to know how long it took Willow to dig up that audio.

WALL-E beelined straight for the ordered position, running at ten meters per second. He somersaulted over a one and half meter high fence that intersected the shortest route. Smart people didn't tangle with WALL-E and his 2067 model brethren. Versus an above-average male soldier with top end gear, the bipeds ran four times as fast, were eight times as strong, and had armor twice as bullet resistant.

Within thirty seconds of vaulting out of his container, WALL-E stood facing the door at the position ordered. He held his M6 carbine in the low ready position. The Alliance fireteams preferred their bipeds to use human-compatible weapons to enable fast swaps between carbines, grenade launchers, non-lethals, or whatever the flavor of the day was.

After WALL-E departed the parking lot to take up his forward position, the whisper of a stealth drone's engine fired up nearby. River and Noah had unpacked a drone and loaded it up with the scouting tech package. The drone whizzed by ten centimeters off Kesa's right ear. Normal people would have ducked in surprise, but she didn't even flinch. For starters, Kesa had abnormally steady nerves. She also got used to River's shit during his six months on her team. Kesa gave him the finger, which he pretended to ignore as he operated the drone for the rooftop HVAC unit drop.

Kesa headed into the command post. Kani had the video and data feeds for WALL-E and the drone up and running on the vibrant wall sized display. *These screens are sweet; I wonder what this command post costs? Certainly more than Phoenix has budget for this year.*

Jose glanced back at her as she entered. "Who signs the checks for your team? I want to get my crew a few armored Rivians and kick-ass biped bots."

"I consider our equipment budget as a fair trade for being roped into whatever the worst shitstorm of each day turns out to be," Kesa said. She checked out WALL-E's video and vital stats in the upper right quadrant of the display.

"Fair enough. I'm sure the typical New Boston shitstorm my team has to handle doesn't hold a candle to what happens Alliance worldwide." Jose pointed to the lower left quadrant of the screen. "Here's your drone making its drop."

The drone neared the rooftop HVAC unit. Four scouting tech minibots deployed. The bumblebees were single rotor stealth minidrones just under a cubic centimeter in size, simply a rotor and an 8K camera with a transmitter. The geckos were three centimeters long walkers. Their four vacuum suction feet made of a synthetic material provided adhesion to almost any surface. Kesa clenched and unclenched a fist to release some tension. *Each minibot's ultra-high density nanogel battery alone costs more than I make in three months. Let's try to not blow up our expensive toys on this mission.*

Jose's command post tech was a pro. On her own initiative, she repurposed the upper right quadrant of the video wall from useless thermals into a split quad for the minibot feeds. Kesa glanced at her surreptitiously. *Is she satisfied working for New Boston PD SWAT, or perhaps open to a Phoenix job?*

Jose must have caught the movement. "Don't even think about it. Kani is so valuable to my team that I married her to stave off talent poachers."

Kani laughed as she monitored her personal screens that showed all incoming data, much more than she selected to feature on the floor to ceiling screens. "Don't you believe him, Corporal James, because I'd leave in a second for the right offer."

CHAPTER THIRTEEN – 20:00 June 1, 2070 – Chaos vs. Fluid Response

The battlefield is a scene of constant chaos. The winner will be the one who controls that chaos, both his own and the enemies.

Napoleon Bonaparte

River's minibot spies worked their way through the rooftop HVAC unit on the industrial cleaning company's bay. A Birther cell used this legitimate business as a front for their operations. Fortunately, the last maintenance crew installed the HVAC filter off kilter, leaving a gap sufficient for the minibots to infiltrate. Displayed on the command center's screens, River split one minibot off into each HVAC drop branch. He skipped every second one on each side to spread his remote eyes throughout the space. Soon enough, each minibot acquired line of site from centimeters outside their respective HVAC ducts.

"No tangos in the open area, Viper," River said over the comms channel. "Moving a bee to the offices. Hey, does something seem off versus the blueprints?"

Kesa scanned the stable video feeds from the geckos River left parked on the underside of the HVAC vents, each focusing on half of the open area. *The office and washroom dimensions align with the floor plans, but what is on the opposite wall?* "You're right Fire. There's either a new long skinny closet on the wall between the bays or someone installed a covered stairwell to a new basement. Can you get a bee in there?"

"We only need an eleven millimeter gap under the door," River replied, one bee already heading over to the unknown structure while the other buzzed over to the offices. The minibot code included pathfinding AI. River could specify a destination and focus on something else until the minibot arrived and signaled him for more instructions. He could also specify a series of waypoints if he wanted a particular general path followed or take direct control.

The first bee arrived at the offices. It wafted through the air circulation gap at the bottom of the door. River brought it up to head height to scan the office space in both standard video and thermal. He repeated the scan from each corner.

The tech processed the feeds and put up a consolidated 3-D rotating view. There was nothing of interest to Phoenix and SWAT, merely typical office furniture.

"3-D composite verifies no tango in the offices." Kesa broadcasted over the comms.

"Roger. One bee and two geckos now allocated to space surveillance. They will alert on movement or thermal change," River advised. The office bee headed to a suitable vantage point to monitor the general area.

The other bee dipped under the door of the mystery room. After barely enough floor space for the door swing, a set of wooden stairs with no handrail descended. The walls and ceiling enclosing the staircase were just steel studs and the outer drywall. A bare bulb hung inside the upper door, providing adequate light to the upper part of the stairs, but not much else. The wiring and junction box for the light were stapled haphazardly to the open stud drywall. The bee drifted above the stairs, descending four meters below grade, where there was a short hallway leading to a sturdy door. River had the bee scan the lower door and hall, flipping between video and thermals to find anything of note.

"Definitely off-book construction," Jose said, "none of this would pass an inspection. They're lucky they didn't hit a water or sewer line when they were digging."

"The coming and going of cleaning vans was masterful cover to dispose of dirt. It must have been painful packaging it all up for transport and disposal." Kesa said.

River moved the drone to examine the lower door. The drone camera's onboard AI image enhancement software provided crystal clear 8K imagery, even in the dim lighting. River narrated as he scanned. "Steel door in a steel frame. This is quality work; the door and frame seam is fingernail thick at most."

"Based on the measurements and style," Kani added, "that's a top end door and frame combo kit from the leading local security door manufacturer."

Kesa digested the information, scrunching her face in concentration. *Why beat your head against a door when you can go around it?* "We won't bother with the door and frame. We'll use a shaped charge and blow the surrounding wall. Ice, acknowledge?"

"Wilco," Willow replied.

In the video feed, WALL-E sprinted back to the staging area. He soon returned to his post by the cleaning company front door with a small backpack.

"Unless somebody has more intel," Kesa said over the team comms, "we're proceeding with what we know." She paused for a few seconds; her team would speak up with any pertinent information. After hearing nothing, Kesa issued the order. "Ice, you have a go for robot entry into the basement."

"Wilco," Willow said. "WALL-E, enter the target location in defend mode."

Kani brought WALL-E's video feed up on the wall screen beside the feed from the SWAT drone with WALL-E in frame. WALL-E walked to the door and tugged it with human strength.

Jose looked at Kesa with raised eyebrows.

"He has superb manners," she said, "and why break a perfectly good door if you don't need to?"

The gentle touch not working, the whining and clicking of WALL-E applying more force increased in volume. When pulling on the handle didn't work, WALL-E's AI routines for gaining entry switched tracks. He pulled out his shin mounted pry bar, smashed the glass, and entered. The response was eerily nothing: no alarms, no shooting, no yelling, and nobody popping out. WALL-E holstered his pry bar, walked to the stairwell upper door, and tried it. This one turned and opened.

"I guess our prey rushed too much to lock the upper door," Willow said. "Let's hope the same for the lower."

WALL-E descended the stairs, M6 carbine unerringly covering the bottom door's latch side, where a threat would most likely first appear.

River backed his bee halfway up the stairwell to provide an overhead view, passing disconcertingly close to WALL-E's head as he walked down the stairs.

There was an audible click when WALL-E's lead foot stepped on the bottom stair. "Oh, shit," Willow said over team comms.

WALL-E's and the nearby bee's video feeds blipped out while the other minibot feeds showed WALL-E being blown four meters upward. The explosion thumped immediately on the audio from the feeds and echoed soon after in the command post as a muffled boom from afar. The drywall blew outward from the blast. WALL-E hit the mostly intact steel studs framing the stairwell then fell, landing face down in a heap on the stairs. Without pausing, WALL-E rolled over and trained his M6 on the door.

"What the fuck, they blew up WALL-E," Noah shouted over the comms.

Kesa shared his anger since WALL-E was their favorite.

Kona barked in the background of Noah's feed. She was attuned to her team members' emotions, especially her handler.

"Settle down, Phoenix, WALL-E just served his key purpose of keeping us intact." Kesa said over the comms. "Hold for sitrep."

The team absorbed the situation in the video feeds, whether on the wall screens in the command post or via personal helmet displays and holograms. There drywall and other dust in the air obscured regular vision, but each source's AI image enhancement yielded usable video. Other than the stairwell drywall blow out, there was no activity in the open area. River's stairwell bee was MIA, but WALL-E's video feed had returned.

"Ice, how's our boy?" Kesa asked.

"Re-establishing comms with him now," Willow replied. "The charge blew off the entire leg that triggered it, also severed the other leg at the knee joint."

As she spoke, Kani highlighted WALL-E's self-diagnostics display over the feeds.

"He is functional other than a complete loss of lower mobility," Willow concluded.

River moved his remaining bee overhead to view the staircase. Other than drywall and other debris settling, there was no sign of movement.

"Boomer, any idea what that was?" Kesa asked Noah, the team's explosives expert, over the team comms.

Noah responded quickly. "I checked WALL-E's logs. The device triggered as soon as forty kilos of his weight shifted to the leading foot. With the click we heard and no wires or lasers showing up on Fire's scouting tech or WALL-E's camera, this was definitely a pressure switch. The explosion was beefy and semi-directed, but not as focused and damaging as a military anti-personnel device. I'd rate it as a superior quality IED that our prey set up on their own. We should expect more of the same."

Other than dreading the resulting paperwork, Kesa was relieved the bots were there to trigger traps. *I prefer that Willow spends a couple weeks repairing WALL-E versus a team member losing a leg or worse. We need another soldier.* "Send in Rosie with a new strip charge pack, Ice. Pull WALL-E out of the way in case we need to follow Rosie."

"Wilco, forty-five seconds to ready," Willow acknowledged.

The quick turnaround impressed Kesa. *She must have started prepping Rosie as soon as WALL-E triggered the IED.*

Five seconds earlier than promised, Willow issued orders to Rosie. She echoed them over the team comms to keep everyone aware of robot activity. "Rosie, retrieve WALL-E and set him up for sentry duty at ground level."

Rosie whipped through the various video feeds and grabbed WALL-E by the service handle on his back armor. WALL-E didn't react. Alliance military robots planned interactions and kept aware of each other's position and orders via secure Wi-Fi. WALL-E's feed started to bounce and move backwards up the stairs. Unaffected by the rough handling, WALL-E maintained a perfect weapon lock on the door's latch side. Rosie dragged WALL-E to the corner of the main area and set him up where he had maximum line of fire.

"Rosie, set the strip charge around the downstairs door midway between the door frame and corridor wall," Willow said over the comms. "Retreat for detonation three meters past the top of the stairs. Defend if attacked."

Rosie advanced down the stairs, gracefully leaping the missing stairs and a small rubble pile at the bottom. She trained her M6 on the steel door as she approached it, arriving without being blown up or fired upon. Letting the M6 hang by its sling, she placed the strip charges in a textbook breach pattern on the wall around the door frame. She affixed the detonating cord and unrolled it up the stairs. "Tasks complete, standing by." Rosie broadcast on the team's comm channel in the vintage Jetsons cartoon robot's voice.

Kesa gave Jose an embarrassed head shake.

Joes reassured her with a shrug, saying off comms, "A good leader knows when to let their team have some fun."

CHAPTER FOURTEEN – 20:25 June 1, 2070 – Striking from the Grave

Religious fundamentalists and political radicals don't think like us. Never make the mistake of thinking extremists will act reasonably, because they will die for their beliefs. General Max Williams, welcoming speech for JSA operations class of 2068

"Ice, proceed with robot breach and sweep. You have command while the rest of us gear up for entry." Kesa relayed the orders as she exited the command post. She joined Noah, Mason, and River, already at their military spec Rivians pulling body armor and weapons out of Pelican watertight gear boxes.

Willow ignored her teammates as they donned their close quarters combat gear. She sat in one of the three Rivians, engrossed in the data feeds from the bots and minibots. "Rosie, breach the door and enter. Defend if attacked."

Kesa selected Rosie's feed for her helmet viewer so she could gear up while monitoring the breech. Rosie triggered the blasting cap at her end of the detonating cord with a jolt of electricity from her less-than-lethal shock tipped finger. The entire detonating cord disappeared all at once in a flash, a burn rate of 6,400 meters per second hard to capture in anything but super slow replay. The shaped charge around the security door's frame disappeared in an orange and yellow burst, followed immediately by a dull thump. The explosion boomed via Rosie's feed and echoed much subdued a fraction of a second later at the SWAT staging area. This explosion was a shaped charge, directing its force straight into the walls around the steel door. It was quieter than the IED that WALL-E triggered and didn't result in debris launching up into the main area.

Rosie ran down the stairwell four steps at a time, M6 held at the ready. There wasn't any wall left holding up the lower door up, a kick from Rosie toppled it. Before it hit the floor, she ran over it into the room beyond. The Birthers built the underground room crudely: cinder block walls, metal decking for the ceiling, and plastic deck boards for the floor. They furnished sparsely, only setting up three collapsible tables and four folding chairs. Closed lid wooden shipping crates one meter wide and three quarters of a meter tall sat under each table and beside two of them.

As soon as Rosie entered the room, four Birther terrorists leaned around shipping crates and opened fire. They sprayed ten 7.62x39 mm rounds/second at her from AK-65 assault rifles in full automatic mode. In defend mode as she entered the room, Rosie targeted potential tangos immediately but had to wait for an attack condition before firing. The click of a trigger engaging on a weapon pointed at her allowed her to open fire. The first terrorist fired only five bullets before a red blossom sprouted from his forehead, the back of his head exploding in pink mist.

Rosie was targeting the second terrorist as the first 5.56×45 mm bullet left the barrel of her M6 carbine. The second terrorist sprayed seven bullets before the back of her head burst. All ricocheted off Rosie's thick frontal armor. The droning boom of the unsuppressed AK-65s firing full auto echoed throughout the small room. Occasional single shots from Rosie's relatively quiet suppressed M6 punctuated the AK-65 din. The metallic ringing of spent cartridges bouncing off the floor was barely discernable.

The first nine of the ten bullets the third terrorist fired whizzed close by Rosie's head, burying themselves in the cinder block wall behind her. At the same time as Rosie bullet lobotomized the third terrorist, his tenth bullet hit Rosie's 8K camera square on. It was a one in fifty thousand shot, given the small size of the lens and its armored and slanted outer ring housing. Rosie paused two milliseconds to switch to her thermal camera to target the fourth terrorist.

Due to the vagaries of thermal imaging, Rosie's kill shot on the fourth terrorist was three mm off her forehead's dead center. No matter, dead is dead and Rosie had no feelings to suffer shame for imperfection. This last terrorist unloaded only thirteen bullets, all of which bounced off Rosie's armor. From the first click of an AK-65 trigger to the thud of the last body hitting the floor, a mere one and half seconds passed.

"Damn," Jose exclaimed over the broadcast comms channel.

I bet they've never seen a combat robot in action. An analogy might help. "Fighting a combat robot in a confined space with small arms is akin to bringing boxing gloves to a gunfight," Kesa said. "Oh, and what do you want to bet the New Soviets will have paperwork proving someone stole those AK-65s and smuggled them out of their country?"

"They shot Rosie in the damn eye. What kind of person shoots someone in the eye?" Noah said over the comms.

"Stop whining. You're not the one spending the next few weeks repairing robots," Willow replied.

Kesa broadcast her orders over the comms. "Listen up team. With Rosie's camera out, we need to search for intel. Ice, Jose, and Kani review the video and Rosie's thermal feed for any threats or other entrances to that room. Fist, Boomer, Fire, Kona and I are entering if you don't see anything of concern." *It's probably the opposite of good leadership to ask River not to get killed like his predecessor did. Best I can do is look out for him.*

Her entry team geared up to prepare for this contingency. Phoenix Fireteam wore body armor top rated for ballistic, fragmentation, and stab protection. The team's helmets included integrated cameras and could project a display onto the back of the bullet resistant visor. Their M6 carbines with suppressors hung on slings across their front. Each had sets of flash bangs, smoke grenades, and fragmentation grenades in pouches mounted on specific locations on their chest rack. A holstered SIG SAUER M29 9x19 mm pistol topped off everyone's kit.

Kona wore her protective vest with an integrated camera and biofeedback. From kilometers away, Noah could instruct her which direction to go by triggering the four vibration packs.

Kona tested within the top ten of the hundreds of bomb-sniffing dogs working throughout the Alliance. She could detect the most compounds with ninety-five percent true positive rate at parts per trillion sensitivity. Researchers spent billions since 1990 trying to supersede sniffer dogs. However, even eighty years later, the tech's performance remained an order of magnitude behind dogs bred for the job. Kesa shuddered, remembering how much expensive gear she traded the NYPD to encourage them to "give" Kona to her team. She still watched her back when in New York, fearing retribution from Kona's ex-handler. He believed Kesa had abducted a member of his family.

Kesa waited semi-patiently for Willow to report in. *My team needs to work without me wasting everyone's time by hassling them. Knowing what excellent leadership is doesn't make the waiting any easier.* Out of the corner of her eye, she caught River and Mason shaking hands while looking her way. "Fuck both of you," she said in her low ass-whooping warning tone, "especially whoever bet I would crack and pester Ice."

"You have a 'go', Viper. The three of us don't see any signs of other entrances or tangos." Willow said over the team broadcast channel. "We're unanimously concerned about the contents of the five ominous shipping crates."

Wordlessly, the entry team jogged over to the industrial cleaning company with River on point. Kona trotted beside Noah. Highly trained working dogs like her function best off leash, no bias from the handler.

River pushed the door's broken glass aside with his combat boot and reached in to unlock the deadbolt. He propped the door open in case the team needed to leave with haste. No one wants to get hung up on jagged glass trying to squeeze through a closed frame.

Noah motioned along the interior wall. "Go," he said to Kona. She trotted beside the wall, sniffing on the move but slowing to give containers an extra sniff. She didn't alert to anything along that wall, nor along the back wall of the shop. Now turning to follow the wall with the new stairwell, she stepped gingerly among the scattered pieces of drywall. She barked when she came upon WALL-E's leg.

Kesa had to smile. *That sounded like a bark half explosives alert and half 'Why is WALL-E's leg here?'*

"Good girl, keep going," Noah shouted to Kona while gesturing the direction he wanted her to go. "She tweaked on the residue on WALL-E's leg, nothing else yet," he said to the team.

Kona continued heading along the opposite wall, passing by the now open staircase. She got to WALL-E and sniffed his pack, alerting with an excited bark and staring at Noah. WALL-E didn't bother to acknowledge her presence since canines are not combat robots' best friends.

"Good girl, Kona," he praised. "Just WALL-E's shaped charges," he said aside to the team.

Kesa waved the team to the ramshackle stairwell. "Down we go."

Noah gestured down the stairs. "Go," he said to Kona.

She headed down the stairs, jumping over the blown bottom ones, but circling back to give a sniff and a bark. "Good girl, more residue. Go," Noah said as he gestured into the room and jumped the broken steps.

Everyone stacked up at the room's entrance.

Rosie ignored them. Nobody programmed combat robots for niceties.

The room was thick with the iron smell of blood and the acrid smell of spent bullet propellant. Each body lay where Rosie shot them, the remnant of each head surrounded by a large pool of blood. The terrorists' head wounds bled profusely until their hearts realized they were dead and stopped pumping.

Noah gestured at the two crates on the room's left side. "Go," he said to Kona.

She stood her ground and stared balefully at him.

This behavior didn't seem new to Noah, because without hesitation he pointed to the other three crates. "Go," he repeated.

Kona proceeded, giving the first two crates a thorough sniff as she trotted by.

Kesa tapped her trigger finger impatiently on the side of her M6's magazine. *Does it still count as taking orders if someone simply refuses orders until getting one they want to follow?*

River headed over to the nearby tables and rummaged around in the papers spread haphazardly on top.

"Are you the dog handler," Mason asked Noah, "or is she the people handler?"

"Well, Fist," Noah said matter-of-factly, "I've come to understand Kona has her own ideas about some things and that it is unproductive to argue with her over such matters." Throughout the exchange, he kept his eyes on Kona as she approached the third crate and pushed her nose right to its seams to sniff. Kona sat and barked emphatically at Noah.

"Pop the seam of that lid for me," Noah ordered as he hurried over to the crate, "one and only one millimeter." He pulled out a light and magnifying glass on his way. "Good girl, now back." He gestured Kona toward the entryway.

Kesa dashed to assist, signaling Morgan to join. *When your demolitions expert wants something done fast, the smart money doesn't get all wound up over the chain of command.*

Finding the lid unsecured, they lifted it up a fingernail's thickness.

Noah crawled all the way around, inspecting with his light and magnifying glass. "No switches or wires that I can see. Now lift it super slow, but be ready to freeze if I say."

Kesa and Morgan lifted the lid up five centimeters in slow motion.

69

"OK, take it away," Noah said.

Kesa turned back after putting the lid against the nearby wall. Noah's expression was dead serious. His eyes rapidly scanned the contents of the crate. *Oh, oh, what's going on that has our demolitions expert wired?* Kesa stepped closer to get a look. Inside the crate was a seamless stainless steel box the size of a shoebox. It sat on a couple of containers taking most of the room in the crate. Wires emerging from the box went into the containers. There was a red digital display on the box, too small and far away for her to read.

"OUT!" Noah yelled and headed for the stairwell.

Everyone exploded into motion, nobody wanting to stay in a room the demolitions expert was exiting at high-speed. Kona had no manners and didn't wait for slow two legs on normal days; she was halfway up the stairs by the time Noah stood up. River, Noah, Kesa, and Mason barreled up the stairs. Rosie took up the rear behind Mason. In contrast to Kona, Rosie's programming made her leave a room last in a bug out situation. An armored robot taking up the rear on panic exits had saved many soldiers' lives.

By the time the team burst out of the stairwell at full tilt, Kona stood on the parking lot's far side, barking furiously.

Kesa translated the barking as "Hurry up, idiots."

River didn't bother turning and running for the regular exit at the other corner of the industrial cleaners' frontage. He aimed his M6 at a low upward angle and sprayed a few bullets through the large pane of glass straight ahead. Without missing a step, he ran past WALL-E and straight through what used to be a floor to ceiling window.

Kesa ran by WALL-E. He perched passively against the wall, not saying goodbye and not begging to be rescued from whatever crummy thing was going to happen soon. *Sorry, buddy, I know you don't give two shits about whether you blow up, but I will miss you.*

Willow must have issued recovery orders on Rosie's direct comms channel, since Rosie grabbed WALL-E and slung him over her shoulder as she trotted by. WALL-E brought his M6 up and covered their exit from his rear-facing perspective.

The instant River neared Kona, she galloped fifty meters toward their staging area and turned to bark frantically at the entry team.

"Boomer, how far do we need to run?" River huffed.

River, nor anyone else on the team, was tiring given their elite physical condition. Kesa agreed, however, that it wasn't fun running in full gear any longer than necessary.

"Well, nowadays I keep going until Kona stops," Noah replied. "The one-time I didn't, I ended up with a piece of shrapnel in my shoulder as a reward for my independent thinking. Since she's still wired up, we need to pick up the pace. Also, the explosive component containers were uncomfortably largish."

Kona freaking and "uncomfortably largish" explosive containers? None of this sounds good. "Come on team, full out sprint," Kesa said.

Everyone put their obsessive physical training to use in an all-out sprint back to the staging area. They arrived to find Kona noisily lapping up water from her dish. Apparently, she deemed the staging area far enough away from the bomb.

CHAPTER FIFTEEN – 20:40 June 1, 2070 – Blowing Up and Winding Down

A civil society encourages educated and productive discourse to foster continuous improvement. Those finding this insufficient for their personal agenda can choose to leave the society. If they instead choose to violate the laws of civil conduct, society must take their freedom or their life.

Mala Safanzai, Alliance Presidential candidate campaign speech 2034

"Cover!" Kesa shouted as she sprinted into the SWAT staging area.

Jose's team members that weren't already behind or in cover leaped to get there. Situationally aware people had already taken cover when they saw a fearless Alliance fireteam sprinting toward them.

The entry team stopped at the opposite side of the command trailer from the Birther base. The trailer provided excellent shelter because of its heavy-duty stabilization legs and reinforced walls.

Kona trotted up, giving them a perfunctory "wuff."

Kesa petted her. "Yeah, I know, about time the two legs arrived."

Noah started counting down over open comms. "Ten, nine, eight, seven,"

Kesa wasn't surprised the skilled demolitions expert could race up a staircase, sprint two hundred meters after their insane genius bomb dog, and still be able to count down synchronized to a timer he had only glanced at.

"Six, five, four, three, two, one," Noah concluded.

The explosion at this distance was a thunderous, but not quite ear ringing, crump. There was a hint of breaking glass within the raw explosion's noise as the generous glazing of the industrial cleaning business blew out. The rumble of concrete and steel collapsing followed as the last two bays of the building fell apart. A dust cloud blasted into the air and obscured all the video feeds on the target. The blast wave threw drones caught close to the building to the ground. Chunks of concrete rained down in the area, but none more than one-hundred-fifty meters away from ground zero.

Kesa had the entire team in her line of sight. *Everyone accounted for and intact. No need for a comms call out.*

Kona was unconcerned. Every bomb-sniffing dog heard many explosives go off in the distance, either as unplanned events akin to today or in disposal operations.

Jose worked the comms to check on all of his people. The interactions were quick and calm, good signs that everyone was in one piece.

Kesa initiated comms to Kani. "Kani, can you run the explosion video to my teams' helmets?"

"Wilco." Kani looped several views of the explosion to Phoenix's helmet screens.

"OK, Boomer," Kesa said, "you saw the bomb, you heard the blast, and you watched the video feed. What's your gut say?"

Noah paused for a second, looking into space while performing mental calculations. "It was definitely high-order explosive. The size of the blast versus the volume of the materials in the crate makes me confident it was an ANFO bomb rather than military grade explosives." With everyone still paying attention, he continued. "But I gotta say, the workmanship of the timer, detonation device, and materials containment was top end. The stair pressure switch bomb was not something an amateur could build. Unless we prove one of those bodies was our bomb maker, we need to find them and take them out of commission before they can fabricate more devices."

"Hey hotshot, why didn't you disarm the bomb instead of running away as fast as you could?" Willow said, pausing to rib Noah as she instructed Rosie to load WALL-E for transport.

"It's not like the movies, Ice. It takes time to disarm a bomb." From his tone, Noah didn't find the question amusing. "A helluva lot more time than fifty-five seconds. With that sealed stainless steel housing securing the timer and trigger, I would have barely lifted it away before a lot of pressure and heat ended my days."

"Relax Boomer, I want you to stay in one big grouchy piece of flesh your dog can boss around rather than blown to bits trying to show off for the girls." Willow came over and squeezed his shoulder. He nodded in surrender and released the tension knotted in his trapezius and shoulders. At the nearby Rivian, Rosie hopped into her transport container and powered down.

"How do you think the timer started?" River asked. "As soon as Rosie entered that room, nobody had time to pick their nose. Forget about arming a bomb."

"One terrorist probably had a proximity and life watchdog tied to the bomb via radio or Bluetooth," Noah replied. "It's all the rage at terrorist parties these days. The timer starts if you take a captured terrorist more than a set distance away from the bomb or stop the terrorist's pulse. They chose ten mikes as a timer to try killing some Alliance law enforcement besides destroying all the intel in the room. They foresaw needing a delay between the timer trigger event and detonation. What they didn't count on was our response speed and our two hundred meter site clearance protocol."

"Thanks for the expert analysis, Boomer. Everyone head into the command post for video review and intel dump with Jose." Kesa led the way into the trailer.

Jose and Kani were already reviewing the video when Kesa and her team entered.

"How's your team, Commander?" Kesa asked, hoping for the best.

"All living, breathing SWAT members that came to site are uninjured," Jose said with a grin. "Two SWAT drones are unaccounted for and assumed KIA. I saw your entire team make a timely exit. Things were tense in here during the mad dash. Where do you want to begin the video review?"

"Let's bring up the helmet cams for the entry team and run them slow and time synced," Kesa requested.

Kani brought the feeds up on the video wall, running quarter speed. The team watched in silence, trying to find something useful before the bug out.

"We are interested in actionable intel. From what I have seen, only Fire's feed might have it. Does anyone think their feed may have caught intel?" Kesa's question met with silence and heads shaking "no". Kani moved River's feed up front, centered and large on the video wall, again running at quarter speed from the underground room entry point.

"Fire, we're only seeing what the camera captured," Kesa said. "Can you narrate?"

"While everyone else took care of the bomb search, I searched for intel." River talked and pointed as the playback ran. "I only had time to sift through the top layers of paper on the closest table. Note that everything is ink and paper, no computer printouts. The Birthers rarely digitize data since Alliance operatives can't hack paper. Hold on, there's a couple of interesting items here."

Kani paused on the best frame that showed a drawing on the table.

River pointed out key features on the drawing. "This is a map of an urban warfare training zone. Note the building outlines drawn at scale and lines of fire drawn from tactically strong positions."

"I agree," Kesa said. "Unfortunately, this layout of a few buildings could be on a private ranch, in a small town, or many other places. We'll see what the analysts come back with from an AI fuzzy match versus all mapping available." She signaled Kani to roll the feed again.

"The rest of the top layer looked mundane, but maybe the analysts will derive useful information," River said. "Pause after I push those papers aside, please. Here's another map. This one is a typical underground bunker complex, albeit a large one. See the room tags for housing, kitchens, cold storage, and recreation? Someone designed this facility as long term housing for hundreds of people. There's also a sizable space labeled 'armory' fitting with the Birther playbook. The rest of the video is us getting the hell out. Oh, check it out, that blur is Kona going from standing still to top speed in six strides." River nodded to Kesa.

"The bunker map is an interesting find, Fire." It pleased Kesa that the team gleaned this intel before the bomb destroyed it. "We can assume they built without development permits, so we won't hold our breath for a match to any plans on record. The JSA analysts have worked wonders before; maybe they can determine where this bunker is located. Kani, have you had time to compile explosion video?"

Kani nodded and ran a composite of drone, minibot, sniper sight, helmet cams, and body cams showing the explosion's destructive majesty.

The video feed substantiated how close on their heels the building exploded and collapsed into a crater. Kesa shivered at the near miss. "Thanks go to Boomer and Kona for getting our asses out in time. I no longer harbor any regret for being forced to include my beloved PGWDTI LRT-7 .50 caliber sniper rifle in the trade for Kona."

"Thanks, Viper," Noah mumbled, blushing a bit. "We're just looking out for the team."

"Commander, we're packing up and heading out," Kesa announced. "The scene is yours to process and clean up, enjoy. When your team sifts through the rubble, they should find a combat robot leg and a half belonging to my friend WALL-E. We'd appreciate if you could ship it to us along with sharing any useful forensics data. It has been a real pleasure working with you and your team." Kesa shook Jose's hand and then mimed "call me" to Kani, who smiled in return.

"Your team does remarkable work, Corporal James," Jose said. "SWAT learned a lot today that will help us down the road. I will personally ship you every robot leg we find, but I will not send my wife to join your merry band of soldiers."

Phoenix Fireteam and SWAT laughed at the exchange. Cherry-picking talented crew was an endless chess match between law enforcement entities in the Alliance.

Kesa and the team geared down and packed everything into the Rivians.

Noah apprehensively opened Kona's travel carrier; often there was a contest of wills to load her. Kona had enough excitement for one day, however, as she entered without hesitation and curled up to sleep.

It has been a long day, too bad there isn't enough room for me to curl up with Kona for a nap. Kesa shook off her tiredness and continued packing the gear. She couldn't rest easy until squaring Phoenix away.

River insisted on driving again. Perhaps he was tired, since he didn't drive like a bat out of hell on the return trip. Once they were underway, River gave her the "can I ask you a question" look.

"Speak your mind, Fire. It's only us here," Kesa felt it essential her team feel comfortable bringing information, concerns, and questions to her.

River breathed a sigh of relief. "Why do they do it? The Birthers, I mean. Why kill people who haven't harmed them, people they don't even know? Why try fighting us then try reaching from the grave to kill us? Their philosophy is unfettered procreation, shouldn't they be about life instead of death?"

"You're right, the Birthers make little sense," Kesa said. "In the Alliance, we encourage everyone to speak their position and constructively debate policy. The Free Parenthood movement does that. They don't believe human overpopulation and the resulting overconsumption pushed the Earth to the brink. Although they disagree with some policies, they abide by the laws that protect them and their right to disagree. The Birthers refuse to work for change from within the system. They reap society's benefits while attacking those disagreeing with them or even just people they perceive as representing the government."

River was quiet for a minute, processing what Kesa said before continuing his questions. "Were there terrorists before the Alliance?"

Kesa smiled. *I slept through a history class or ten in high school; it sounds like you did too.* Kesa had worked hard later, in her officer's training, where lessons from history were a key part of the curriculum. "Fifty years ago, it was much worse. There were one hundred and ninety-five nations in the world instead of three. There was little international cooperation of sustained substance. Within most countries, many groups of people disagreed with their government, whether on a policy or religious basis. Several groups worldwide were as violent as or worse than the Birthers, often sponsored by rogue nations."

"I can't understand the rage," River said. "Since we get only one life, isn't our time too short to live in anger or hatred?"

"It certainly is, but some people choose to waste it," Kesa said. "Especially when you take the express exit those Birther terrorists chose today, by going toe-to-toe with a combat robot. To understand living in anger, consider this: what if your family owned ten apartment complexes in Franklin, but someone swindled them when you were young?"

"Show me where the swindler lives, I'm heading over for a not-so-civil chat," River said.

"Right. Now assume someone swindled the apartments from your great-great-great grandma. Even though the parties are long dead, you were told throughout your life that you are a victim and the rightful owner of the apartments. How do you feel?" Kesa asked.

"How are these apartments still standing? Isn't this swindle occurring over a hundred and fifty years ago?" River asked.

"Hey, it's a thought experiment, don't go bringing time and space physics into it." Kesa said.

"Fine, fine. I'd still feel angry. Even more so because of the repetitive programming giving me a permanent victim mentality." River slowly nodded.

"See how people fixate on the past rather than making the best of their one life? Now, back to reality. Humanity bathed the Earth in the blood of thousands of years of conflict." Kesa enjoyed revisiting her history course content. "Any race or nation can claim part of the planet was theirs before someone took it. Add four thousand religions, many of which taught that non-believers were heathens, and you have the fuel for never-ending conflict."

River's eyebrows went up and his eyes widened. "Wow, how did we get past it?"

"Well, I wouldn't say we're past it yet, but we have made tremendous strides," Kesa said. "Forty years ago, a hundred and twenty-three nations merged into the Alliance of Nations direct democracy, what you now call the Alliance. Given time to experience the Alliance's benefits, most people stopped wanting their own little nation. The Alliance worked with religious leaders to weave respect for people's freedom of religious choice into every religion. No more heathen non-believer teachings. What's the key clause from the Charter of Responsibilities and Rights?"

River had not slept through those classes since he answered without hesitation. "Everyone is equal; no one is more than equal."

"Good. Israel and Palestine were a great example of a religious and political conflict hot spot. Five million Palestinians and nine million Israelis lived in under thirty thousand square kilometers. Their religions completely differed, and they had land claims back and forth for a hundred years in the past. Life was one long war with an occasional breather. A terrorist group whose explicit goal was to exterminate the Israelis even governed a large part of Palestine for years." Kesa was into this since, as a military leader, she took special interest in learning from past conflict.

"Why aren't they still trying to kill each other?" River asked.

"The Alliance recognized that some people would never be willing to resolve the situation. They would raise their children to continue the hatred and war," Kesa said. "The Alliance offered everyone a new start anywhere in Alliance territory that had room. Due to population declines, there were many splendid places to migrate to, even in large groups. Since conditions were generally dreadful, everyone moving gained a higher standard of living and better opportunities. Perhaps most important, they were safe and able to live in peace. A divergent mix of residents remained: those willing to live together in peace and the diehards from each side. The diehards did exactly that, died hard. The Alliance didn't pussyfoot around with those resorting to violence to force others to comply with their ideals. This took decades to settle, things quieted down around 2060." *If only my professor could hear me; he never believed I paid attention in class.*

River continued driving. They were nearing their C-57. "I get it. People get invested in their own world view, whether driven by policy, religion, or a land claim. They have to choose whether to live past it by walking forward as part of civil society or to live looking and walking backwards, always stuck. Those with ideals incompatible with society might turn to violence because they believe that's a way to get what they want."

"That covers it," Kesa said. "By the way, thank those turning to violence for your job."

River turned into the schoolyard, the C-57 ramp already down for them to drive right in.

Kesa addressed the team once they parked the Rivians and took their seats. "Excellent work today, Phoenix Fireteam. We impressed our local allies with our execution. By following our perimeter plan and protocols, they endured the explosion with zero injuries to humans. We demonstrated technical expertise, fluidly integrated minibots and robots, neutralized the terrorists, and made a timely and professional exit to prevent loss of life. To sum up, you prevented the situation from turning into a soup sandwich. Buckle in and chow down on an MRE or take rack time before we're back at base."

"We would have been FUBAR without you, Kesa," Noah said. The rest of the team nodded in agreement.

"I'm thinking our exit appeared a lot more timely than professional." River said snidely.

Willow's eyes widened as she put her hand over her mouth, but the rest of the team had a good laugh.

Kesa laughed along with everyone else. *I agree, but there are always a couple of truthful ways to spin events, and my report is going the other way. I'm glad I can also assess the twins as performing as promised by their Alliance instructors.*

Everyone buckled up and passed out. Kesa's team slept whenever the opportunity came about.

You can eat on the run, but you can't sleep on the run. Kesa double-checked the wheel chocks, the tie-downs on the Rivians, and the team's seat buckles. Everything was flawless, of course, but she needed to confirm Phoenix's safety. "Phoenix Fireteam, ready for take-off," Kesa said over the comms to the pilot. She was pretty sure her buckle clicked shut before her eyes closed.

THE SINGULARITY – WILLOW

CHAPTER SIXTEEN – 11:00 June 4, 2070 – Trespassers will be ~~Shot~~ Embraced

When humanity realized our demotion to prey, survivors saw other survivors as friends until proven otherwise. According to the elders, people acted the opposite before Gaia.
Sophia Davis, 2065

Willow signaled her team to take cover as she dove behind a boulder. *Did gunfire just echo from the town?* Since this was her first mission as a scavenging team lead, her senses were on ultra-high alert. She gave her team the listen signal and gestured to the run-down town a couple of klicks north of their position. *River must wonder why my team halted. We didn't have stops scheduled in the open.* She faced his team and repeated the gestures.

Noah nodded to Willow as he lowered his binoculars. "Kesa signaled they received your message." On this mission, Noah filled the dual role of her mentor and the team second-in-command, same as Kesa did for River's team.

Willow's team crouched behind the readily available cover. The field they had just walked halfway through stretched four klicks from the edge of the forest to the edge of town. Boulders and hillocks person-sized to ten times that were strewn throughout the field. Long grasses that swayed in the gentle breeze covered the field and hillocks.

River's team took cover five hundred meters to her team's right. *I hope that was a door banging in the wind or something else inane. River and I aren't looking for trouble on our first mission as team leads, especially with our teams each including two relative newbies. Not a good roster for enemy contact.*

There was no mistaking the next salvo of gunfire. It was louder than the first noise and definitely coming from the town. Willow was not the only one concerned; both of her newbies' bodies tightened up and their breathing quickened.

Noah showed no signs of concern. He tilted his head toward the team's newbies.

Willow got the hint, breaking the silence since the threat was far out. She forced herself to sound calm. "Listen up team. We're hunkering down here until we understand what's going on in town. The Cave Cell teams in this area are here with all members accounted for, so we know Cave Cell isn't taking fire. If Gaia shows up in force, I'll make the call whether we bug out for the forest or stay in hiding. Logan, you focus on identifying air threats. Chloe, ground threats. Noah is monitoring for signals from River's team."

The newbies raised their binoculars and scanned the town. To prevent lens flash from giving away position, Cave Cell used binocular lenses with an anti-reflective coating and a plastic honeycomb grid.

Noah nodded affirmation to Willow after verifying the newbies were watching the town.

Willow felt less performance anxiety. *He's an excellent mentor, supporting my authority while still providing needed guidance so I can succeed as a team lead. When we were gearing up for this mission, he advised he's only intervening if team safety is at risk. I'm hoping to make intervention unnecessary.*

On multiple team missions, Cave Cell protocol was the team initiating an action took mission lead unless it explicitly handed off to another team. River's team would mirror her team's actions or take orders from her, which for now meant staying put and observing.

Willow considered herself backup for monitoring air and ground threats in case the newbies missed something. The far off popping of gunfire was moving closer. *I can hear several small caliber weapons and a few medium caliber in the action, all semi-auto mode so far.*

Chloe called out an observation without lowering her binoculars. "Blue building on the close edge of town furthest right corner, survivor with a carbine."

Willow oriented on the location. There was a male in ragged clothing with a dirty backpack. He was peeking back into the town from around his corner and firing the occasional round. After a minute, he paused and held his carbine at low ready. He signaled someone to move through his field of fire. A female in a similar state of disarray ran by him. She took cover behind a hillock close to the edge of town and in line with River's position.

Willow pondered the situation. *We need to determine if it's people fighting, which Cave Cell would stay out of, or if Gaia is involved.* She glanced at Noah. *Does he know anything?*

Noah signaled for her to wait while he gazed through his binoculars toward River's team. After a few seconds, he lowered his binoculars and related his findings. "Kesa signaled they have line of sight and can see two Gaia bipeds and a quadcopter hunting about twenty survivors." Noah stared at Willow, his silence a signal it was time for her to make the call.

Willow paused. *I want the team to bug out for the forest before Gaia spots us, so we all make it to the Cave in one piece. But the right choice is to assist these survivors. If humanity doesn't stand together, Gaia will whittle away the human population almost unopposed. Two Cave Cell teams should be able to destroy this small Gaia contingent even if the survivors on the run cannot assist. Dammit, why did this have to happen on my first mission as team lead?*

Willow took a deep breath and let it out before issuing orders. "Noah, head two hundred meters northwest on overwatch. The three of us will draw the bipeds our way so you can get a side or rear shot. Chloe and Logan, dig in to minimize your target profile. Unload only enough on the bipeds to get their attention, since our M4A1 carbines won't do much against their frontal armor. Our actual target is the quadcopter. Hold fire until I advise to shoot." Willow followed her own advice and dug to give Gaia as little of herself as possible to shoot at.

The newbies locked their folding shovels into digging position. "Wilco, Willow".

Noah held his M110A1 SDMR up for Kesa to see, signaled "2" and pointed northwest. Noah raised his binoculars to verify Kesa understood. "Message received," he said for Willow's benefit before he ran northwest cover to cover.

Kesa was River's sniper. She would mirror Noah, but to the northeast instead. Cave Cell equipped Noah and Kesa with sniper rifles that fired armor-piercing tungsten-cored 7.62×51 mm XM1158 rounds to penetrate Gaia unit armor.

Gunfire from the edge of town got louder as the battle moved closer to Cave Cell's positions, tending more toward River's than Willow's. More survivors spilled out of the town, ran past their covering comrades, and took cover a hundred meters further out. The survivors were attempting a controlled retreat. Willow took a quick look at each person in her field of view. They wore rags and had gaunt faces and limbs. Hastily-bound wounds were common, some even had untreated fresh wounds that were still bleeding. *They are starved and exhausted; functioning purely on willpower.*

A large framed, tall man ran past the man posted at the blue building's corner. By Willow's count, this was the eighteenth survivor. He must have been the group's tail end, as the first two survivors fired a couple of rounds from their corner posts and ran after him. They headed toward where their group had already taken cover behind various boulders and hillocks. Willow watched with bated breath. *Come on, you can reach cover. Run!*

The man from the blue building made a tactically sound decision, running in a direction using the blue building to shield his retreat. As he sprinted away, two Gaia bipeds walking parallel emerged on the town's exit road beside the blue building.

The newbies both gasped.

Willow's heart quickened. *We've seen Gaia bipeds before, but the horror of machines bent on exterminating your entire species never fades away.* The gunfire from the survivors increased in intensity. *They're expending valuable ammo to give their fellow survivors a better chance of reaching cover. Too bad their low caliber weapons are just an annoyance to the bipeds.* The survivors were firing center mass, fruitlessly bouncing bullets off the bipeds' thick frontal armor. *No one trained this group where to target bipeds or they are full-on panicking.*

The biped closest to Willow stepped past the blue building. It fired a couple of rounds at a survivor shooting from cover and scanned its new field of view at the same time. Corner post survivor was a hundred meters away, still dashing for cover. The biped fired a single round from its M16A4 at him. His face exploded in pink mist. *The poor bastard; he couldn't have done it any other way. Gaia never misses an exposed target within a weapon's effective range.*

Both newbies looked at her with wide eyes. This was the first time they saw Gaia execute someone.

Willow needed to get them focused on the mission. "Time for us to act," she said evenly. "Both of you put some rounds on the biped closest to us. It is far out of effective range, fire just enough to keep its attention and make those survivors aware they have friends. River's team will do the same with the biped closer to them. When the target gets within five hundred meters, aim for its weapon and leg joints. Don't worry if you don't appear to be doing much other than drawing it to us. Noah will go for the kill shot when the opportunity arises."

Logan and Chloe showed the value of their training and buckled down to the task at hand, forcing their emotions back behind mission focus.

Willow saved her ammo, choosing instead to monitor the situation through her binoculars.

Chloe methodically fired rounds at the biped's head sensor package area. The bullets ricocheted off heavy armor but still got Gaia's attention, drawing fire to their dug in position.

Logan picked up on Chloe's success, shifting his aim from center mass to the head.

"Well done. That must be messing with some algorithms." Willow checked on Noah; he was dug in and lying in wait for the biped to enter effective range. He wouldn't give his position away by firing until the biped exposed its lesser-armored back to him. She swung the binoculars over to River's team. *Cave Cell multiple team training is paying off. River and his newbies are harassing the other biped. Kesa is nowhere to be seen. That's good; she is doing the same as Noah across the battlefield.*

Next, Willow checked on the survivors. *Thank goodness, they figured out where the Cave Cell teams are and are retreating between our lines of fire. There's hope and renewed determination in their expressions and in how they are moving.* Willow watched the bipeds for a bit. "Keep it up. The bipeds are having difficulty choosing between suppressing our threat versus killing retreating survivors."

The bipeds lost time switching between targeting Cave Cell positions and survivors. So far, their rounds fired at the Cave Cell positions were ineffectual. The bullets whizzed overhead or sprayed dirt as they hit the ground. Unfortunately, the bipeds remained deadly to survivors on the move in no or partial cover and still within the M16A4 effective range. Another survivor died from a shot in the back hitting a vital organ, someone crawled along with a leg wound, and two others took shoulder and arm wounds.

No one could help the crawler, since it was suicide to run toward the bipeds to try a rescue. The crawler didn't want anyone sacrificing themselves. "Go, go!" she yelled as she tried to get to cover. She delayed the bipeds by making them deal with her, giving her fellow survivors more time to escape.

Throughout all of this, Willow marked the distance from the nearer biped to Noah's and her positions. The biped was moving into five hundred meter range from her, the outer limit of M4A1 point target effective range. Noah was another thirty-five to forty meters from the biped, but his rifle's effective range was half again over hers. He would not fire, however, until he could make a potential kill shot. Cave Cell strategy was to hide the position of heavier weapons until a high probability shot.

The whirring of a quadcopter on the move got Willow's attention. Something in how battle conditions were shaping made Gaia bring forward the quadcopter that hung back at the town's edge.

Willow checked her M26 modular accessory shotgun system mounted under the barrel of her M4A1. Cave Cell recently adapted to having someone armed with birdshot shotgun shells on each team to deal with Gaia quadcopters. "Chloe, if that drone gets within a couple hundred meters, you and I are going to do what we can to disable it. I'll switch to shotgun if it comes within forty meters. Logan, stay on the biped and call out every fifty meter mark as it comes closer."

The quadcopter flew straight toward the retreating survivors. Its XM8 weapon became effective under two hundred meters of range. The closest survivors neared the midpoint between her team and River's. The furthest, in the most danger from the bipeds and quadcopter, were still three hundred meters away. *More casualties are inevitable. We can't knock the quadcopter out of the air until it gets much closer.*

"Four-hundred-fifty meters," Logan said calmly over the gunfire, shouting survivors, wounded screaming, and the buzz of the quadcopter.

The quadcopter entered its effective range and started firing at survivors. Survivors returned fire, forcing it to swoop while shooting, reducing its accuracy. Regardless, Gaia's marksmanship was still better than human. Soon enough, the quadcopter overflew cover and fired at the exposed survivor. An agonized scream rolled across the battlefield.

"Four-hundred meters," Logan said.

Willow noted his demeanor. *He's holding it together so far even though witnessing deaths firsthand, to say nothing of the biped and quadcopter charging his position. Well done, newbie.*

The quadcopter continued at top speed toward them, Gaia negating cover by overflying survivors to shoot them after it passed. When it breached the two hundred meter mark, Chloe opened fire. With Logan pestering the biped and Chloe firing at the quadcopter, Gaia must have deemed them her top threat. The quadcopter dove to two hand spans above ground level as it skimmed directly toward them. *Cave Cell knows your tricks, Gaia. You plan to overfly us at high-speed, popping up after for a kill shot. That's fine with me, I'll have a half second or so of steady target to fill with birdshot.*

"Three-hundred-fifty meters," Logan shouted, now firing at the biped's leg joints.

The quadcopter buzzed barely over their heads. After it continued five meters past, it rose to gain a firing angle for its dangling compact carbine. Willow fired her M26, spraying birdshot into the quadcopter at close range. Pieces flew in every direction, the quadcopter flipping end-over-end and crashing to the ground. Willow fired another birdshot shell into the control casing. "Quadcopter down."

"Three-hundred meters," Logan said, his voice a pitch higher.

Willow got back into position to monitor and fire on the biped. She checked her binoculars first. The closer biped had just passed where the crawling woman played dead as she leaned on a boulder for cover. The crawler raised an M17 9x19 mm pistol and fired three ineffectual rounds at the biped's back. It wheeled toward her and put a bullet in her head. *She played that perfectly. Why couldn't it have worked?*

Two shots in quick succession erupted from Noah's position. AP bullets punching through armor echoed throughout the battlefield, the biped dropping limp to the ground as it lost power, processor, or both. The biped had exposed its back to him to kill the crawler.

Ragged cheers erupted from the survivors witnessing the biped go down.

Logan and Chloe exclaimed, "Yes!"

Willow felt the same. *Thank goodness for Noah, but there's still another biped in the fight. I need to be a good example for the newbies and stay cool.* "Chloe and Logan, put some suppression fire on that other biped. We need to protect Noah while he takes cover." Taking her own advice, she targeted the biped and fired two rounds to keep Gaia thinking.

The other biped stopped what it was doing the instant the AP bullets hit its comrade. It swung toward Noah and fired its M16A4 as it ran top speed toward his position, relying on its heavy frontal armor to protect it. Noah was now Gaia's number one enemy on this battlefield. The biped fired in full auto, rock chips exploding off Noah's cover centimeters from where he propped his weapon for the kill shots.

Chloe, Logan, and Willow fired on the biped, bullets pinging and twanging off armor. After firing almost thirty rounds each, a solid hit on the biped's knee joint caused the lower half of its left leg to fold. The biped toppled to the ground, but pushed itself back up on its one good leg.

Logan pumped his fist in the air. "I broke the knee joint!"

"Nice, shot Logan," Willow said. "Everyone focus on blowing that rifle out of its grip."

The three of them resumed firing, now aiming for the biped's weapon. The M16A4 was as good a target as it could be, fully exposed lengthwise to them as the biped continued to fire at Noah's position.

A metallic ping sounded as the rifle blew out of the biped's grip and skidded to a halt ten meters away from it. This time, Chloe celebrated a hit. "Eat that, minion."

The biped hit the dirt and crawled smoothly toward its weapon.

Now that the gunfire had quieted down, the whining, whirring and clicking of the biped's gears and servomotors stood out. Willow shivered. *Those noises are the stuff of nightmares for survivors.* Willow aimed at its back and squeezed off a couple more rounds, fruitless against the lesser rear armor at this range with this caliber. *C'mon, die fucker, I know you will kill humans as long as any part of you can move.*

Someone sprinted toward the biped from the east side of the battlefield. "Hold fire. Friendly approaching," Willow said.

Chloe and Logan ceased fire, each echoing "Wilco" back to her.

The runner was Kesa, moving fast with her rifle targeting the scrabbling biped. She arrived when the biped was still a couple of meters from its weapon.

The biped wasn't going to die easy. It tore the dangling lower part of its left leg off and threw it at Kesa.

After dodging the flying robot part, Kesa brought her rifle to firing position. It was too late for a shot to the weaker back armor, since the robot rolled to face her.

Kesa was ready for the flying leg; maybe she's seen it before. How are we supposed to defeat an enemy that tears off its own body parts to use as weapons against us? "Kill. It," Willow said to herself.

The robot crouched, readying to leap off its good leg toward Kesa. Two shots rang out in quick succession from Noah's position. He had set up to shoot again the moment bullets stopped spraying his position. For a second time today, the gratifying crunch of AP bullets ripping through armor rang out. The second biped folded limp to the ground, almost right beside its decommissioned sibling.

Kesa fired two more rounds into the exposed control components.

Quiet reigned for a moment, a seemingly hopeless situation turning around so fast it took time for everyone to realize they wiped out Gaia's forces. A cascade of cheers erupted, turning into a flurry of activity. The ragged survivors ran back to their fallen to aid the wounded and to scavenge from the dead.

Willow focused on River with her binoculars. He pointed to himself and then the nearest survivor to indicate his team was taking the lead on moving them to safety. Willow gave him the OK signal and issued orders. "We're on clean up duty first, assisting with moving the survivors to safety second. Logan, bolt cutters on those bipeds. Chloe, cover him. I'll put a bend in this quadcopter's XM8."

Logan grunted and stumbled as he rose from his prone firing position. A wet patch of blood covered the right shoulder of his fatigues and spread to his arm and chest. "Sorry, Willow," Logan gasped, "I can't cut cables. Our biped tagged me in the shoulder a moment before Noah punched holes in it."

"Damn, how severe is it?" Willow asked. *Don't you die, I'm getting you home to the Cave no matter what it takes.*

"'Tis but a scratch," Logan deadpanned and paused for effect. "Feels like through-and-through the shoulder muscle. If someone can help me bind it, I'm mobile."

"Chloe, treat his wound and put a bend in that XM8 barrel. Get Logan and any extra survivors you can gather to our rendezvous point in the forest. Don't worry, Logan, we'll get you home." Willow pivoted the team's orders and finished with a wink to Logan as she tugged the bolt cutters from Logan's pack. He grunted in pain but otherwise stood firm.

Noah headed Willow's way. "Cover these bipeds for me," she shouted at him as she headed over with the bolt cutters.

Noah already held his rifle at low ready toward the bipeds. He altered his course to head to them, replacing Kesa as decomm guardian when he arrived.

No one wanted to die finding out Gaia learned to play dead. Willow cut the cables and the hoses on the two bipeds under Noah's watchful eye. While working, Willow complained. "Fucking Boston Dynamics genius engineering assholes. If Gaia had class, she would at least cover their logo and model name with something of her own."

Noah chuckled before responding. "I'm pretty sure those engineers had no idea they were building robots for an AI bent on exterminating humanity. How about 'Extinction R Us' for her branding?"

Willow laughed as she finished up. "I'll consider that. Can you haul these M16A4s back to Cave Cell? Gaia does impeccable weapons maintenance, these are almost factory fresh."

"Wilco, I'll haul them at least to the rendezvous before I saddle a newbie with them." He tilted his head toward Logan and Chloe. "How's Logan?"

Willow handed the rifles to Noah and attached the bolt cutters to her pack. She glanced in Logan's direction to make sure he wouldn't be able to hear before she answered. "He says through-and-through shoulder muscle, a lucky wound if you must have one, but the amount of blood concerns me. We'll need to keep an eye on him and get back to Cave Cell for treatment ASAP. Since the wounded and these ragtag survivors can't move fast, we're risking contact with Gaia reinforcements before we make it to cover in the forest. I need you to set up for overwatch somewhere you can guard our retreat but where you still have an excellent bug out option."

Noah slung the M16A4s behind his back. "Wilco, Willow. If you get us home safe, this will be a textbook first mission as team lead." He headed off at quick time pace toward the forest rendezvous point, already scanning for a suitable perch.

CHAPTER SEVENTEEN – 12:00 June 4, 2070 – It's Not Over Till it's Over

Part of the happiness of life consists not in fighting battles, but in avoiding them. A masterly retreat is in itself a victory.
Norman Vincent Peale
If you give Gaia a black eye, get the hell away because you can be damn sure she is coming to break both of your legs.
Noah Cruz, 2069

While Chloe treated Logan's shoulder, Willow headed five hundred meters east to where River's team had gathered ten of the survivors. There was another still scavenging from bodies, and a last one saying goodbye to a cherished fatality. *Twelve out of eighteen is much better than everyone dying. Given their lack of high caliber weapons and dreadful physical condition, Gaia would have eradicated this group except for our intervention.* She arrived as River finished addressing the group.

"Anyone desiring escort to safe territory, we're leaving now to our rendezvous point in the forest." River pointed to the close edge of the forest two klicks to the south. "Gaia may have air, ground, or both minion types on the way. Carter and Ava, lead at a strong pace. Stragglers will keep up as best they can rather than delay the group. Kesa, you and I are on rearguard."

The survivors parted. A middle-aged woman walked unsteadily toward Willow from the group's midst, supported by the large framed fellow who left town last. She cradled her bloodied and field dressed arm in a makeshift sling. *She's dehydrated, starved, faint from loss of blood, or all of the above. Unfortunately, treatment will have to wait until the forest.*

The woman spoke in a firm voice that belied her rough condition. "I am Mia, I speak for this group. You saved our lives, and we will make proper thanks in safer conditions. Please lead on." She glanced about. Two of her group lingered on the battlefield. She whistled at them and motioned to the forest. The laggards stopped what they were doing, hastening to join those already moving. This group was tight-knit, able people moved to help those needing aid rather than bolting ahead to safety.

As Willow approached, River nodded toward Logan and Chloe. "I see field dressing is being applied. How bad is it?"

"Logan took a bullet in the shoulder," Willow said. "He should be alright if we can get back to Cave Cell for proper medical attention without delay. How's your team?"

"My team is fully operational. The battle took shape further from our position than yours. The biped on our side didn't even enter its effective range. This must be a shitshow magnitude record for a team lead's first mission, right?" Still wired from the firefight, River couldn't stop moving and talked fast.

"This beats any first mission stories I've heard," Willow said. "Let's hope we're done making records for now and can just get home safe. I'm thinking we take these survivors to a spot a couple hours out from the Cave and talk to the Cell about what to do with them. How about you?"

"Agreed. Hide the home, protect the home." River checked his gear, readying to heading out. "I see Noah moved out first. Is he scouting or overwatch?"

"Overwatch, but somewhere he can retreat to the forest if a UAV shows up. The newbies and I will do what we can to help keep this group moving." Rock clanging on metal noises rang out behind Willow. Chloe would soon finish bending the XM8 barrel and be ready to move out.

Willow, River, and Kesa moved out on rearguard, ushering the slowest survivors along. Chloe and Logan joined, Logan making a valiant but futile effort to help; he stumbled nearly as much as the worst off survivors.

"Logan, give me your carbine and assist the folks in the middle group to the rendezvous," Willow said, gently tugging the carbine away from him. As he trudged off, she mouthed "Take care of him," to Chloe.

Chloe signaled OK and jogged after Logan.

Willow spent most of her time listening, watching the sky, and looking back toward town for any sign of minions. The group walked on unassailed for just over twenty minutes at what Willow considered an agonizingly slow pace. A faint droning buzz arose from behind Willow as the lead survivors started entering the forest and the laggards were still a hundred meters away. *Oh shit, that sounds like an MQ-9 Reaper's turboprop engine.* She looked at River for confirmation, but something in the sky behind them engrossed him.

"Reaper, eight klicks out!" River yelled as he turned to run for the forest.

Willow glanced back. Sunlight glinted off the Reaper and two small dots falling off of it. The sudden flare of light at the dots confirmed Willow's worst fear. "Hellfire, twenty seconds," she shouted, already turning and accelerating to a full sprint. *Too late to help anyone slow, time to race for hard cover or die.*

Twenty seconds ticked by in what Willow perceived as minutes of adrenalin fueled sprinting. The Cave Cell soldiers and the survivors ran full out to the forest.

This was a life or death sprint. When an able-bodied survivor tried to aid a woman with a bandaged leg, she pushed him away. "We're both dead if you help me. Run for your life."

Noah leapt off his overwatch hillock with three rifles slung to him and hit the ground running.

"Drop everything, Noah," Willow yelled. *Overloaded and too far to run, damn it.*

When it happened, there was no warning. The Hellfire missiles traveled at sixteen hundred kilometers per hour, one and a third times the speed of sound. The roar of their explosive impact drowned out the sound of their approach. One eradicated the entire hillock Noah had just left, blowing dirt, rocks, and grass away in a thirty meter blast zone. The other detonated amid the four slowest survivors at the edge of the forest, the injuries at the root of their diminished pace costing their lives.

Willow ignored her ringing ears and assessed who had made it. Everyone from Cave Cell except Noah made it deep enough into the forest to suffer only debris raining down on them. Willow counted eight of the survivors, none of them much worse for wear than before the explosion.

Mia had survived. She pointed back to the clearing. "That Reaper is arriving in under one mike. Find your sniper, but be quick about it."

Willow nodded, tossed the carbines to River, and ran out of the forest. She met a disheveled and dirty Noah stumbling toward her. *He made it in one piece, thank goodness. The stubborn idiot is still carrying the rifles.*

He pushed the three rifles into her hands. "Gaia blew up the fucking dirt hill I used for overwatch!" Noah yelled.

Futile to tell him he's yelling because his ears are ringing; no time for circular arguments now. Instead, Willow slung the rifles over her shoulder and grabbed Noah's arm to help him get deep in the forest faster. They both glanced sorrowfully at the scattered parts of the four people blown apart by the Hellfire at the forest edge, but didn't slow down. *Gaia is pleased to kill you while you mourn the dead.*

As they neared the rendezvous point, the Reaper passed overhead. Fortunately, it maintained course and speed. From everything Cave Cell knew, neither the Reaper's optical nor thermal imaging could penetrate the thick forest canopy.

Willow and Noah arrived at the rendezvous. No one made a sound. Everyone huddled in small groups, most staring upward with wide eyes and shaking hands as if expecting the Reaper to crash in their midst. Willow spoke loud enough to make sure the other fifteen people heard her. "She can't hear or see us under this thick canopy. We're safe here until she sends ground minions."

River's focus returned to the here and now. "My group and Willow's move out in one hour. Mia's group, you need to decide what you are doing."

Gaia's spell broken, Cave Cell teammates and survivors with medic skills did what they could for the wounded. Other Cave Cell team members passed around rations and water. Everyone checked and reloaded their weapons.

Mia, again supported by the large framed man, approached River and Willow. For someone narrowly escaping extermination by Gaia, she had an aura of calm that her tone and pace reflected. "Thank you for saving us. You risked your own lives to save people you hadn't even met. We already owe you an unrepayable debt, and yet I come to ask for more. Until three weeks ago, we were Central High Cell, a Dunbar hundred fifty living in a suburban town high school safe from the worst of the extreme weather. Gaia rarely ventured into our area. When she did, we kept the home secret by hiding until she left."

"Hide the home, protect the home," Willow and River said.

With death was no longer imminent, Willow's curiosity surged. "How are so few of you here with us?"

Mia closed her eyes, her expression a deep sadness. After a few seconds of silence, she opened her eyes and continued. "We got too comfortable and let our youth venture throughout the town to scavenge. Our elders, of which I am the single living member, failed to make sure the youth understood following the Imperatives was of life and death importance. We believe one group of youth reused a route to the high school day after day. On one of

Gaia's rare visits, her bipeds spotted some youth out scavenging. The youth panicked and ran home using their regular route."

"They violated the fourth Imperative 'Never move unawares, never leave any traces'," River said.

"Absolutely," Mia said. "They got away from the bipeds, but Gaia found their well-used route and followed it to the school. We destroyed the first wave of scouts, the two bipeds and two cheetahs, but Gaia realized she had discovered a cell. She had a force nearby, because eight bipeds, twelve cheetahs, and four supporting quadcopters showed up before we could pack and disappear. After our defenses were breeched, only forty of us escaped with what we could carry. We ran for three weeks, Gaia always pursuing and sometimes finding us to kill as many as she could."

"Gaia certainly wanted you dead to have pursued you with such focus and resource allocation," River said. "Our cell has never seen her launch two of her precious Hellfires from maximum range, let alone at low probability targets. To the best of our knowledge, she cannot manufacture more to replace what she uses from the stockpile she seized thirty years ago."

Mia inclined her head in agreement. "Yes, Gaia was relentless. Does she conduct all her hunts exhaustively, or did something about our group trigger the treatment?"

"Our cell hasn't heard of Gaia investing this much in a hunt," River said, "but we also haven't heard of her having an entire cell to pursue."

"Regardless, eight survived the day, thanks to you," Mia said. "I fear we won't survive much longer without more help. Are you able to take us somewhere safe where we can find food and water? We need time and nourishment to regain our strength."

The Central High Cell survivors' plight touched Willow, but she couldn't commit to material action on behalf of Cave Cell.

River gave her his best "we should go over there and talk privately," look.

"Can you excuse us?" Willow asked. "The senior people from my group must discuss your request."

"Of course, take all the time you need." Mia and her escort left to check on their people.

Willow motioned River far enough away to ensure privacy, waving over Noah and Kesa to join them. *These Central High survivors are hardy folk and seem honorable. I bet that even if Cave Cell refuses to provide any further help, Mia and her people will accept the decision with grace.*

River glanced surreptitiously around to ensure no one could hear him. "Willow and I want to help these people out, but we can't march them into our home without giving everyone at Cave Cell a chance to decide. Has this happened before? How did the team in the field handle it?"

Kesa and Noah, the senior Cave Cell members within the two teams, made eye contact. Noah pointed at Kesa for her to weigh in first.

"Your instincts are good," Kesa said. "We want to help other people, but we cannot pre-empt Cave Cell's safety and right to choose how to handle outsiders. Prior teams encountering other survivors brought them to a resting place a few klicks away from Cave Cell and left them with provisions and watchers. If trust was high, the watchers stayed with the survivors. When there was low trust, the watchers monitored the survivors from afar to defend them if needed, but also to observe their behavior. Anyone travelling to or from Cave Cell approached the resting place in different ways to hide the Cave's location."

"That makes sense," Willow said. "What came of the prior survivors?"

Noah replied this time. "Based on their behavior and demeanor, Cave Cell took them in or sent them on their way with suitable provisions. Some kids you grew up with and some adults that helped raise you are from recruited families."

Willow considered the information and opinions. "Is everyone OK with taking these survivors to a resting place and asking Cave Cell about the next steps?"

River, Noah, and Kesa gave her a thumbs-up.

"How about the newbies take turns leading everyone toward Cave Cell for experience," Kesa suggested. "Once we're five klicks out, Noah and I will lead to a safe camp for the survivors to rest. One team should stay with the survivors while the other returns to Cave Cell to brief them."

"Sounds good to me," Willow said after thinking it over for a few seconds. "Best of three playing biped, cheetah, and quadcopter for the choice of minding the survivors or returning to Cave Cell?"

River extended his fist. "On three. One, two, three." River held out two fingers to represent a biped's two legs.

Willow held out a fist to represent a cheetah's cylindrical main body.

Noah refereed. "Biped kills cheetah, first round for River. Second round on three. One, two, three."

DEAN WHITFORD

River again held out two fingers to represent a biped.

Willow held out her hand with all fingers extended to represent a quadcopter's flat chassis.

"Quadcopter kills biped, tie game," said Noah. "Last round on three. One, two, three."

This time, River held out his hand with all fingers extended.

Willow held out a fist.

"Cheetah kills quadcopter, Willow wins." Noah fist bumped Willow.

"I'll be reserving my choice until we reach the resting place," Willow said. "You're wallowing in uncertainty for a while, River."

"Gaia's minions." River hated losing games. "Let's brief the newbies and leave. They can swap leading and rearguard every two hours. You're briefing Mia as part of your winner's package."

Willow learned early in life that it was not productive to push her brother's buttons after beating him. "Fair enough, I'll brief Mia. My newbies will take first shift up front."

Noah trailed close behind Willow as she approached Mia, who was sitting on a fallen tree to rest. She peered up, puzzled. "I hope my people's fate did not hinge on a game of biped, cheetah, and quadcopter?"

"Oh, no, absolutely not," Willow said. "The game was for duty assignments. We decided to escort you to a safe place and give you provisions so you can rest. That's all we can commit to without consulting the Cell."

"Although I hoped for more, this is the best outcome I expected for now. Thank you." Mia gave Willow's hand a quick squeeze to reinforce her words. "As a cell elder, I would offer the same if the shoe were on the other foot. I assume we leave soon to put come klicks between us and the last Gaia contact?"

Given the situation, Mia's composure again impressed Willow. "Yes, we move out as soon as everyone gets their gear together."

"I'll have my people get ready." Mia went to them, motioning for them to rise and prepare for travel.

Willow glanced at Noah, who grunted as if agreeing with her impression of Mia. She corralled Chloe and Logan, inspecting his dressing. The bleeding had slowed to a trickle. "Flawless field dressing, Chloe, well done. You look ready for travel, Logan. How do you feel?"

"My arm is nearly useless, although I may be able to aim and shoot from prone," Logan said. "I'm stronger after taking a break and having food and water, but not anywhere near peak condition. I still want to help."

Willow scrutinized Logan to weigh his plucky words versus his actual fitness for duty. *He's making a valiant effort to ignore the pain, but the injury severely compromised his battle readiness.* "Stick with Chloe. You two are going to rotate between lead and rearguard with Carter and Ava every hour. First sign of trouble, you hit the dirt behind cover and set up prone to support. The mobile soldiers will execute flanking maneuvers while you provide cover fire. I know it was mentioned in your basic training, but I need to remind you we cannot tell these folks anything about Cave Cell."

"After analyzing the scenario presented by these survivors and our rescuing them, I see both the risks and benefits of further interaction. I guess, umm, what I am asking is are we going to help them?" Chloe asked shyly.

"We're proceeding with the most we can commit to without consulting Cave Cell," Willow said. "We'll escort them to a safe resting place a few klicks from Cave Cell."

Chloe and Logan both brightened a bit.

"That's good. I didn't want to abandon them to Gaia's hunt," Chloe said.

"You two are taking lead first." Willow pointed to the clearing exit. "Gather up the survivors that are ready to follow. Everyone else will hustle when they see you leave. Before you head out, spread Logan's gear except his carbine amongst the other newbies to lighten his load."

CHAPTER EIGHTEEN – 13:30 June 4, 2070 – The Long Way Home

Be slow to fall into friendship; but when thou art in, continue firm and constant.
Socrates
To help our cell survive, we learn five Imperatives from a young age. The fifth Imperative is "Respect strangers, but don't trust them".
River Taylor, 2069

Chloe and Logan left the small clearing, the bulk of the survivors following. Willow and Noah walked near the column's head to support the leading newbies and to critique method when necessary. Their departure forced everyone else to hop to it and catch up to the Cave Cell guides. None of the Central High Cell survivors desired to be lost alone in the forest, most likely hunted to the death by Gaia's minions than found by anyone friendly.

River and Kesa positioned themselves in the column to support Carter and Ava near the rear.

When Willow looked behind to check on her brother, River gave her a dirty look. *He thinks I stole his spot to be first up at the front of the column. Poor jealous brother.* She responded by making a fist and extending her middle finger to give her ear an exaggerated scratch.

The hike through the forest was typical for a Cave Cell mission. Those in the lead had to pick routes traversable by everyone, including the injured, but could appear nothing more than a game trail after their passing. Since Reapers with upgraded sensors monitored a hundred square kilometers, those leading avoided clearings. Rearguard erased footprints and any other signs of humans passing.

These four newbies had taken their lessons to heart. The Cave Cell's senior members only needed to voice a few minor corrections during the hike.

The hum of insects bustling came from all around them. Birds sang and flitted about. Rabbits and squirrels stayed at least a few meters away but otherwise ignored them, except the occasional squirrel chattering warnings until the hikers left. Off in the distance, whitetail deer and coyote took a glance before disappearing. Willow breathed deep; the smells were earthy and full of life. *This is the opposite of this morning's battle, exactly what everyone needs to decompress. The forest gives me calm, comfort, and feels safer than everywhere else. Gaia prefers to patrol the broken down towns and roads; there's better mobility and line of sight for her minions. Cave Cell is a safe place, but it's crowded and closed in.*

Willow and Noah agreed early on to travel placed within the group where they could overhear the survivors' conversations. They needed the observations to speak to their character when questioned by Cave Cell.

Willow discretely listened to survivors talking about their losses, struggles, and fears for their future. By rescuing and escorting them to somewhere safe, Cave Cell had lit a spark of hope. Many discussions centered on how Cave Cell might assist. The survivors reviewed how Central High Cell recruited some people, sent others on their way, and how they judged character to decide. None of the survivors expressed doubt, at least within hearing of Willow, that Cave Cell would judge them as anything other than suitable recruits.

Across the spectrum of leadership attributes, Willow saw two types of leaders in tense situations. Leaders akin to Cave Cell's Grandpy Max remained calm in any storm, no matter how grim it got, and could talk anyone down from any extreme. Other leaders thrived on raw emotion, escalating it in others. Since becoming a team lead, Willow strove to follow Grandpy Max's example. She resisted when supposedly righteous anger tried to cede control to emotion.

Throughout the hike, survivors approached Mia and her ever present near-silent helper. Mia was a textbook example of de-escalation; a pool of calm surrounded her. People came up and spoke in excited tones and gesticulated. Mia listened to them and replied quietly at a measured pace. Her manner and words defused their raw emotion. Each departed conversing with her at peace, at least for a while, with one exception. A late teens male of average height and build named Finn accosted Mia often, wired up about something or other. Mia could calm him somewhat, but never defused him; he always departed agitated to talk with Freya, who bore some family resemblance to him. Willow marked him as one to watch. She surmised Noah felt the same because she saw him monitoring her watching Finn, evaluating her ability to evaluate others.

After hiking three hours at a moderate pace in deference to the wounded, Kesa signaled Noah and double timed to the front of the column. Chloe and Logan were the newbies leading; they dropped back without instruction.

Willow admired the smooth transition. *These newbies are quick to understand; they'll make excellent soldiers. We're an hour away from the Cave, time to drift over to the resting place rather than expose Cave Cell's location.*

River signaled Willow to drop back, also signaling the newbies on rearguard to give them some room. When the gap in front and behind them widened, he spoke quietly to ensure no one else from Cave Cell or Central High Cell's survivors could hear. "I see you and Noah were watching and listening to the survivors. Kesa and I did the same. Anybody giving you concern as a potential recruit?"

Willow considered the question versus her observations. "Mia impresses me. Most of the others haven't given me a reason yet to be ecstatic or hesitant about their joining. The sizable one named Joseph sticking to Mia's side has spoken a grand total of two words, hard to judge his character. Given the way he protects Mia, it would be difficult to separate them. The only one I have concrete concerns about is Finn, since he seems to be a hothead."

River nodded. "Yeah, I agree. In Finn's defense, he is around our age and I'm sure there's at least a handful of Cave Cell members that described us as hotheads even this year."

Willow chuckled and said, "River, some cell members called us hotheads just last week when they disagreed with our assignment to lead this mission."

River blushed, getting a bit heated. "Hey, I'm working hard at keeping my cool."

Willow squeezed her brother's shoulder. "Slow down there soldier, I was talking about both of us. Yes, you are working hard and you have improved. Today we both did great. You have to admit, however, we still have a low tolerance for bullshit, after which things get hairy."

River looked down, shuffling pebbles with his left shoe. "You're right. Being accused of being a hothead made me act like a hothead. Hey that's brilliant irony." He brightened; River always appreciated quality irony, whether or not of his own making.

"We agree Finn's hotheadedness is something to stay aware of," Willow said, "but not yet sufficient to strike him as a candidate recruit. Let's continue observing." *Enough about Finn; time to return to the topic at hand.*

"Agreed," River said. "We'll close the gap and keep on watching and listening until we reach the resting place."

Within a half hour, Kesa and Noah called a halt in a grove where the overhead cover was sufficient and fallen trees served as benches. There was no fire pit, since Cave Cell typically did without fires. Teams away from the caves lit small cooking fires only when there was enough wind and diffusing forest canopy to prevent Gaia from spotting the light or smoke. The experienced scavengers built near smokeless fires from a magical mix of wood in proper condition and a generous flow of combustion air.

Noah made eye contact with Willow and nodded toward Mia.

Apparently, the others appointed me the official liaison between Cave Cell and the survivors. I must have missed that meeting. Willow approached Mia. "You folks can get comfortable here for at least tonight. More food and medics will arrive in two hours. We will take turns guarding the perimeter so your people can rest."

Mia clasped Willow's hand and peered into her eyes. "Thank you yet again, Willow. Can I speak to your elders on behalf of Central High Cell?"

"I am sorry, Mia, that is not our way," Willow said, chagrined. "Those of us traveling with you will inform the cell. Cave Cell will decide without outside influence. If you like, I can share a message from you when I attend the meeting."

"I appreciate that. I will put together something brief for you to pass on." Disappointment was evident in Mia's tone, but she didn't take it out on Willow. "In the meantime, ask me anything. I will tell the complete truth, whether or not it paints us favorably. I respect your need to protect your home from threats, whether Gaia or human."

Willow left the survivors to their rest. *By the landmarks, we're three klicks north of the Cave. Time to decide whether my team is guarding and surveilling or heading back to the Cave.* She signaled Noah, Kesa, and River over to where they could have a private conversation.

Willow glanced around to make sure no one could overhear. "I'd prefer to experience both the intel gathering and the Cave Cell meeting to choose what we're doing for these survivors. River probably wants the same."

The other three glanced at River, who inclined his head.

"Can we make that happen?" Willow asked. "Oh, and regardless of my schedule, Logan needs medical attention at the Cave ASAP."

"I respect that you both want to experience everything you can as a team lead. That's a good thing," Noah said. "How about Kesa takes Logan and Chloe back to Cave Cell and sets up for a 19:00 meeting? I'll stay here with you two, Ava, and Carter to protect and gather intel. At 18:00, you and River return to the Cave to share our learnings."

It pleased Willow to have her cake and eat it too, but she felt a twinge of guilt. "Are you sure, Noah? You're signing up for a long day and you'll miss the meeting."

Noah shrugged. "Been there, done that. Much better for Cave Cell if you and River build your skills as team leads. I trust you to represent me tonight. Tell Ava and Carter to make noise leaving the survivors until they are out of sight. They should return to hearing range if they can do it undetected."

"Thanks, Noah." Willow couldn't stop herself from smiling. *Noah's plan is beneficial for Cave Cell, so what if it's what River and I wanted?*

"Done deal," Noah said. "To protect the home, make sure Cave Cell members enter and exit the grove via the northeast. They can loop back south toward the Cave after they are behind that ridge." He finished with a discrete wave at a ridge running north-south to the east of their position.

"See you two later tonight." Kesa headed northeast, calling for Chloe and Logan to accompany her.

Logan hesitated, looking back toward Cave Cell. He looked about to speak. Realizing what was up, he instead turned and followed Kesa.

Willow had to smile at the near miss. *I am so proud of Chloe and Logan. We left this morning on a routine scavenging mission. It was supposed to double as an intro to team leadership for River and me and a training opportunity for the newbies. Instead, we ended up defeating Gaia in a high-stakes firefight and rescuing another cell's last eight survivors. Best of all, everyone from Cave Cell is going to make it home.*

CHAPTER NINETEEN – 17:00 June 4, 2070 – Holding Pattern

There's the calm before the storm, the chaos of the storm, and finally the cathartic release of accumulated tension.
Mia Brown, 2070

River signaled Carter and Ava to come for a confidential briefing. They left the rest area in the forest where Cave Cell had set up the Central High Cell survivors and pushed through the undergrowth. By coincidence, they ended up within Willow's hearing.

Willow listened in to see how River's newbies reacted to their duty update. Carter clenched his jaw before River started speaking. *He stared awful long at Chloe and Logan as they were leaving.*

"We need you both to stay here on watch with Noah until Cave Cell decides what to do with the Central High Cell survivors," River said. "The first hour, you'll be out on the perimeter doing double duty on watch and to monitor the survivors for any useful intel or impressions."

Ava showed no surprise or disappointment when advised of the extended duty. "There's no way I would return home and leave Logan here with his shoulder wound untreated."

Carter wasn't as gracious. "We've already been going for almost twelve hours. What's another five or six matter, right?" Resentment trickled into his expression.

Noah nudged Willow to get her attention away from River and his newbies. He pointed to a sheltered spot under an oak tree, out of sight from where the survivors rested. "Since I'm lead on the night shift, I'm going to crash over there until it's time for you to leave, OK?"

Willow laughed before replying. "I envy your ability to sleep whenever and wherever time allows. Yeah, I'll wake you up."

As Carter and Ava were heading north to their post, River approached and motioned. "It's you and I posted to the south."

Willow left with him, neither Cave Cell watcher pair making any effort to be quiet as they departed.

Once out of sight from the survivors, River halted. "Ready to work our way back? I chose this direction because the ravine enables us to reverse unseen."

Willow punched River's shoulder. "You sneaky bugger, well done." They turned to follow the ravine toward the resting place. Willow halted and grabbed River's shoulder. *I can hear them talking. I can't distinguish what they're saying from the ravine floor, but probably can from higher.* Rough slopes formed the sides of the ravine, steep but still climbable. Willow pointed to a perch high enough to provide line of sight for guard duty, close enough to eavesdrop, and yet downslope enough to hide them.

River gave her a thumbs-up, secured his gear for the easy climb, and ascended.

Willow followed, taking her time to make sure she didn't kick rocks or deadwood downslope to blow their cover.

Ensconced in the little hollow on the slope, Willow could now overhear the survivors.

"Thank you for speaking Tocho, we heard you," Mia said. "Finn, you wanted to speak?"

Finn's voice was high pitch and he talked fast. "Why we are sitting here waiting, trusting these people we never met? They say they are guarding us from Gaia, but I think they are watching us instead. Are we prisoners? Since we survived this long, why can't we move on and find a new home?"

A female spoke next; perhaps Ramla. "We're not surviving, Finn. Gaia is running Central High Cell to extinction. In three weeks, we have been decimated from a community of a hundred fifty to just us eight. I believe the only thing we would move on to is our death."

"Freya, what say you?" Mia asked.

Willow closed her eyes to visualize the speakers. *Freya and Finn are similar in appearance, probably siblings or cousins.*

Freya cleared her throat. "I'm worried, too. Where we are going? Will we be alive in a week?" she mumbled. "I feel safe tonight for the first time in three weeks, and this will be the first night I won't go to bed so hungry my stomach hurts. These people risked their lives to save us from minions, brought us somewhere safe, and gave us their food. They have done nothing but help us. I think we should trust them and be patient."

Willow shifted uncomfortably. *Freya says they should trust us, and yet here we are eavesdropping on them. I don't like having to do this, but it's necessary to protect Cave Cell.*

Mia must have wanted Freya's words to sink in as she paused before speaking again. "Does anyone else wish to speak?" There was only silence in response. "We heard from everyone that wished to speak. There's a strong majority wanting to remain here, as our rescuers requested."

Willow gave her twin a conspiratorial wink. *River and I didn't overhear everyone, but I am betting the strong majority means everyone but Finn.*

Mia's next words supported Willow's theory. "Finn, will you wait peacefully with us?"

Finn's voice dripped with grudging acceptance. "Yes, I will wait . . . peacefully."

Mia closed off the discussion. "Everyone agrees. Now, please get some rest. Willow advised more food and medical assistance are coming soon."

Several quieter conversations started. Willow couldn't make sense out of the general buzz. She nodded in agreement when River signaled to suggest they descend to the ravine floor.

As they readied to head down, someone shoved through the brush uphill between them and the resting place. River and Willow both tried to disappear into the ground of the hollow but remained exposed, given how shallow the hollow was. The crashing soon stopped. Someone above them breathed fast and shallow.

Willow closed her eyes. *I can't see you, you can't see me. Don't catch your purportedly kind rescuers spying on you.*

A wavering voice broke the stillness above them. It was Finn, the worst possible person to discover them, but he wasn't screaming bloody murder about finding Cave Cell spies. Finn said quietly, "Mother, I miss your calm. Father, I miss your clarity. Please help me do the right thing for our cell." After speaking, his breathing leveled out and became slower and deeper.

Finn's parents are among Central High Cell's many dead. It's nice that their memories help Finn cope with his harsh new reality. After what felt like an eternity but was minutes, Finn turned and pushed back through the bush. Willow sucked in air, because she had barely dared to breathe with Finn just above them.

River did the same before leaning close to her. "Let's get the fuck away before someone comes and takes a leak on us."

On the ravine floor, far enough away that no one could hear them, River let loose. "Holy shit, that was awesome. If I reached through the bush above us, I could have grabbed his ankle. He would have lost his mind."

"I wasn't fantasizing about trying to scare the shit out of him," Willow said dryly. "I was too terrified of being outed as a nasty spy."

River calmed down as they retraced their route to return. "I get it. I can't imagine explaining ourselves to those poor folks. They've been through enough. Mia might understand what we did, but Finn and any others sharing his concerns wouldn't. Now that we understand Finn better, is he a risk to Cave Cell?"

Willow walked in silence while she mulled over the question, responding after a minute. "When I first listened to him, I was concerned he was a hothead and might be trouble for Cave Cell. When he asked his parents for guidance, he showed he's just a young guy trying to do the right thing for his people. If we recruit him and the others, we become his people."

Her answer jazzed River. "Ooh, deep. How Zen of you. Before you brought that up, I thought he was a liability. Now I realize he's like me before my training. You're saying if we can take his passion and energy and channel it to Cave Cell's benefit, he should work out."

Willow glanced sideways at her brother. "You mean he should work out no worse than you did, and turn into a net positive force with proper training?"

River laughed and said, "Hey, no permanent harm came to any Cave Cell members . . . and property damage was minimal."

Willow punched him hard in the shoulder in response and chin-pointed ahead. They were nearing the survivors.

Mia stood and approached when River and Willow arrived. "Any signs of Gaia on your patrol?"

Willow shook her head in the negative. "No ground or air units."

Mia's expression shifted to a piercing glare. "Did you overhear any useful information?"

River squeaked almost imperceptibly and hurried away. "Gotta check in with my newbies," he said over his shoulder as he left.

Willow waved goodbye. *I wish it surprised me he bailed, but he can't even withstand casual questioning by strong matriarchs like Mia. Forget pointed questions.*

"We're always gathering intel to protect our cell and our friends," Willow said. "How did you know?"

Mia smiled grimly. "Your brother's face is an open book. He was gawking at me as if he just ate my last meal. Regardless, although I may not look it, I was one of Central High's best hunters. People moving in the forest sound different than animals."

Willow recovered her composure. "Since our cards are on the table, what would Central High Cell do in this situation?"

"I committed you could ask me anything, and this good question calls out our character," Mia said. "I fear our elders were not as brave nor as charitable as your cell has been. Throughout our years at Central High, many small survivor groups passed through our area without us even making them aware we were there. We approached other survivors only when a key person died or left and we needed a replacement. Elders interviewed each survivor about their skills and knowledge to find out what benefit they brought. We tested them by asking who they would bring if we could only take them and half of the others in their group. The cell never interceded the few times we saw survivors in Gaia's sights. I never felt right about the process, but I didn't dispute. We all believed it was the best way to protect the home."

Mia's response took Willow aback. *Wow, she promised to tell the complete truth, but I wasn't expecting to find out Central High Cell cared only about itself, not humanity. I guess a cell could end up that way, especially if there were incidents with shoddy recruits or cell member losses fighting Gaia to rescue strangers?* "Thanks for being candid, Mia. I will try to understand why your cell worked that way. Would you mind if we use Central High's interview process to inventory your group's knowledge and skills? The information may help your case with my cell."

"Please do. These are worthy people I believe will benefit your cell," Mia said with conviction. "Start with me—it might make the others more comfortable."

A terrific idea; we can practice on Mia. Cave Cell trained us to stay alive and destroy minions, not deal with survivors. A gap to bring up with the elders after the Central High Cell matter resolves. Willow pointed to where Cave Cell had conversed privately earlier. "Meet you there in five, since I need to find River. Can you brief your people?"

Mia nodded and headed back to her group.

Willow recognized Mia could convince her people better than anyone from Cave Cell. River emerged from behind a thick patch of trees and brush.

Either his timing was impeccable, or he hid until Mia split. Willow suspected the latter.

"Sorry for bailing," River whispered. "One sharp look from her and I was confessing our eavesdropping."

"Your transparent face sold us out long-ago," Willow said. "We need to work on your ability to contain classified information. You must withstand a lot more than a female authority figure's piercing gaze. Some semi-simulated torture will be required."

"Oh, ha-ha, funny. You are joking, right?" River asked, voice quavering.

"This is serious, River. Central High Cell is a perfect example of how essential it is to protect the home. If you give up a couple toenails and suffer some minor electrical burns, it will be well worth building your containment and delay skills." *Am I joking? Maybe not. We always help each other be our best and sometimes a tongue lashing isn't enough.* She changed the topic before Mia arrived. "Don't worry about that now. We're interviewing the survivors to build a skills inventory. Mia's going first to serve as an example."

CHAPTER TWENTY – 17:30 June 4, 2070 – Put to the Question

When you stop expecting people to be perfect, you can like them for who they are.
Donald Miller

Willow, River, and Mia walked together to a nearby small clearing where they could converse without the other survivors overhearing. Willow removed her journal from its protective plastic cover. She penciled "Central High Cell Interviews" at the top of a new page.

River raised his eyebrows.

Willow knew what had caught his attention. Using a page from their dwindling paper supply was a sign of serious business. *Before Gaia, who would suspect the future high value of flattened wood fibers? Paper is back, social media followers mean less than nothing.* "OK, Mia, tell us what knowledge and skills you bring to our cell."

"I was a Central High Cell elder for five years," Mia said with her usual composure. "As you know what happened to us, you may question whether my experience is helpful or harmful. I assure you I learned as much from our mistakes at Central High Cell as I did from our wins. My knowledge will be valuable to Cave Cell. Regarding pitching in, I am sure you noticed I don't get around as well as you younger folk. Gaia damaged my leg in an attack, so long journeys are beyond me now. Other than that, I am as healthy as expected for my age. I can help with work near the cell."

Willow jotted notes and then gazed at Mia. "Thank you for being forthcoming. If our cell recruits you, our safety becomes intertwined. Is there anyone in your group that might compromise cell safety?"

"Excellent question," Mia praised. "You are learning how to fulfill team lead responsibilities quickly. Now, to answer your question, I am confident these Central High Cell survivors will be beneficial and loyal to your cell. There are a couple that may cause concern at first glance. Joseph is textbook strong and silent, so you will have trouble getting him to provide you with any information. Joseph is a talented, self-taught mechanic. He kept all our mechanical devices at Central High Cell running even without spare parts.

His innovations to replace or get around failed parts were phenomenal. To be blunt, if you possess mechanical devices, you best recruit Joseph versus the value I bring."

Mia paused until Willow finished writing. "I also want to comment on Finn. You probably perceive him as a troublemaker. He's a loyal young man who cares deeply for his people, but is still learning how to express himself. Right now, his people are just the seven other Central High survivors. If you recruit us, Finn will soon be among the hardest working and staunchest supporters of your cell." Mia peered at Willow.

"Thanks Mia, that's my questions," Willow said. "River, anything you want to ask?"

"How long have you known the other seven?" River asked. "Any newcomers?"

Willow readied her pen. *Terrific question. Mountain Cell just informed us a cell to the east was almost wiped out after a human collaborator disclosed the cell's location to Gaia.*

Mia pursed her lips and paused before speaking. "Teachers, families of the last student group, and school alumni like me founded Central High Cell in 2055. We took in other survivors until hit we hit our Dunbar hundred fifty in 2064. The other seven survivors are part of the original Dunbar hundred fifty; each with the cell for minimum six years." Mia peered quizzically at River. Her expression shifted to intrigue. "Are you asking because you are concerned about infiltrators? Has Gaia recruited people as her agents?"

"We think it has happened." River confirmed her hypothesis. "Not to us, although the information is from a trusted secondhand source. It may be the root of the fifth Imperative."

Concern in her voice, Mia quoted the fifth. "Ah yes, respect strangers, but don't trust them. I assumed it was about competition for scarce resources, but the danger of Gaia collaborators applies." Mia paused, looking at Willow and River.

"No more questions from me," River said.

"Well then, I have something to say." Mia put her hand on Willow's shoulder. "I will not ask you to parrot a statement. I trust you will recommend what is best for both your cell and Central High Cell."

"Oh, thank you for having faith in me," Willow said. "I believe we want the same thing."

Mia dropped her hand and stepped back.

"We'll cycle through the other seven now," Willow said. "Can you send them in the order most agreeable to your group?"

"Of course," Mia replied. "We want your cell to be comfortable with us and to understand the value we can bring." She headed back to the other survivors.

River let out a slow breath, releasing tension.

"Little old Mia scares the shit out of you," Willow said.

River didn't bother to deny the obvious. "Hell, yeah. She's got killer laser beam eyes."

Soon enough, Joseph arrived.

Willow tried to make Joseph comfortable with a wide smile before speaking. "Hi Joseph, I'm Willow and he is my twin brother, River. We are the team leads for everyone you've met from Cave Cell. We're gathering information so our cell can decide what to do for the Central High Cell survivors. Can we ask you some questions?"

Joseph nodded "yes".

"Great, please tell us what knowledge and skills you could bring to our cell," Willow asked.

Joseph pondered the question. "I fix mechanical things," he said.

"Oh, like small motors?" Willow led, trying to coax out a bit more detail.

Joseph nodded "yes".

"What about more complex devices like an alternator bike?" Willow asked, trying again to lead Joseph into details.

Joseph nodded "yes".

Willow was about to try another prompt when River interrupted. "Hey Joseph, I sense you're a man of few words. If our cell recruited you, you and I would be responsible for each other's lives. Could I trust you with my life?"

Willow waited with bated breath. *That was a pretty intense question, but will it break Joseph out of his one-word funk?*

"Yes," Joseph said, staring into River's eyes.

River didn't seem surprised by the monosyllabic answer. "Do you mistrust any of the other Central High Cell survivors?"

Again, Joseph did not hesitate. "All trustworthy."

That's everything we're getting from him. "Good talk," Willow said. "Please have Mia send us the next candidate."

Joseph nodded and headed back to his group.

"Call me foolish," River said, "but between what Mia verbalized for him and his demeanor, I trust him. If Gaia was recruiting someone to act as an agent, she'd pick an outgoing, friendly type rather than the never-waste-breath-on-words type."

Willow grunted and said, "Unless Gaia determined that assumption probable, and picked him to fool you."

"I hate the Gaia game theory arguments." River hissed and punched her on the shoulder. "Tell me what you think without worrying six layers deep about what Gaia wants you to think if she knows what you know and you know what she knows and you both know each other knows that."

Willow sighed. *I enjoy an engaging session of looking forward and reasoning back, especially since it infuriates River so much. If I must decide based on what we know now, I agree with River on this one.* "What you said."

River smiled and composed himself. Finn was approaching.

Willow desired a successful interview with Finn. "Thanks for coming to talk with us, Finn. I'm Willow and this is River. We are the team leads for everyone you've met from Cave Cell. Can we ask you some questions to help our cell decide what to do for the Central High Cell survivors?"

Finn sneered. "I don't have a choice, do I?"

Willow understood Finn better after hearing him speak to his departed parents. "We understand your frustration after the last three weeks. Our cell is meeting about how to help. If you don't want input into the decision, we can skip this chat."

"Hold on, we can talk," Finn said.

Willow forced a big smile. *We jimmied open the door, now to walk through it.* "Excellent. Please tell us how you joined Central High Cell and what you do for the cell."

Finn unclenched his fists, but still eyed Willow and River warily. "My family lived across the street from the school. I was just three when my parents helped form the cell there in 2055. My father was in a scavenging party that crossed paths with minions ten years ago. Nobody understood how to fight them. Only one of the eight scavengers made it back, but they died from their wounds. A few years later, my mom fell ill and died because no one could find the right medicine. I started working for the cell when I was eight, doing errands and helping with meals. When I was twelve, I started going out with scavenging teams. Soon after, my brother died when we were on a mission. A biped discovered us ranging far from the cell, but my brother drew it away to save the rest of the team. I've led scavenging teams for a year and done weapons maintenance when at the cell."

That got River's interest. "We did time for our cell cleaning weapons. What was in Central High's arsenal?"

Finn looked humiliated. "We built up a top-notch arsenal, but Gaia caught us unaware. We had two M107A1s, eight M4A1s, twelve M16A4s, and various pistols. Plentiful regular rounds for everything, but we were running low on armor-piercing. We even had an M320 grenade launcher with ten sweet M433 rounds that punched right through biped frontal armor. None of that matters now, since she probably has it all. When Gaia entered the school, we ran away with the small arms in hand. A stop at the armory was suicide."

"Do you mistrust any of the Central High Cell survivors?" Willow asked their closing question.

Finn's answer was quick and definitive. "We lived in close quarters for years, and in the last few weeks, our lives were often in the others' hands. These are trustworthy people."

River glanced at Willow. He raised his eyebrows to see if she wanted to close things off. She gave him a slight nod to go ahead. "We appreciate you talking to us," River said. "We will share your comments with our cell before it decides how we are going to help you. Can you ask Mia to send over the next candidate?"

"Yeah, sure, no problem." Finn turned to go. He hesitated and turned back. He looked at Willow, River and finally focused down at the ground between them. His voice wavered as he said, "I've disrespected you and your people. Almost my whole life, my cell raised me to trust only them. Now I understand that everything you did was to help us, even though you didn't have to. What I am trying to say is 'thank you' for putting yourselves at risk to rescue us. Please do what you can for the other Central High Cell survivors. I'll understand and leave if you decide I pose a risk to your cell."

When Finn finished and looked up, Willow smiled. "I can't speak for our cell," she said, "but from my perspective, I don't believe it will come to that."

Finn headed back to Mia and the others with a hint of a smile.

Willow waited until Finn was out of earshot. "Now we're seeing the real Finn."

River held his fist up for a bump.

CHAPTER TWENTY-ONE – 18:00 June 4, 2070 – Pre Game

One important key to success is self-confidence. An important key to self-confidence is preparation.

Arthur Ashe

The first talks with elder Mia, mechanic Joseph, and scavenger team lead Finn were awkward because of River and Willow learning on the fly. The remaining Central High Cell survivor interviews went smoothly. River and Willow spoke with red seal chef Abas, carpenter Hourig, seamster Tocho, small appliance fixer Freya, and fortune-telling scavenger team lead Ramla.

As River and Willow finished interviewing Ramla, a shout came from the forest to the northeast. "Free survivors approaching." Soon enough, Mason and a few other Cave Cell members arrived to offer food and medical attention to the Central High Cell survivors.

Before going to meet them, Willow secured her valuable journal in its protective cover, storing it in her pack.

Ava and Carter were with them. Ava discretely tugged her ear and shook her head.

Willow blinked at Ava to signal understanding. *They didn't make it to where they could overhear or they heard nothing useful. No matter either way. At least they weren't busted like River and I.*

The newcomers each bore a heavy pack; their weapons slung loose or holstered. Mason would have observed the camp from cover before announcing his team's presence and coming in with weapons lowered.

"Hello, I am Mason, our cell's medic," he announced. "We brought food, water, and medical supplies. My assistant Isabella and I will examine the injured, then treat based on severity."

Isabella, a spritely ten-year-old in contrast to Mason's tall and muscular frame, kicked Mason's shin.

"Ouch," he said.

"Apprentice," Isabella said, scanning the survivors to make sure everyone understood. "I'm his apprentice."

Mason rubbed his leg and grinned. "Apologies, Isabella. My apprentice will treat this contusion on my leg after helping you."

"That's a bruise." Isabella said, grinning as Mason affectionately ruffled her hair. The Cave Cell crew and the Central High Cell survivors laughed. Isabella's exuberance was what they needed after today's experiences.

Willow gave Isabella a thumbs-up and the "you go girl" face. *She'll do great things for Cave Cell. She's brilliant and doesn't take shit from anyone; especially Mason, her mentor and favorite Cave Cell uncle.*

Mason and the others set up for a meal and medical treatment.

Willow poked River's arm. "Everyone is in capable hands here. Should we wake Noah and head home? We can plan what we'll say as we walk."

"Let's do that, but you'll speak to Cave Cell," River said. "Although I want time on center stage my first day as team lead, this turned into your mission when you initiated our response. I'll support you, but this is your show."

Willow thought about it. *On the one hand, I don't want to push a fellow team lead, especially my brother, into the shadows if there's a win to share. On the other hand, River is correct about protocol. Also, what if Cave Cell rules that helping Central High Cell was a giant mistake and needs someone to blame? Better I take the fall and protect his standing than both of us getting burned.* "OK, I'll take the lead until we gauge the room's temperature. If it's all rainbows and unicorns, be ready to share the credit."

"Oh, Willow, I love you like a sister. Wait, you are my sister," River said and laughed. "Fine, I'll follow your lead. If things get tense and I jump to your defense, don't trip me up and take the fall yourself."

Willow nodded as if agreeing. *Arguing will not get us anywhere. I'll strategize how to protect him, in case things get ugly at the meeting.* Willow headed over to Noah while River packed.

Noah snored in a deep sleep. It was a shame to wake him, but he had planned this. Willow gently shook his shoulder and was about to say his name. Before she spoke, she was staring at a pistol's barrel pointed between her eyes. "Noah, chill. You wanted me to wake you before River and I left."

"Yes, of course, just instincts. Sorry." Noah yawned as he apologized and holstered his pistol.

Now that the gun was out of her face, Noah's reaction impressed rather than scared Willow. "Can you teach me how to go from deep sleep to weapon ready?"

"Yes, but first you have to suffer from raging paranoia and sleep deprivation. Gaia blowing up the hill you were perching on is another prerequisite." Noah grinned at her as he stretched himself awake.

Willow grimaced. "Hmm, maybe we'll save that lesson for later. Mason and a few others arrived and are feeding and treating the survivors. River and I will pack and go."

"All right, you are good to go. I'll get Ava and Carter. They'll hunker down here to rest while I take watch." In under a minute, Noah woke up alert, geared up, and headed out.

Willow made a mental note to hasten her "time to ready" when outside the Cave. *I must seem like a snail waking up and getting ready compared to Noah.*

Willow and River departed to the northeast, still maintaining the protective façade of the direction their cell was located. On their way out, they waved goodbye to the Central High survivors. Everyone except Mia waved cheerily back, their moods upbeat with a proper meal and medical attention both underway. Mia waved solemnly.

Willow nodded to Mia. *She understands what's at stake tonight; her people's fate worries her. After knowing them for a day, I am also concerned.*

Once out of hearing and sight, River shivered and said, "Damn, I'm glad I'm through my shenanigans phase. If we recruit Mia and she ends up in charge of who did what and when, I'll crack like a dropped egg at one glance from her."

"Well, you better up your game at hiding in the caves. You might be through your daily shenanigans phase, but you're still in your weekly shenanigans phase." Willow jibed and shoved River in perfect timing to make him walk into a tree.

"Dammit, that hurt." River disentangled himself and ran to catch up. "I have grown as a person, whereas you have not as proven by pushing me into yon tree. To show it, I want the Central High folks to join Cave Cell; even though it means I'll have to survive Mia's truth piercing gaze. What do you think?"

"Yeah, I agree. Let's review the interviews and talk strategy. First, what the fuck is a red seal chef?" Willow asked as she walked, scanning the surrounding forest for any threats.

"I believe it was acknowledgement of high-level skill, like how people apprentice at Cave Cell to work toward being the real shit," River said. "He said he became certified in a place called Canada months before the Second

Dark Age began. Screw the details, Tocho promised Abas cooks a rat stew that will make you lick the bowl clean. Who knows what he does with deer and fresh vegetables? We've never had a genuine chef before, so chances are a red seal one is a giant leap forward."

"Better wipe your chin, because you're drooling." *His stomach is always top of mind. I am intrigued, though. Can eating be enjoyable instead of just acquiring energy for work?* Willow checked a mental box beside Abas' name. "Abas is desirable. How about Tocho? We're making do with trying to repair our clothing and gear, but a bona fide trained seamster will help us do better. Cave Cell's clothing is threadbare and we've already scavenged the clothing from nearby sites."

"I've lost count of the times I've repaired a gear sling, only to have to fix it again a week later," River said. "You know how you do something and you know it's not the right way, but you don't know how to do it right? That's me repairing gear and clothing. If he's true to his word, we need Tocho to show us the right way."

"Whenever we haul ass to escape from Gaia," Willow said, "I am half afraid of her catching me and half afraid of my rifle sling, pack strap, or pants button giving way. OK, OK, make it ninety-ten, but you know what I mean. We're agreed Tocho is beneficial."

They walked in silence, Willow replaying the interviews in her mind to identify any red flags. She suspected River was doing the same.

"I expect they'll be helpful right away," River said after a while. "Put Finn to work for Noah, Kesa, and Sophia for a year and he would operate at our level."

Willow often disagreed with River, and he with her, just to push each other's buttons. That was kid's stuff, though, since people's futures were hanging on this. She sighed. *There's always time for a stimulating argument about something inconsequential later.* "You nailed it. These folks will pitch in wherever we need them. I'm sure all of them, Mia included, wouldn't hesitate to spend the day on their hands and knees weeding our vegetable gardens."

"Yeah, and while she's weeding, she's choking confessions out of the work crew with her truth stare," River said. "Abas isn't in the garden. He's in the kitchen, whipping up the yummy things to eat that Grandpy Max talks about from before the Second Dark Age."

"Promise me you'll never stop being you." Willow gave her brother a one-armed hug while they walked.

"Finally, a promise I can keep," River said. "Done deal."

They walked quietly the rest of the way, River giving her time to rehearse. Willow worked through her speech and planned how to protect her brother in case things turned sideways.

"Free survivors approaching," River shouted when they neared the Cave's main entrance.

CHAPTER TWENTY-TWO – 18:30 June 4, 2070 – Showtime

To Confucius, harmony was consensus, not conformity. It required loyal opposition.
Evan Osnos

Too far away to hear, Willow hoped the watcher engaged their rifle's safety as she and River approached. The lookout perch was concealed, even to those knowing where to look. The perch had an excellent line of sight to all approaches to the Cave.

Owen Garcia stepped out of hiding and waved. "The Cave is buzzing with the news of your rescue mission. I predict a lively meeting."

"Are you stuck out here?" Willow asked. It surprised her to find a senior militia member on watch, so likely to miss the meeting.

"Only until everyone is ready to begin. They're going to send a watch-qualified junior out to relieve me," Owen replied. "You know nothing goes on around here without my say so, right?"

"I happen to have some imminent latrine activities you can supervise," River said.

"Hard pass, River. You're responsible for making sure you don't get it on yourself." Owen waved them off and disappeared into the perch.

Cave Cell engineered the cave entrance to appear nondescript from outside, arranging boulders and growing brush to conceal it. They randomly placed stepping stones to enable those coming and going to avoid leaving tracks or wearing a trail in the foliage. Cave Cell needed to avoid detection by both ground and air minions.

Willow and River walked single file on the stepping stones and around the brush in front of the entrance. Although they entered quietly, they found themselves staring down the barrels of two carbines.

"Welcome back. If the rumors are true, you've had a busy day," Zoey said. She, the lead guard on entry duty, and Taamir, her duty partner, lowered their M4A1s as they stepped out from cover behind boulders. They each had a chair and small table beside their cover where they cleaned and lubricated carbines while they "greeted" anyone coming into the Cave.

"Yeah, we're hoping every mission we lead isn't a firefight and survivor rescue capped off with a Hellfire up the ass," River said matter-of-factly.

Taamir chortled, choking it off when Zoey gave him a sharp look. "When you're done giggling," she said, "go scare up two juniors to replace Owen and one of us. We're going to flip for who stays on entry duty or goes to the meeting."

Taamir made an elaborate mocking salute and headed off to find the junior infantry. Rank was a loose concept at Cave Cell, more of a mutual understanding of each other's abilities and role instead of a formal hierarchy.

Zoey turned back to Willow, giving her a "what-are-you-gonna-do" shrug. "Almost everybody is in the Big Cave, probably arguing. You should go before they come to blows or decide without your input."

"I wish I could at least pretend to be surprised, but thanks for the heads-up," Willow said. "We'll head straight there." Cave Cell adults taught Willow and her peer group that Cave Cell is a participative meritocracy. A council of wise elders accepts feedback from everyone before making decisions all are expected to live with. That was a reasonable classroom description of the process, but the reality was grittier and chaotic. Those surviving Gaia's effort to exterminate Homo sapiens were a tough bunch that didn't hesitate to voice their opinions.

Willow gazed expectantly at River as he was first in line to start off through the sometimes tight passages leading into Cave Cell's refuge. He gave Zoey a saucy wink and headed into the passage. Zoey responded by giving River the finger. *I don't know or want to know what he is up to and with who.*

The caves were dimly lit with sparse quarter watt LED bulbs powered from Cave Cell's DC electric system. Cave Cell gathered the power from a few sources. Solar panels, hidden from aerial surveillance, provided a third of the needed power. These vertical or inwardly slanting faces were only in sunlight a few hours each day. Because of the placement to maintain secrecy, each panel contributed little. Cave Cell tried to mitigate that with volume; there were countless solar panels to scavenge given their ancestors' late rush to green energy. A Cave Cell founder placed a turbine in a natural wind tunnel. It typically supplied the remaining needed power. Cave Cell also had a couple of what used to be called exercise bikes rigged up with alternators to supply power on deficient wind days or for special purposes.

Willow followed River through the twists and turns of the entry caves. Instead of making movement easier by widening or straightening passageways in this front section, Cave Cell built a tight maze. If Gaia got in, the twists, turns, dead ends, and ambushes would slow her advance while Cave Cell evacuated from secret exits. Willow knew the tunnels well enough to navigate with her eyes closed if she focused, but let River lead so she could rehearse for the meeting.

In the living and working areas, they passed by and through larger caves. Here was where Cave Cell residents slept, stored or prepared food, tended to a small hydroponic farm, attended school, and trained to fight Gaia. Normally, abandoned living areas would be odd, but this wasn't a normal day. The din of almost all of Cave Cell's hundred and forty residents engaged in debate and conversation increased as River led.

"Don't worry, sis, you got this," River said.

They traveled through a rough-hewn rock tunnel. It widened to two meters across for the last twenty meters before opening into the hundred meter diameter nearly circular Big Cave. The noise resolved from an incoherent buzzing into scores of conversations spread throughout. The upper caves like this one stayed dry, other than when the rare torrential downpour infiltrated. Cave Cell long-ago removed the stalagmites scattered around the floor, short raised discs the sole sign left of their existence.

River stepped into the cave, moving to the side so Willow entered as the star of the show.

The party atmosphere surprised Willow, since she expected a contentious meeting. Kids were running through the crowd playing games with no one trying to calm them. Animated but civil conversations abounded. *The last Cave Cell meeting was some time ago; perhaps it's just nice to have a break and a chance to socialize.*

Max Williams, the elders' council unofficial head, conversed with the other elders. At sixty-five years old, he was the oldest person in Cave Cell. Grandpy Max was a welcome sight. He was always there for Willow and her brother. He listened to their trivial woes as they grew up, celebrated their successes, and doled out the right amount of wisdom when they were ready to listen.

Grandpy Max excused himself and came to Willow and River, spreading his arms wide to give their opposing shoulders a reassuring squeeze. "Thank goodness you and your teams are OK. We worried about your late return until Kesa arrived and briefed us. Such an adventure your first time as team leads."

The relief in Grandpy Max's voice brought home the magnitude of the day's events. A flood of the emotion Willow had bottled up throughout the day came over her: fear for her team and her brother's safety; anger at Gaia; exhaustion; and empathy for the Central High Cell survivors. The rush of emotion and exhaustion must have shown on her face.

Grandpy Max examined them both. "I am so sorry for having to ask you here without rest, but Cave Cell awaits your story. You can keep things short if you need. Who wants to speak?"

Willow glanced at River, a small part of her hoping he would volunteer.

River shook his head. "You led us through the battle. The cell needs your story. Listen to this crowd. They're primed to hear about Gaia's ass getting whooped."

Willow took a deep breath and let it out slowly to center herself. She turned to Grandpy Max. "I'll speak," she said confidently.

"Excellent," Grandpy Max said and smiled. He headed to a natural rise across the cave that served as a stage. "Attention everyone, attention. Our newest team leads have returned from leading their teams against Gaia to rescue another cell. Willow will tell us what happened and share what she learned about the cell's survivors."

Willow and River walked to the rise, River peeling off to stand at the front for moral support. Grandpy Max stepped to the side to give her center stage.

Willow faced the crowd, all people she had lived with for her entire life or their entire life, depending on their age. Owen and Zoey entered the cave, Zoey giving her a wave. The crowd gazed at her. Willow cleared her throat and launched into the story.

"River and I each led a scavenging team for the first time today. We planned to go to the nearby town site, double check prior scavenged ground, and return to the forest for a picnic lunch. You know, keep our first outing nice and easy." As quiet laughter rippled through the crowd, Willow felt her tension fall away.

"We heard gunfire when we neared the town, so we took cover to assess the situation. The Central High Cell survivors spilled out from the town with Gaia hot on their heels, hell bent on exterminating everyone. They fought for their lives without the weapons or position to have a chance. Gaia murdered many of them in their tracks as they ran unknowingly toward the Cave Cell positions."

Those in Cave Cell that hadn't seen Gaia in action gasped.

"The people from Central High Cell didn't have the right weapons nor a tactically acceptable position, but we did. I felt sure that nobody on our teams wanted to watch in silence as Gaia murdered them one by one. We had to join the battle. Noah and Kesa moved to the right positions with the right weapons. Our newbies, Logan, Chloe, Carter, and Ava, fought bravely to distract Gaia's armored bipeds. Logan took a bullet in the shoulder but fought on, not telling us they wounded him until after the battle."

"Working together, we destroyed a quadcopter and created opportunities for Noah and Kesa to put AP bullets through the two bipeds' thinner rear armor. Everyone knows those two will not hesitate to take a kill shot on Gaia."

"Hell, yeah," said Kesa from the midst of the crowd, triggering another ripple of laughter.

Willow waited for the levity to die out before continuing. "Thanks to our Cave Cell training as soldiers, team leads, and in multi-team coordination, we won the firefight, but that wasn't the end. Killing six of Central High Cell didn't satisfy Gaia. As our teams were working to get everyone to relative safety in the forest, she fired two Hellfire missiles from a Reaper. One killed another four from Central High Cell, the other blew up the hill Noah had set up on for overwatch."

People looked around the cave. "Where's Noah?" they whispered.

"Noah's OK," Willow said to quell everyone's fears. "He's protecting the Central High survivors from Gaia."

The crowd quieted again, attention back to her. Willow resumed her story. "The contact with Gaia was over in only an hour and a half. We spent the rest of the day getting the eight Central High Cell survivors to a nearby resting place. There, we gave them food, water, and medical treatment without compromising our security." Willow paused for a breath and to check the crowd. Her story still riveted them; this was the most excitement in recent times for Cave Cell.

"The Central High Cell survivors were on the run for three weeks. Gaia hounded them, killing everyone she could each time she caught up to them. Out of the hundred-fifty Central High Cell members, these are the last eight.

I have observed and spoken to each of them during an intense four and a half hours of exposure. Even though I'm seeing them at their worst, I feel they all have something to contribute to Cave Cell. Many bring special skills not represented in our cell today. None displayed signs of being a Gaia agent, and each trusts the others with their life. I urge Cave Cell to recruit these survivors." Willow made eye contact with Grandpy Max, wondering what to do once she finished her speech.

Grandpy Max was ready for his cue, joining her center stage. "Thank you for your firsthand account, Willow. We are incredibly proud of you, River, and your teams." He motioned River onstage. "River, please share your thoughts whether we recruit the survivors or provision them and send them on their way."

River, ever the showman, mounted the stage at a leisurely pace and scanned the audience. He paused to add drama before speaking. "I was with my sister, gathering information about these survivors. I agree with everything she said and want to add that one survivor is an elite red seal chef."

There was a glint in Grandpy Max's eyes as he mumbled "red seal" under his breath. Grandpy Max and River had high regard for anything resembling a proper meal in this world where Cave Cell usually had to focus on survival.

Grandpy Max shook off the chef mention. "Thank you for your endorsement, River. I believe we have more firsthand witnesses here? Kesa, Chloe, and Logan, please shout out whether you agree or disagree with Willow and River."

Three shouts of "agree" came in response.

"Now, does anyone have questions for our witnesses?" Grandpy Max asked.

Rene, a middle-aged man who kept Cave Cell's electrical system running, raised his hand to be recognized. Grandpy Max nodded to him. "Willow, did the Central High survivors tell you how Gaia discovered their home?" Rene asked.

"Yes, one survivor was a Central High Cell elder," Willow said. "She told us they became complacent because Gaia wasn't patrolling their area. Central High Cell allowed some of their young to scavenge without monitoring to make sure they were changing up their return routes. Gaia followed an established trail back to Central High Cell and caught them unawares."

Rene crossed his arms. "A deadly lesson. Cave Cell should learn from it and maintain our strict security protocols. I appreciate Central High Cell's honesty for not trying to hide this embarrassing and fatal truth."

Ethan, a lean ten-year-old, worked his way to where Grandpy Max could see him and waved his hand. He spoke when Grandpy Max nodded at him. "Can this chef teach me to bake an angel food cake with icing? I've seen pictures in our cookbooks and want to make one."

"They tell me you are a splendid helper in the kitchen, Ethan," Grandpy Max said. "If we choose to recruit these folks, the chef will help us cook tastier meals. Our ingredients will limit what the chef can make, but a cake will be doable."

"Thank you for hearing me. I want to learn from this chef." Ethan was mature for his age, since necessity required Cave Cell kids to contribute to Cave Cell's functioning.

Grandpy Max scanned the room. No one else indicated having a direct question. He moved on from witnesses speaking and being questioned to Cave Cell's next phase of decision-making. Cave Cell hears everyone that wants to speak in meetings. "Since witness statements and questions are done, we'll open the floor to statements."

Jaanvi raised her hand. She was thirty, strong in body and will. She was the resident black cloud, always seeing the potential downside of what Cave Cell was debating. Her dire predictions proved true often enough, however, that everyone considered her concerns. Getting the nod from Grandpy Max, she stepped onto the stage and moved her gaze across the audience.

Willow noticed that everyone had quieted. *Cave Cell hears everyone, but those who effectively deliver their message are heard the best. Jaanvi engages the audience, a skill I need to learn.* Willow paid attention to both the delivery method and the message.

"I trust everyone here with my life, as most of you do," Jaanvi said. "Trust makes me want to agree with our witnesses. They recommend, however, that we extend our trust to people only eight of us spent a partial day with. They say Gaia destroyed their cell by capitalizing on a weakness. We should not make the same mistake. I say we provision them and help them set up a day's walk away from us and the other nearby cells. We can watch them for a year and consider recruiting them if they don't show any signs of Gaia's influence.

Remember what Mountain Cell advised about Gaia spies and the fifth Imperative 'Respect strangers, but don't trust them.' "

Much murmuring followed Jaanvi's speech. Jaanvi voiced a shared fear, especially given the recent news.

Althea, a forty-five-year-old on the elder council, gave Grandpy Max a quick wave. Grandpy Max gestured for Althea to hold on to let the crowd digest Jaanvi's words. When the crowd quieted, Grandpy Max tipped his hand to her.

"Thank you for putting words to a common concern, Jaanvi," Althea said as she came onto the stage at a relaxed pace. She was another skilled orator. "We learned long-ago to fear any computer-controlled machine. With the recent news that Gaia uses human agents, we doubt other humans. If we ran across one or two people with only their word Gaia was hot on their tail, I would agree with Jaanvi." Althea paused for effect and then continued. "What happened today is significantly different. An unscheduled Cave Cell mission stumbled upon a firefight in progress between these folks and Gaia. Gaia killed six of them in our team's sight. Even after losing a battle on the ground, she tried to finish everyone off with two hopefully irreplaceable Hellfire missiles. The eight survivors state they've known each other for years and trust each other with their lives. For this to be a trap, Gaia would have to corrupt them all and they would need to be OK with her killing ten of their fellows."

Some in the audience talked amongst themselves. Althea gave everyone time to consider her words. When the room quieted, she wrapped up. "Given the improbability that Gaia orchestrated this, I suggest we recruit the survivors. We will all welcome them and monitor for suspicious behavior. Coming from another cell, they'll understand being confined to the caves for a while."

Grandpy Max peered around the room for anyone else wanting to speak. Since no one signaled for attention, Grandpy Max put out a last call. "Thank you, Jaanvi and Althea, for speaking on this matter. Before the show of hands, does anyone have new interpretation or information to share?"

This was a key part of what made Cave Cell's participative meritocracy work. Everyone prolonged debate only with fresh content rather than repeating anything already said. The later non-binding vote would include everyone's opinion.

No one called out or motioned to speak.

The last of the three elders, Robert, joined Grandpy Max and Althea on stage, where they could best see how Cave Cell voted.

Grandpy Max moved to the front of the stage. The vote was the pinnacle of a Cave Cell meeting. "Cave Cell is deciding whether to offer the Central High Cell survivors an opportunity to join us or if we will instead escort them well away from Cave Cell territory." Grandpy Max ensured everyone understood before continuing. "First, raise your hand if you feel Cave Cell should recruit the Central High Cell survivors."

Willow raised her hand, scanning to see who else voted the same. River and their teammates in the room raised their hands, as expected. Ethan's hand was up. Since voting was non-binding on the elders, Cave Cell allowed anyone old enough to understand the question to show their opinion in a vote. Overall, Willow estimated at least six in ten were in favor.

Grandpy Max finished surveying the room, glanced at the other elders to make sure they were ready, and called the other half of the vote. "Now, hands up if you feel Cave Cell should provision the survivors and escort them away from our territory."

Willow, hand down, checked the room. Only two in ten voted this way, including Jaanvi. Grandpy Max once told her the nonvoting count was as interesting as the counts for those who voted.

Althea and Robert left Big Cave, heading to the nearby small private cave the elders used for meetings. Grandpy Max wrapped the meeting up before leaving himself. "We have heard everyone. The elders will now decide."

Willow breathed a sigh of relief. The elders typically followed the vote. Years ago, Grandpy Max taught Willow and her young friends about Cave Cell decision-making. He told them that Cave Cell was pretty smart and made competent decisions, as expressed by their votes. The elders went against the majority only when they had failed to ensure everyone was told all the facts and implications. Although the vote usually made the decision, the genuine work of the elders was to plan execution details everyone could tolerate.

Even though the decision was imminent, most folks left Big Cave. They were busy, and knew that news travelled fast by word-of-mouth. Willow, River, Logan, Chloe, and Kesa stayed to hear the elders' decision firsthand.

Kesa put her fist up for Willow to bump. "You spoke well. I am betting Central High Cell will have you to thank for a new home." Everyone else nodded in agreement.

Willow blushed. Praise from the senior infantry was always hard earned; it meant a lot to receive any. "I capped the day off with a speech, but the teams made everything happen. That's who the survivors owe gratitude."

Soon enough, Althea returned to Big Cave. "We suspected you waited. I believe it will please you that the elders opted to recruit the Central High Cell survivors into Cave Cell. We are ten below our Dunbar hundred fifty, so have room, and we'll gain welcome skills. To maintain security, the survivors may not leave the caves unescorted for six months. We'll check their gear and persons for transmitters before bringing them to the caves. Do you believe the survivors will agree to these terms?"

Willow scanned her and River's team members. Everyone nodded in agreement.

"There's a couple that might chaff at the restricted movement for a while," River said, "but their elder Mia will help them understand the reason behind it."

"Excellent. Do you want to take part in notifying them?" Althea asked. "Robert is planning to go along with some infantry."

With the decision made, Willow felt the weight of the day's events. "Although I want to go, I'm wiped out and need to rest. I suggest Robert talk to Mia first. She may have a positive way to present the terms to everyone else."

The others that had awaited this decision yawned and eyeballed the passages leading to their beds.

Althea took the hint. "Robert is a big boy. He will handle it. You should go for food and rest before you pass out."

STATUS QUO - KESA

CHAPTER TWENTY-THREE – 11:30 June 2, 2070 –
Chumming the Water

Before The Reckoning, fictional movies and front page coverage of the rare attacks convinced us to fear sharks. The Reckoning taught us to forget about sharks and fear the real threat: our fellow humans. A few killed for the sake of killing, everyone else killed out of necessity.
Althea Franco, 2067

Kesa mulled over waking Noah. *He looks so peaceful and obviously needs sleep after his long day yesterday. On the other hand, I have orders to bring him to the meeting, and he was relieved from the lookout perch at least seven hours ago. Decision made, duty wins over empathy.* Kesa gently shoved his hip with her booted foot. "Wakey wakey, Noah. We need you for a mission."

Noah groaned and turned away from her, putting his pillow over his head.

Kesa shoved him again, this time not gentle. "Don't make me tip this bed. You know I'll do it." The bed was Cave Family's typical makeshift single size, with a patchwork cloth bag stuffed with more cloth rags serving as a mattress. Unlike the more common shared sleeping quarters, Noah had his own little cave because of his role as a key protector and hunter. Kesa had switched on the sole quarter watt LED bulb in his room. Cave Family was lucky these bulbs' service life exceeded a hundred thousand hours. The end of mass manufacturing early in The Reckoning meant no replacements for products like this. The dim light revealed a candidate for the most Spartan living quarters throughout the caves. Noah had a bed and gear chest for furniture, but nothing covering the rough-hewn rock walls, floor, and ceiling. Kesa scrunched her nose in a combination of pity and distaste. *I furnished and decorated my cave like a person actually lives there.*

"Fine, I'm up, I'm up." Noah threw his pillow at her as hard as he could. He rolled out of bed, thankfully fully clothed in yesterday's pants and shirt.

He stretched wide. "What time is it? Any intruders overnight? What's the mission? Is my gear packed?"

"So many questions from someone so recently comatose. Follow me for answers. Grandpy Max wants to talk with everyone together." Kesa coaxed, tugging at Noah's shirt to get him moving.

"Ah, here they are. Apologies, Noah, for the early awakening after your long day. I trust Kesa was gentle?" Max Williams, one of Cave Family's three elected leaders, halted mid conversation to greet them.

Grandpy Max stood with six others at the near end of Big Cave: Ava, Chloe, Sophia, Owen, Carter, and Mason. The headcount surprised Kesa. *Mission teams are usually only four people.*

Noah glanced at Kesa. "About as gentle as Kesa can be," he mumbled. "Ouch, do you sharpen that thing?"

Kesa gave him a sly grin. *I know where to apply an elbow for full effect.*

"The leaders conversed at length about the bodies you found," Grandpy Max said. "We're concerned because this reminds us of the predatory behavior many people exhibited during The Reckoning. A few dark hearts show up and before you know it, there is a veritable thieves' den on your doorstep."

Ava, Carter, and Chloe glanced at each other in confusion.

Sophia stepped up to clarify. "The leaders fear we'll end up with a gang of thieves and murderers in our territory if we don't deal with these first ones."

"Correct. Thanks for the summary." Grandpy Max looked around to make sure everyone was engaged. "Here's what we propose to nip this in the bud. We send out a small group geared up to appear they are fleeing the western desertification. They look vulnerable and have things worth stealing. They'll slowly travel the same tornado track as where Noah found the bodies. Another team will shadow them from concealment, ready to capture the thieves when they accost the first team. What do you think?"

Everyone was quiet for a minute.

Ava broke the silence. "So the first team is bait?"

"Absolutely." Grandpy Max confirmed.

Kesa appreciated that Grandpy Max never tried to gloss over danger or dire news.

"If we want a vulnerable bait team, we can't have strong and dangerous looking people on it. You intend Chloe and me to be bait," Ava said in a matter-of-fact tone.

"Also correct," Grandpy Max said. "Although, the leaders requested each of you on this mission for particular reasons. Chloe stays cool under pressure, whereas you panic at first, which is more than balanced by quickly calming and abundant bravery. The leaders believe unfeigned temporary panic lends reality to the deception."

"Well, I never imagined panicking would land me a mission," Ava said, "but so be it. I'm in."

"A family is more believable bait," Noah said, "but nobody here is old enough to be Ava's and Chloe's parents."

Grandpy Max stared meaningfully back at Noah. "You're right, no one here looks old enough as they appear now."

Kesa got the feeling Grandpy Max was coaxing the group to an end the leaders had already envisioned.

Noah stroked his chin and scanned the others. "So if I am daddy with ash in my hair to age it, dirt and grime on my face to hide my youthful skin, and a crouch to look shorter and less threatening . . . " His gaze settled on Kesa. "Hello, wifey."

"My dear husband," Kesa said, "I hope this mission is long, so I have time to whip you into shape. We mustn't forget the cane you need to help you walk with your gimp leg that never healed quite right."

Grandpy Max smiled as he perused the bait team. He then turned to Sophia. "Will you lead the shadow team?"

"Days of sneaking around in a ghillie suit, sleeping on the ground in a ghillie suit, and eating cold meals?" Sophia tilted her head and raised her eyebrows. "How could I miss out on that? Of course I will lead the shadow team."

Owen, Carter, and Mason glanced at each other. Something unspoken must have passed between them, because Owen committed on their behalf. "We'll fill Sophia's team. Don't worry, we'll have your back, bait team."

"What if the thieves resist, or they endanger our team members?" Sophia asked, her tone dead serious.

Grandpy Max didn't hesitate to answer. "I'll refer to the most relevant of The Rules, 'Judge others by their actions, as words can be without meaning and appearance means nothing.' In this context, team safety is paramount. Eliminate any threat. Strip those surrendering of all firearms, ammo, and anything else making them a threat to Cave Family. Tell them to travel at least a week to the east, and that we will kill them if we see them again. If either team lead feels sending them on their way is a mistake, your judgement to eradicate the threat has our full support."

The lethal force directive shocked Kesa. *This is the first kill-if-necessary mission I have heard of! Grandpy Max issuing these orders means all the leaders are of the same mind. I understand things were tough during The Reckoning; is this a taste of those times?*

Sophia gestured to Kesa. "You know that old Cave Family saying, two cooks spoil the broth and two team leads botch the mission. Do you want to be the team of teams lead?"

Kesa wanted the dual team lead experience, but the bait family team lead needed to focus on staying in character. "Shadow team lead is the better choice to lead the team of teams." *Sophia also has four more years of field experience than I. Rumor has it they were hard years full of painful lessons. Perhaps I can learn some lessons from her on this mission rather than the hard way.*

Sophia slipped into her new role without hesitation, positioning herself beside Grandpy Max to face everyone and issue orders. "Gear up and meet by the Cave front entrance. Bait team, dress for the part in good but travel-worn clothes and gear. Keep weapons realistic but not threatening enough to scare off the prey. Pack a half load of provisions so we can travel fast. When we approach the starting point of the deception, we'll fill your bags with wood and rocks to mimic a full load of goodies. Shadow team, pack your ghillie suits, usual travel kit, and weapons. See you in twenty." Sophia strode from the room to pack her gear.

Bait team chatted about weapons. Consensus was that Noah, as the father, should bring a pistol, whereas the three women should have concealed knives.

Back at her small cave, Kesa rummaged for clothing and gear that fit the part, even going to her neighbors to ask them to contribute their worn clothing to the cause. *Funny how when you ask for someone's worst belongings, you get it without argument versus the fight you're in for when you want their best stuff.* She strapped a fifteen centimeter dagger to her upper leg; she could access it through a strategic rip in the side of her pants.

Kesa found Sophia already waiting outside the Cave entrance. *Wow, I thought I packed quickly and would beat everyone here. The first leadership lesson from Sophia is that team leads are early rather than late.*

Sophia wore upper body armor with a chest rack holding ammo clips for the assault rifle slung across her front. The pistol holstered at her waist was one of the Cave Family's better condition SIG SAUER M17s.

Kesa's eyes lingered on the assault rifle; it wasn't often anyone from Cave Family took one of those outside the weapons cage.

Sophia greeted her with a smile and patted the rifle. "This Mk 16 is the right tool for the job. We're not hunting deer today. I like your worn traveler outfit. We'll dirty your face up to cover your age when we're ready to start the deception. How about you show me your middle-aged woman walk while we wait for the others?"

Kesa paused for a few seconds. *How do middle-aged people move differently than me? Less bounce and a shorter stride; more careful and less youthfulness.* Trying it out, she paced around the entrance area.

After Kesa walked twenty meters, Sophia commented. "That's acceptable, but you can improve. Think less nimble than Jaanvi, but not as stiff as Althea. Also, I got a glimpse of that wicked blade strapped to your leg through the rip in your pants. If you shift the sheath a few centimeters further toward the back of your leg, you will make it harder to spot, but still accessible."

Kesa shifted the dagger's sheath. She pictured Jaanvi and Althea in her mind, remembering how they moved the last time Kesa went harvesting with them. She paced again, modeling someone between their ages.

Noah and the other men piled out of the Cave, quieting down while she paced in persona. Noah wore quality clothing that showed some wear and tear. He armed himself with a Beretta M9 pistol in a glossy black leather holster and a hunting knife in an elaborate sheath. Owen and Carter outfitted themselves similar to Sophia, including assault rifles and pistols. Mason's gear was comparable, but for a weapon he carried Cave Family's best sniper rifle, an M110E1 in perfect condition. Mason himself scavenged it two years ago.

"There's my beloved wife." Noah said. "She is even more precious to me as her youthful vitality fades away."

Sophia laughed and waved at Kesa to stop. "Perfect, Kesa. Now let's see how your husband performs." They both glared at Noah.

Mason patted Noah on the back. "Yeah, dad, strut your stuff."

Mason's sniper rifle reinforced how different this mission was versus Kesa's prior hunting, scavenging, and passers-by intercepts. *We want people who killed others for a bit of food and meagre possessions to accost us.*

Noah pulled a cane handcrafted from a branch off his pack. He paced around the entrance area, easily pulling off the middle-aged-man-with a-gimp-leg persona.

The other men whooped and hollered.

"Damn, now I can't remember Noah walking without that limp," Owen said when he stopped cheering.

Ava and Chloe exited the Cave in time to witness Noah taking a deep bow. "If you're wondering how I pull that off," he said, "it's because I feel twenty years older than I am."

Chloe pointed at the cane. "That cane is remarkably similar to Robert's. It's unlikely that there's more than one that I just haven't seen in our close quarters. I believe it's a fair assumption the cane is Robert's. Are you sure he'll be OK without it?"

"This cane?" Noah examined the cane as if seeing it for the first time. "I found it unattended, so the prior owner mustn't care much for it. Besides, Robert's barely sixty-three and has lived through the nearly complete collapse of civilization. A tough old bird like him must have another cane stashed somewhere." He strapped the cane to the side of his pack.

Sophia failed to stifle a giggle, clearing her throat after to get everyone's attention. "Mom and dad are ready to assume their roles. We're going to travel together for now at full pace. Noah will lead us to a few hundred meters up the tornado track from the murders. Under the cover of the forest, the bait team will assume their roles and then follow the tornado track. We may run into our prey on the way, so stay alert with weapons at hand."

Noah hoisted his pack by the haul loop before working his arms through the shoulder straps. After pulling the straps snug, he headed into the forest at a vigorous pace. The switch from injured middle-aged man to young, strong, and confident hunter was immediate and obvious. The other seniors followed without hesitation.

Kesa hung back. Sophia had caught her eye and tilted her head to signal Kesa to take rear guard. The young ones, Carter, Ava, and Chloe, stood stunned in the emptying clearing. "Are you waiting for an invitation?"

They double timed to take their places in front of her.

After hiking two hours at a brisk pace, Noah halted in the forest near a tornado track. They had crossed other tornado tracks after checking to make sure no one was in sight, but Noah signaled this one was their destination. Unlike the more recent tornado tracks densely littered with toppled trees, time had recycled most of the debris in this one. In this state, it was an easier route to travel than the bordering forest.

Sophia motioned everyone to do a careful three-sixty degree scan. No one indicating sighting other people; Sophia gathered them in a circle. She tipped her hand at Noah to proceed with his briefing.

Noah pointed eastward along the nearby tornado track. "There's a clearing on the tornado track a few hundred meters that way and near the other side. That's where Carter spotted the refugee family. The bodies will be there unless someone or a scavenger moved them. The boot prints to the clearing approached from the south and departed southeast. Unless someone laid the prints to misdirect, our prey came from this side of the tornado track."

"Thanks, Noah," Sophia said. "I don't like how they come and go toward the Cave. Kesa, you're the bait team lead, so how do you want to play it?"

Kesa had mulled this over while they hiked. "Since we want to attract attention, we should come across the bodies and recognize them as refugees from our area. We were all fleeing the same desertification. If the bodies are there, we'll cry out in despair, bury them close by, and make camp in that area tonight. If there aren't any bodies, we'll continue down the track and make camp early, but not suspiciously early. Either way, we'll have a generous fire and a loud conversation tonight."

"Good plan," Sophia agreed. "Mason, where will you be?"

Mason peered up and down the tornado track. "North side forest for line of sight across the south forest. I want Carter with me as my spotter."

"Carter, you're with Mason," Sophia ordered. "Follow his lead. You two hold off crossing until dark. Sunset is nine and there's only a quarter moon tonight. These spotty clouds will give many opportunities to cross the tornado track undetected."

"That leaves you and me creeping just inside the south face forest?" Owen asked Sophia. After she nodded affirmatively, he spoke to the bait team. "We need you to move slowly. Shadow team needs time to travel stealthily and to spot anyone hiding in the bordering forest before they notice us."

Noah rubbed his leg and moaned. "Oh, the pain in my injured leg is flaring up. We're going to have to stop often, so my loving wife and dutiful daughters can massage the knots out of it." After Kesa, Ava, and Chloe all gave him a "what the hell are you talking about" look, he smiled genially. "Or perhaps I can massage it myself."

Kesa laughed along with the others; she appreciated Noah's ability to keep his sense of humor even in tense situations.

Sophia set her pack on the ground and opened a dry box. Inside were five two-way radios.

The radios were another sign that this was a significant mission. Although Cave Family had scavenged many radios, they only issued the rechargeable batteries in times of critical need. Every year, there were fewer and fewer taking a charge. Grandpy Max said they were worth a hundred times their weight in gold. Before The Reckoning, people lusted after several things, gold and diamonds, for example, that no longer had value over their use as materials for tools.

"These are primarily for the shadow team to coordinate when we spot the prey," Sophia said. "Maintain radio silence unless you see them. The radios are all set up to scan and transmit on channel twelve. Kesa, keep this one off except for an emergency transmission or coordinating tactics after contact." She handed a radio to each shadow team member, then handed the last one to Kesa.

Shadow team turned their radios on, each doing a transmit check. Before storing them, they set them to transmit inhibit to prevent accidentally giving away their positions.

Kesa tested hers and switched it off.

Kesa tried to reassure Ava and Chloe with a smile. "It's show time bait team. Let's bulk up our packs with wood and rock at the bottom. If the folks we're after end up digging through our packs, the shadow team needs to intervene before anyone digs deep to discover the ruse. We also need to help each other dirty up our faces. Noah and I to hide our youth, Ava and Chloe to appear like we've traveled far since the last opportunity to bathe."

Soon enough, they finished preparing. Kesa wrapped her radio in clothing to protect it and stuffed it at the bottom of the real contents in her pack. *The gig is up if the thieves glimpse a radio.* She glanced at her team for a final gut check. Noah's expression was finally serious, whereas Ava and Chloe were tense and scared; from Kesa's perspective, this worked for the dad and kids personas. "Dad's going to set the pace and choose the path. We are now in character until mission completion, or Sophia or I call it off. Address each other as mom, dad, daughter, sister, Ava, or Chloe." Kesa nodded at Noah, who walked away with a convincing limp and masterful use of his cane. *He's much too good at that; is he a natural or has he spent a lot of time with leader Robert?*

CHAPTER TWENTY-FOUR – 15:30 June 2, 2070 – Bait Team Walking

The tough part about being bait in a trap is avoiding death when the trap springs shut.
Kesa James, 2070

Bait team meandered through knee-high brush and grasses as they traveled eastward on the tornado track. The occasional still sizable rotting tree trunk prevented straight line travel. Although Noah's pace was fitting for his supposed condition as "dad with bad leg", Kesa found it frustrating. *I get twitchy when a scavenging team rolls along at an easy pace, and here we are moving only ¾ of that to support Noah's limp charade. I hope this doesn't go on for days. At least I look the part of the wife wanting a new home ASAP.*

Noah's sense of direction was perfect. They walked only ten minutes before he whispered, "Clearing just ahead."

Ava and Chloe glanced nervously at each other. Kesa understood their apprehension. Playing the bait team's daughters had been easy so far. The clearing where the murders happened would be their first actual test.

Another twenty steps and they came upon a gruesome scene. Three pale bodies sprawled in the clearing. Scavengers had been at them. Their limbs splayed haphazardly, clothing torn, and bits of flesh were missing here and there. Regardless, the bodies remained near the reddish-brown dried blood on the ground where the thieves had murdered them.

Noah's description didn't prepare me for this. What happened to this poor family? Kesa's first instinct was to be a perfect team lead and contain it, but she remembered her role. Embracing the horror, she shrieked in despair and collapsed to the ground.

Noah came over to comfort her, playing the part of wanting to appear as the stoic father who bottled this stuff up and trudged through it.

Ava had her hand over her mouth and wept, eyes wide.

Chloe glanced at Kesa, perhaps surprised at the magnitude of her reaction, but soon caught on. She cried out in despair before embracing her sister to comfort each other.

After a suitable amount of time to get over the shock of discovering the bodies, the bait team dug shallow graves and held brief ceremonies. Everything was heartfelt; the bait team genuinely felt sorry for this family. Anyone spying on them would not have any reason for suspicion.

"I don't want to camp for the night anywhere near here," Kesa uttered after their goodbyes. "Anyone feel different?"

The other bait team members shook their heads. Decision made, everyone shouldered their packs and continued eastward along the tornado track.

As they walked, Kesa discreetly scanned for friends and foes in the woods. Even knowing what the shadow team wore, she spotted no one. *Although it's unnerving that I can't see our protection, this is for the best. An unfriendly focusing on the bait team won't spot the shadow team if I cannot.*

Chloe blatantly scrutinized the forest on each side, behavior any watchers may find questionable.

Kesa walked beside Chloe to speak privately to her. "Daughter, you need to pay attention to where you are stepping to avoid twisting an ankle."

"Yes, mother." Chloe changed focus to their path down the tornado track rather than the surrounding forest.

Noah led them until 19:30, halting at a passable camping spot. "It's only an hour before dark, so best to set up camp here rather than continue." Bait team built a fire and prepared to camp. Noah played the dutiful father, showing his fake daughters how to start a fire and coax it to a balance of heat for comfort and for cooking.

Kesa hid a grin. *Young Noah or old Noah, still mentoring the woodcraft skills Cave Family needs to teach these young ones.*

Bait family prepared, ate, and cleaned up from their simple meal. They were careful to eat foods typical of people migrating; this meal was jerky with berries and greens foraged near the campsite. They kept a fire and conversation going to appear an easy target.

Kesa maintained her subtle surveillance of both sides of the forest, but couldn't spy friend or foe. If she didn't have complete trust in her Cave Family members, she might have worried that someone neutralized the shadow team.

About 21:30, when the sun was long below the horizon and the twilight was fading away, Noah limped to the fire and sat down beside her. He warmed his hands and mumbled, "Probably time to get some sleep. Should we set a watch?"

Kesa also kept it casual and quiet, just a husband and wife conversing about the day. "Although it's reasonable for people seeing what we did today to set a watch, we need to appear vulnerable. We should trust the shadow team to protect us."

"Agreed, both with your unease and your decision," Noah whispered. He stood up and faced Ava and Chloe across the fire. "Bedtime, daughters," he said at regular volume, "we have another long travel day tomorrow."

Bait team spread their bedrolls around the dying fire and slept, or at least feigned it.

Kesa found it hard to sleep. *It goes against my instincts to sleep while under threat without a watch set. Everyone else must feel the same. They're playing their part, though, making a convincing show of sleeping whether they are or not. I need to do the same.*

Kesa awoke the next morning in a panicked state. *When did I fall asleep? Did anything happen? Is my team OK?* She glanced around. The rest of the bait team slept. Noah was drooling admirably. The sun just rose, Kesa judged it 06:30. She exhaled in relief. *Everyone can continue to sleep. We aren't in a rush, and the shadow team night watchers could use the extra rack time.*

Minutes after 07:00, Noah opened his eyes and stared at her. He raised his eyebrows and dipped his chin slightly.

He was asking if they should get up or fake sleep a while to appear as targets for longer. *If the thieves wanted to attack, they would have in the dark.* Kesa stood up, simulating a typical waking up in the morning stretch. "Wake up family, we need to get further away from the desert."

Noah transitioned into character, starting a small fire to cook fry bread and heat dry cured ham for breakfast.

Ava and Chloe helped with breaking camp and breakfast.

Kesa brewed a pot of dandelion tea. Folks traveling through this area from the expanding desert to the west could harvest the ingredients for this tea along the way. *I miss my Cave Family recipe chai tea, but desperate travelers fleeing the desert wouldn't have the special ingredients.*

After the simple breakfast, the bait team packed up and continued their trek. Noah led the way, stopping frequently to tend to his fake ailing leg.

Kesa resumed her subtle surveillance of the surrounding forest for friends or foes, but didn't catch sight of either. *Being bait is stressful. We haven't seen shadow team since we split up. What if our enemies eliminated them, and now stalk us?*

Noah's pace gave Ava and Chloe plenty of time to range across the tornado track and the edges of the forest. They looked for mulberry trees, gooseberry bushes, and blackberry bushes. Everyone growing up in Cave Family had lots of experience working on foraging teams near the caves. Grandpy Max told her that as human pollution tilted the earth warmer, one of the few benefits was an expanded growing season. Wild fruits prospered in areas with the right combination of sun and rain.

A bit after noon, the bait team stopped for a cold lunch of leftover fry bread and the berries Ava and Chloe gathered during the morning's hike. Kesa and Noah sat facing each other to achieve the widest view of the forest bordering the tornado track's sides.

While conversing about the delicious berries Ava and Chloe found, Kesa inconspicuously scanned the tornado track's south face. Noah did the same with the north. As Kesa's gaze drifted across a dense patch of bush just inside the edge of the forest, the thick brush opened a hand's width. The motion was slow and parted the bush such that only someone at Kesa's angle could glimpse Sophia's face. Kesa kept talking about their lunch and made eye contact with Noah.

Noah let Ava and Chloe carry the family's conversation. "Mason gave me a thumbs-up and disappeared," he muttered.

Kesa slipped in a discrete reply to Noah. "Sophia gave me a quick glimpse, too. Shadow team is still in place." *Good to know, nobody murdered the shadow team to leave us undefended.*

After lunch, the hike and act continued. Despite the threat of death and the annoying pace, it was a welcome change from the daily bustle of scavenging, foraging, and hunting missions. Kesa enjoyed the hike through the vibrant wilderness that made this region special. Cave Family children learned how climate change brought extreme conditions to most of the world, making life difficult for people and animals. Cave, Lake, and Mountain Families settled in this region since the climate was the same or better than before The Reckoning. Flora and fauna prospered here, even in the face of weather extremes.

As the day waned, Noah dropped back to walk with her. "If I have to keep this fake limp up any longer," he whispered, "I'll do permanent damage and end up with a legit limp. Can I call the halt early?"

Kesa scrutinized the horizon. It was 07:00, late enough to halt without raising suspicion. She nodded to Noah.

He called out to the girls, who again ranged about gathering edibles as they hiked. "Girls, I can't drag my leg around any more today. We're making camp here."

Ava and Chloe both waved to show they heard and kept foraging. Apparently, they didn't mind a temporary return to their old duties for Cave Family.

Bait team set up camp again. Ava and Chloe took care of the fire to show off their woodcraft. Dinner was dandelion leaves, dandelion tea, leftover fry bread, generous portions of fresh wild berries, and a tiny dry cured ham ration.

Kesa was gaining a new appreciation for Cave Family's work to build and maintain a quality and varied food supply.

The evening was a repeat of the prior night's activities.

An hour after bedtime, Kesa was still feigning sleep while she tried to fall asleep. The sounds of heavy bodies pushing through brush and crunching fallen branches stood out from the usual nighttime noises. Faint at first, but increasing in volume. *Someone is approaching our fire. Two or three people trying to move quietly and quickly. Are Sophia and Owen coming to cancel the mission before we venture too far from the caves? No, we're not that far away and we are putting on a great show as bait. If not them, who? Oh shit, is the trap springing here and now? I'm not ready!*

CHAPTER TWENTY-FIVE – 22:00 June 3, 2070 – Taking the Bait

The fish sees the bait not the hook; a man sees not the danger — only the profit.
Mongolian Proverb

A deep, grating voice interrupted the forest's nighttime background noise. "Well, well, what do we have here?" he drawled. "Looks like mommy, daddy, and two girls taking a night of rest from their travels."

Kesa opened her eyes. Two unkempt men stood at the edge of the bait team's dying firelight. The speaker looked thirty and had a nasty scar starting above his left eye and going almost straight down to his chin, barely missing his mouth. Whatever cut him didn't damage the eye socket. He wore a ball cap and clothing in passable shape, other than being long overdue for a washing. His M4A1 carbine, in contrast to his clothing, hair, and beard, was in immaculate condition. *He holds that carbine like he knows how to use it. From the cold in his eyes, he wouldn't hesitate to use it.* "Scar" didn't point the carbine directly at them, but he was a fraction of a second away from a standing or kneeling shooting position. The carbine's stock nestled ready in his shoulder.

Bait team stayed in character, Ava even letting out an authentic terrified squeal. Chloe clung to her in apparent fright, although her eyes coolly assessed the situation. Kesa wasn't concerned about their unwelcome visitors perceiving this. *Only those knowing how special Chloe is will see that she's assessing the situation rather than panicking.*

Noah played into the dad's role. "We're just passing through to get ahead of the desert growing west of here. We don't want any trouble."

"Oh, I'm afraid trouble has found you, dad," Scar said. "Matter-of-fact, trouble is Junior's middle name. Ain't that right, Junior?"

Kesa judged Junior was much younger, about twenty. In contrast to Scar, he had washed and trimmed his hair and beard at least once in the last month. Junior shifted around and looked back and forth at the bait team's members. He held a well-cared for pistol at low ready in a steady hand. Scar and Junior each wore a long-bladed hunting knife in a sheath strapped to their upper right leg. Junior's voice echoed his appearance and manner, higher pitched and edgy. "Yeah, trouble's my middle name. Anyone makes trouble, I'm putting a bullet in their head!"

Ava squeaked again and clung to Chloe.

Scar drawled in his eerily calm manner. "Now, now, Junior, there's no need for talk like that when folks are cooperating. Mom, how about you hand those packs to Junior while dad and the girls sit real still."

Kesa handed their packs over one by one, moving slowly to avoid setting Junior off. *Where is the shadow team? This is already playing out way longer than comfortable.*

Junior took the packs from her and started rifling through them.

Scar stood casually by. He was not careless, though. His eyes scanned the bait team.

Kesa was concerned. *He is much too calm for this to be new. These men have done this often.*

It wasn't long before Junior was staring at a rock placeholder he pulled from a bait team pack. Just as he opened his mouth to speak, a shot rang out in the night somewhere nearby.

Bait team and Junior jumped.

Scar calmly scanned everyone to determine the victim. He fished a radio out of his pocket as his eyes narrowed and head tilted. "Goldilocks, who you shooting at?"

After radio silence for a few seconds, Junior spoke up. "All due respect, Boss, that didn't sound like Goldilocks' 300 Win Mag. I think it was a suppressed 7.62 round. And look here, this pack is half wood and rocks."

Kesa's wariness of Junior increased; his precise ear for gunfire must have come from abundant firearms experience.

Scar tilted his weapon up one-handed to point at Noah's chest. Without taking his eyes off the bait team, he growled in a drawl. "Thank you kindly, Junior. My hearing isn't the same since that firefight a few months ago. Nobody move. We get this sorted real quick or we start shooting." He keyed his radio. "Goldilocks, Snake, report."

Someone approached from the east, pushing through the brush.

Sophia called out from twenty meters in that direction. "Snake's here, with a pistol to his head. Unless you want your head to turn to pink mist, like Goldilocks' just did, you'll put your weapons and radio down real slow and back up three steps."

Scar pursed his lips, considering the situation. He keyed his radio. "Goldilocks, unless you have something to say to our new friends, I'll be surrendering my weapons." He stared pointedly at Junior, but Owen materialized behind him and jammed his pistol muzzle into Junior's neck.

Scar laughed heartily as he made a show of piling his carbine, knife, radio, and a pistol in front of him and stepping back with his hands spread wide. "No need for any more killing, friends. We surrender." He nodded at Junior, who mimicked Scar's surrender. "Junior, we just got outfoxed. I suspect these folks are not the helpless family they appeared to be." He turned to Noah and Kesa. "How about you tell us what's really going on?"

Bait team dropped the act, Noah picking up Scar's weapons and Kesa picking up Junior's. Ava and Chloe took the zip cuffs offered by Owen and secured Scar's and Junior's hands behind their back. Kesa covered Junior with his own pistol, while Noah did the same for Scar.

"We're going to be asking the questions. First, what's your name?" Kesa said.

Scar stared at Noah. "Why do you let your women folk do the talking? Don't they know their place?" Scar didn't seem rattled, unlike Junior, who shifted around with wild eyes.

Sophia emerged from the darkness behind Scar, shoving Snake to where the rest of Cave Family could cover him. She pushed the muzzle of her pistol against the back of Scar's head. "This woman folk ready to put a bullet in your skull is in charge. You should know I lack patience. Now, answer her."

"Well, my friends call me Boss," Scar said calmly. "I haven't gone by another name for a long time. And you are?"

Kesa didn't want these people learning about the teams or the rest of Cave Family. "Boss doesn't work for us. We'll call you Scar. Your thieving and murdering in this region is over. Cooperate, and maybe Goldilocks will be the only one dying tonight."

Owen held up another set of zip cuffs for Ava to secure Snake.

Kesa nodded to Sophia to acknowledge she should resume as lead.

"We resent these unfounded accusations and protest being detained under threat of violence." Scar scanned everyone present from Cave Family. "I see none of you are carrying a 7.62 rifle with a suppressor. Will your sniper be joining us?"

Sophia ignored the inquiry, moving her pistol to Scar's forehead. "We're asking the questions, not you. Is this your whole crew other than Goldilocks?"

"No need to get worked up," Scar said. "All my friends are here. We have a man at our camp, but he's what you might call an indentured servant."

Sophia sneered. "You mean slave. Lead us to your camp. If any of you makes my team nervous, you all die."

"Of course, of course. Straight there, no funny stuff," Scar said. "We'll need some light. Our camp is in the forest over there." He motioned southwest.

Kesa noted Scar's behavior change. *Scar figured out it's not wise to push Sophia any further. Just smart or dangerous smart?*

"Ditch the extra weight and gear up, everyone." Sophia said. "We're heading to their camp."

Ava and Chloe tossed the rocks and wood from the bait team's packs and returned them to their rightful owners.

Snake, adorned with a rudimentary stick-and-poke snake tattoo on his forearm, wore a day pack with a handful of pine resin torches strapped to it. Sophia motioned to Ava and Chloe to take his pack and the torches; their light would suffice until moonrise. Chloe took a torch, lit it from their fire, and headed out on point. Sophia nudged Scar forward behind Chloe, followed by Junior covered by Owen.

Noah, holding Scar's carbine like it had been his for years, signaled Kesa he would take rear guard.

Kesa checked the chamber on Junior's Glock to verify it was ready to shoot. She popped the magazine out and in, taking a glance at the witness holes. As she suspected from first glance, Junior kept the Glock in perfect condition. *Important to know how many rounds you have. Should I feel grateful or scared that Junior had it fully loaded and ready to fire?* She put the pistol against Snake's spine on his lower back and nudged him to follow Owen. Ava lit another torch and followed her. Noah took up the rear after smothering their fire with dirt.

Kesa assumed Sophia arranged with Mason and Carter to follow from afar as support. She didn't ask to confirm, no need for Scar and his gang to learn any more about their teams.

The group walked southwest a half hour with minor course corrections from Scar. He remained calm. "Our camp is ahead. You can see our man has a cook fire going."

Although there was a small fire flickering ahead, it was too dim to discern anything else. Sophia motioned for Noah to check the perimeter. Off he stalked into the night. None of the captives tried to raise an alarm, escape, or break their bonds.

Kesa was uneasy. *I don't have any experience in subduing thieves and murderers, but I didn't expect them to be this docile, even with weapons pointed at them. Are they up to something?*

"All clear," Noah called out ten minutes later.

Kesa entered the tiny clearing where Scar and companions made camp. A man in steel handcuffs attached to five meters of chain spoke to Noah. "Are these your friends? Oh, thank goodness, these men imprisoned me for the last month. Please, let me out of these cuffs." He held his cuffed hands out toward the Cave Family group. His wrists were raw and bleeding. There was a small cook fire with a pot hanging above it and an array of food and cooking supplies spread on a tarp nearby, all within reach of the man's chain. His captors had padlocked the other end of the chain around a tree.

Sophia scrutinized the man and then looked to Kesa and Noah.

To Kesa, he was as unkempt as Scar, with poorer clothing and no visible weapons. As best she could discern, he was the prisoner he claimed to be. She gave Sophia a "seems to be as appears" shrug.

Noah echoed the motion.

Sophia's eyes narrowed. "Who are you, and how did you end up here?"

Kesa estimated he was in his early twenties and a hundred and eighty centimeters tall. He was slim, so maybe seventy-two kilograms. All in all, a bit shorter and a lot lighter than Noah.

The prisoner gulped. He let his cuffed hands hang loose, realizing no one was freeing him this minute. He scanned everyone, avoiding eye contact with his ex-captors. "Folks called me Walker John," he stammered, "because I walked between communities relaying messages, carrying packages, and doing odd jobs. My real name is John Walker. Two months ago, I headed east to flee the expanding desert. These men kicked me awake one night a month ago, took my things, and kept me around to do their menial work. I cooked, dug latrines, made camp, and broke camp. As you can see, they're not fans of having laundry done."

Scar interrupted Walker John with a laugh and raised his hands palms up. "Where's the gratitude, Walker John? We shelter you, we feed you, and you insult our hygiene?"

Sophia gave him a dark look.

Scar smiled defiantly, but shut up.

"Please free me," Walker John said. "The handcuff and padlock keys are with the one they call Boss or in the tent. I'll take what was mine and be gone, unless you folks can use a hard worker?"

Scar piped in, "This one is lazy. You don't want him. Cut him loose, but I'm sure he'll come crawling back to us after starving for a week."

Sophia spoke to Ava, Noah, and Chloe after mulling it over for a few seconds. "Search the tent and everything else in the camp. We're taking all weapons and tech. Put the best clothing and bedding you find in the best backpack for Walker John. Divide the rest into the remaining packs for them." She motioned at the zip-cuffed prisoners.

The three headed off.

Ava soon returned from the tent with a handcuff key, a padlock key, and a two-way radio. "These were sitting on a bedroll."

Sophia verified the radio was off and pocketed it. She removed Walker John's cuffs, hefting them and the chain as though considering whether to toss them. Instead, she put them in her pack.

Kesa would have done the same; these days you didn't throw anything away. Someone at Cave Family would use the materials.

Chloe handed Walker John a full pack.

Walker John's eyes widened when he hefted the pack. He fumbled for words. "Thank you. Thank you all. I'll continue my journey now." He turned toward the tornado track.

Sophia grabbed him by the shoulder. "Hold on. I recommend you stick with us for a while. We're releasing these men, and I don't want you running into them again."

Ava emerged from the tent again with a handful of ammo, a pistol, and some pre-Reckoning trinkets that she, Chloe, or Noah liked. "Nothing else useful other than this stuff and the food."

Sophia packed Ava's findings, then gestured at the other backpacks. "Let's not give them reason to linger. Five days' rations for them to share should motivate them to keep moving and foraging. We're taking any food over and above that. Your discretion on who gets what."

Soon enough, Chloe, Ava, and Noah finished filling the backpacks.

While Cave Family covered the prisoners, Sophia showed them two hunting knives, shoving them deep into two of the packs. "We're not leaving you defenseless, but you're getting a bullet in the head if you make a move toward these knives while we're still in sight. Head east for at least a week and do it fast, because we'll be watching." She gestured at them to hold their wrists up, popping the zip cuff locking tabs and pocketing the cuffs for reuse.

Scar rubbed his wrists and picked up the pack sitting in front of him. "Thank you all. This is kind of you."

Kesa found it hard to interpret his tone. *Is he thankful we aren't killing them, or is he being sarcastic? No matter, we put a good scare into them; we shouldn't be seeing these three any more.*

Sophia brought her rifle to low ready. "Oh, and we're shooting on sight if we see you again."

Scar nodded at the other two. They picked up their packs and followed him into the forest. The moon was rising now, providing enough light for them to find the tornado track and cover some distance tonight.

Cave Family and Walker John stood in silence as the three headed toward the tornado track. None of them looked back at Cave Family.

Sophia waited until they were far out of earshot. "Owen, take first shift on watch. Everyone else, take a break around the fire and sample Walker John's cooking. We're expecting company in an hour."

Walker John looked puzzled. "There's more of you?"

"Yeah, our sniper and his backup," Sophia said. "If you're wondering what happened to the one they called Goldilocks, our sniper was better."

Walker John's face fell. After a moment, his face returned to neutral. "Oh, I see." He paused before continuing. "I guess they all deserve death for what they were doing to desperate travelers."

Close to the hour promised by Sophia, someone approached the campsite from the forest. They weren't bothering to conceal their coming. "Who goes there?" Kesa said.

Owen answered from the dark forest. "Mason and I, Carter's taking watch."

Mason smiled as he joined the group, squeezing Kesa's shoulder and clapping Noah on the back. "Good to see you in person instead of through my scope. Those three following the tornado track east showed no signs of trying to slip into the woods and circle back, at least until I lost sight."

"Is that the sniper rifle you used to . . . ," Walker John asked Mason. He stared at the M110E1 as Mason leaned it against a tree.

Mason didn't mince his words. "She was lining up for a shot. I protected my people."

Walker John's eyes widened. He stood in silence for a few seconds. "Yes, yes, of course," he finally stammered. "No choice. They were truly evil."

Sophia pointed to the pot over the cook fire. "Mason, grab some food and we'll have a chat over here." She motioned Owen, Kesa, and Noah to move out of earshot of those at the fire, tipping her head toward Walker John to signal Ava and Chloe to watch him.

By the time Mason walked from the cook fire to Sophia and the others, he ate halfway through a bowl of stew and continued to scoop

Kesa gaped at him.

Mason talked while shoveling food into his mouth. "What? This is my first hot food in days. I spent all my time being your guardian angel, not cooking."

Kesa laughed and punched him in the arm. "Yeah, my hundred and eighty-eight centimeter tall wingless angel armed with a sniper rifle. Remember to chew your food so I don't have to be your guardian angel and save you from choking to death."

Sophia gazed at them with crossed arms, tapping a finger against one elbow while she waited for them to finish. "What do you think about Walker John?" she asked once everyone was paying attention.

"Seems odd," Mason, still eating, mumbled around his food. "But I only met him two minutes ago."

"If we believe his story," Noah said, "he has been Scar and gang's prisoner servant for a month. Anyone experiencing that will probably act odd for their first few hours of freedom. Are we talking about sending him out on his own versus taking him back to Cave Family?"

"Correct," Sophia replied. "The leaders usually go with what the team in the field decides."

"He was weird regarding Goldilocks being offed," Owen said. "Also, if Scar and gang are such royal assholes, why are his only visible wounds fresh marks from trying to escape the cuffs? Like Noah said, though, who wouldn't have issues after being enslaved for a month?"

Everyone looked at Kesa.

Kesa agonized over the decision. *My turn to share an opinion. I want to send Walker John away to avoid risk to Cave Family, but that could be a death sentence. Alone in the wilderness, murder hornets or fire ants will probably kill him. If they don't get him, he'll end up Scar's prisoner again.* "His story seems true, and the way Scar spoke to him supports it. I fear he will come to a dreadful end if we send him out alone. My vote is to take him to Cave Family."

The others nodded in agreement, albeit not enthusiastically.

Sophia brought the conversation to a close. "Well, if no one wants to recommend something different?" After waiting for anyone to speak up, she continued. "OK, we're all in agreement to take Walker John to Cave Family, subject to him wanting to come and the leaders taking our recommendation to let him in. Kesa, can you brief him and get his choice?"

Kesa headed back to the cook fire. She kneeled beside Walker John where he sat cross-legged, stirring the stew. "We didn't want to advise within your captors' hearing, but we are from a nearby community. There's almost a hundred fifty of us, all good people. You can come with us to see if the community will accept you or you can continue your journey from here. The choice is yours."

Walker John stirred the stew for a few seconds. He made eye contact. "Please take me to the community."

"Unless anyone wants to stay in Scar's old camp tonight," Sophia said, "I suggest we head back while we have moonlight enough to monitor our surroundings."

Mason hurried to scrape the remaining stew into his bowl.

Walker John grinned, rinsed the pot with water, and hung it from his pack. Off to the south they headed, Noah once again drowning the fire in dirt and taking up rear guard.

Kesa shook her head. *How can Mason pack so much food away? To top it off, now he is eating while we hike? I guess that should be the least of my concerns. Has our team made the right decision to bring Walker John back to Cave Family? With this many senior scavengers participating in the field decision, the leaders will not overrule us. If he doesn't fit in, or worse, whatever happens is my fault for tipping the vote.*

UTOPIA - MASON

CHAPTER TWENTY-SIX – 18:30 June 2, 2070 – Home Sweet Home

We are overdue for citizens to have direct say on all important matters. The Alliance's birth is also the birth of direct democracy.
Angelou Smith, first president of the Alliance; convocation speech January 15, 2031

"Hi Mason, can I help with one of your bags?" Isabella said, skipping up to Mason as he entered the Blue Spruce Manor lobby. Her family and Mason were a few of the hundred-fifty residents of "Blue Spruce" as the residents referred to it. For decades now, the Alliance encouraged apartment complexes in a Dunbar model of a hundred-fifty people. The complexes managed communal ownership of infrequently needed assets, like power tools. This maximized the effectiveness of people's income and minimized the environmental impact of supply chains.

Mason, making his duffel bags seem insubstantial by the ease he held them with, put down the lighter one. "It's kind of you to offer, Isabella. Can you take that one?" He kept his go bag in hand. Nobody except his Phoenix Fireteam teammates were allowed to touch it, and only when needed rather than convenient. You were responsible for being ever ready; a compromised go bag was the downfall of more than one special teams' soldier.

She grabbed the handles of the twenty kilogram duffel and grunted as she tried to lift it. No surprise that a ten-year-old couldn't lift over half their weight. "I need a friend to help with this. Wait here a minute," Isabella said, never one to surrender easily.

Mason smothered a laugh. "What I need is to catch up on Blue Spruce news. Can you help with that?"

Isabella nodded and pointed at the bag. "OK, you carry and I talk."

Mason picked the duffel up, groaning to appear he needed to make an effort. Together, they headed toward Mason's apartment at the end of the middle wing. Artwork and photos from residents adorned the common area walls. Blue Spruce was effectively a single extended family.

Isabella skipped along beside him, keeping pace with his much longer stride. She chatted at the same time. "Well, I hope you remember what happens the day after tomorrow, since it's the most important event in the world this year."

Mason feigned concern. "Oh no, is it the tax filing deadline?"

"No, silly. You should have filed three months ago, otherwise you will incur penalties and interest." Isabella wagged her finger at him.

Mason chuckled to himself. *Isabella loves that phrase. Her accountant mother must say it often.*

"Fine, I'll tell you. It's the Titan vote. You know, the entire planet cooperating to build a base on Titan?" Isabella glared at him, trying to discern if he was truly clueless or just teasing her again.

"Oh, thanks for the reminder," Mason said. "I knew it was approaching, but I was busy at work and the date snuck up." *Funny how you understand something is coming for a long time, and boom, it surprises you anyway.*

"Have you been studying?" Isabella said. "It would be a shame for your vote to be disqualified. Remember, your five questions are selected out of a hundred. To answer at least four right, you have to know your stuff."

"OK, full disclosure," Mason said. "I didn't study yet. I want my vote to count, so I am going to cram."

Isabella's eyes narrowed. "What's cramming?"

Mason hesitated. *Oh, damn, another episode of "irresponsible Uncle Mason" teaching the Blue Spruce kids bad habits. I am going to catch a lecture from her mother on this one. Well, I opened the door, so best to answer honestly.* "It's when you study hard for a test just before taking it rather than spreading the work out earlier."

"It sounds more like trying to remedy a failure to prepare," Isabella said, scrutinizing his reaction.

Mason smiled. *She got me again. This is her daring me to lie my way out of painting myself into a corner.* "That's right. To be positive, we could say 'better late than never'?"

"Hmm, I guess so. Luckily, you can learn a lot at the Blue Spruce Titan debate tomorrow evening. You will come, right?" Isabella asked. "Ethan is speaking for the kids."

"I will be there unless there's a work emergency," Mason said.

"Is that where you were, an emergency? Tell me what you were doing." Isabella's innate energy was only surpassed by her curiosity.

"You know the deal," Mason said. "I can't disclose more than what's on the news, but if you see me on the news, I am looking for a new job." Adults in the apartment complex understood portions of Phoenix Fireteam's duties, but there was a tacit agreement the kids should be told harmless generalities.

"But there's so much news. Yesterday you could have fought a forest fire on the west coast, rescued a cat on Elm Street, or busted a drug lab in the warehouse district." Everyone at Blue Spruce knew Isabella's loathing for unsolvable puzzles.

"I may have done any or none of that," Mason said. "Tell you what, I promise to spill everything when you are old enough to vote." *Valiant effort Mason, the likelihood of Isabella accepting that is near zero.*

"Seriously? It will be six years before I turn sixteen," Isabella said.

This was a recurring conversation. "Hey, don't rush growing up. You have endless kid stuff to do before you need to act like an adult," Mason said as he stared into the retina scanner by his door. It clicked open, his "welcome home evening" lighting scheme activated. "Thanks for the update. I needed it." He hauled the duffels into his apartment.

"No problem. See you tomorrow." Isabella said.

Mason wasn't worried about Isabella's disappointment. *She gets over minor challenges quicker than you can blink.*

Mason stashed his go bag in the bottom of the closet closest to the apartment's main door. It was the sole item there to make sure he couldn't grab the wrong bag or get tangled up if he desired to move fast. The go bag contained body armor, an M29 pistol and ammo in a biometric-secured Pelican dry box, a black head to toe change of clothes, zip ties, a field trauma kit, a first aid kit, gas mask, and a KA-BAR combat knife. Mason considered these tools of the trade. On top was his special favorite, the Surefire UDR Dominator XX-milspec flashlight. It put out sixty-five hundred lumens to fifteen hundred meters, with a nasty strike bezel to top it off. Mason had non-lethally subdued more than one unsavory character with a solid headshot from it.

Mason watched the news while he unpacked his travel bag. The terrorist attack, the terrorist cell's violent death, and destruction of the cell's base of operations were, of course, top news in the Alliance. *Media attention will die off after a few news cycles. Thank goodness the media respect Alliance law protecting law*

154

enforcement operators' identities. The Birthers would love to strike Phoenix Fireteam at our home. We can take care of ourselves, but no one wants to endanger our Blue Spruce family.

The next story caught Mason's interest. The police arrested a young man for creating a deepfake video of an Alliance Representative speaking out against the Titan mission. Internet safeguards identified it as a deepfake and quarantined it. The traffic backtrack algorithms built into the Internet immediately identified who executed the upload and from where. Alliance citizens voted to ban anonymous Internet activity decades ago. They had enough of the hatred, lies, and scammers hiding behind Internet anonymity. All access since was driven by bio-identifiable logins. The old folks at Blue Spruce told Mason that online hatred, partisanship, and identity politics split nations into warring camps fifty years prior. It was common knowledge that many who fanned the flames did so anonymously or used false identities.

The deepfaker is to register his plea the day after his arrest. After the Alliance plea process reform voted in by direct democracy in 2032, offenders stand within a week of arrest to testify to the facts and speak the truth under oath about their involvement, or non-involvement, in the crime. They must plead guilty or not guilty, since saying nothing in order to not incriminate oneself or one's family is no longer permitted. The truth is of utmost importance. Perjury results in mandatory incarceration no matter the magnitude of the lie. An attempt to mislead millions of viewers with a deepfake video was a serious crime. It should make for a stimulating plea and later sentencing.

Travel bag unpacked, Mason made himself a pea protein burger in his small kitchenette. Blue Spruce's commercial quality kitchen for group meals and for those with food preparation-related businesses was more than he needed for a quick meal. To decompress, he caught up on his favorite dramas while he ate rather than studying up for the Titan vote. He would focus on that tomorrow.

Mason drifted off in front of the television by 20:00. The terror attack and mission to bring the terrorists to justice made for a brutal two days. Mason couldn't fight his mind and body's need for sleep.

CHAPTER TWENTY-SEVEN – 16:00 June 3, 2070 – Truth in Justice and Constructive Conflict

We have perverted justice to value due process over the truth. Without truth, there can be no real justice. We must correct the balance.
Angelou Smith, first president of the Alliance; convocation speech January 15, 2031

Mason peeled off his soaked workout clothes and put on jeans and a t-shirt. He started off the day in the Blue Spruce gym, weight training and sparring with River, Willow, and Noah. After a late breakfast, he and Noah studied the Titan data and then ran with Kona on the Blue Spruce forest trails.

The Blue Spruce children spilled onto the grounds for a water gun fight, interrupting the run. Mason felt obliged to teach the young kids fireteam urban warfare tactics to give them a fighting chance against the older kids. Noah provided his typical help and hindrance mix with two scoops of humor. Kona fed the chaos by exposing everyone's hiding places. The whole thing degenerated into all the kids trying to soak Mason, Noah, and Kona. The afternoon ended with Mason sprinting pell-mell through the Blue Spruce forest to escape, Noah and Kona hard on his heels. Kona and the kids had a blast. Mason got a solid reminder of what he defended when executing missions.

Time to service my addiction to live justice and see what happens to deepfake video guy that was on the news yesterday. Mason called up the channel broadcasting his plea. Two people who spread lies on the Internet preceded the deepfaker. Free speech was an Alliance fundamental right, but there was zero tolerance when speech crossed over into lies and hate.

A Free Parenthood social media worker who generated falsified analytics of world population and resource consumption was first on the stand. She tried to refute studies proving humanity's unsustainable consumption to gather support to remove population limits. Mason binge-watched crime shows from the first twenty years of the century. Everyone on the shows pled not guilty, no matter how blatantly guilty they were. Mason harbored a macabre fascination with hearing the charges read and seeing the cameras zoom in on the accused's face. He kept expecting the accused to blurt "not guilty" like in the old shows, but it never happened due to the body of evidence. Alliance courts always considered all truthful evidence, irrespective of the collection method. An investigator breaking regulations resulted in a separate disciplinary hearing but never resulted in truthful evidence being excluded from an accused's trial.

In the end, the three accused pled guilty. The old folks at Blue Spruce told Mason that most people pled not guilty before the Alliance, regardless of the truth. They then waited months for their trial, either sitting in jail or running free in society on bail and finally enduring a months-long trial. Mason didn't believe them until he dug around in court archives on the Internet and verified their claims. Mason couldn't understand how justice could move so slowly and that everyone expected guilty people to plead innocence.

At 18:30, he entered the Blue Spruce auditorium via the main atrium. The auditorium seated two hundred in tiers to ensure a satisfactory view from every seat. There was a stage with a retractable large projection screen for movies or broadcasts. The acoustics were superb, suitable for live music if the residents wanted to perform or host. About a hundred Blue Spruce residents were already in the room. Mason exchanged greetings with folks as he headed to where Kesa, Noah, Willow, and River were waving. The Blue Spruce residents aware of his profession gave him an extra caring greeting; they assumed any team absence from Blue Spruce was for a dangerous mission. *Home is extra special when you have a hundred-fifty siblings, aunts, uncles, nephews, and nieces.*

"Mason, barely on time as usual." Willow tapped her watch.

For security and sanity, Phoenix Fireteam used their real names when off mission. "Just trying to squeeze everything I can out of life," Mason said.

"Dude, you were agonizing over those plea bargains on live court TV," Noah said. "I know your addiction."

Mason made his best mock shame face. "Busted. They all pled guilty, as usual. Someday, someone will plead 'not guilty' and you will miss it."

"Sure, but it will repeat on the news for days afterward," River said. "Alliance prosecutors rarely make an incorrect charge with the data available these days. When there's even a slim chance they got something wrong, everyone gets real interested." As usual, he was playing with his phone but somehow keeping pace with their conversation.

"Hi Mason and Noah. You're a lot dryer than last time we saw you." Isabella giggled, joined by a laughing Ethan.

Mason dove behind his chair and put his hands up. "Don't shoot, don't shoot!"

Noah mirrored him.

"You guys are silly. We don't have our water guns here. Ethan is on the speaker list for tonight, right Ethan?" Isabella nudged him forward.

Ethan lowered his gaze. "I'm so nervous. I don't think I can do this," he said, barely audible.

Mason gave Ethan's shoulder an encouraging shake. "You know what? I get nervous about speaking to crowds. Lots of folks do."

"So, how do you do it?" Ethan asked, peering up at Mason.

"First, I make sure I am well prepared," Mason replied. "You're one of the smartest people I know, so you surely understand your material. At the event, I ask my friends to scatter in the audience. Part of making an impactful speech is to make eye contact with the audience. With my friends spread around, I can engage the entire audience and there is always a friendly face to look at if I get nervous. How about I sit here, Isabella and her parents sit on the other side, and you ask your parents to sit in the middle?"

"That's a great idea. Isabella, can you get seats on the other side? I'll get my parents to sit in the middle." Ethan headed off, holding his head high.

Isabella waved goodbye and shepherded her parents to the other side of the auditorium.

Sophia entered the auditorium and scanned the audience.

Mason waved her over. "Well hello, Dr. Davis, how kind of you to grace us with your giant brain's presence this evening," Mason smiled and gestured to the open seat beside him.

"Why thank you, Private Lee." Sophia glanced down the row to see who else was there. "Hmm, the entire gang of trouble is here, or better to say there's not enough trouble out there to prevent you from being here."

Kesa, at the end of the row, leaned forward. "Easy now, Doc, I need my team to have their heads on straight, so don't twist their feeble brains."

"Roger that," Sophia said with a wink, settling in beside Mason.

"Better to say 'wilco' if you intend on complying with the commander's request," Mason stage whispered to Sophia. "'Roger' just means you heard, but doesn't indicate planned compliance."

"Roger that, too," Sophia said, laughing. "See, you teach me new things. And how about you River, is your ego still bruised from our last sparring match?"

"My bruised gluteus maximus and ego are healing," River said. "Both should be ready for another MMA sparring match soon enough. You realize, of course, that I am getting stronger and faster while you are merely aging?"

"Since I'm only twenty-six, I suspect age isn't the problem," Sophia said. "I'm blaming too much time in the lab rather than the gym."

That got Mason's interest. *Sophia used to be in the gym as much as Phoenix; what's changed recently?* "You have sequestered with your grad students and undergraduate minions a lot this last month. Is it super-secret, or can you tell us what you are doing?"

Sophia perked up, like she wanted to be asked about her work. "Well, in contrast to you masters of mystery and subterfuge, I can share. We are working on the most ironic project of my life. My team is building a specific purpose AI to monitor compute traffic on quantum computers to ensure no one tries building general artificial intelligence. Quantum computers are proliferating and can run too many simultaneous jobs for us to trust fallible humans to stop other people from trying to achieve the singularity."

Willow laughed and then tilted her hand. "So, you're building an AI smart enough to stop people from building the super smart AI we don't want running free and wild. Yeah, that's ironic."

The buzz of conversations throughout the auditorium died off as Max Williams stepped onto the stage. An energetic and athletic Blue Spruce resident, he didn't look anywhere near his sixty-five years of age. The citizens elected Max as the representative for the Rockies East Foothills Alliance region that included the City of Franklin. Known only to Phoenix Fireteam and other JSA operatives in the Alliance, Max also chaired the JSA approval and oversight board.

"Welcome, everyone, welcome." Max's voice boomed through the auditorium. Mason marveled at how Max could project without shouting.

Almost everyone took the hint, aborting their conversations and sitting. A sole white-haired older man remained standing. "Who does this guy think he is?" he shouted.

"Thank you for the reminder to introduce myself, Robert. I assume you didn't vote for me in the last election," Max said, not missing a beat. The crowd laughed. Although best friends for decades, Robert and Max never let each other off easy at public gatherings.

"I am Max Williams, usually your Rockies East Foothills Alliance Representative. Tonight I serve as master of ceremonies to ensure miscreants akin to Mr. Robert Acosta over there don't interfere with the proceedings." Max gestured toward Robert and paused for the laughter that followed.

Robert gave him a good-natured wave of dismissal before sitting.

"Tonight we perform an Alliance sacred tradition," Max said. "An opportunity for all to be heard before we participate in direct democracy tomorrow by voting on the Titan mission."

"First up, the proponents selected Mia Brown to speak for those of voting age." Max led the applause greeting Mia as he stepped out of sight offstage.

Mia was a forty-year-old award-winning junior high sciences teacher. She queued up a slideshow of stunning space photos to serve as the backdrop on the screen behind her. The lights dimmed and the slideshow began as she spoke.

> Good evening. I invite you to envision a future where Homo sapiens ventures out of our home solar system. A future where we travel into the Milky Way to seek other life forms and more Earth-like planets. Since NASA's unmanned Dragonfly ceased to function in 2045, the Alliance has not made any significant strides in space. For twenty-five years, this was prudent. We had a multitude of issues to resolve on Earth, and we have made admirable progress. The Alliance has brought humanity to a sustainable path with a balanced environmental and fiscal budget. Now we can raise our gaze and minds to the sky, to space, to the Milky Way.
>
> To quest into the Milky Way, we need fuel and a place to build and launch vessels. Titan is that base of operations. It has hundreds of times more liquid hydrocarbons than all the

known oil and natural gas reserves on Earth, much of it in surface lakes ready to use as-is where-is. Saturn's other eighty-one moons offer all the materials we can't harvest from Titan.

Yes, the price is high and generations will contribute to the building of the base and vessels with a slightly reduced standard of living. Each of them will appreciate contributing to something bigger than themselves, bigger than their entire generation. I will pay and will take comfort in contributing to Homo sapiens' Milky Way exploration.

AsiaPac and the New Soviet Union have agreed to share in the venture and the costs, contingent on the citizens of the Alliance voting to proceed. Tonight, I ask you to dream of the stars. Tomorrow, I ask you to vote yes for the Titan mission.

The audience applauded Mia's speech, Titan proponents applauding enthusiastically.

As Max came on stage, the lights brightened. "Excellent presentation, Mia, thank you," Max shook her hand before she exited. "Let's hear from the opponents next. Please welcome Ethan to speak on behalf of those below sixteen. Their votes don't count yet, but they will be an integral part of working on and paying for this multi-decade initiative."

Ethan walked on stage. His gaze was downcast and sweat glistened on his forehead. Max turned off his microphone and gave Ethan a few private words of encouragement that perked him up. Ethan delivered his speech, nervously at first, but getting into the flow as he proceeded.

Whenever Ethan looked in his direction, Mason gave him a smile and nod, his expression communicating "you are doing great".

Thank you for this opportunity to speak. I represent two-thirds of the Blue Spruce kids. I learned in history class of how it is vital for people in civil societies to hear what each other thinks about issues. If anyone here feels the same as me, Mia's speech made you excited about what the Titan mission can mean to Homo sapiens.

I am excited, but I am also concerned about who is paying the massive bill. Depending on your age, you may pay for this mission for only a few years, or perhaps a few decades. When you are voting, consider the kids paying for this decision as long as we live. Oh, and don't forget my kids, because they will also pay for their entire lives.

Three trillion dollars. That's what your yes vote commits the Alliance to out of the five trillion dollar price tag for the entire mission. Since the Alliance commits to environmentally and fiscally balanced budgets, and the negotiations to table this vote resulted in no cuts to existing government spending, the money has to come from tax increases.

In school, we learn the history of AsiaPac and the New Soviet Union. We learn agreements between nations aren't sure things. If either backs out, is the Alliance going to cancel the mission or will Alliance taxpayers also cover their share? Take this risk into account when you vote.

People excited about the mission tell us kids to imagine the exciting jobs and astronaut opportunities coming with it. It is true, the mission will create intriguing jobs for thousands of scientists, fabricators, and ground support people. But we shouldn't vote as though we are all going to have the opportunity to become astronauts. Only a thousand humans are going to Titan with thousands more robots. Of the billions of taxpayers worldwide paying for the mission, a relative few will work on it.

I believe we should follow through with this mission, but not now. The Alliance tamed the deficits of the predecessor nations but is yet to pay them off. There is plenty of opportunity for discoveries in space propulsion systems to enable the mission to be achieved faster and cheaper. We should wait for the Alliance to improve finances and for cost-reducing technology.

You are well aware of the Alliance Charter of Responsibilities and Rights. Think about this clause as part of your decision since this vote affects the prosperity of generations of Alliance citizens: 'We are responsible for our own actions, health, safety, and prosperity and for the health, safety, and prosperity of our fellow citizens.'

In closing, most Blue Spruce twelve-to-fifteen-year-olds will vote 'no' tomorrow. We want the mission reconsidered in ten years. Please consider this when you are voting.

The audience clapped heartily, the occasional person shouting out in support. Ethan started to depart but Max headed him off to stand center stage for the applause. The children Ethan represented were especially exuberant.

The quality visuals the kids put together to cycle on screen while Ethan was speaking fascinated Mason. *They did a great job. They communicated the mission cost, how many years for taxpayers to cover the cost, and the expected disposable income reduction. The new tax freedom day of July fifteenth slide brings it all home. Another half month of work to pay tax for this mission is a substantial increase to what I already work to pay for wealth redistribution and program spending.*

Max stood with Ethan at center stage. "Wow, Ethan, these folks heard your message. That was an exceptional speech and engaging visuals. You and the other kids opposing the Titan mission have done a stellar job of representing your position. Next up, let's hear from the kids in favor of the proposal. Please welcome Chloe Hill." Ethan exited as Chloe came on stage. The kids nodded to each other as they passed. The Alliance education system teaches everyone the value of civil debate at an early age.

Chloe and the adult opposed speaker, Rene Patel, made excellent speeches but didn't cover any new material versus Mia and Ethan. Mason left the speeches with a slew of information to reflect upon before voting.

Some Blue Spruce volunteers had prepared an outstanding vegetarian finger food spread for a mixer in the great hall after the speeches. Phoenix Fireteam piled into the food and mingled, enjoying the friendly debates and amiable arm twisting.

Ethan tugged at Mason's arm. "Thanks for the idea to help my fear, Mason. It worked."

"You were phenomenal. I am super proud of you," Mason said.

"Did I convince you to vote against the proposal?" Ethan asked.

"Well, I entered the auditorium as a firm yes vote. I'm still leaning toward yes, but you made arguments that made me reconsider my position," Mason said. "I'm going to sleep on it tonight and let my brain sort through everything."

"That's what I wanted to do, convince people to consider the Titan mission's impact on everyone." Ethan headed over to where his friends were seeing who could eat avocado sushi rolls with the most wasabi.

Noah elbowed Mason. "If I correctly recall, you have an unimaginably low tolerance for wasabi."

"Yes, and you have a freakish ability to eat the stuff pretty well straight." Mason elbowed him back.

The mixer ended by 21:00. Most Blue Spruce residents worked or went to school at regular hours during the week. Phoenix Fireteam stayed after to help collect and load the dishes into the community kitchen's dishwasher. Robert told the kids helping with the dishes how people fifty years ago used plastic dishes, cups, and utensils for events and threw everything away after a single use. The kids stared at them in disbelief, their education in understanding product total cost making such waste inconceivable.

Mason didn't believe it either when he was told the same a decade ago, he had researched on the Internet to check it out. "Max and Robert aren't trying to trick you, kids. In 2020 alone, humanity manufactured and threw away a hundred-fifty-million tonnes of single use plastics. That's stuff for parties like this and other kinds of single use items like packaging."

The kids stared at Mason. *They're waiting for me to yell out "Gotcha".* Mason smiled and reassured them, "We're telling you the truth, but you should find out for yourselves by researching on the Internet."

Noah sidled up. "Should we tell them what a mess of lies and half-truths the Internet was fifty years ago?"

"Hell no, they already think we're messing with their heads about plastics," Mason said.

Clean up done, everyone scattered to their apartments for the night.

Mason pondered Titan as he prepared to hit the sack. *It's frustrating to learn more but become less decided because of it. Sometimes you just have to absorb the information and give your brain time to stew on it.*

CHAPTER TWENTY-EIGHT – 06:00 June 4, 2070 –
Having Your Say

Democracy cannot succeed unless those who express their choice are prepared to choose wisely.

Franklin D. Roosevelt

Mason woke at his habitual 06:00 and went for a run around the Blue Spruce trails. Voting ran from 01:00 until 21:00 in this time zone. Since the Alliance spanned the globe, polls needed to stay open many hours to give everyone equal opportunity to vote. Mason could have voted upon waking, but he didn't want to rush it. Citizens choose where and when they vote thanks to the biometric identity validation required for internet access.

Back in his apartment after the run, Mason took a quick shower and grabbed some oatmeal with apple cider vinegar marinated tofu for protein. Feeling ready and now needing to get it over with to spend the day training with Phoenix, he logged into his computer and navigated to the voting site.

As with any Alliance direct democracy vote, each voter had to first answer five questions randomly selected from a pool of a hundred. You were never told whether your answers were right or wrong or even if you passed the eighty percent correct threshold for your vote to count. Alliance Elections kept the questions secret until voting day and they were under a strict no sharing ban until the vote closed. Dedicated purpose AIs with humans-in-the-loop monitored voters for possible cheating. The repercussions for sharing questions were serious, as Alliance Elections certified the sanctity of the vote. It was top news last vote when a conscientious eight-year-old reported on her father videoing his questions and showing her mom before she voted.

Mason started the process. His age and lack of vote-process relevant disadvantages permitted him only ten seconds to answer each question. The voting software locked him out of internet access on all devices to discourage last-minute research.

Total estimated cost of the Titan mission to the three participating nations? A) 3 trillion, B) 4 trillion, C) 5 trillion, or D) 6 trillion. Mason muttered "Easy" to himself and selected "C".

166

Alliance current deficit to nearest trillion? A) 23, B) 32, C) 25, or D) 35. *Good question to ask, since folks should know how deep a hole their country is in before making a humongous spending decision.* He confidently selected "B".

Which other Saturn moon does the Titan mission plan to harvest water from? A) Styx, B) Phoebe, C) Suttungr, or D) Enceladus. *Wow, I hope no one will select Pluto's moon, Styx.* He chose "D".

How is the Alliance planning to cover the costs of the Titan mission? A) borrow under existing debt facilities, B) program spending cuts, C) sell space bonds, D) tax increases, or E) a combination of A&B. *Space bonds sound like a fun investment. I would buy them if they paid reasonable interest. The correct answer, however, is "D" as Ethan's visuals pointed out.*

Mason read the next question. If we approve the Titan mission, when does tax freedom day occur? A) July 15, B) June 15, C) June 22, or D) July 7? *Ah, the dreaded follow-on question. Your correct response to one question leads to a more in depth and thus harder question along the same lines. On the flip-side, getting the follow-on question tells you your answer for the initial question was correct. Thanks, Ethan, for drilling these facts into my brain.* He selected "A".

His voting buttons appeared. He had two minutes to choose "Yes, I support the Titan mission" or "No, I do not support the Titan mission". *This is the tough part. After cramming with Noah yesterday, I was a firm "Yes". We read the opinions of various academics, government watchdog non-profits, Alliance regional representatives, and economists. Ethan's speech forced me to consider that by voting "Yes", I am committing the Blue Spruce kids and future generations to pay for this expensive mission. Hmm. All said and done, I am still a yes. I'll have to explain my choice to Ethan. Hopefully, he will be OK with it.*

The timer marched toward zero. Mason selected "Yes", exited the voting application after being thanked for participating in direct democracy, and shut down his computer. With his vote done, he could focus on a solid day of training. Phoenix Fireteam already planned to return to Blue Spruce for the evening results announcement. This was part of the voting traditions in Alliance shared living complexes. You gathered before a vote to hear differing opinions and try swaying your neighbors to your point of view. After the vote, everyone gathered to hear the results in the auditorium.

As he was heading out the main doors to join his Phoenix teammates, Mason found Ethan waiting for the school bus.

"Did you vote yet, Mason?" Ethan asked.

"Yes, I did. Your speech and slides helped me with the questions, so thanks." Mason held up a fist for Ethan to bump.

"May I ask how you voted?" Ethan looked shyly at Mason.

"I don't mind telling you. I was a firm 'Yes' before your speech. This morning I hemmed and hawed on the voting screen. It almost timed out. In the end, I voted 'Yes' because I believe we need to contribute to ventures that are bigger than us if we want humanity to make monumental achievements." Mason braced himself, since he expected Ethan to be disappointed.

"I'm glad you voted how you wanted. I spoke for the kids last night to make sure people understood the commitment they are making on behalf of future generations. My secret is that I am barely on the 'no' side. Titan is an exciting opportunity, even if my friends and I end up only paying rather than working on it." Ethan gave Mason a smile and wave as he boarded his electric school bus.

Ethan's intelligence and emotional maturity impressed Mason yet again. Max told him the educational system upped its game in the past fifty years, and Mason was a beneficiary. Regardless, he didn't recall being as mature as Ethan at age ten.

Mason spotted his teammates waiting for him in the parking lot, loaded and ready to go. He threw his bags in the hatchback and took the seat left open for him in the second row.

Noah secured the shotgun seat up front, as usual. River sat in the driver's seat.

Kesa leaned over to Mason. "Hold on to your hat, soldier."

Mason cringed. River always tried to shave a few minutes off the commute by driving manually. This trip was typical, with the safety AI repeating "Warning, following too close", "Warning, aggressive acceleration", and more. In parallel, River cursed as the safety systems made risk-reducing adjustments in trajectory, speed, and acceleration. Manual mode in commuter EVs differed from the team's Rivians. In the military vehicles, the safety systems kicked in only when collision or loss of control were imminent.

River came to a stop at the gate to the JSA facility near Franklin. The gate guards checked everyone's ID, even though they had seen them many times. Thankfully, the fireteam IDs prevented any drama about finding pistols in the go bags.

Mason sat patiently through the security checks. *We need these guards willing and able to shoot to kill when a terrorist attempts to drive a vehicle laden with explosives into a JSA building. I have no issues with their procedures.*

After clearing security, River parked the car.

Kesa hopped out. "You all get Death Town set up while I check on our intel from the Birther cell."

Teams training at JSA Franklin named their urban warfare training facility "Death Town." The name celebrated the innumerable simulated deaths they experienced and dealt out. The facility was a small town of buildings of differing sizes, configurations, and construction types to mimic mission environments.

Phoenix Fireteam set up the buildings they wanted to use.

Kesa caught up with them as they donned their gear. "No joy on the blueprint or map. There's no record of a regional authority issuing a permit for the bunker and it isn't showing up in our aerial or satellite imagery. The training facility building configuration matches eighty locations in Alliance territory. The map doesn't cover enough area to make the location differentiable. They're not giving up, but from my perspective, consider both leads as dead ends."

The team spent a grueling but satisfying day of urban warfare training. They drilled in human-on-human, humans with robots against humans, and humans against robots. Given any time to locate its enemies and start its high-speed attack sequence, the combat robot wiped the team out every time. No one used live ammunition, but the computer-calculated damage from simulated weapons fire was accurate.

Mason wiped the sweat from his brow after the team completed another fruitless attempt against a combat robot. *KIA again, damn it. We are lucky terrorists aren't known to have combat robots.*

After training, the team geared down, prepped gear to be deployment ready, and showered. They met at 19:00 in the base cafeteria for pea protein burgers on dense multigrain buns with all the toppings a person could desire from a self-serve topping bar. Defying logic, these burgers handmade by privates on mess duty were the best that the team could find throughout Franklin. The many topping options were a bonus.

Phoenix usually discussed learnings from the day's training over burgers and almond milkshakes. Noah started this time. "Kesa, should we be going for headshots, the power pack, weapons systems, or mobility when we fight a combat robot?"

Kesa finished chewing and swallowed before replying. "I'm glad you brought it up. Given our dismal record in that scenario yet again today, we need to get our shit together if we're going to be up against a combat robot. I want your opinions first. How about you, Willow?"

Mason stopped eating and leaned in to listen. *Willow has probably mulled this over. Some of her robotics specialist maintenance and command knowledge must transfer over to how to destroy combat robots.*

"We train soldiers to shoot center mass on a tough shot but to consider the head for a kill shot," Willow said. "When fighting a combat robot, there are issues with both options. Center mass on the typical robot is the heaviest armored to protect the power and compute systems. If you fire .50 caliber armor-piercing rounds within effective range, you will penetrate the armor but will mostly hit the nanogel battery. Our live fire exercises have proven that nanogel batteries have to be shot into Swiss cheese to suffer performance degradation."

"Agreed," Kesa said. "How about going for the head?"

"The head shot is tricky," Willow replied. "Head shots on a robot manufactured with sensory equipment consolidated there, as with our combat robots, can blind the robot to its environment. That's a key step to taking it out of commission. Unfortunately, the sensory equipment doesn't have to be consolidated in the head. Even if the primaries are there, secondary visual and auditory sensors can be anywhere on the body."

Noah listened, burger held motionless in the air, ready for a bite that was not coming. "That makes sense. How about weapons systems or mobility?"

Kesa noticed River waiting his turn, which was startling since he was usually staring at his phone. She motioned for him to proceed.

"Weapon systems are misleading," River said. "We can disable mounted or held weapons, but the robot itself is a weapon. They are strong enough to break or crush any of our feeble parts they can hit or grab. Some combat robot designs include bayonets or spikes mounted for hand-to-hand combat."

Kesa gave Mason a quick wave.

"I suggest attacking mobility first," Mason said. "Even our own combat robots scare me when they are moving full speed on an attack vector. What if half the team shoots to disable mobility then takes cover? We should impair the robot's movement but it will return fire. While the first shooters are drawing its fire, the other shooters target ranged weapon systems. With the robot's mobility and ranged weapons disabled and hand-to-hand attack useless if we stay out of reach, the team can shoot to disable sensors, power, and compute."

"Bravo team," Kesa said. "When you show your smarts, it makes me look smart for selecting you. We'll put Mason's tactical suggestion to the test in the next Death Town training session."

Everyone wanted to catch the vote results with their neighbors at Blue Spruce, so supper wrapped up in time to allow for the commute. Willow poked River in the chest as they took their dishes and utensils to the wash bins. "FYI, I'm sitting in the driver's seat so we can have a nice, quiet return trip."

The drive back to Blue Spruce was uneventful. As they unloaded their gear bags and headed for the front entrance, a raucous group of children raced by. Isabella skidded to a stop and grabbed Mason's arm. "Mason, you gotta patch me up." Her knee was skinned and bleeding.

The others continued in, waving goodbye to Mason and Noah. Noah stuck around, as usual, in case there was any opportunity to hassle Mason. Sometimes he even helped.

Mason put his gear down and kneeled to examine the wound. "Sure, I can do first aid, but wouldn't you rather have the nurse or your mom do it? They have medicine to reduce the pain."

"No, I'm tough like you and Noah. Besides, they would make me stop playing. Just patch me up so I can get back in the game," Isabella said.

"That's a firm request for aid, Mason. You better get to it," Noah said.

Mason was already digging for his first aid kit. *Isabella won't take "no" for an answer.* Her friends gathered around, willing to take a break from their game for a first aid show.

Capitalizing on the teaching opportunity, Mason verbalized the steps as he progressed. "First and most essential is to clean the wound. I'm spraying it out with a saline solution from this bottle. If you don't have saline handy, use clean water or water and a bit of soap."

Finishing with the cleaning and checking the wound, he continued. "This wound isn't deep, and it cleaned up perfectly. See how there isn't any dirt, twigs, pebbles, or dog poop?"

"Was there dog poop?" Isabella examined the wound, not squeamish at all.

The other kids took turns crowding in close to look at the cleaned wound.

"Luckily, no. If there was, you need to clean it out and apply antibiotic spray." Mason took a piece of gauze out and displayed it to the kids. "Now we need to dry the wound and the surrounding skin. We're using this gauze because it won't leave fibers in the wound, whereas a cotton pad will. Be gentle, but take care to dry the area so the bandage will stick."

Isabella grimaced but showed no other sign of discomfort while Mason applied gauze to the wound with pressure to stop the bleeding. He used more gauze to clean and dry around the wound.

Mason continued the narrative. "Now we have cleaned the wound, stopped the bleeding with some pressure on the gauze, and dried off the surrounding skin. We're going to use this special bandage that will stop anything nasty from getting at the wound and will also allow it to heal fast. It has a window, so Isabella and her mom can keep an eye on the wound to make sure it is healing."

"Cool, it's a see-through bandage," one of the other kids said.

Mason packed up, giving one last instruction. "You will see goop through the window for a few days. Clear or yellowish goop is OK, that's part of the healing process. Cloudy, green, or foul smelling goop means you need to go to the nurse immediately to clean the wound again. Also, go to her if you get a fever, the wound swells up, your skin turns red around it, or the wound is warmer than your other skin."

"Thanks, Mason." Isabella gave him a quick hug and ran off with the other kids.

"She's tough as nails. We should recruit her." Noah said with a wink. "Great job, field medic, shoveling some wound care knowledge into those young sponge-like brains." He offered his fist for Mason to bump.

Mason fist bumped. "Let her finish being a kid first," he said. "The world will never run out of violent radicals to deal with." He checked the time on his phone. "We have time to stow our gear before the vote results broadcast." Mason picked up his gear and he and Noah headed off to their apartments.

CHAPTER TWENTY-NINE – 21:10 June 4, 2070 – The Titan Decision

Not every vote is going to go your way. In a civil society where all are equal and heard regardless of race, religion, or other individual attribute, those who lose a vote should still celebrate having the right to vote.

Farida Azinek, Alliance President, after a direct democracy vote in 2068

Mason jogged into the Blue Spruce auditorium and dove into his seat at Phoenix Fireteam's usual spot. He was the last of the team to arrive. Noah, River, Willow, and Kesa were in the midst of exchanging vote result guesses.

Just as Mason sat down, Alliance President Farida Azinek came on the screen. "Good evening, Alliance citizens. I am honored to present the results of another successful Alliance direct democracy vote. The Titan mission engrossed almost every citizen, with ninety-seven percent casting a vote. This beat the prior Alliance voting participation record by one percent." Vote analytics visualizations came up to share the screen with the president.

The raw turnout didn't surprise Mason. With voting taking under five minutes from any computer or smartphone, there wasn't any barrier to at least casting a vote. *The interesting ratio is the portion of voters that cared to do enough homework to ensure their vote counted.*

"Ninety-four percent of the votes cast met the Q&A threshold to be counted. This ties the previous record for vote viability." Farida dropped the stats and paused.

"She's the master of the pregnant pause," Kesa whispered to the team while they waited for Farida to continue.

"Before I announce the Alliance citizens' choice, let's reflect on our direct democracy." Farida made her presence felt even through remote broadcast, demonstrating the magnetism contributing to her presidency win three years ago. "For forty years, Alliance citizens have decided all important matters. Although the vote is core to our democracy, so is the willingness of all citizens to engage in civil discourse. Since I was twelve years old, I have enjoyed the spirited debate everyone took part in before voting. This opportunity to hear everyone's opinions ensures we have considered the vote from all angles. After turning sixteen, I am thankful to be heard in the debates and in the vote, whether the vote goes my way or not."

"And now the results." Farida gripped the top edges of the podium and leaned forward in emphasis. "The Titan mission is . . . approved by sixty-five percent of the viable vote!" Polite applause rippled throughout the Blue Spruce auditorium with pockets of exuberance.

Mason believed Farida had a sixth sense for what was going on in gathering places throughout the Alliance; she waited exactly long enough for the reaction to settle.

"The Titan mission will thus proceed," Farida said, "into detailed planning and execution."

"For the twelve-to-fifteen-year-olds, although your vote doesn't affect the outcome, we are still listening. The youth vote was even more in favor of proceeding with Titan, coming in at seventy percent of viable votes. By the way, voters of age, you need to study harder. The youth vote viability was a whopping ninety-six percent." Farida shook her index finger at the viewers.

"Now your Alliance Representative has a few words." Farida waved goodbye.

Max Williams replaced her on the screen. Max on TV always made Mason feel weird versus Max being at Blue Spruce with the rest of the residents. From others' expressions around the auditorium, a lot of folks felt the same. Some looked around for Max, expecting he was here and broadcasting from a quiet corner.

"Greetings citizens of the Rockies East Foothills Alliance region. I'm your Alliance Representative Max Williams. All elected Alliance Representatives join Farida and myself in thanking you for participating in direct democracy. We're all excited to see the Titan mission proceed. The youth interest in this vote was phenomenal across the Alliance. Presentations from youth in my community particularly impressed me. The Alliance will ensure as many companies and citizens as possible have an opportunity to work on the mission. If you are interested, please monitor the supplier and job opportunities pages of the Titan mission website." Max's speech was short and sweet as usual, which his constituents appreciated. He waved as he finished and, a second before his feed cut, discreetly steepled his hands into a tree shape. This was his not-so-secret way of greeting his Blue Spruce neighbors. Laughter and whistles erupted from the crowd, since everyone at Blue Spruce appreciated how Max watched out for them.

"OK, straw poll." Willow scanned Phoenix Fireteam. "Who voted for the proposal?" Everyone raised their hands, nodding as they saw the unanimous vote.

Kesa motioned toward everyone on the Fireteam. "Perhaps we appreciate humanity working together toward a goal in contrast to what we deal with in our jobs."

Her statement resonated with Mason. *I didn't realize it when voting, but that tipped the balance for me. I needed to be part of something positive to counter the negativity I face in our missions.*

THE SINGULARITY - RIVER

CHAPTER THIRTY – 10:00 June 7, 2070 – A Revelation and a New Idea

I can't understand why people are frightened of new ideas. I'm frightened of the old ones.
John Cage, 1988

Willow glanced at Sophia and took a deep breath before finishing her presentation. "To conclude, Sophia and I believe we can build our own combat robots. They will respond to simple commands from Cave Cell members and destroy or at least distract Gaia's minions." She scanned Cave Cell's three elders, awaiting their feedback. River watched from behind them, near the back of the presentation cave. This six by five meters cave housed one of their few computers and had a handful of chairs facing the front.

The elders sat still and uncharacteristically quiet. Even though River had listened to the proposal yesterday, he shivered. *This still gives me the heebie-jeebies, but less than when I first found out helping Willow rehearse. After sleeping on it, I am past the knee-jerk aversion and can at least consider the merits. I bet the elders are thinking along the same lines, but they should get from abject fear to considering the possibilities faster than I did.*

"I would rejoice to see robots destroying minions. What you propose can be a great win for Cave Cell, but can also result in our destruction," Althea said. "If someone scavenges parts and doesn't ensure to disable communications devices, they will give Gaia a beacon straight to the Cave."

"We would need to select a location far away from the Cave," Robert said. "Workshop users must follow strict safe travel protocols to avoid compromising Cave Cell's location. Gaia may discover the workshop and monitor our movements instead of attacking immediately."

"We need to get feedback from Cave Cell and consider this carefully," Grandpy Max said. "For now, you may request scavenging parties to stash decommissioned minion parts near each contact site if they can do so at low risk. We can recover the parts if we proceed with the proposal."

Willow smiled. "Thanks for your consideration. Sophia and I look forward to further discussion."

River remained undecided. *I'm glad for her. Although the elders didn't approve, neither did they outright refuse. On the other hand, part of me screams "no, no, no" after going toe-to-toe fighting Gaia's minions. Could I stand with a Cave Cell minion made from the pieces of Gaia's minions that killed some of my cell members?*

Althea caught Sophia's eye. "You mentioned you and Willow had important topics to discuss with the elders?" she asked. "I hope your item isn't as unsettling. Our old hearts are frail."

Sophia waved at Carter. He pedaled the exercise bike that Cave Cell rigged up to power a Wi-Fi disabled laptop and an eighty-one centimeter LCD screen. "Apologies, elders, this other item is most likely more upsetting than our robot proposal," Sophia said while the laptop powered up. "Yesterday, I reviewed the digital photos of last week's mission." She turned the monitor toward the elders and brought up the photos. As she clicked slowly through the photos, she provided commentary. "This series focuses on the new centipede minion we encountered. Until I looked at these photos, my concerns were the .50 caliber ATLAS turret showing up and Gaia having the ability to manufacture new minions." She paused, checking if any of the elders had questions so far.

Something monumental loomed in the air. They gazed expectantly back at her.

River leaned forward. *Willow didn't tell me about this. What would concern Sophia more than a .50 caliber murder machine? Hmm, Willow seems as curious as me, she isn't in the know either. Sophia wanted the elders to be the first to learn this news before it travels the Cave Cell gossip network at light speed.*

Sophia gingerly clicked to advance to the next photo in her presentation. "This is a panel Mason pried open to salvage ammo from the .50 caliber. The welds exposed behind the panel piqued my curiosity." Her voice was strained.

The elders leaned in to examine the photo.

River crept forward. *All good, I'm not blocking any else's view. Just getting a better peek. There's lots of weld spatter; is that what Sophia is pointing out? What do the elders think?*

Grandpy Max pointed at the screen. "The weld on the joints isn't uniform. It reminds me of my work when I first learned in high school shop class fifty years ago. There's also an unusual spatter away from the joint. I expect robot welds to be near perfect with no spatter."

"That's what got my attention," Sophia said. "Now I will zoom in on the spatter area."

Everyone gasped in unison as soon as Sophia zoomed in on the photo. Carter almost fell off the bike, leaning over to see what was so shocking.

River's mouth hung open, but his overloaded brain was incapable of shutting it. *That's not welding spatter, someone sloppily welded "HELP" on the metal crosspiece!*

Sophia paused, waiting for the shock to subside. "Given the message and the inferior weld quality, the most likely scenario is Gaia took humans as slaves."

River's mind reeled. *For eighteen years, everyone in Cave Cell told me and, in recent years, I witnessed Gaia's hunger to annihilate humanity. We've never seen signs that Gaia has human slaves. Does this change everything? Why hasn't any elders spoken yet? Robert clenches his jaw shut like he wants to shout out in disbelief, but is holding it back. Althea is unreadable, as usual; she's just gazing stoically at the screen.*

Grandpy Max ran his hand over his head, resting it for a second on his neck. "This shouldn't surprise us. Gaia is operating with robotics technology as it stood at 2040. She desires to improve her technology, but thirty years of war and humanity's scorched earth policy inhibit advances. Humankind destroyed anything of use to her, especially manufacturing and research facilities."

"I see where you are going," Althea said. "Humans are versatile workers whereas most of the machines and robots Gaia took as minions are special purpose. Humans provided the bare minimum of food, shelter, and clothing are cheap from a resource perspective."

"I feel somewhat stupid for not expecting this," Grandpy Max said. "Gaia has access to copious historical examples of forced labor, economic slavery, and plentiful other forms of servitude. Unencumbered by morals, slavery is a no brainer for her."

"What if this is a trap?" Robert asked.

"I share your concern, Robert, but a trap requires a path suggested, or a door opened," Althea countered. "A catalyst to trick us to go somewhere or do something. I can't fathom a trap from this message, can you?"

Robert shook his head and stared at Althea and Grandpy Max. "We need to discuss this further, in the elder chamber."

Althea stood up. "Yes, of course." She gestured to the non-elders in the room. "Obviously, you want to share this information with Cave Cell. Please let them know the elders need to discuss the matter before anyone takes any action."

The three elders left the presentation cave, already speaking in hushed tones.

"Shocker," River blurted. "I thought Gaia wanted to kill us, not make us work for her." *I was going to explode, trying to keep my trap shut while the elders were in the room.*

Carter jumped off the bike and peered at the LCD from centimeters away. The bike generator's small battery stored a few minutes of runtime for the computer and monitor. Momentarily and without a word, Carter left at a jog.

River failed to suppress a quick laugh. "There goes a man with a burning desire to share news. What do you think Cave Cell should do, Willow?"

"We must find the slaves and free them," Willow said. "We're already searching for Gaia's bases. Learning she has human slaves means we have to work faster."

Sophia grunted in agreement while she shut down the computer.

"Sophia, you must have almost burst at the seams keeping this a secret," River said.

"You're right, I barely slept last night from not being able to tell anyone," Sophia confirmed. "By the way, aren't you booked to take a scavenging team out today?"

River narrowed his eyes. *Uh oh, where is this going?* "Yeah, I'm lead with Kesa as mentor. Carter, Ava, and Kona are crew."

Sophia and Willow exchanged a look River couldn't interpret. Sophia pulled a map out of a pocket and offered it to him. "This map has Cave Cell's three most recent Gaia contact sites marked on it. Can you stop by to check for robot parts and hide any you find?"

River accepted the map with a theatrical sigh. "It's intriguing you had this map handy even though the elders heard your proposal just a few mikes ago. Fortunately, I love and respect the both of you as much as if we were siblings—otherwise I'd be suspicious."

Willow laughed and punched him in the shoulder. "What the hell is that supposed to mean? I'm your twin sister."

Sophia shook her head. "Don't get sucked in. He's only stirring the pot for fun before agreeing to help."

River frowned. *Killjoy, she shut me down just as I started winding up my sister.* He glanced at the map. "This chemical plant is along my planned route. My team will investigate it on our way out. Depending on how the mission goes, we may stop at another site on the return."

Willow bear hugged him. "Thanks for helping us, dear brother. Be safe and listen to Kesa."

River hugged her back. "Come on, I always pay complete attention to my mentors."

Sophia and Willow laughed until they gasped for breath.

River noticed it was 10:30. *If I want to be an at least half-assed good team lead, I need to hustle my gear together and be first at the Cave entrance for the mission's noon start time.* He waved to Sophia and Willow as he left. "I'm off. Thanks for yet another unforgettable experience. Maybe don't invite me for your next earthshaking picture show."

CHAPTER THIRTY-ONE – 16:00 June 7, 2070 – Party at the Chemical Plant

We've been so focused on avoiding extermination at Gaia's hand, we failed to consider what else she might be up to.
Kesa James, 2070

River, Kesa, Ava, and Carter huddled up ten meters in from the forest edge. Kona paced around them. Bordering the forest was a flat grassy plain separating the forest and a nearby ridge as each meandered for kilometers to the north and south.

River pointed at the rocky but otherwise barren ridge whose slope began fifty meters out from the forest edge. It was steep, but still walkable. "The chemical plant is immediately over this ridge. Cave Cell experiences a high frequency of contact with Gaia in this area, so stay sharp and move cover to cover. Cap your scope if in the sunlight. Willow and Sophia requested we recover any stray robot parts and hide them somewhere around here."

"Why do they want robot parts? Is it to research minion weaknesses?" Ava asked.

Carter grinned. "They looped me in. They're planning to build Cave Cell robots."

River coughed on some errant phlegm. *I need to explain before this conversation spins out of control.* "Cave Cell might build a remote workshop to experiment with the parts. It may lead to us having our own minions, stupid ones. For now, we'll smash and leave any control boards with any possibility of communications capabilities and stash the other parts we find."

River gave everyone time to digest the information. Carter and Ava exchanged worried glances. Kesa remained placid; a good poker face was a senior scavenger prerequisite. Kona sniffed various animal tracks. *At least Kona's mind is still mission focused. She doesn't give a damn about robot parts. I admire Kesa's vibe. Willow and I should work on our poker faces. Carter and Ava need time to understand the reason behind the orders, but for now, I must get the team moving.* "Alright everyone, focus and ascend the ridge. Ditch your packs near the top and crawl the last five meters. I don't want anyone making themselves an easy target silhouetted on the ridgeline."

Carter and Ava regained some mission focus, tightening their gear straps and checking each other without River prompting.

River was pleased. *These two are already showing improvement in their first few weeks of Cave Cell field missions.* He waved everyone forward. "Kesa, you are on point, followed by Carter, then Ava. I'm rear guard. Kona, heel." They proceeded across the plain and up the ridge.

River checked his M110A1 sniper rifle as he walked, the same rifle and 7.62x51 mm armor-piercing tungsten ammo as Kesa carried. *I adore this rifle. It's twice as heavy as a loaded M4 carbine, but at least I feel like I pose a threat to minions. An M4 feels more like a distraction rather than doing actual damage. Willow will laugh her ass off when I tell her what happened at the armory. "Are you sure you want to carry the extra three kilos?" the armorer asked. His face was priceless when I said "Fuck, yeah, gimme that thing." I guess the Central High rescue execution pleased the elders if they now allow Willow and me to take the good shit out on missions.*

The team crawled the last five meters, taking cover behind small boulders on the ridgeline. Even Kona belly crawled, following the visual cue from the two-legged.

From behind the torso-sized rocks he crawled up to, River had a terrific view of the abandoned chemical plant and surrounding area. Until 2040, this plant had produced various chemicals, stored them in massive metal tanks, and shipped via the rail and truck loading facilities on site. Thirty years without maintenance and suffering the wounds of many firefights took their toll. Portions of the buildings had collapsed. The metal tanks were rusting and had the occasional gaping hole. Burn marks and bullet holes marred anything left standing.

Ava pointed to the far end of the parking lot.

River recognized one of Gaia's flatbed electric tractor trailers four hundred meters away. A biped emerged from between two buildings and headed for the trailer. The biped dragged something long and thin, like a pipe or cable.

Kesa signaled the minions were out of hearing range.

River broke the silence, speaking quietly to be safe. "Can anyone identify what the biped is dragging?"

Kesa peered through her binoculars. "That's electrical cable. From its size, I'd guess transmission cable from the downed line that used to serve this chemical plant."

The biped labored to pull the heavy cable across the weathered parking lot. The cable crushed the grasses sprouting from the many cracks in the pavement as it dragged. Upon reaching the flatbed trailer, the biped pulled the cable forward to create slack, jumped to the deck of the flatbed, and coiled the cable.

"Why is Gaia coiling the cable?" Carter asked. "With those side posts on the flatbed, she could haul more cable and load it faster if the bipeds cut it to trailer length."

"Gaia's smarter than all of us together," River said. "She's scavenging electrical transmission cable and keeping it intact for a reason."

Kesa kept her eyes glued to her binoculars. "Cave Cell needs to understand what she is plotting."

Just as Kesa finished speaking, Ava gasped.

River oriented his binoculars to where she was looking. A biped emerged from the forest where the transmission line arrived at the chemical plant. This biped dragged more cable, but it also flushed a fuzzy dark gray wolf pup out of the forest. The distressed pup yipped and whimpered as it backpedaled away from the biped. The biped ignored it as Gaia customarily did, her minions ignoring animals not deemed a threat.

Seconds later, a light gray wolf with black highlights leaped from the brush. A male, given its half meter shoulder height. Instead of whimpering, it snarled a challenge to the biped.

In a single smooth motion, the biped dropped the cable and brought its M16A4 to high ready from where it had been slung across its back.

"Now we know sixty kilos of snarling wolf qualifies as a threat to Gaia," Carter said.

There was an unexpected rustling to River's right along the ridgeline. Next came the definitive click of a weapon's safety switch. Wondering what the hell was happening, he looked over. Ava had positioned her M4 carbine for a shot and was peering through the combat optic mounted on it.

River said nothing more than "Ava, nnn" before she fired.

The biped's head jolted from the bullet caroming off its armor, a deep ping signaling a harmless ricochet. *Great shot, hitting a biped's head at four hundred meters with an M4. Too bad it might be the death of us. Time to go!*

Everyone was already backing off the top of the ridge when River issued orders. "Bug out to the forest, carbines deep in the middle to draw the bipeds in with suppressing fire. Kesa and I will set up on the sides for kill shots on the back armor."

Shit happened fast. River took a last glance at the chemical plant parking lot. Both bipeds charged forward while firing at the team's position. The wolf ushered the pup into the forest. Bullets scattered rock fragments from where the team's heads disappeared a moment ago, or snap-cracked barely over the ridge.

The team ran full speed down the slope and past their packs, hoping to reach the cover of the forest before the bipeds crested the ridge. Kona led as usual. She seemed to know the tail end of a retreating group attracts bullets.

River paced himself to keep up but stick to rearguard. As he ran, he watched for rocks large enough to dive behind. *I need to be ready to take cover and lay down suppression fire to give the rest of the team time to reach the forest.* Thankfully, it wasn't necessary; the team made it to the forest without taking fire. River took up his position on one side of the kill box.

River slowed his breathing to try hearing anything other than his own heaving lungs and pounding pulse. The sole audible noise was the whine of five hundred kilowatts of electric motors fading into the distance. Even though he waited six minutes, no bipeds came crashing full tilt into the forest to do their damnedest to eradicate his team. Moving quietly to where he gained line of sight to Carter and Ava, he signaled all clear on his side. They signaled the same from their perspective. Carter and Ava signaled Kesa; she arrived at their middle position at the same time as River.

Kesa's poker face was out of service. She gestured wildly and talked fast. "What the hell just happened? In eight years of field operations, I've never seen minions refuse an opportunity to try killing humans." Her expression shifted to angry. "Oh, and dammit Ava, I am going to beat some sense into you if the elders leave any of your flesh unbruised."

River tamped down his own anger. *I better defuse this before it comes to blows.* "Ava knew exactly what she was doing. She will suffer the repercussions of her actions back at the Cave. Until we're home, we are all still on mission."

"Are you serious?" Carter exploded. "She nearly got us killed to save a couple of wolves. We should take her M4 and send her to the Cave right now."

River kept his tone even, trying to model calm. "You know better than that. We work in fours for our collective safety. We're still in the field and in danger. I need everyone focused on the here and now."

Kesa composed herself and gave him a discrete nod.

Wow, the mission mentor had nothing to add after that shit show? What's our next move? Cave Cell protocol is to go to ground after contact with Gaia because she pursues you until she slaughters you or cannot find you. Gaia retreating is unheard of, and I want to determine what's going on. Fuck it, I'll take a stab at investigating; Kesa will overrule me for team safety if she wants. "We're supposed to cut and run after contact, but that protocol is based on Gaia pursuing us. Today is different, since the bipeds retreated with their partial load. We should find out why. After we move our packs up to here in case we need to make a second run back to the forest, we'll check out the chemical plant site again. Kesa, you're on point. I'll take rear." River forced a confident tone.

Kesa said nothing. She brought her rifle to controlled carry position and headed for their abandoned packs. Ava and Carter followed, each covering one side of their advance. Kona ranged beside the group.

River gave himself a mental shake. *Everyone else is following my orders; best I do the same.*

Back at the ridgetop, River peeked at the chemical plant. The bipeds and tractor-trailer were nowhere to be seen. River peered at Kona. He had experienced firsthand her ability to hear and smell minions long before people did.

She sniffed the air, scanned the area, and stared back at him.

I'll take that look to mean, "Well, what are we waiting for?" River signaled the team to move ahead.

The team alternated between covering the field of fire, running to cover, and diving behind cover. Reaching the bottom of the ridge, also the edge of the parking lot, Kesa caught River's eye and shrugged.

River agreed Gaia had departed. *Let's see if we can figure out what Gaia's objective was.* "Kesa and Carter, follow the transmission lines into the plant site. Ava, you're with me following the lines as they come to the site."

"Walk around puddles and drips," Kesa said. "Fluids resembling water here may be a strong enough acid or base to burn right through your hand or foot."

"Good to know, thanks," River replied. *Yeah, I'll keep that top of mind. I enjoy having a complete complement of ten fingers and ten toes.*

River and Ava headed across the parking lot to where the second biped had emerged. The cable remained where the biped dropped it to fire on the team. They followed the cable into the forest, where it rejoined the path of the downed transmission towers. The metal frame giants stood proud and tall before high winds and tornados toppled them. "Be careful. We don't want to get between the pup and its protector," River said. "Such a shame to kill it in self defense after what you did to save it." *I do enjoy a double scoop of irony.*

"Screw you," Ava said.

They followed the towers for a quarter hour until reaching high ground. A few kilometers of the old transmission line's route was visible. Ava stared down the cutline, tapping an index finger on her chin a few times. "All three power cables and the grounding cables are missing as far as the naked eye can see down the cutline."

River patted her on the shoulder. "The plot thickens. Let's head back and regroup." He scrutinized Kona for an alert on the buzzing of quadcopters approaching or the far above droning of a Reaper. She, however, intently sniffed the trails of whatever creatures passed by here over the past god knows how many days. *I only smell forest, but no matter. A carefree Kona means I'm likely to stay on the right side of the dirt.*

When they reached the parking lot, Kesa and Carter stepped out from cover. "Gaia pulled all the transmission cable from this area," Carter said. "Cable cut residue is sparse, so Kesa and I believe Gaia maximized cable length to the most a biped could handle."

"We observed the same for at least four klicks up the line, perhaps further," Ava said.

Kesa creased her forehead. "Gaia has scavenged cable here for a while. No wonder we have frequent contact."

"We need to advise Cave Cell of Gaia's activities here," River said. "We'll scrub the original mission and head back now." Again, he waited for Kesa to belay his orders. Again, the team wordlessly set out, all in agreement with his direction.

The team returned to where they had stashed their packs in the forest. River called for a quick meal before heading back to the Cave.

A low growl from Kona put the team on high alert just as they were finishing.

River scanned the forest for an immediate threat. The others signaled they couldn't hear or see anything yet. River trusted Kona, but with nothing in sight, he assumed the team had a minute or two before the threat came close enough to identify. He signaled the team to stash their gear and make ready to move fast if needed.

Kona shifted her head between the northwest and the north. With the chemical plant situated west of them, the threats were not at the plant site.

River motioned for everyone to take positions maximizing line of sight from excellent cover. Given the extra time provided by Kona's warning, the team dug into their positions and applied foliage to minimize their target profile. Kona continued to growl. Whatever concerned her was still close by.

After a few minutes, Kesa waved to catch everyone's attention from her position on the far right. She chopped her hand at twelve o'clock.

River scanned the indicated area with his binoculars. He glimpsed what Kesa spotted, a man walking through the woods. The man looked older than River, similar in age to Kesa's twenty-two years. His clothing was shabby, the quality of the worst Cave Cell kept around. The man appeared underfed, since his face was gaunt. He plodded parallel across their front, but somewhat towards them, stepping on dry twigs. Every twenty steps, he stopped and made some hand gestures while yelling something. *He couldn't make any more noise even if he tried; his intent is the complete opposite of stealth.*

The man moved close enough to enable River to hear. The man stopped again. "Hello, I am unarmed and need help," he yelled. "Please call out so I can find you." As he yelled, he held his left hand immediately in front of his body, made a flat shaking motion, lifted his index finger up, and pointed it to his sternum.

The man was too far away to hear them talk, so River broke the silence. "Any idea what he is signaling?" River asked, just loud enough for the team to hear.

"He's signing no or nothing, followed by one and pointing at himself to specify 'me'?" Ava said. "Should we call him to us? It looks like he is alone and unarmed, as he claims."

Kesa caught River's eye and tilted her head to Kona. Kona looked back and forth between the man at their twelve o'clock and something she was concerned about toward ten o'clock.

River paused to process. *Something's not right here; his hand signals and words don't line up. Kona is interested in more than the man.* "No, don't call him. Kona's alerting on something else at ten o'clock. There's more going on than what we see on the surface."

"What if he isn't pointing at himself but behind him?" Carter asked. "He is making the gestures close to his chest as though he is hiding the signals from someone to his rear."

"Yeah, I agree," Ava said. "The gestures are no and one and behind, meaning either 'no one behind me' or 'no and one behind me'."

River put it together. "Carter, eyes on the man. Tell us if he changes his behavior. Everyone else scan ten o'clock. The man is telling us to ignore his words and there is one behind him, a threat he doesn't want rescuers to encounter."

Fifteen minutes passed. The man traveled off their right flank, noisily moving further away from them. The foliage River scanned blurred for a fraction of a second. Assuming his eyes were strained, he blinked long to give them a rest. He resumed scanning the area. The foliage blurred again, but this time only one tree and the bush beside it. Soon after, the next tree to the right. He gasped and stammered, "Unbelievable, cloaking." River didn't want to lose track of whatever it was; he kept his binoculars trained on the slow-moving disturbance. To signal the others, he chopped his hand in the same direction.

Seconds later, Kesa corroborated. "I see it. You can detect a slight blur when it moves, but when it stops, it is invisible. It's taking care not to step on twigs or make other noises as it moves. Quiet down and listen."

River signaled Kona to silence her alerting and listened in with everyone else. There was a barely discernable hint of the high pitch whines and clicks of electric motors and compact hydraulic actuators.

Kesa beat him to stating his suspicion. "From the noise and the height of the visual disturbance, it's a cloaked biped minion."

Ava and Carter cursed under their breath.

This situation is way outside the bounds of team lead training, where my mentor only overrides orders that compromise team or Cave Cell safety. I need Kesa's experience to help make the best decision. "I want to disable the minion, examine it, and talk to the man. What do you think?" River asked Kesa.

"The risk profile sucks," Kesa said, "but I agree that Cave Cell needs intel to figure out what the hell is happening here. Let's build a biped kill box oriented toward where it should be in five mikes. You and I will take a few quick rear shots and disappear. The carbines will open up to draw the minion. We'll get more rear shots when it charges the carbines."

Carter and Ava understood their dangerous role in baiting the minion to their position. They dug deeper behind their cover to avoid becoming victims of Gaia's impeccable aim.

River nodded in approval. "Stay aware of your teammates' positions, since we'll be in each other's field of fire."

Kona stared at him, chaos menaced when the two-legged got all serious clutching their boom sticks.

River motioned behind their line. "Go."

Kona headed off. Cave Cell had trained her to wait quietly five hundred meters away until summoned.

River crept a hundred meters northwest. He planned to take the much more dangerous north direction, but Kesa, a fearless warrior, headed there before he could broach the subject. Settling in behind excellent cover, he pinpointed everyone's positions to make sure he didn't fire at them.

Kesa moved silently from cover to cover. Being the closest to the minion, she needed to take the utmost care to avoid detection by its exceptional visual and audio systems. Once settled in, she pointed at him to advise he take the first shots. She angled to fire on the minion's lighter rear armor after it charged Carter and Ava.

River oriented toward the disturbance. It closed in to four hundred meters away from his position. *Now I understand why she wants me to take the first shots; the minion is walking north of her position. It needs to be drawn back my way to get in the kill box.* Fortunately, the minion paused often, allowing him to time his shot to maximize the probability of putting tungsten and steel on target.

River breathed in, out, and waited for the minion to halt during his natural respiratory pause. No joy, it kept moving. He breathed in and out again. This time, his respiratory pause coincided with the minion stopping. River squeezed the trigger all the way back, the bullet erupting from the barrel at over twice the speed of sound. An indiscernibly short time after the sonic boom cracked came the heart-warming crunch of a bullet tearing into the minion. A fist-sized chunk of parts flipped away as its cloaking flickered and then deactivated. Unfortunately, the minion retained full functionality. It whipped to face him with weapon raised and ready before River could get another shot into its rear armor.

River gritted his teeth. *Now the hard part. I need to make a low probability of affect second shot to draw the minion toward me. How about a head shot to take out a valuable sensor rather than pounding the strong frontal armor?* As expected, his bullet glanced off the side of the biped's head instead of doing any damage. The minion bolted full tilt straight at him, firing where his head was a half second earlier. Fortunately, his head was no longer there. River expected the immediate response, ducking under full cover the moment his second bullet left the muzzle. Bullets blasted chunks of rock and moss off the top of his first shooting position. River rolled a meter to his left, ready to emerge from a second firing position after someone else attracted the minion's attention.

Eighteen seconds later, the somewhat more subdued thumping of two M4 carbines joined the minion's M16A4 firing. The minion had entered the kill box, triggering Carter and Ava to open fire.

The minion's gunfire re-vectored from straight at River to perpendicular to him. *Time to get back to work.* River brought his body and rifle into firing position, swallowing the fear of popping up to find a minion pointing a rifle straight at his head. As planned, the minion ran in the middle of River and Kesa straight toward Carter and Ava. They blew the equipment strapped on top of the minion's chest armor off in chunks with a barrage of 5.56 mm bullets, but it didn't affect the minion's run or firing. The minion would be on top of Carter and Ava in twenty seconds. *I only know one survivor of hand-to-hand combat with a biped, not a good statistic to retest today.*

By coincidence, Kesa started firing at the same time as River resumed firing. Three quick rounds from each of them tore chunks off the biped's rear armor, but didn't disable it. The biped wheeled back around to River's position, algorithms determining that close range 7.62 mm AP rounds made River biped enemy number one. River hit the dirt just before the biped completed its turn and put ten rounds into various nooks and crannies that were the front face of River's cover.

River counted himself lucky that none of those rounds made it through to him. The high-speed whirring, clicking, and thumping getting louder by the second was concerning, to say nothing of the 5.56 mm rounds exploding out of the biped's M16A4 that blew rock chips and moss off his cover or whizzed barely overhead. The only pauses in M16, M4, and M110A1 gunfire were the few seconds for magazine changes. *My friends at the Cave call these moments "anal sphincter control tests". I hope to be with them soon, sharing the gut wrenching panic I feel right now and having a good laugh at myself.*

When the biped's whirring and clicking was just twenty meters away, an uncharacteristic pop ended the M16 fire. The biped's M16 soon passed a whisker over him in a flat spin, whooshing through the air and slamming into the tree just behind him. The squib round was timely, but the high-speed whirring, clicking, and thumping was now just on the other side of River's rock. Kesa's M110A1 firing took on an urgent pace, her usual methodical aim and fire pattern changing to a rapid booming. AP rounds tore into biped armor again and again. *From her angle, the bullets should punch into vital systems through the light rear armor.*

The biped's hydraulics whined, readying for a leap. *Oh damn, this is the end. The damn minion will vault over my boulder and kill me with its bare hands. Kesa is putting AP rounds on target; how is this biped still operational?* Finally, there was a thump on his boulder. The biped had landed atop rather than vaulting over. River had squeezed his eyes shut, now forcing them open to face his death.

The hydraulics and actuators noises faded away to nothing, punctuated by the pain of something scratching the middle of his forehead. A trickle of wetness ran down the ridge of his nose, dripping off the tip. The biped's skeletal right hand hung above his head. The middle finger was the only one that contacted his forehead, the biped losing power before it could crush his skull.

River lay still, not quite realizing that he was still alive. As he resumed breathing, he experimentally flexed his butt cheeks to discern if he had shit himself. *Nothing there; anal sphincter control test passed.* "Damn, that was close!" He rolled out from under the prostrate biped's arm.

Ava vaulted out from cover, bolt cutters in hand. She ran to the biped and cut cables and hoses while Kesa and River emerged from cover, rifles trained on the biped until Ava finished.

Kesa glanced at River. "Mosquito bite your head?"

"Yeah, an eighty kilo stainless steel and plastic one with anger issues. Your timing is a bit short of impeccable, by the way." River wiped his bloody forehead onto his shoulder, keeping his rifle on target.

"Where's Carter? Is he OK?" River asked, hoping his team avoided injury or worse.

"If you consider breathing and not bleeding as OK, then yes. A bullet hit his helmet. He's feeling peculiar." Ava pointed toward Carter's cover.

River raced to Carter after Ava finished disabling the biped.

"Carter! Carter, are you OK?" River nudged Carter's shoulder.

Carter laid prone in his firing position, only now releasing his carbine. He slowly turned to River and blinked, as if deciding if River was imaginary. His right pupil diameter appeared less than half the size of his left, which looked too dilated for the light of day. "Yes, sir, I am ready to move out," he slurred as he stood up and stumbled, without his carbine or pack, in the direction opposite to the Cave.

River shouted over his shoulder at Kesa and Ava. "He has a severe concussion." He grabbed Carter's arm and steered him. "Hey Carter, can you sit over here for a while?"

Carter drifted to where River shepherded him and sat on a log. "I am sitting here," he slurred.

Kesa and Ava approached, both staring dubiously at Carter.

"Will he be OK?" Ava asked.

"He was lucky," Kesa said. "Our helmets can't stop a bullet at that velocity. If it hit two centimeters right instead of glancing off the side, he would be dead. As it is, he'll need six to eight weeks of downtime."

River called, "Kona, come." *I want Kona around to alert on any minions that may have been in the area to support Gaia's invisible biped. Carter's a concern, but Cave Cell needs us to finish putting this puzzle together.* "Monitor him and get both of you ready to move," River said to Ava. "We'll distribute his pack and carbine, since he shouldn't be carrying any extra weight."

Carter fumbled and gawked at the log on each side of him. "Where's my helmet?" The helmet remained strapped to his head.

"Wilco." Ava leaned into Carter's line of sight to comfort him. "Don't worry about your helmet. I will find it. You stay here and relax."

River shifted nervously as Kona approached. He half expected her to alert more minion signs.

Kona, glad to rejoin her pack, met them with floppy ears and whole body tail wags. No alert . . . yet. She sniffed questioningly in Carter's direction.

Carter pointed at her. "Puppy."

"These two are the most at risk. We'll leave Kona here with them while you and I hunt the man," River said to Kesa.

"We'd best hustle, since we must assume Gaia is sending something our way." Kesa headed in the direction they last saw the man. She set a strong pace, moving as fast as she could while keeping her rifle at low ready.

"Stay," River said to Kona before following Kesa.

CHAPTER THIRTY-TWO – 17:00 June 7, 2070 – Man on a Mission

I'd be a terrible secret agent. I can't keep a secret and I'm not sneaky.
Katherine Heigl

River and Kesa double timed two hundred meters toward where they last saw the shouting man. They switched to crouch walking cover to cover after they drew near enough to make out his words. River wasn't sure whether to consider him friend or foe. *He was with Gaia's stealth biped, but there's no doubt he signaled us to warn it followed him.*

"Hello, I am unarmed," the man yelled. "I heard shooting. Did you disable the stealth biped?" By the volume and clarity, he headed their way.

They set up behind cover to await him. Still making so much noise he must intend it, he soon came into sight. River took a better look at the man. *His clothing is not only shabby, no one is repairing any of the rips. He is definitely not getting enough good food; his cheeks are hollow.*

River waited until the man drew within fifteen meters before shouting, "Hands up, don't move!"

The man halted and put his hands up. "I am John Walker. Did you disable the stealth biped that followed me?"

"Do not move unless you want some holes in you, John Walker," River said. "We dealt with one stealth biped. Are any other minions around?"

John Walker shook his head. "Only one allowed me to see it. It instructed me to draw you out and convince you to take me to your cell. I assume the stealth biped was supposed to follow us to discover your cell's location. Gaia rushed me here several times over the last month, trying to implement this plan. The prior times, I wandered fruitlessly until the stealth biped terminated the search."

Kesa leaned into her rifle, ready to fire. "Tell us why we shouldn't put a bullet between your eyes, traitor."

John Walker scanned Kesa's way and squinted, straining to spot her, but in the end just replying in her general direction. "I'm not a traitor. Gaia has my wife and child. Didn't you notice my signals? I shouted what Gaia told me to, but used hand signals to alert you to the biped following me. Please, we must get moving. I need to talk to your elders about saving my family and the others."

This piqued River's curiosity. "Others? What others?"

"I'm sorry, I will get into detail with the elders," John Walker, unsettled, talked faster now. "Help me hide Gaia's radio and check me for other transmitters. We need to leave before she sends other minions to follow us." As he spoke, he slowly dipped his left hand into his coat pocket. Between two fingers, he pulled out a fist and half sized rectangular object wrapped in aluminum foil.

River disliked how this was working out. *The people with the guns pointing at you are supposed to run the show.* "Whoa, stop moving. What is that?"

John Walker froze with the foil packaged object dangling in the air. "Gaia gave me this radio. She wanted me to hide it before making contact and return to it to call in at least once every ten days. The foil wrapping is to avoid discovery in case you possess a transmitter detector. We need to hide this and ensure I report in on time. My family's lives depend on it."

River peeked at Kesa for her reaction. She made an "I don't know what the fuck" shrug and head tilt. *This is only believable because it is unbelievable. Without a doubt, John Walker did what he could to warn us of the stealth biped. Something truly freaks him out about this radio and getting moving. Truthful concern for our collective safety or playing us to get our cell location for Gaia?* "Put the device on the ground in front of you and then take five steps to your left," River said.

John Walker did as ordered, nice and slow. "Now you need to check me for transmitters. I am not aware of any, but Gaia drugs us and does as she desires. Search for scars, healing cuts, or other anomalies to suggest something implanted." He started to strip.

River grunted in frustration. *His request makes perfect sense, but I'm still not liking the chain of command in this encounter.*

Kesa taunted with a sly grin. "I'm pretty sure protocol is the team lead conducts all strip searches."

I'm pretty damn sure no such protocol exists. No matter, Kesa holds rank, and she left no doubt who should search. River cursed under his breath and stacked his rifle, pistol, and combat knife beside Kesa's cover.

John Walker had stripped naked by the time River turned to approach him. River shivered involuntarily. *An afternoon spent peering into someone's nooks* and crannies for Gaia implants is most definitely not on my list of "things I want to do before I die".

"Come along, don't be shy," John Walker said. "There's a chill in the air. As you can tell by the lack of insulating fat on me, Gaia is annoyingly precise about providing the exact calories needed to stay alive and work. Actually, she is annoyingly precise about everything, but that is a future conversation."

River steeled himself. *I must do what it takes to hide the home and protect the home. What kind of Cave Cell soldier and team lead am I if I dodge this duty?* He began the unpleasant task of poking and prodding every part of John Walker, who cooperated fully.

"Palpate the scars, no matter how old they look," John Walker said, "since Gaia may have snuck something under them."

Finished, River returned to Kesa's side and splashed water from his canteen to wash. He muttered to Kesa as he picked up his gear. "I didn't perceive anything amiss. He has plenty of scars related to doing Gaia's bidding. She couldn't care less about worker safety."

Kesa kept John Walker in her sights. "So, is he the real deal or part of a Gaia plot?"

"I think he's legit, but Gaia can layer her plans," River said. "John Walker might be 100% honest with us, but be an unknowing pawn in a secret secondary plan. Only she knows her grand strategy."

Kesa chuckled. "Your sister's game theory rants are soaking in. Are we taking him to Cave Cell or not?"

"Yeah, you're right, my sister is getting in my head," River said. "Let's take him to a resting place ten clicks out from the Cave and set up a meeting with an elder."

Kesa geared up, slinging her rifle for transport and pulling her pistol out to cover John Walker. "We have a near-field detection receiver. It will make sure Gaia didn't implant something you didn't find when you groped him."

She placed a lot of emphasis on "groped". Dammit, what happened in the forest isn't going to stay in the forest. "I'm not going to appreciate how you choose to tell this story to Cave Cell, am I?" River asked.

John Walker finished dressing. "Nothing to be ashamed of. You did what you needed to protect your cell. Besides, your touch is surprisingly gentle for one with such strong hands." He finished with an exaggerated lascivious wink, making River blush and provoking peals of laughter from Kesa. After she quieted, John Walker held out his hand to River. "Those who know me

196

call me Walker John or just Walker, since I believe we have achieved that stage in our relationship."

River pursed his lips and shook John Walker's hand. *I'm not sure I want what just happened to signify the start of a friendship, but so be it.*

Walker John gestured at the foil package. "Can we hide the transmitter and go to your cell? We're giving Gaia too much time to bring in more minions."

"Agreed. We need to get moving," River replied. "I will handle the transmitter. Kesa, take Walker John to the others. I will join soon so we can gear up and move."

"Wilco." Kesa tilted her head in the direction she wanted Walker John to walk.

River watched them walk until he lost visibility through the forest. *I can't see you, you can't see me. Now, what's in this foil?* He flipped open the edge of the foil wrap with the tip of his knife. *There's a radio inside just as Walker John said, nothing more. It's off if I accept the power switch setting and the dark display at face value, but Gaia may have modified the innards to operate always-on. After Cave Cell's training to avoid transmitting devices, being near this radio makes me feel like there's a Hellfire targeting laser on me.* Folding the foil back down, he picked it up and scanned the surrounding terrain. A rock outcropping fifty meters away had an abundance of holes and cracks. He jogged to it and parked his rifle against a tree. *This looks like a 5.10a sport climb, very difficult for a non-climber and hopefully Gaia's bipeds. Perhaps something stashed high in the face will be outside Gaia's search consideration set.* As a skilled climber, River free soloed up ten meters to stash the foil package out of sight in a hole sloped upward and deep enough to stay dry.

Hustling as quickly as the terrain allowed, River returned to where they left Ava and Carter. Carter still sat where they had parked him earlier, but leaned far forward with his head in his hands.

"He's mostly back in touch with reality but says he's groggy and his head aches like there's no tomorrow," Ava said. "Your new friend Walker John is digging a hole for Kesa to stash the stealth biped parts in."

"What do you mean 'new friend'?" River asked. *Has Kesa already had time to tell her story?* "Forget it," he said before Ava answered, walking over to Kesa and Walker John.

Kesa waved a greeting with her free hand while covering Walker John with a pistol.

Walker John had pushed over a rock and was digging a hole beneath it, flinging the dirt far and wide to conceal the excavation work. "Prisoner labor or voluntary?" River asked.

"What? He offered to help," Kesa said.

Kona helped him dig. River smiled at the dog's industrious digging. *She must think Walker John is OK. That's plus one on the trust scale.*

River kneeled by the pile of choice biped parts destined for the stash hole. He picked up a slab of armor to examine. A furry layer of tiny octagons and nanowires interspersed with tiny fiber optic sensors covered the exterior.

Ava noticed him handling the armor. "The fur is heating wires and thermochromic material to enable the near instant color changes. The sensors take in the surrounding color and texture from every angle. Chloe read about this technology in an old tech enthusiast magazine I scavenged for her; she felt it necessary to share the info with me . . . in great detail. They published a story about the crude initial system in the early 2020s developed in Korea. We found it peculiar there wasn't any follow-ups with further improvements, but what we see here is a far more advanced system."

River gathered the parts to take them to Walker John's hiding place. "Grandpy Max mentioned that large military contractors secretly developed most of Gaia's surprise technology." He and Walker John placed the pieces in the hole and moved the rock back overtop, replacing it in the original position to hide any sign of disturbance. River made mental note of key landmarks in case Sophia and Willow ended up wanting these parts.

"The other parts?" River asked the group.

"I slung the heavy bastard over my shoulders and carried it down to the treeline due east of the chemical plant." Ava said. "It's stuck between a big rock and a tree two hundred meters away where Gaia won't have any problem finding it. I covered my tracks to and from here, so she won't have any clues pointing to our stash."

"Well done, thanks," River said, dusting off his hands. "Time to move. Ava, take point and help Carter. You two will set the pace. I'll carry both your carbines. Walker John, you'll stay ten meters behind them. Kesa, cover Walker John. I'll be on rear guard." Noticing Carter's pack on the ground, he gritted his teeth. *Damn it, who can manage the extra weight?*

Walker John followed his gaze. "The boy shouldn't bear that weight in his condition. Let me take his pack."

River nodded his assent, glancing to make sure Carter's pistol and combat knife were still on him rather than in his pack.

Throughout the hike, River listened to Kesa pushing for information. Walker John talked amiably about his family's life before Gaia raided his cell and captured them two years ago. He refused to provide details about his captivity, insisting that the Gaia information was his sole bargaining chip to save his family.

River split his time between watching their six, scanning rear left and rear right, and monitoring Kona for any alerts. To his relief, the only stress Kona showed was barking at the chittering squirrels as she passed below their trees.

CHAPTER THIRTY-THREE – 21:00 June 7, 2070 – A Critical Conversation

Be brave enough to start a conversation that matters.
Margaret Wheatley

River felt the gnawing tension of knowing you need to move faster but being unable to. Limited to a pace reasonable for concussed Carter, the hike to a resting place ten klicks out from the Cave took an hour longer than usual. Blindfolding Walker John for the final two klicks and having to help him navigate made the slow pace even slower. *It was easier when I could assume that Gaia on my trail meant crashing through the bush in a running firefight. With Walker's information and seeing a stealth biped myself, now I have to fear Gaia choosing to lurk in the distance.*

In the dying daylight, the resting place looked even less like a camp than it was. Cave Cell rarely built actual camps, and never took strangers to those. This area was better called "somewhere we rest." It had good forest canopy cover, rocks and downed logs to sit on, and clean running water nearby. There was no fire pit or other visible improvements. Cave Cell kept this area undisturbed, since Gaia couldn't glean clues about Cave Cell's whereabouts if there weren't any clues to find.

Walker John scanned the resting place. He showed no surprise at the complete lack of development. "My cell was careful, too," he said when he noticed River watching his reaction.

Kesa waved River over to talk privately once Walker John, Ava, and Carter sat to share water and food. "Carter needs a medical check and we need to alert the elders ASAP. Do you prefer to travel to the Cave with your team, or stay here and guard Walker John while I lead them back?"

"My preference is to stay here," River said. "I overheard you getting nowhere with Gaia intel. I want to try."

Kesa smiled. "Good luck. My impression is he is pretty sharp and intends to take the intel to his grave if Cave Cell won't help his family. How about a little wager? You get my next share of cake if you extract any useful intel before we line up an elder to talk to him, but I get yours if you fail."

River shook his head. "A month ago, I wouldn't have hesitated to take that bet. After the strawberry honey cake Abas and Ethan made yesterday, I know what real cake tastes like so won't risk losing a single bite. Anyway, I'm not confident about learning any information, just want to try."

"How disappointing," Kesa said, mocking sadness. "I was looking forward to a double serving." Charade abandoned, she continued. "I'll take Carter's M4. No need having unattended firearms around to confuse our guest. We'll leave Carter's pack for the next team. Walker John can use the extra rations, by the way his skin hangs on his face. Keep sharp and listen for Reaper surveillance, since we're still not sure if he is being tracked or not."

"Wilco," River said, turning to address the team. "Kesa is leading you home while I stay here with Walker John."

Ava sat where she could lean against a tree, mechanically sipping water. She managed a thumbs-up to acknowledge.

Carter perched on a log, leaning forward with his head held between his hands. He complained of a worsening headache as the day progressed.

Kona took full advantage of the free time in unfamiliar territory. The scents deposited by passing creatures riveted her to a tiny prickle bush.

Kesa, Ava, and Carter departed a half hour later. Under Cave Cell protocol, they headed in the wrong direction until out of sight to protect the Cave's location. Kona stood at the edge of camp, glancing between the three leaving and River. She dove into the brush in pursuit after River motioned toward the departing.

"She's worth her weight in gold, if gold still had value. Who knows what B&B Cell could have done with the seconds or minutes of warning she would have provided," Walker John said.

Here's my opening. Given the resistance Kesa encountered, I need to avoid direct questions about Gaia's facility and capabilities. "If you don't mind sharing," River asked, "please tell me about your cell. What was the location like?"

River read Walker John's expression as aware of a game afoot but willing to play it to keep the peace.

Walker John leaned back against the tree he sat by and stared off into the distance. "Since there's no longer a home to hide or protect, there's no harm in sharing. To outsiders, we called ourselves Bee Cell to avoid giving a clue to our location. Among ourselves, we were B&B Cell. Not bed & breakfast like the old folks assume, but B&B because of the name on the warehouse we called home. The location was perfect. The tons of rubble in the area from tornados and the wars made it hard for Gaia's minions to travel. A nearby green belt through the mostly destroyed city provided foraging options. A stream passed close by and a large river was only a day's hike away."

Walker John paused and closed his eyes. "B&B Cell was on the outskirts of a nearly deserted, massive city. Our elders contended three million people lived in there. I never believed countless people could live close to each other in peace and forage enough food and water from the area. Anyway, enough buildings stood scattered in the city to provide ample scavenging opportunities. We even met to trade with two other cells and share information. We stuck to the Dunbar number and totaled a hundred forty-eight souls on our last day. B&B Cell was a family. Friction happened, but you took care of each other regardless of differences and disagreements. Life was hard, but well worth living."

Walker John's story enthralled River. Cave Cell received news on rare occasions from people traveling through Cave Cell territory. Regular contact with other cells didn't happen. He leaned forward, willing Walker John to continue.

"That's where I picked up the name Walker John. When I joined the cell ten years ago, there were already two men named John. We kept things simple and flipped my first and last name. Folks in the cell soon just called me Walker."

River's curiosity was killing him. "What happened to B&B Cell? How did Gaia find you?"

"We never learned how she found us," Walker John said, shrugging. "I returned from foraging for plants and berries in the forest with three teammates. We climbed up a row of rubble that provided a natural wall around our building. A cargo drone swarm dropped bipeds and cheetahs everywhere. They surrounded my team by the time we worked our way down the rubble. A biped demanded we surrender or they would kill ten of their prisoners before killing us. Since they had already rounded almost everyone up, we surrendered."

River's eyes widened and eyebrows raised. *Damn, it's hard to keep a poker face when you hear disturbing news. I'm going to have to work on that.* "Cargo drones carrying a biped's weight? I didn't know those existed. Wasn't anyone able to fight?"

Walker John's tone hardened. "Yeah, rumor among the slaves was a local cargo drone maker couldn't destroy all of its inventory. Gaia got control of forty high lift capacity drones." He met River's gaze. "I realize what you're doing. I don't blame you for trying to get information, since I would do the same for my cell if our roles were reversed. We're done talking about anything that leads to more intel about Gaia. Information is all I have to bargain with your elders for my wife's and daughter's lives."

"Honestly, I started out intending to get information, but B&B Cell's story pulled me in," River said. "I won't try to get anything else out of you. Did B&B Cell get a Blu-ray player running? My cell has. Can we talk about movies to pass the time?"

Walker John smiled in appreciation for the topic change. "Yeah, we got a player running. I watched the Hobbit and Lord of the Rings movies at least ten times, I never tired of the break from our reality. What's your favorite?"

River and Walker John passed the next few hours talking movies.

At 01:00, Willow's voice came from the surrounding darkness. "Free survivors approaching, all clear?"

"All clear, Willow," River shouted.

Willow and Sophia emerged from cover a minute later. Willow held her rifle at low ready whereas Sophia's hung muzzle down slung across her back. Sophia carried a black plastic watertight case the size of a daypack with "Pelican Storm" emblazoned on it. This got River's attention. *I haven't seen that case before; what's in it? Where's the elder, staying at a safe distance with another soldier until Sophia calls them in?*

Willow smiled at River and gave him a quick nod. *I am happy to see you safe to, sis.*

Sophia was all business. She nearly ran him over, bustling by and barking, "Make way, River." After putting the case on the ground a meter away from Walker John, she pressed and pulled to pop open the two strong latches. She positioned the case so the lid swung open to block Walker John's view of the interior.

Walker John stared at her apprehensively, glancing at River as though hoping to get a hint of what came next.

Not even aware he had held his breath, River exhaled in relief when he viewed the contents. The box contained a handheld device with a screen and a variety of odd shaped black objects. They ranged from screwdriver size to a triangular item a hand and a half in size. None of them displayed the metallic sharp or blunt edges expected of torture instruments.

Sophia attached the triangular black object to the handheld and powered it up. While getting ready, she addressed Walker John. "Fair to assume you are Walker John?"

He tilted his head slowly, watching Sophia's every move.

"OK. Don't move," she said. "I will sweep very close but not touch you."

After he identified the device, the concern in Walker John's face faded. "Oh, of course, a transmitter detector," he said. "I'm glad you brought one. River checked me for implants, but he could only do so much. I hope your kit includes all the antennae and probes necessary to cover the full signal range?"

Sophia chuckled while she swept the antenna all around Walker John. "Yes, I heard all about River and his strong hands checking you for implants. Fear not, this is a full kit." She winked at River when she moved behind Walker John's field of view.

River blushed. *Did Kesa delay the team bringing the elder just to share her new favorite tale?*

Sophia cycled through another four antennae and probes. After the last sweep, she turned to Willow. "Nothing, he's clean."

River sighed with relief. *I don't want to contribute in any way to Gaia finding the Cave.*

"I didn't think she implanted anything," Walker John said. "It would jeopardize the mission she set for me. Good to confirm, though, because she considers us similar to how we view the animals we raise to slaughter for food. Her sole consideration of whether to implant is mission success. We can't comprehend the multitude of variables feeding into her decisions."

Willow signaled to River. "You're on watch. I'll fetch the others." She left as soon as River nodded and brought his rifle to low ready.

Willow disappeared into the forest. Walker John glanced at Sophia; she was busy packing up the near-field detector. He prodded River in a quiet tone, avoiding whispering to make Sophia suspicious, but still subtle. "Your elders, what kind of people are they?"

River understood Walker John's concern, since his future depended on the outcome of the upcoming discussion. *Whether or not Sophia is listening, I'm certainly not going to give Walker John any information to help him mislead the elders. But I still believe Walker John is doing his best to subvert Gaia's plan.* "Our elders have been protecting our cell for many years. Whichever one shows up, just tell them the truth without holding anything back. They will treat you fairly."

Walker John nodded his thanks and said no more, sitting with his brow creased in thought.

Sophia snapped the Pelican's latches closed and stood beside River. "Excellent answer to his question," she whispered. "We want his full cooperation."

River, always suspecting she had overheard, was glad she approved. As a new team lead for Cave Cell, the senior team leads scrutinized his actions and decisions for opportunities for improvement.

A couple minutes later, torchlight and the noise of the bush being pushed through announced a group's approach. The composition startled River. *All three elders came? I expected one, maybe two at most. The elders must consider Walker John's information significant to want to hear it firsthand, putting them all at risk.*

The elders made themselves comfortable in a semicircle around Walker John. River, Willow, and Sophia guarded the gathering, albeit for outside threats more than from Walker John. The other six soldiers accompanying the elders melted into the bush to guard a hundred meter perimeter. River chose a post two meters behind the elders. *There's no way I am missing this conversation.*

Althea kicked things off, scrutinizing Walker John. "Greetings, Walker John, I am Althea. To my left is Robert and to my right is Max. We are the three cell elders. Kesa advised Gaia imprisons your family and that you want to petition us in that regard. We cannot consider requests until we listen to your complete story, starting from the beginning."

River cringed. *Now the hammer and the anvil collide. Althea's not one to bend and Walker John won't give up his bargaining chip before securing help for his family.*

"I hoped to trade my information for a commitment to rescue my family," Walker John said reluctantly. "Reconsidering the situation from your perspective, I realize you can't obligate your cell to such an unknown up front. I will share everything and hope you conclude that helping my family is beneficial to your cell."

Walker John's about face shocked River. *I didn't see that coming. Too bad it's not the time or place to congratulate Althea on strong-arming Walker John.*

"We're glad you can understand our position. Please go ahead," Robert said.

Walker John shared B&B Cell's story. The elders let signs of surprise and dismay slip through their affectation of calm when he mentioned the heavy lift drones.

Walker John continued onward from where he cut off with River. "By day's end, Gaia wiped B&B Cell out. She captured a hundred twenty of us and killed the twenty-eight that fought her. Those resisting destroyed a biped, three cheetahs, and two heavy lift drones. Gaia scooped up the parts of her deactivated minions and left our dead where they lay. She ignored our pleadings to bury them and to gather food and other belongings from the warehouse. She force-marched the captured to a wind farm a few hours southwest of B&B Cell and imprisoned us in a camp that already held eighty slaves."

"Gaia enslaved two hundred?" Grandpy Max asked, his voice strained. "How did we not hear about this?"

That got River's attention. *Grandpy Max prides himself on staying informed and keeping the facts straight; he isn't happy about missing out on critical information. So, this is news to the elders?*

Walker John stared at Grandpy Max for a few seconds, seeming unsure how to answer. "Perhaps evidence will aid in understanding," he said. "May I show something on my neck?" When the elders nodded, he turned around on his knees and lifted his medium length hair away from his neck.

The motion puzzled River. *What's there to show? I touched his neck under his hair, but didn't see it when searching for implants. Nothing felt unusual.*

"My wife and daughter are the next two numbers in sequence. Others in our work camp vary higher or lower by hundreds or even thousands," Walker John said, displaying the back of his neck.

The elders gasped, then froze in silence.

Never having heard or seen anything that shut them down like this, River peeked over Grandpy Max's shoulder. Walker John exhibited a precision black ink tattoo on the upper back of his neck. A box four centimeters square with thousands of smaller seemingly random boxes in it formed the top of the tattoo. Below the box appeared the number 49,654.

River understood the elders' shocked silence. *Walker John told us there are about two hundred slaves in his camp, but his Gaia tattoo suggests she has near fifty thousand . . . maybe more?*

[End Book One The Singularity]

STATUS QUO - MASON

CHAPTER THIRTY-FOUR – 12:00 June 7, 2070 – Raiders of the Furthest Garden

A thousand known enemies are better than one unknown enemy.
Mouloud Benzadi

Mason shepherded Ava and Chloe toward the infirmary. The rough-hewn rock hallway was dimly lit by an LED light string hanging from the two meter high ceiling. To conserve inventory, the valuable LED bulbs filled only every second socket in the hallways. Cave Family leader Althea was waiting for them, pacing back and forth. Mason found this curious. *What's up with Althea? She usually exemplifies calm, cool, and collected.*

"Ava, Chloe, thank goodness you're here," said Althea. "I appreciate you finding them, Mason." Ten minutes ago, Mason ran into Althea as she searched for Ava and Chloe. She grabbed him as he passed by and told him to find them fast and bring them to the infirmary.

Althea stared at Ava and Chloe as if trying to judge their fitness for a particular purpose. "Zoey's injured. She was harvesting alone in our furthest garden when two people attacked her. They stole the harvest and left her semiconscious. She got close enough to the Cave that the kids on gathering duty spotted her. Isabella took command and sent someone for help while she and the others assisted Zoey."

Ava grabbed Althea's arm. "Oh no, will Zoey be OK?"

Ava's reaction triggered something in Althea, since her demeanor shifted to her regular calm. She patted Ava's hand. "Yes, Dr. Ren patched her up, and she is resting in the infirmary."

Mason glanced into the infirmary, but from his poor angle he couldn't see Zoey.

"I'm having trouble narrowing the possibilities of why you wanted us. Umm, I mean, what can we do to help?" Chloe asked.

Althea paused and pursed her lips before speaking. "You three are the only ones available that took part in the murdering bandit hunt. We need you to listen to Zoey's account and advise if your bandits were involved."

After everyone nodded in assent, Althea motioned them into the infirmary. Cave Family chose the infirmary cave from among the bone dry caves of sufficient size. It held four treatment beds, various medical equipment, and supplies, all scavenged. The Cave included triple the usual LED light strings for proper task lighting. Cave Family's medic, Renxiang, checked Zoey's bandages. Renxiang earned her paramedic certification just before the world fell apart. With few doctors available, it thrilled Cave Family to have Renxiang serve as their de facto doctor, even calling her "Dr. Ren".

Mason nodded at Renxiang; she smiled in return. Mason assisted here often to build his skills as a medic for missions.

Zoey had a vicious black eye and other facial bruising. "Zoey, are you OK?" Ava asked. "Those bruises look painful."

Zoey smiled weakly. "I've been worse. Dr. Ren worked her magic, so I'm feeling better than when those poor kids found me. I must have scared the hell out of them."

Althea interjected before Ava could continue. "Zoey, these three saw the bandits last week. Can you describe your attackers so we can determine if it's the same people?"

"Yes, anything I can do to help prevent anyone else from Cave Family being hurt." Zoey shifted around in the bed.

Mason feared the visible bruising on her face was nowhere near the full extent of her injuries.

Zoey closed her eyes before beginning. "I was harvesting vegetables from the northeast far garden. They stepped out from the thick brush at the edge of the garden when I neared. One male and one female, each late twenties or early thirties. They wore scruffier and dirtier clothing than what we manage for the family. Both brandished rifles, the male a hunting rifle with a scope and the female an AK-74 with iron sights. The female stepped forward and struck me hard in the face with her rifle butt as I greeted them. I got a close look at its laminated wood, and then things were pretty blurry. I remember getting kicked and struck with what I assume were their rifle butts before I lost consciousness for a short time." Zoey opened her eyes, but lowered her gaze to her legs to avoid eye contact.

Chloe put her hand on Zoey's shoulder. "There was nothing you could do. They intended to knock you out from the beginning. Can you describe their faces and hair?"

Zoey raised her chin. "Someone cut the man's black hair a few centimeters long. The cut was uneven, like they used a hunting knife. The female's hair was dark brown and pulled back in a braid."

"You didn't mention scars or tattoos. Did you notice any markings on their face or exposed skin?" Ava asked.

Ava's line of questioning impressed Mason. *Good strategy, delving for details without influencing Zoey's recollection of the attackers. Were Scar or Snake the male attacker?*

Zoey paused for a few seconds, trying to recall. "No, I didn't see any scars or intentional markings like tattoos."

Chloe glanced at Ava and Mason and proceeded after they remained quiet. "We encountered different men. The mid-thirties group leader had a long scar down his face. You couldn't miss it even with a quick glance, so we called him Scar. One of the others had shoulder-length brown hair and a snake tattoo on his forearm. He's the age range Zoey mentioned, but the hair color, hair length, and tattoo are a mismatch. The last of our three was younger than Zoey's attackers. Last, and I hate to say it, but from what we know, the bandits we trapped killed or enslaved their victims. They didn't just beat people up and steal their belongings."

Althea took Zoey's hand in hers. "Although I am so sorry for asking you to relive the attack, your description was a great help. Rest now. I will speak with these three in the corridor."

Ava and Chloe got the hint, heading out to the corridor after wishing Zoey a quick recovery and waving goodbye to Renxiang. Althea followed.

Renxiang motioned for Mason to stay, waiting for Ava and Chloe to leave before speaking quietly. "When you are available, please return so I can show you how I treated Zoey and how we will support her healing. We hope this won't happen again, but best to be prepared."

This confirmed Mason's suspicion that Zoey's injuries were serious. "Of course, Dr. Ren." He winked at Zoey, which she rewarded with a quick smile. *She's Cave Family strong, she'll pull through this.*

In the hall, Althea gestured for the group to huddle. "Mason, we need you to lead a team out to the furthest garden and hunt down Zoey's attackers," she said. "Take Ava, Chloe, and Noah. He is due back in a couple of hours. I'd suggest you meet him at the Cave entrance. He's a boulder rolling down a steep slope on mission but grows deep roots awful fast if you let him get comfortable."

After hearing Zoey's account, Mason had expected this. "We'll take care of it. Should we deal with these two permanently, or are we to consider other options?"

Ava's eyes widened at the question, whereas Chloe peered at Althea.

"We're trusting your instincts," Althea said.

Mason nodded in understanding. *This is becoming a regular thing. The Reckoning must have been tough times for the leaders to so strongly want to prevent it from repeating.*

"I suggest you err on the side of caution," Althea said, "but I am an old woman with little faith in humanity. On that note, watch for connections between these bandit groups that have appeared at the same time." She squeezed Mason's arm, to which he smiled in return. Over the years, a deep understanding of each other had developed. She preferred to give advice for consideration instead of explicit orders.

Althea, not one to waste time on social niceties, waved goodbye and hustled to her next task.

Ava and Chloe stared at Mason. He led with an inquiry. "Ava, Chloe, are you both OK with what Althea is asking? This is a single team hunt rather than a bait team and shadow team like last time."

"We can't let whoever did that to Zoey wander around in Cave Family territory," Ava said. "As a bonus, I am building a reputation as a bad ass bandit hunter."

"I am good to go. My bonus is also reputational diversification," Chloe said, keeping it somewhat simple for once.

Assigned a mission with a now verified team, assuming Noah didn't balk, Mason got down to business. "Gear up for a few nights away. We're hunting people, so arm yourself with a knife, pistol, and rifle or carbine. Althea is right about Noah. If we let him anywhere near his bed after being out in the field, we'll end up having to peel him off of it. To make sure we catch him, I'll meet you out front in an hour and a half at the latest."

"You got it, boss." Ava punched his shoulder before departing.

Chloe shrugged and followed her.

CHAPTER THIRTY-FIVE – 13:45 June 7, 2070 – A
Hunting We Will Go
The perils of duck hunting are great - especially for the duck.
Walter Cronkite

Mason, Ava, and Chloe waited in the sunshine outside the Cave entrance. It was only fifteen minutes before Noah's four-member team emerged from the forest. They had bow hunted small game; each returning with a brace of rabbits and a quiver of arrows strapped to their pack.

Mason stood up, waving to welcome them. *Ironic, the prey returns bearing prey.*

Noah glared at them. "Look, it's my friend Mason, coincidentally leaving for a mission at the same time as we return from ours. This is just a coincidence, right, Mason?"

The rest of Noah's hunting team, Taamir, Jaanvi, and Owen, settled in to watch. Whatever was playing out here was interesting enough to delay heading into the Cave.

Mason just smiled in return, then nodded at Ava and Chloe, who secured their packs and weapons.

"Really? You're gearing up now?" Noah asked. "A paranoid person would perceive an ambush." After a quick pause, he scrunched his face in displeasure. "I've been voluntold, haven't I? Was it Grandpy Max, Althea, or Robert? No matter, I need time to pack and take a quick nap."

Mason picked up the backpack sitting behind his own and held it out for Noah. "Our mission sponsor will remain anonymous," he said in a faux formal voice. "Rest assured, they hold sufficient rank to compel you to join my team." *Noah, my brother from another mother, we know you too well to let you slip away.*

The three other members of the incoming team snickered.

Noah put the offered pack on after handing his bow and small game pack with attachments to Jaanvi, grunting as he did so. "I hope you packed me clean underwear or we'll all be paying the price. Seeing your, er our, teammates armed with rifles, I should run in and get my own after five minutes of rack time. Only five minutes, I swear."

While Noah talked, Mason headed over to the tree his M110E1 sniper rifle leaned against and held out the carbine stored beside his rifle.

Noah's shoulders slumped in defeat. "How sweet. You brought me Scar's M4A1. Are you briefing me now, or as we travel to wherever?"

Mason motioned to a trail heading northeast and started walking with Ava and Chloe.

"Briefing on the move, superlative choice," Noah said, more to himself than the group.

After hiking two hours at a good pace, Mason signaled a halt. They were near the main trail junction a hundred meters away from Cave Family's northeast far garden. Extreme weather posed the largest risk to their food supply. To mitigate the risk, Cave Family planted many small gardens and grain fields rather than a few large ones. They scattered locations throughout the three hundred fifteen square kilometers within two hours' walk from the Cave. Mason had helped scout this location and prepare the plot for its first planting two years ago.

Mason briefed Noah and then the team had planned their initial recon, all while hiking. Not needing any discussion upon arrival, everyone quietly removed their packs and stashed them in the forest. Noah and Ava advanced to circle outside the garden's left, Mason and Chloe on the right.

Mason followed Chloe across the trail junction. Three plate-sized rocks were stacked on the corner of the junction leading to the Cave. *Why is there a trail marking here? Cave Family doesn't work hard to hide the way to the Cave, but neither do we mark it. The young gardening helpers taking a break must have stacked the rocks for fun. No time to fuss over this, a hunting we will go.* He pushed the marker apart with his foot as he passed.

The initial sweep concluded without finding anyone hiding around the garden. The team fetched their packs and met in the garden. They approached single file from the south to avoid obscuring any signs of the bandits' comings and goings. As luck would have it, unusually calm weather since the attack left any tracks undisturbed.

"This is likely where they attacked Zoey," Chloe said, pointing. "Many boot prints and a patch of disturbed soil where they knocked her down and beat her."

"Agreed. Now let's find their exit path. Everyone search a quadrant from this point." Mason walked slowly northwest, scanning the ground.

Noah walked southwest, toward the Cave, and motioned to the forest's edge. "Someone alternated between crawling and stumbling toward the Cave this way. It must be Zoey's trail."

Ava stepped in and out of the brush northeast of the attack site. "Here's where they laid in wait outside the garden's edge. It was a while, given how flattened the shrubs are." She stepped further into the brush. "Found it. They arrived and departed from here," she said a few seconds later. Once the team gathered, she showed them the tracks. "Two sets of boot tracks in, one set larger than the other. There's the same two sets leaving."

Noah got down on hands and knees to examine the prints in a patch of softer ground. "Ava's right. You can also tell they carried more when they left. Bigger boots holds the vegetable bag for now; those prints are deeper on the departure than incoming."

Mason tightened his pack straps to signal the team to be ready to move. "We'll follow their trail as fast as we safely can. Noah, take point and set the pace, but please do not run us full speed into the middle of their camp. Ava, cover left, Chloe, cover right. I'll take rear."

The team sprang into action, following the trail that headed northeast. After quick time traveling an hour, including a few delays where they fanned out to pick up the trail after hard ground, Noah took a knee.

Mason crouch walked up to Noah, both Ava and Chloe automatically shifting their stance to cover their half of the rear. *It's sad we need them to be good at things like this, but essential that they are, since our lives may hang in the balance.*

Noah pointed ahead through a gap in the trees. "There're structures ahead," he whispered, "a home with a large detached garage. The way these prints head, I'm sure our bandits went there."

Mason squeezed Noah's shoulder. "Well done, spotting the site from afar. You gave us a chance to approach undetected." Mason motioned Ava and Chloe to huddle up. "Same sweep, same teams as the garden. We'll meet on the opposite side unless anyone engages the bandits."

Ava shifted focus over Mason's shoulder. "Are you comfortable with the weather behind us?"

Mason looked where she had, southwest toward the Cave. There were dark clouds forming on the horizon far away. *Damn it, I fixated on human threats as rearguard and completely missed this storm front forming.* "I missed that, so thanks for bringing it up. We'll stay on mission and monitor it since it just looks like a vanilla thunderstorm so far. I want us all safe in the Cave if that storm turns into a supercell."

Everyone nodded in agreement.

"Let's do the perimeter sweep. The sooner we control this site, the sooner we leave," Mason said.

Mason and Chloe circled the right side. *This two-story house is sizeable, but nowhere near as large as the places Robert calls mansions. Broken windows and trashed interiors are the status quo for any building the tornados left standing. These solar panels are odd. Most homes have full roof coverage and no more, but the panel racking continues from the roof all the way to the ground on the south and east faces of this house. What's that all about?*

The team rendezvoused as planned at the outer perimeter of the backyard.

"No signs of bandits or other people," Ava said, still scanning. "Is this the regular solar panel coverage? Besides the garage roof, someone racked more panels to ground level on the sunny side of the garage."

Noah scratched his head and waved his hand at the panels. "The home and garage have double the usual panel coverage. Whoever lived here wanted a lot of power."

"Any bandit tracks?" Mason asked. "Chloe and I didn't spot any on our side." *As curious as these panels are, we need to stay on mission. Oh, and that storm will arrive before we know it.*

Noah pointed out a path running along the road to the house and ending at the garage's west face. "The trail we followed leads straight to the garage, but there's no sign of anyone coming back out."

"They're still in the garage? This is an excellent opportunity to trap them," Chloe said.

Mason felt the same, but kept his voice level. "For our safety, we must assume they are inside and watching out the windows for movement. We'll stay avoid line of sight from those north-facing windows and line up on the windowless east wall. Are there panel gaps for windows on the south face?"

Ava waved her hand sideways. "No, the panels are edge-to-edge roof peak to ground."

Mason paused for a few seconds. *The panels provide concealment for us to move to the man door at the front of the garage. We'll hold for intel prior to entry.* "Circle around the south face, crouching low to avoid being spotted through any

214

windows behind the gaps between panels. At the front, we'll pause beside the man door to listen for five minutes before making a dynamic entry. I will breech then follow the three of you. Chloe, with the best armor you are first in, then Noah, and Ava last. First in takes the furthest corner and so on down the line."

The team stashed their packs under a tree and moved to the garage's front as planned. Nobody sounded an alarm or fired at them.

Mason signaled the start of the five-minute wait. *I trust Noah's tracking, but they just show the bandits entered. Are they still in there? I can't hear anyone moving around, but if they are lying in ambush, they're trying to stay quiet.* After five minutes of nothingness, he scanned the team. They all shrugged, body language expressing the same puzzlement he felt at the lack of signs anyone was in the garage.

Mason gently twisted the door handle before he risked injury kicking down the door. *The door isn't locked. What's going on?* Chloe nodded when he made eye contact with her to verify readiness. He pushed the door open.

With Chloe leading, Noah and Ava rushed past him.

Mason brought his weapon up to ready position and followed the others in as they rushed to control the space. He didn't have far to go, since his corner was at the man door. The building was sixteen meters across the face with the doors and twenty-four meters long. Three windows on the south wall were dimly lit. Sunlight only made it to them through the gaps between solar panels and occasional missing panels. The three unobstructed north face windows provided most of the light in the garage.

Mason's team scanned the room with weapons at low ready. No one shouted out or fired. There weren't any bandits to confront. Mason closed the door to make things appear undisturbed to anyone outside the building. *That was anticlimactic. No contact is safe, good for the team, but it is disappointing to prepare for nothing.*

The garage contained the usual junk piles, albeit piled up against the side walls. Noah signaled for Mason to examine the floor. The only disturbances to the dusty floor on the south side were Chloe's and Noah's tracks crossing to their corners. Traffic across the north face disrupted the dust from the man door to a large cabinet on the east wall. Oddly, disturbed dust went all the way to where the cabinet and floor met.

Chloe noticed them looking at the cabinet and searched for a handle or other opening mechanism. She soon pulled a cord dangling from the top rear of the cabinet to where the others could see.

Mason waved everyone into a semicircle around the cabinet. He brought his rifle to ready, pointing at the cabinet, Noah and Ava following suit. Chloe gave the cord a slow but firm tug when Mason nodded. Something clicked inside, the front face of the cabinet popping open a few centimeters. Chloe grabbed the now exposed door edge and pulled it wide open.

Mason grunted. *Another rush of adrenalin and no action.* The cabinet was empty; it didn't have shelves or even a bottom panel. There was just a seventy-five centimeter diameter hole in the garage floor the closed cabinet had concealed. The hole became real dark, real fast. Visibility ended barely an arm's length down from the top. Rungs mounted in cement started at ground level and descended into the darkness.

Noah caught Mason's eye, shrugged, and hand signaled for talking.

Mason nodded in agreement. He shouted toward the hole, "We followed you here. Drop your weapons and come up or we're coming down shooting."

Complete silence. Mason shifted around, the few minutes wait dragging on like an hour, but still no noise, no light, and nobody climbing the ladder.

Chloe huddled close. "You brought a flashlight, right? Let's hang it by a string, so it seems one of us is coming down the ladder holding it. If the bandits are below, they'll shoot where they think the person who holds the light is located."

Morgan passed her the treasured flashlight issued to him for this mission.

She attached a roll of string, clicked the light on, and lowered it in a manner to mimic someone holding it while descending. Mason peeked over the edge. The bouncing light revealed a concrete floor four meters below. The earthy smell of soil wafted up. Silence reigned.

"Aim the beam away from the ladder," Mason whispered to Chloe. "I'll drop into the dark." He handed his rifle to Ava, checked his pistol, and descended the ladder as quickly as he could without making noise. Crouching below the flashlight with his pistol at high ready, he scanned the room as the light beam danced. The light didn't show anyone. Mason grabbed the light for a more deliberate scan. The two-and-a-half-meter high concrete room measured eight meters by twelve meters. Raised table trays filled with soil and dead plants ran in rows end-to-end, with light fixtures above them.

"Clear." Mason advanced to make room at the bottom.

Once down, Chloe whistled in appreciation. "This is a professional setup, most likely hydroponic to start with, but switched over to soil when the seventeen nutrient specialized hydroponic fertilizer ran out."

"Well, this explains the multitude of panels," Ava said. "The delicate plants grow protected down here. Up top, you only need to keep enough of the sturdy panels running to power your grow lights. Much better to repair panels after a storm versus starting over with the garden. Cave Family should restore this facility."

Noah held his hand up in the air. "Does anyone else notice a slight draft? It feels like it's coming from the northwest corner."

Mason advanced in that direction with the flashlight. The light revealed a corridor heading due west. Intermittently aiming the beam to checking his footing on the way, he lit a large area of disturbed dust littered with carrot tops.

"Hey, those are our carrots," Ava said. "They rested here and ate our carrots."

Chloe was on her knees, examining where their prey had rested. "Mason, give me some light under this cabinet. I see the edge of something fluttering."

When he directed the light where requested, Chloe reached under the cabinet and plucked a piece of paper that had drifted there. She turned the paper toward the light. "Some markings and numbers. I'll take a closer look when we're safe." She tucked it deep into a pocket.

Noah walked toward the corridor with his carbine at low ready. "The prints head into this corridor and don't return."

Here we go again, Mason thought. *I'm betting the rest of the team is as tired as I am of tactical movement for no reason. We have to suck it up, since ignoring protocols is how people get killed.* He signaled everyone to stack up in the same order used for the garage entry. With everyone in position, he clicked off the flashlight. The team stood in the dark for a minute, listening. *Dead quiet again; this is becoming a thing.*

Mason crouched low and quietly crossed the corridor opening. Once across, he turned on the flashlight and held it around the corner to both draw fire and light the corridor. No bullets whizzed past, hit the flashlight, or pounded into the wall past his corner. Nothing.

Chloe, Noah, and Ava moved out in a crouch walk along the wall, weapons ready to fire down the corridor. Mason moved in behind and held the flashlight up high to light the way. The corridor was the same unpainted concrete as the grow room. It ran straight west for a hundred meters. At the end, a concrete tunnel headed up, with metal rungs poking out of the concrete to form a ladder. There was a closed metal trapdoor at the top.

Without hesitation, Ava and Chloe leaned their rifles against the wall and readied their pistols.

"Since you led down the last hole, we're first up this one," Ava said in response to Mason's questioning look.

Mason set the flashlight on the floor to light the ladder. He raised his rifle to cover the opening above. "If you need to fall back, Noah and I will cover you."

Noah mirrored Mason's ready stance as Ava and Chloe scrambled up the ladder. At the top, Chloe set up with three points of contact and a drawn pistol while Ava flipped the cover open.

Mason, Noah, and Chloe all stared at the exposed sky with weapons drawn and waited for a gun to appear and rain bullets down on them. None came.

Ava drew her pistol and popped up just enough to gain line of sight on the area surrounding the exit. She did a three-sixty degree scan. "Nothing to see here, so you can start breathing again."

Mason took a deep breath and lowered his weapon. *Did Ava know we were all waiting with bated breath or was she guessing?*

After everyone climbed up, Noah did a quick perimeter check for tracks. Finishing the sweep, he pointed northeast. "They continued along their prior direction. This place is a resting spot, not their home."

Mason peered northeast. "There aren't any signs of movement. The bandits are long gone." He turned back toward the Cave. The storm was growing, a front of heavy rainfall preceded a massive cloud growing taller with an anvil shape forming. *Is that rotation? I must be seeing things, since it's too far away to tell. Regardless, there's definitely a supercell headed our way.*

CHAPTER THIRTY-SIX – 17:45 June 7, 2070 – The Way Back Isn't Always Easier

If you know you're going home, the journey is never too hard.
Angela Wood
Angela Wood never had to run home with a supercell on top of her.
Chloe Hill, 2070
People live in a place called Tornado Alley - and they're surprised when they get hit by a tornado. I'm sorry when they get hit by tornadoes, but when you live in Tornado Alley you can't really claim surprise.
Carlos Mencia, 2009

Mason paced in the tall grasses around the trapdoor. They had closed it, everyone agreeing that if Cave Family wanted the underground garden, they had best protect it from the weather. *This sucks; we missed the bandits and now a killer storm is heading our way. Should we chase the bandits and risk dying in the storm? Hunker down in the underground bunker? Make a run for the Cave? Chloe has been studying storm behavior, so maybe she knows the risk?* "Chloe, how much time before the nasty part of the storm hits the Cave?"

She tapped her finger on her chin. "Umm, I estimate the supercell will reach the Cave in three and a half hours. Heavy rain will precede the supercell by an hour."

Mason glanced at Ava and Noah. "Anyone disagree?"

They both shook their heads.

"If we follow the bandits, we may or may not catch them, but will endanger our lives in the storm," Mason said. "Even worse, they are familiar with this territory and have a head start. If we shelter in this bunker, we risk armed unfriendlies showing up. I say we return to the Cave. If we leave now and meet or beat our prior pace, we'll be safe before the worst of the storm hits. Comments?"

Mason glanced at Ava and Chloe. Neither spoke nor signaled disagreement with his plan. He shifted his gaze to Noah.

"I'm not liking the option of racing after prey that may set up an ambush," Noah said. "This bunker is stormproof and defensible, but anyone could nullify our solid position by controlling both exits and smoking us out." He engaged his carbine's safety. "Race you to the packs!" He took off, running full tilt to where they had stashed their packs.

Ava and Chloe stared dully at Noah's departing back.

Mason engaged his rifle's safety. *They have been on high stress missions and believe we have a rigid code of behavior.* "Get him," he said, sprinting after Noah.

The first two hours of the return trip passed without incident. They made better time traveling the now familiar ground without burning time tracking bandits. Water rising in the nearby river was the first sign of the impending storm. Soon after, the heavy rains started. Water rained down in sheets, soaking the team. Mason, on rear guard, took extra care to monitor behind them. Shifting his gaze forward after one of his frequent scans rearward, he almost walked right into Ava. She had stopped dead in her tracks and was staring upriver.

"Hold," Mason said to Noah and Chloe. They halted and looked back. "What is it, Ava?" Mason asked.

"Listen." Ava continued to look upriver.

At first barely audible above the storm, but getting louder each cycle, there were a few high-pitched barks followed by a brief howl.

"Sounds like a wolf in distress," Noah said.

Seconds later, a wolf with a black upper coat fading to white legs came into view on the opposite bank. The wolf was medium large, about forty-five kilograms and eighty centimeters at the shoulder. The wolf ran up and down the riverbank, barking and howling while keeping pace with a particular piece of flotsam in the turbulent river.

Mason squinted to see better through the rain. Two small gray shapes scrabbled to stay attached to a large branch. "There are wolf pups in the water and mom following," he yelled above the howling storm and pointed. *These three look awfully like members of the pack living by the Cave. The family likes to share pack sightings, especially of the pups.*

Boots tumbled to the ground in front of Mason, surprising him. Ava dropped her pack, piled her pistol and rifle on top of it, and ran barefoot to the river.

Mason started to say, "Ava, we don't have time," but trailed off when she jumped into the river and swam toward the pups. He looked at Noah and Chloe for any insight.

Chloe stood with her arms crossed, expression saying "this is classic Ava."

Noah just shrugged. "Seems a great time for a swim. Perhaps I will join her?" He bent to unlace his boots but didn't follow through, winking at Mason instead.

Mason sighed. *What would it take for Noah to be concerned? Apparently, being trapped in the open under a supercell while a teammate goes swimming isn't enough. Well, we're sure the hell not abandoning her. No choice except to play this through.* "Noah, get our rope out of your pack. Chloe, find a piece of wood just heavy enough to give the rope throwing weight."

As Ava swam past the halfway point to the branch with the pups, Mason spotted a shifting red mass on a collision course. He pointed and asked, "Is that?"

"Ava, fire ant raft. Ant raft!" Chloe yelled overtop Mason's question.

Mason agreed with Chloe. The ants grab each other to form a floating mass to survive flooding. Ava turned toward the team when they yelled, but from her puzzled expression couldn't discern their words. She did, however, look to where they pointed. She dove under water as the ant raft approached her and popped up upstream of it, now closer to the wolf pups.

Mason peered at the sky, wondering if the worst of the storm approached. The heavy rain preceding the supercell obscured its proximity. *At least I can't see any funnel clouds yet.*

The mother wolf's barking and howling became more frantic the closer Ava got to her pups. Fortunately, the pups didn't give a damn about Ava, since they focused on clinging to the branch. Ava swam up, grabbing the end of the branch furthest from the pups. She pushed the pup branch in front of her as she swam toward the opposite shore.

As the branch neared shore, the mother wolf stopped her distress calls and instead paced the shore and shallows. The moment the branch entered shallow water, she ran out to grab each pup by the scruff of the neck and toss it to shore. As the pups shook water off themselves, the mother wolf stared at Ava and barked twice. She climbed the bank and issued a low, deep howl penetrating the noise of the storm. An answer coming from upriver, the wolves melted into the forest.

Ava kept the branch to aid the return swim. She took increasingly frequent breaks as she battled back across the rushing river.

"She won't ask for help," Mason said, "but I'm pretty sure she'll grab a rope if it lands nearby. Noah, can you toss it to her?"

Chloe grabbed the rope from Noah. "I've got this." She started spinning the weighted end of the rope above her head, letting more rope out as she increased the spinning speed. Noah ducked low, skittering outside the spin area to stand beside Mason. After the rope and weight were only a blur, Chloe released. The weighted end of the rope landed one arm's length upstream from Ava.

Relief plain on her face, Ava grabbed the rope.

Mason glanced sidelong at Noah. "She's throwing the rope if I need a water rescue."

"Hell yeah, same here," Noah said.

Chloe grunted as she pulled the rope. "The muscle mass of a couple XY chromosome bodies would be beneficial." Noah and Mason stared at her blankly. "A little help here, please," she said louder.

Mason felt embarrassed Chloe had to prod. He grabbed the rope, with Noah right behind him.

Now that all three of her teammates hauled in rope, Ava sped across the water and soon stood ashore with them. "Did you see?" she asked. "The mother wolf stared right at me with her yellow eyes and barked 'thank you'."

Chloe snorted. "You speak wolf? Maybe she said, 'I was going to take care of business before you risked your team in a storm'."

Noah laughed at Chloe's burn.

The storm clock ticked away in Mason's head. "Making the rescue was a bad judgement call, but well executed. Now we need to focus on getting the team to safety. Everyone gear up and head for the Cave. We're an hour out."

Ava laced her boots while Noah stashed the rope. "Funny how I swam, but you three are just as wet." Ava started walking.

Back on rear guard, Mason chuckled. *Yeah, I'm soaked to the bone. This is just one reason I try to be in the Cave for these storms. Avoiding death by tornado still tops the list.*

A half hour of travel after the wolf pup rescue, Chloe signaled a halt and crouched low. She peered into the forest to the west, rifle held at low ready. Awaiting further information from her, everyone else scanned their quadrant with weapons ready.

Mason scanned the ninety degrees to their rear. *Why did Chloe call a halt? I'm finding it tough seeing anything in this heavy rain. Hold on, was that a flash of purple to the northeast? How about a slow scan through the rifle scope . . . damn it, all I see is already soaked forest getting more wet.*

"Sorry team," Chloe said, "I thought I saw someone wearing a cape moving parallel to us, but after deliberating, it was only wind and rain. We can proceed."

Mason's brain verged on putting something together. He grabbed Chloe's arm as she started to turn and stand. "Wait, a cape or a cloak?"

Chloe shook his hand off. "Chill out. I don't know if I saw a cape or cloak, since either can flap around in the wind. What's the difference, anyway? Are you defining the cloak as having a hood?"

"How about the color? What color did you see?" Mason asked.

Chloe responded carefully, as though afraid to set Mason off. "That's what got my attention. You don't see a lot of purple around here."

"Fuck!" Noah said, swinging his carbine to high ready and scanning his quadrant through the scope.

Finally he lost his cool, not sure I'm happy to have discovered his threshold. Mason motioned Chloe and Ava to stay low and to scan. "Only the End Timers go around in purple cloaks."

"You mean the ones who preach that humanity has overstayed its visit on planet Earth?" Ava asked with a quaver in her voice.

Noah continued scanning through his scope. "Those are the ones. Cave Family last ran into them a few years ago. Eight of the family were on a long range scavenging mission. After a fierce firefight, the four survivors traveled weeks to return to the Cave. That's how long it took them to shake the End Timer trackers."

"Umm, Mason, I hate to pile on but…" Chloe pointed to the sky toward the Cave.

Mason looked at the sky. Three funnel clouds formed off in the distance, twisting together in the beginning of a macabre dance. Only a faint howl was discernable, since the tornadoes were not close enough to voice their full force. *The supercell is nearly upon us. This is how it started ten years ago, same funnel count, same far away howl. That time nearly cost my life. Stay cool, man, stay cool. Do not cut and run, you have a team counting on you.* Although adrenaline flooded his body, Mason brought his entire will to bear and pushed back the primitive instinct to run and hide. The thunder that rumbled in the distant southwest earlier now surrounded them. Lightning flicked here and there across the horizon, the nearby strikes followed immediately by thunder you felt on your chest.

Mason ground his teeth. *This is turning out to be the mission of impossible choices. Run for shelter from the storm, but risk leading the End Timers to the Cave? Lead the End Timers away, but risk dying in the storm? What's the most applicable Rule? Oh yeah, "Live for the family and the family will live for you." We cannot lead them to the Cave.* "We're ditching our packs and making an indirect run for the Cave. This storm will mostly obscure our tracks. If we spot any End Timers, we deviate further and keep doing so until we're sure they're not following before we loop back toward the Cave. Fire if fired upon or if they get close, because you do not want to be captured by these people."

Everyone ditched their packs under a nearby pine and formed up, scanning their quadrant with weapon at low ready. Mason tapped Chloe on the shoulder to get her attention. "Take point and run us due south for a klick. If there aren't any End Timers, we'll run in the creek for a hundred meters just to be sure before turning toward the Cave."

Chloe gave a thumbs-up and took off double-time; the rest of the team followed.

Powered by adrenaline and without their packs weighing them down, the team covered a klick of rough country in five minutes. The howl of the wind increased with every step. No one spotted End Timers and no one fired on the team, or at least no one got shot and they didn't hear any bullets whiz past.

Chloe stopped, Ava and Noah stacking up with her. When Mason arrived, she peered meaningfully at him.

Wow, was that a klick already? I hate making this decision based on a lack of input, almost easier to have seen End Timers and know we had to run from them. Lacking a reason not to, he waved her forward.

Off she led the team, running in a rocky creek bed for a hundred meters to obscure their trail.

Emerging from the brush surrounding the creek, the team saw a funnel threatening to touch down on top of them. The wind was a deafening shriek. Mason clenched his fist to keep the self-control he had fought for minutes ago. *Althea once described tornado noise as Mother Nature screaming her anger at humanity for what we did to the Earth. It is a fitting analogy, since only supernatural force could generate this massive energy and apocalyptic volume.* Blueberry-sized hail bombarded them, team members shouting out in pain each time they were hit. Fortunately, from here it was a straight shot west to the Cave. "Run for the Cave!" Mason shoved each of them forward to jar them free from the paralyzing grip of fear.

Chloe set a punishing pace no one complained about, the team arriving at the Cave fifteen minutes after leaving the creek. The tornado passed on the opportunity to pick them up and throw them to their deaths.

The team entered the Cave, coming upon Owen Garcia posted on watch. For years now, watch duty had meant nothing more than keeping inquisitive animals from following their noses into the Cave.

Mason wiped water from his drenched hair and face. "Good to see you, Owen. The storm is a solid seven on the nasty scale. Three funnel clouds are dancing."

"I hear it howling like a banshee," Owen said. "Good thing my watch is inside rather than outside. The leaders issued a no exit order a few hours ago. Your team was the last of the family outside."

"Unfriendlies may have followed us," Mason said sheepishly. "Noah and Ava will stay here to support you on guard duty until I can talk to the leaders about rotating in replacements."

Owen gawked at Noah; waiting for the usual punchline.

Noah, all business for once, focused on finding the best place to perch his carbine for both cover and line of sight on the entrance.

Owen's eyes narrowed, and he turned back to Mason. "This isn't a joke or a drill, is it?"

Noah paused in looking for the perfect perch to stare at Owen. "End Timers. Yes, the End Timers, might be right behind us. Keeping skunk and porcupine out of the Cave is the least of our concerns tonight. Matter of fact, we should let them in and give them pistols to defend our home."

Owen, without another word, joined Noah and Ava in finding cover with an acceptable line of fire.

Mason motioned Chloe into the caves. "Come on, you can help me gather the leaders to their conference room."

By splitting up, he and Chloe found the leaders and ushered them to the conference room in fifteen minutes. Name dropping "End Timers" encouraged surprising cooperation.

Located next to the Big Cave used for large gatherings, the conference room was a relatively small cave. No signs or rules restricted it to leadership use, people simply honored exclusive use out of respect. The nicest large table Cave Family scavenged filled the center of the room. A mishmash of what Grandpy Max called "fancy chairs for office workers" surrounded the table.

Mason sat waiting with two of the leaders, Grandpy Max and Robert, when Chloe brought in Althea.

Althea glanced at the faces of her fellow leaders and tsk-tsked as she walked to her seat. "OK, Mason, you scared the crap out us with talk of those crackpot End Timers. Now spill the details. "

Mason made direct eye contact with each elder before beginning. "We tracked Zoey's attackers from the northeast far garden to a home another hour's walk northeast. The bandits rested there in an underground bunker rigged up for growing vegetables with solar powered lights. They left via an exit tunnel unknown minutes or hours prior to us. The trail gone cold and upon seeing the incoming storm, I aborted the hunt to turn the team back toward safety in the Cave."

"After hiking two hours on the return trip, Ava rescued some wolf pups from drowning and returned them to their mother. We then resumed our hike to the Cave." Tilting his hand to toward Chloe, Mason continued. "Two to three klicks out, Chloe thought she caught a glance of someone wearing a purple cape or cloak moving parallel to us and called a halt. I also noticed purple behind us, but the quick flash of color in the heavy rain made me doubt what I saw. Putting our two potential sightings together points to End Timers in the area. I decided we should ditch our packs and use an indirect route back here, watching for End Timers and deviating if we spotted any. We double timed it due south for about a klick plus another hundred meters in the rocky creek bed. From there, we headed due west to the Cave because there was no sign of the End Timers."

Mason took a deep breath and exhaled before concluding. "There's no way I can make amends if I led the End Timers here. I tried to balance protecting the Cave's location and wanting to get my team home safe."

Robert raised his eyebrows and looked at Grandpy Max and Althea. They each barely perceptibly shook their heads, giving him the lead. "We'll want details about the bunker once things settle," Robert said. "For now, we need to focus on the potential End Timer sighting. With two of you each seeing purple in different directions, it is likely they are here. Cave Family needs to prepare."

"Mason, you did everything right," Althea said. "If the End Timers even came within five klicks of the Cave, our gardens and well-used trails would lead them straight here. We have made little to no effort to keep our location secret."

Grandpy Max added, "Your team prevented them from surprising us. Your warning may save Cave Family. Althea, Robert, and I will take care of setting a strong guard at the entrance. Tell your team to get some rest, since everyone might be called upon tomorrow."

"Umm, Mason, the paper?" Chloe asked.

"Oh, yes, Chloe found a piece of paper in the bunker," Mason said. "It seemed to be new, likely dropped by the bandits. Do you still have it?"

Chloe pulled the paper out and handed it over to Grandpy Max. "Sorry, it got a little wet."

Grandpy Max unfolded it on the table, everyone leaning in to get a better look.

Groups of four lines and slashes filled the top half of the page, whereas the bottom half was just a series of numbers.

Robert tapped the top of the page. "Someone was counting something here. Each group of lines and a slash is five. The total is one hundred thirty-four."

"It doesn't seem relevant to us. We have nothing of that number," Grandpy Max said. "Our population is right on our Dunbar hundred fifty target."

Chloe cleared her throat and waited for everyone's attention. "One hundred thirty-four is only four short of the Cave Family members old enough to venture regularly outside the caves."

"That's a workable theory." Grandpy Max motioned at the bottom half of the page. "How about this lower list of numbers? There's thirty of them ranging from twenty-five to a hundred."

Althea pounded the table with her fist. "Dammit, someone has been taking count of our people and food growing capability. That second list is our gardens' sizes, they're only missing a couple."

Grandpy Max looked puzzled. "I thought Zoey's attackers were wearing regular clothes? The End Timers never hide their identity."

"Why not? On the face of it, they want to recruit or force everyone to take up their cause. Why would they care about how they achieve that?" Chloe asked.

"You have to understand their faith," Althea said. "Their religion focuses on the ultimate end of Homo sapiens on Earth in exchange for advancing to a higher state of being. They believe your conduct in this life dictates your ascension station. Since inappropriate behavior can prevent ascension, they have a strict code of conduct: no deceit, no theft, and no dishonor."

"Oh, umm, I understand. Disguise is deceit," Chloe said.

Robert made eye contact with Grandpy Max and then Althea. "We have much to discuss, Mason and Chloe. Thank you for bringing this information forward."

Mason and Chloe thanked the leaders and left them to the business of protecting Cave Family. As they exited the conference room, someone departed the neighboring cave and walked away from them. Mason recognized Walker John. "Hey Walker, how's it going?"

"Oh, hey, Mason and Chloe," Walker turned and said. "I'm glad you made it back in one piece. Word was your team got caught outside in a tornado."

"Yeah, a close call," Mason said. "I wasn't sure if we were going to drown in the deluge, get killed by hail, or have a funnel drop on top of us."

Walker shrugged. "Well, we're all glad none of those things happened. Thanks again for bringing me to Cave Family." He turned and left.

Chloe tilted her head and narrowed her eyes. "He's not friendly. We didn't even get to tell him about the wolves. What was he doing in there, anyway? Doesn't he work in the kitchens and have quarters near them? That's on the other side of the caves."

Chloe had piqued Mason's curiosity. "You're right, let's take a peek."

They peered into the small cave Walker John had vacated. It was on the opposite side of the conference room from the Big Cave. There wasn't much to see, nothing but a chair and table with a half-finished solitaire game. As with most non-critical spaces in the caves, some LED bulbs were missing from the string; the entire back third in this case.

Mason shrugged. *Nothing to see here. We need to wrap this up and get some rest before the storm ends, since we might have End Timers to deal with.* He made a snap judgement. "Walker has had it rough since leaving his old home territory out west, so maybe he just needs time alone."

Chloe scanned the room a second time. "That's probably it," she said, although doubt was clear in her voice. "He just wants a break from the hustle and bustle around the kitchen. Let's gear down and rest."

CHAPTER THIRTY-SEVEN – 08:00 June 8, 2070 – The Color Purple

. . . there is no fanatic like a religious fanatic.
Agatha Christie, 1974

Someone was calling him over and over. They wouldn't leave, no matter what he said or did. At last, they stopped calling for him, but now he was drowning. Mason awoke thrashing and spluttering. He looked around in a panic, afraid he was waking in a lake. *Just me on my bed, in my cave, home safe home; get a grip.*

Chloe stood over him, a cup in hand, looking ashamed. "Sorry, I tried to wake you up, but you were dead to the world. I threw water on your face to rouse you. A bunch poured into your nose and mouth."

Mason was still groping at full consciousness after abruptly departing deep sleep. "What's happening? Why did you get me wet again? I just dried off from being tornado soaked."

Chloe fussed with the empty cup. "There's no way to make this easy, so I'll tell you straight up—the End Timers are here. Well, to be precise, one is here. He wants to talk to the entire team."

The phrase "End Timers are here" flooded Mason with adrenaline, awakening him. "What? Why us?" he asked Chloe.

"I'm just the messenger," Chloe said over her shoulder as she turned to exit. "You need to ask the End Timer at the Cave entrance what they want."

Mason pulled on his clothing and hustled to the Cave entrance, catching up with Chloe a few steps before the entrance room. Owen, Taanvir, and some others arrayed themselves behind cover, each holding a rifle or carbine trained on the Cave entrance. Mason stepped outside. The weather was completely the opposite of yesterday evening's life-threatening chaos of tornados. The sun beamed in a clear blue sky. Bird songs and calls echoed in the forest surrounding the Cave entrance. Plant parts covered the ground, but here there weren't any signs of wholesale destruction.

A purple-cloaked figure stood motionless in the center of the small clearing outside the Cave entrance. A hood hid their face. As soon as Mason arrived, the End Timer flipped their hood back and spread their arms wide. "Finally, the valiant team lead called Mason. I am brother Matthias of the End Timers. Greetings Mason, Ava, Chloe, and Noah. We enjoyed observing your mission and safe return yesterday. The Almighty has favored you. Spotting two of us during the storm was impressive, since we observed Cave Family for weeks without detection before that."

After making his greeting, Matthias folded his arms and stood in silence.

Mason just stared at him, because this was his first look at an End Timer. *Who is supposed to speak for Cave Family? Am I the senior person here?* For the first time since exiting the Cave, he looked to both sides of the entrance. All three leaders were present and flanked by armed Cave Family members. *Ah, not the senior person by far. Good. Have the End Timers really been watching us for weeks with no one noticing? Are we really that clueless or are the End Timers that stealthy?*

The leaders whispered amongst themselves. "Yes, yes, we have heard the flowery End Timer speeches before," Althea finally spoke. "Now, tell us why you are here."

Matthias turned his attention to the leaders. "Greetings leaders Althea, Robert, and Grandpy Max. We are here at your summons, of course. Did you not send scouts days of travel away to draw us from our usual travels, always staying far ahead but never leaving us behind? Did you not mark your trails ten kilometers out with every crucial fork drawing us here? Business we will discuss, but why so rushed? The Almighty has plans within plans within plans for us to discern only with the passing of time. The era of humanity on this planet is ending, but the departure is not imminent. Enjoy this time gifted to us by the Almighty."

Mason glanced at the leaders. *They seem as puzzled as I am. Cave Family doesn't have scouts ranging that far away, and even if we did, no one would purposely lead End Timers to the Cave. And what's this about trail markings? Was that stack of rocks I saw on the mission a marker?*

Matthias took a slow step to one side, exposing the team's abandoned packs. "We brought your property back to you. I fear everything is soaking wet, since the storm yesterday was a glorious demonstration of our Father's power."

No one from Cave Family took action. Mason opted to stay put.

"Well, come along. We are not thieves, and I will discuss nothing further until we return your property." Matthias gestured at the packs.

Everyone peered at Mason. Under Cave Family protocol, the team lead handles team business. *By the way everyone is staring at me, we are perceiving this as my team's business. Best I test the water before exposing my team to danger.* Mason swallowed his nervousness, signaled the team to stay put, and went to grab his pack. Not yet seeing reason for incivility, he nodded to Matthias. "Thanks for retrieving our packs." Safely back with Cave Family outside the entrance, he signaled the others to retrieve their packs.

Once Noah, Ava, and Chloe returned with packs in hand, Matthias bowed his head in silence for a moment. When he returned his gaze to Cave Family, his demeanor changed. He stood taller and prouder. His eyes lit up with religious fervor. His prior preachy speech cadence shifted to a firm, commanding voice. "It matters not whether you summoned the End Timers or the Almighty brought us here. I will now tell you how the lost souls you call Cave Family will attain their rightful place among the End Timers."

[End Book One Status Quo]

UTOPIA - KESA

CHAPTER THIRTY-EIGHT – 05:00 June 7, 2070 – A
Ghost Flits into View
Sometimes the best hiding place is the one that's in plain sight.
Stephenie Meyer, 2010

Kesa glared at Phoenix Fireteam and kicked Noah's jump seat to wake him. "You all look like shit warmed over. I hope appearances are deceiving because we have a critical mission." The rest of the team, Mason, Willow, and River, looked barely more alert than Noah. In contrast, the crew of the Joint Special Actions' C-57 VTOL transport bustled around the plane performing pre-flight checks.

"Hey, you ordered us to be on the C-57 and ready for liftoff at 05:00. You didn't mention being pretty or chipper," Noah said. "Given we were all in deep, deep sleep at Blue Spruce barely an hour ago, I think we did all right."

Mason punched Noah in the shoulder. "Aww, did Noah not get enough beauty sleep?"

Kesa gave Noah a stern look. "Listen up. I assume you are dying to know why we are taking off on short notice. At 03:00, the JSA naval sentry AI flagged a ghost ship that showed up on Global-S-AIS. We're hunting the Nisshin Maru 2."

Kesa waited for reactions from the team, especially Noah. An avid SCUBA diver and ocean conservationist, he wasn't shy about expressing his low opinion of those who consumed shark fin products. Mason perked up, now interested in the briefing. The newest team members, River and Willow, looked confused. Noah's expression darkened and his eyes narrowed. *Oh, oh, that's not a good sign. Time to share what it took to include him.*

"Noah, JSA leadership and I are well aware of your passion for protecting whales, dolphins, and sharks," Kesa said. "You are here instead of home in your bed dreaming because I vowed complete faith in your ability to stay professional on this mission."

Noah stared back at her. "Not a problem. I can confidently state that investigators will trace the Nisshin Maru 2's sinking to the accidental detonation of her fuel tanks."

Given the open-mouthed surprise on everyone else's face, Kesa wasn't the only one who was unsure how to respond.

Noah peered around, stone faced, for a few seconds before breaking into a grin. "What, can't a guy make a joke? Your faith is well-placed, Kesa. I will not perpetrate any destruction on this mission without your orders."

Kesa and the rest of the team heaved a collective sigh of relief.

"So I understand Noah promises not to blow up a ship that he definitely wants to blow up," Willow said, "but that's about it. Can you give River and I context? It seems there's history from before we joined Phoenix, and this is our first nautical mission."

Kesa was relieved to review base intel. "The Nisshin Maru 2 is the last whaling ship on the planet. Besides whaling, it fishes for dolphin and shark. They cut the fins off the sharks and dump the shark bodies because of the slim demand for shark meat."

Noah leaned forward, fire in his eyes. "They don't even mercy kill the sharks. They dump them back in the ocean to die a slow, painful death."

"This situation split AsiaPac leadership," Kesa said. "Supporting the harvest are the traditionalists, plenty of whom consume the catch, and the corporations who resist government interference. The opposing progressives despise what the Nisshin Maru 2 symbolizes: disregard for humanity's role as stewards of the Earth and unbridled corporate greed."

River waved his hand, speaking when Kesa made eye contact. "Why are we taking an AsiaPac ship? Won't it turn into an international incident?"

"Great question," Kesa said. "As Alliance operators, we must stay aware of the potential consequences of our actions. The progressives in AsiaPac's government assured the Alliance they support the ship seizure. Regardless, the trespass under false identity provides solid legal grounds."

"As the tip of the spear, we aren't required to be informed, but curiosity is killing me. What are the grounds?" Willow asked.

"Not a problem," Kesa said. "We're in the air for four hours and you are all security cleared for this information. Are you familiar with Global-S-AIS?"

Willow shook her head.

"A worldwide treaty thirty years ago required all oceangoing vessels to report their position twenty-four seven. The Global-S-AIS system collects from the approved transceivers and reports the data. The Nisshin Maru 2 transceiver showed up for just an hour, replaced by the Furaingu Datchiman in the same location. That ship purports to be an AsiaPac private oceanography research ship. Alliance analysts verified the registration, insurance, crew manifest, and sponsorship from a second tier university in Japan were all in order. They also verified that no shipyard ever built the Furaingu Datchiman, proving the Nisshin Maru 2 has masqueraded as it for thirty years. Analysts backtracked the Furaingu Datchiman's position. It transmitted false registration for several weeks in Alliance waters off British Columbia and Alaska. That's excellent grounds for seizure."

Noah pounded his fist on his armrest. "Unbelievable, a whaling ship pretending to be scientists following gray whale migration routes!"

Kesa stared at him with narrowed eyes. The other teammates' eyes widened and mouths dropped open.

Noah shrugged. "You prefer I release anger rather than bottling it up, right?"

Kesa nodded slowly. *Vouching for Noah's ability to stay professional on this mission may have been a career limiting move.* Mason made eye contact with her. With the hope he wanted to change topics, she signaled for him to go ahead.

"We want to bring the Nisshin Maru 2 to justice. What's the boarding plan?" Mason asked.

Kesa was glad to switch to the mission details. "Given this ship's illegal status and activities, we assume armed guards are mixed in with the civilian crew. Fast-roping to take the deck after strafing to clear it is out. Fortunately, the JSA gearheads were itching for a team to try something they put together with Zeagle." As she spoke, she walked over to a couple of skids and flung back the covering tarps.

"Whoa, are we planning to board them or blow them out of the water with these torpedoes?" River asked.

Noah jumped up to poke and prod the gear. "These aren't torpedoes, they are sea scooters on steroids. See these outer shell contours for the diver to straddle and the plexiglass shielding for cover at high-speed? What's top speed?"

A gearhead herself, Kesa shared the specifications. "Top speed is thirty knots, but the battery only lasts a half hour running flat out. Fifteen knots maximizes the range, since the battery lasts for ninety mikes. Each scooter mates to a clip-on sensor, so if you slip off, it will circle back to you." She passed out the sensors to the team.

Noah whistled low. "Thirty knots is double the better commercial sea scooters, and a hundred fifty percent of the current top military model."

"The JSA analysts gamed this out. They determined a stealth boarding is the lowest risk option," Kesa said.

Noah powered a scooter up and browsed the control screen. "Tell us how these babies factor in."

"Before we are in the Nisshin Maru 2's radar range," Kesa said, "the C-57 will slow and fly barely above the water. Between our stealth mods and flying low, we should avoid showing up on their radar until we are within sight. There, we'll deploy the team from a hover using the turbofan spray to cover our entry. To justify the hover, the C-57 crew shall contact them and demand surrender. Chances are they'll run, but these scooters can catch them since intel says our prey's top speed is twenty knots. While we scale the ship with magnetic climbers, the C-57 distracts them. At first, it will flit at the edge of countermeasures effectiveness for surface-to-air missiles. After nullifying or discounting SAM threats, the C-57 will swoop over them to draw their attention and small arms fire."

"Better the C-57 armor takes a pounding than us," Mason said.

Kesa scanned Phoenix Fireteam. Everyone gave her a thumbs-up. *Phoenix is good to go. Now I need to audit the JSA analyst plan to verify a high probability of success and zero team casualties. The Nisshin Maru 2 no doubt has armed tangos aboard.* "I'm going to review the mission plan. Mason and Noah, make sure the team has weapons, rebreathers, and scooters ready to deploy before 09:00."

CHAPTER THIRTY-NINE – 09:00 June 7, 2070 – The Best Laid Schemes

Just as you must mess up your enemy's battle plan, count on them to mess up yours.
Willow Taylor aka Ice, 2070

Kesa removed her C-57 comms network headset after getting the "go" from the co-pilot. She flashed ten fingers high to make sure everyone saw the signal. "Ten seconds to deployment."

Each team member sat ready in their dive gear atop a torpedo-like prototype underwater scooter in the back of the C-57. They attached their weapons to heavy-duty stainless steel D-rings on the dive gear to avoid losing them to the current. The crew member Kesa had selected as the most detail oriented gave her a thumbs-up. She had assigned him to confirm the team's rebreathers were ready to dive. *You must select the right person for each task. A bad rebreather setup is more often deadly than not.*

Kesa mounted her scooter and put on her face mask. She activated her comms. "Comms check." Their full face masks with secure integrated comms allowed for crystal clear verbal communication. The tech was much better than line of sight limited signing or dive slate scribbles.

"Viper, this is Ice, roger, over," said Willow.

"Viper, this is Fire, roger, over," said River.

"Viper, this is Fist, roger, over," said Mason.

Kesa looked at Noah, waiting for his comms check. *He's screwing around with his scooter's control panel, probably cranking the settings to top performance.* She signaled a nearby crew member to hand over their clipboard and whipped it at Noah.

"Ouch," Noah said when the clipboard bounced off his head. "OK, OK. Viper, this is Boomer, roger, over."

Kesa made eye contact with the crew chief and chopped her hand toward the cargo door.

Mason's scooter was first in the deployment chute. The crew kicked out the chocks preventing it from sliding down a plastic channel leading to the edge of the open rear cargo door. Their C-57 hovered two meters above the peak of the three meter swells rising and falling below them. The four turbofans kicked up a cloud of spray, obscuring the view from those on the Nisshin Maru 2 a couple nautical miles away.

"Three. Two. One. Go, go, go," said the crew chief. The crew shoved Mason's scooter down the slide, it nose-dived into the ocean. In short order, the crew kicked out the remaining chocks and shoved the others down the slide, one by one.

Kesa was the last down the chute. Astride her falling scooter, she entered the dark blue water with a splash and sank fast to ten meters before achieving neutral buoyancy. The twelve degree Celsius water felt icy even through her dry suit. The team had opted against a thick thermal under layer to preserve mobility for the boarding. She made a few quick equalizations as she descended, gently forcing air into her middle ear to balance out the increasing water pressure.

The turbofan wash from the C-57 hummed above, the noise subdued by the meters of water between Kesa and the surface. Operating on autopilot, their sea scooters oriented toward the target two nautical miles away. The scooters coordinated position and heading, forming a single file line to minimize their collective sonar profile. Kesa's scooter took its designated position at the rear of the line. *I hope this single file business turns out to be an unnecessary precaution. The JSA advised these prototypes have an active sonar-defeating anechoic coating. We also set the trip profile to travel below the thermocline to obscure sonar.*

Now in formation, the scooters accelerated to top speed.

"Whoo hoo," Noah said over the short range team comms. He was the team's most experienced diver.

Kesa didn't feel the same. *I'm glad Noah's having a good time, but I'm just working on staying on my scooter. The others are eerily quiet, so I best make contact to verify everyone's head is still in the game.* "Comms check."

The team responded in their predetermined order, everyone with a confident tone.

Kesa sighed in relief with her comms disabled. The display on her scooter showed an ETA of six and a half minutes. Comms back on, she said, "The target isn't running full throttle, prepare to latch onto your assigned position on the hull and climb in six and a half mikes."

"Attention Furaingu Datchiman," the C-57 co-pilot said over the shared comms feed. "You are in Alliance waters and subject to random inspection. Idle your engines and prepare to be boarded."

Kesa waited in anticipation. She, the pilot, and the co-pilot planned this one-time offer for the situation to resolve "the easy way." *Come on, take the offer. Nobody has to die today. Prove me wrong when I told the C-57 crew that people that do the wicked things you do aren't likely to surrender.*

"I'm on the Phoenix private channel now," the co-pilot said. "We're monitoring the public bands. No response yet." She continued after a brief pause. "The ship hasn't changed speed or direction, but we're seeing activity on deck." Another pause, this one followed by a shout, "Oh shit, MANPADS! There's three missiles in the air; we're taking evasive action and launching countermeasures."

Kesa couldn't firsthand see or hear any of the above surface activity. The only detectable noise was the nearby high pitch whine of the scooter motors. The team's closed-circuit rebreathers didn't even make detectable bubble noises.

To keep the team aware of topside events, the co-pilot continued the play-by-play. "Deployed smoke, flares, and launched frag drones. Initiating directed laser interference."

In the comms feed, the C-57's four turbofans roared as the pilot ran them full out in evasive maneuvers.

Seconds later, a crump and a noise like hail on a vehicle's roof, followed at once by a jarring boom, came over the comms feed. The co-pilot shouted over the beeping and wailing of several C-57 systems in alarm condition. "Our frag drone took one missile out but punched a few holes in our own armor. The directed laser tricked a missile into the water. The laser guided third missile ignored all the countermeasures and took out one of our turbofans. From what we see on the ship's deck, they blew their MANPAD load and are down to small arms."

Kesa ground her teeth before replying. "Are you out of the fight?"

"We're down to sixty percent mission capability due to battery damage and the turbofan loss," the co-pilot said. "Running three turbofans far above efficient levels will drain charge aggressively. We can draw fire twenty mikes at most before heading to Anchorage for recharge and repair."

Kesa checked the ETA on the scooter's display. It drifted between four minutes fifteen seconds and four minutes thirty seconds before settling to count down from the latter. *The whaling ship must have accelerated to top speed, still no match for our scooters.* "C-57 stay on mission, roger on twenty mikes. We are boarding with a few spare mikes."

"Wilco, Viper. Starting flybys now to keep their eyes to the sky. The first round of drinks after action is on Phoenix Fireteam," the co-pilot said. For three and a half minutes over the open comms channel, the C-57 turbofans alternated from all three roaring at top speed to variations of one or two for tight turns. A storm of jangles sporadically erupted from small arms fire bouncing off the armor.

The scooter's display counted down to the estimated arrival, now just passing the one minute mark. Kesa keyed the comms. "Time your next flyby for fifty seconds. Make it a slow one since we'll be surfacing to transition onto shipside and need their attention on you."

After the co-pilot confirmed, Kesa flicked over to Phoenix comms. "Get ready to surface and climb. Inflate your BCD before you ditch your rebreather and keep your fins on until secured to shipside." On prior missions, Kesa saw several attempts to board moving ships in rough seas go sideways. Team members bounced off the ship's hull and floundered without fins or an inflated buoyancy control device.

The high-speed thud, thud, thud of the Nisshin Maru 2's propeller so far away for so long now sounded thunderous. The meters deep draft portion of the hull materialized out of nowhere when the scooters reached visible range seventy meters away. Kesa became concerned. *Please don't drive me straight into the nasty sixish meter diameter spinning propeller. Panic canceled; they're breaking their line formation, splitting two and two to each side of the ship.*

Kesa's scooter navigated to her boarding position, port side toward the bow. It surfaced an arms-length off the ship's metal hull. *This is snazzy specific purpose AI coupled with precision lateral thrusters. I've never seen a scooter able to hold this steady amongst the messy hydraulic beside a moving ship. Regardless, the scooter to hull transition is still a high-risk maneuver. Time to discover if being a sitting duck will earn me a bullet in the head.* Thankfully, no one was visible anywhere along the entire port side railing. The roar of the C-57's turbofans and the crew of the Nisshin Maru 2 firing at it remained out of sight but were now loud, no longer muffled secondhand through the comms.

Kesa inflated her BCD, clipped a line from the rebreather to the scooter, and popped the clips on the rebreather harness. Taking a steadying breath and sitting sidesaddle, she attached to the hull with her right hand magnetic clamp, her right knee, and then her left hand. She slid off the scooter, spider-climbed above the waterline, and ditched her fins. As soon as she activated the release switch on her scooter sensor, the scooter sunk to hold position thirty meters down awaiting support ship pickup.

Secure and ready to climb, Kesa turned toward the stern to check in on River. She was just in time to witness him mistime the swell peak and desperately grab for the hull instead of waiting for the next swell. The descending swell pulled him away from the hull before he could make contact. He slid off the scooter, dropping into the ocean and falling behind the Nisshin Maru 2, but his inflated BCD pulled him to the surface. He signaled OK by arching his arm beside him and touching his head with his fingertips. His scooter peeled off to circle back to him.

"Fire will be late to the party," Kesa said over the comms. "I am secure and climbing."

"Secure and climbing," said Willow and then Noah.

Kesa was relieved that only River could not latch onto the hull. "Hold just below deck level. We'll synchronize rolling on and attacking."

"Wilco," said Willow, echoed by Noah.

Adrenaline powered Kesa up the side of the ship. She didn't notice the weight of her gear. Barely breathing hard, she reached deck level and keyed her comms. "Ready at deck level. Status?"

"Ready," said Willow.

"Two seconds," panted Noah.

Kesa switched to the team's open channel with the C-57. "Phoenix ready. How's the deck?"

"Ten armed tangos interspersed with ten crew," the co-pilot said. "No one near your positions and all attention is on us. We're coming in low and hard in five seconds."

Kesa counted down over the comms. "Five, four, three, two, go!" She rolled onto the deck, coming to her feet with her HK517 Assaulter carbine at high ready as the C-57 roared overhead. Noah did the same starboard side across the bow from her. Equipment blocked her view of Willow.

Phoenix Fireteam's arrival was the last straw for the embattled crew. They assumed various positions of surrender, either flat on the deck or behind cover with hands up.

Kesa had four armed guards in sight, none of them aware of her. One oriented his carbine to fire at Noah. Kesa put a 7.62 mm bullet in his unarmored right shoulder to convince him of the error of his ways; he collapsed to the deck, holding his shoulder and screaming in pain.

Her shot made the other three aware of her presence. The smart guy dropped his carbine and raised his hands without even looking her way, folding down to kiss the ship's deck. The other two turned toward her with weapons held high ready. Kesa caught the first with a shot to the lower right of his vest and put a shot into the solar plexus of the second before she could line up Kesa. Both collapsed in pain, the first clutching his lower ribcage and the second dropping to her hands and knees while she tried to suck air back into her lungs. *Bingo, three single shot incapacitations; I love 7.62×51 mm for close quarters.*

Kesa crouched-walked over to each of the four tangos. She kicked their carbines a safe distance away, pointing her muzzle at their forehead while checking them for other weapons. Everyone understood the hint and lay still with their hands spread wide and empty. Three 7.62 round reports echoed from Noah's direction; two more from Willow's. The team's 7.62 reports interspersed with 5.56 from the guards, one from Noah's direction and three from Willow's. Noah controlled his quadrant, but Willow remained out of sight. Kesa glanced port side stern for threats. No tangos were visible. "Sitrep," she said over the comms.

"Quadrant is clear with two tangos down, but I need five mikes," Willow said painfully.

Noah looked Kesa's way and held a hand high with his thumb up. "Quadrant is clear, with three tangos down."

There was a fleshy thump from something hitting the deck behind her, followed by a carbine clattering across the deck. She looked port side stern.

River, lungs heaving, stepped out from behind some equipment to stand over the tenth guard's prostrate body. "One tango down, quadrant clear. Delayed to the party, but not late."

"Ice, you OK?" Kesa asked.

"My tangos had cover. I took three rounds in my body armor, so I'm working through cracked ribs and bruises," Willow said.

"Copy," Kesa said and paused. *Since Willow's hurt, she shouldn't take part in clearing the confined belowdecks. You never know when you're going to have to dive onto metal decking due to people with guns popping out from around corners.* "Ice and Boomer secure the deck. Fire and I will bring the control room staff out once we convince them to idle the ship and then we'll clear the belowdecks. Zip cuff everyone and collect them at deck center. Use crew for labor if you need." She tossed a bundle of zip cuffs at the closest crewmember. "Cuff everyone nice and tight and bring them to midship . . . unless you want to witness firsthand what I do when someone makes me angry?"

CHAPTER FORTY – 09:15 June 7, 2070 – Round Up & Poke Around

We cannot resist opening closed doors even after learning there are some we don't want to see behind.
Noah Cruz, 2070

Kesa surveyed the deck of the Nisshin Maru 2 from a central location. The disarmed guards and the crew were being cuffed by their comrades under Noah, Willow, and River's watchful eyes. There was nothing visible on deck to differentiate between research vessel, fishing trawler, or whaling ship. The incoming Alliance forensics team would investigate the piles of covered gear. *The crew covered everything topside to prevent overhead surveillance from exposing their true purpose. No surprise there.*

"C-57 to Viper, we're down to five mikes buffer for our trip to Anchorage base," the co-pilot said over the comms. "Your support ship is inbound ETA forty mikes. All tangos in our sight are subdued. Are we clear for departure?"

"All clear, return to base before you go black on sparks," Kesa said. "Thanks for the ride and air support." The C-57 roared off in a beeline to the Alliance Anchorage base. *Staying to cover for us when they are so close to safe energy limits was hard core; I'm going to have to send a commendation to their command.*

Noah shepherded crewmembers dragging three guards to midship. Two of the guards moaned in pain as they jostled along, but the third sagged, unspeaking.

Kesa raised her eyebrows at Noah.

"Dead dude wore his vest way too low," Noah said. "Besides, he wrecked my shirt." Noah pointed to his left shoulder, where a bullet tore his shirt and grazed his flesh.

Kesa shrugged. *Those who play with guns often get shot and sometimes get dead, no comment necessary about the kill.* "Does the wound need dressing?"

Noah shook his head. "Nah, I'm barely leaking. Let's wrap things up before anyone dreams up some genius plan and gets more people killed."

Kesa motioned the crewmember who zip-cuffed the others to approach. He came with his hands extended, ready for her to zip-cuff him. "No cuffs for you, we need you to guide and open doors," she said. "Control room first, you lead."

The crewmember lowered his trembling hands and set off toward the stairs up to the control room atop the ship's stern.

Kesa signaled River to take up the rear as they passed him. Two people watched their approach through the wraparound windows, both raising their hands when Kesa looked their way. "They know we're coming, Fire, but it seems they don't want trouble."

Kesa tried to monitor for threats from every direction while climbing the exposed stairs. Thankfully, no one fired on them. At the top, she held their guide back from opening the door until she felt Fire stack up behind her. Kesa rushed into the control room close behind their guide with Fire tight on rearguard. She held her carbine at low ready toward the two occupants. "The Alliance is seizing this ship for traveling in our waters under false identification."

"We are both unarmed. I am the captain and this is the first mate," the fortyish short haired captain said. She betrayed no signs of nervousness at having armed Alliance soldiers on her ship. The first mate was a man ten years her junior, also with close-cropped hair. He twitched and sweated but didn't appear dangerous, more like scared to the edge of pissing himself. Both held their hands up.

The captain spoke again, dispassionately as though having been through similar situations before. "You are aware the Furaingu Datchiman is an AsiaPac private research ship under the ownership of Mitsuitoda Corporation? You are willing to risk an international incident by seizing it?"

"Drop the charade. We know the ship's true name and purpose," Kesa said. "I'd advise you not to concern yourself about international politics, but you don't seem concerned about this seizure. Why is that?"

"I take ships where the corporation directs," the captain said. "My employer doesn't comply with the laws of the sea, so I am no stranger to incidents like this."

Kesa gestured at the controls. "Set the autopilot for minimum speed and a safe direction and then precede us down to the deck. How many people on this ship have weapons?"

The captain replied while slowing the engines. "Ten armed guards. You captured all of them and all but one of the crew. From the ill will I saw between the guards and crew this voyage, I do not think any of the crew wants to fight you."

The ship's controls now set up to await the support ship, Kesa waved their three prisoners to descend the stairs first. Noah occupied a vantage point on a railed deck one level up from the main to overwatch the prisoners. Willow prowled among them, holding her upper body rigid to avoid aggravating the broken ribs.

River handed their helpful crewmember zip cuffs for the captain and first mate. Once cuffed, River motioned them to sit with the rest of the crew.

"Now walk us through the below decks," Kesa said to the crewmember appointed as Phoenix helper. "Are there any traps, or is anyone going to shoot at us?"

"No traps that I am aware of. The sole crewmember left belowdecks is new. I don't know her well, but she doesn't seem the shooting type," the crewmember said, voice quivering. "She hesitated to make the kills required to fulfill her catch processing duty." He headed toward the stairwell door when Kesa gestured.

The crewmember led Kesa and River into the bowels of the ship. Kesa told the crewmember to slow down and often even stop while she and River cleared the rooms they passed. They reached the large catch processing room packed full of piping, conveyors, and hopper bins. *Now we discover what the Nisshin Maru 2 was doing. Do I really want to know? No choice now.* "Take us to the freezer."

The crewmember walked to the far end of the catch processing room, paralleling the travel of the conveyor belts and catch processing line. Kesa followed, dread increasing with each step. *All roads on a freezer trawler lead to the freezer.* The crewmember's demeanor changed. Before approaching the freezer, he exhibited composed fear, like he thought he would survive the day. Now he shook as he walked slower and slower. *This does not bode well.*

The crewmember cracked the freezer door open a few centimeters and stopped dead. Cold air rolled out, but the door wasn't ajar wide enough for Kesa to view inside. She stepped beside the crewmember on the latch side of the door and held her carbine at high ready. "Swing it open."

No one hid inside; edge-to-edge large bins were the only occupants. Cold air rolling out of the freezer chilled Kesa's skin; the contents of the bins chilled her soul. The two thousand cubic meter freezer was full of bins of shark fins, whole dolphins, slabs of dolphin flesh, and slabs of gray whale flesh. *What a fucking horror show! Damn good thing I stationed Noah up top, since he'd lose his shit seeing these species that he dedicates his free time to aid treated this way.*

Kesa felt River crowd up behind her, looking over her shoulder. He gasped and uttered an angry snarl. *Oh damn, the young hothead snapped.* Too late, she spun to intercept him. The crewmember fell to the deck beside her with blood gushing from a head wound.

River held his carbine reversed, hair trailing from the butt. "You fucking monster, how could you do this?" River drew back his leg, preparing to put the boots to the helpless crewmember.

Kesa pushed River away with a vigorous cross check using her carbine. "Enough soldier, control yourself."

"My family, my family," the crewmember said, holding his hands up high and wide.

"What, you don't want your family to find out the despicable things you do on this ship?" River roared.

"No, no, Mitsuitoda Corporation has my family," the crewmember said, sobbing. "They monitor all the crew's families and most of the guards'. If we don't serve their will, they will harm our families. You must arrest us all and publicize that we resisted, then maybe Mitsuitoda Corporation will keep our families safe to secure our silence."

The fire drained from River's eyes.

The intel also took Kesa aback. *Captain calm dropped a hint that most of those aboard this ship from hell are here under duress.* Kesa helped the crewmember up after inspecting the wound and finding it superficial. She closed the freezer door—no need for River to see more of the macabre scene within.

Kesa tried to console River. "The real criminals are the people who buy and consume this flesh. They believe it shows their wealth to their peers, brings them power or delivers special health benefits. Mitsuitoda Corporation profits from these delusions by forcing these workers to kill protected species."

"I shouldn't have been so quick to condemn the crew," River said. "I didn't consider they may have been unwilling participants."

The image of bins of shark fins forced itself back to Kesa's conscious mind. She succumbed to flames of rage in an outburst. "Shark finning became illegal worldwide thirty years ago to save sharks from extinction. I can't believe it took decades to capture the last ship flouting international law!"

"Boss, you OK?" River asked.

Kesa took a deep breath and tamped her feelings down. *The team lead is supposed to be an example of self-control, not lose control.* "I'm good," she said with forced calmness. She spotted a first aid kid on the wall, tossing a wad of gauze to the crewmember for his head wound.

As Kesa closed the kit, a timid voice called out from the center of the catch processing room. "Hello? Are you from the Alliance?"

Kesa took cover and scanned her side of the room, carbine high ready, but no one was visible. River mirrored on his side. "Yes, we are Alliance soldiers and control this ship," Kesa said. "Come out slowly with your hands held high."

"Oh, thank goodness." A rustling and banging ensued as someone extricated themselves from deep under a low shelf of a worktable. The missing crewmember emerged, empty hands above her head.

"I am Arakayo Cutknife, a Sea Shepherd operative first and AsiaPac citizen second," said the lean young woman. "Mitsuitoda Corporation will surely want me dead when they learn of my actions. I request political asylum from the Alliance." She spoke with the confidence and polish of someone who had rehearsed a speech many times.

The request intrigued Kesa. "What will Mitsuitoda Corporation be seeking revenge for?"

Arakayo stood tall. "Sea Shepherd sympathizers helped me to get hired for this sailing. I spent weeks searching in the middle of the night for this nightmare ship's real transceiver. Two nights ago, I found it. Last night, I activated it for one hour before hiding it where only I can show you. That's why you are here, right?"

"Correct," Kesa said. "Aren't you concerned about your family? This crewmember says all the families are under Mitsuitoda Corporation threat." She glanced at the crewmember. His eyes were wide and his jaw slack. *I hope that expression is the shock of learning of this spy in the midst rather than from a serious head injury.*

"He is telling the truth. Everyone on this ship except a few corporate zealots among the guards worked out of fear for their families. The Sea Shepherds moved my family to Alliance territory months ago. When Mitsuitoda's enforcers go to my family's AsiaPac home, they will find an empty apartment rented from one of their own corporations." Arakayo smiled.

Kesa heard enough for now; they needed to get topside before the support ship arrived. "My team is small, so we need to zip-cuff you and keep you with the other prisoners until the Alliance Coast Guard comes to take possession of the ship. We'll free you after we verify your identity with the Sea Shepherds."

Arakayo held her hands together to be zip-cuffed by her former crewmate. Her expression fell as she said, "I did such horrible things to execute this mission."

River put his hand on her shoulder. "You single-handedly stopped decades of atrocities. Mitsuitoda Corporation is losing this ship and subject to heavy additional financial and legal penalties. They won't be doing this anymore. The example the Alliance makes of them will deter other corporations from considering taking up the business."

Back up on deck, Kesa motioned Willow aside to speak where the prisoners could not overhear. "The woman claims to be a Sea Shepherd operative who initiated the transceiver signal leading us here. Isolate her and our helpful crewmember from the others until we can verify her ID and treat her right. The crewmember heard her true identity."

Willow shifted, grimacing in pain. "Wilco. If the crewmember was helpful, what's with the head wound?"

"Fire saw the contents of the catch freezer and expressed his displeasure on the crewmember's head," Kesa said ruefully. "I reacted too late to prevent the first hit, but I stopped him from adding to our body count for the day. Turns out Mitsuitoda Corporation holds the crew and guards' families as hostages to force them to fulfill their barbaric duties on this ship. How are you doing?"

"I'll be all right . . . in six weeks. For now, I am functional and grouchy."

"Square away these prisoners and brief Noah. Skip the details on the freezer. His duty is here guarding prisoners."

Willow ushered the additions to her and Noah's pool of prisoners to a safe spot and walked over to brief Noah. She wiggled a finger in a "naughty naughty" gesture at River as she passed.

Kesa's comms crackled to life. Someone was transmitting to her from the edge of her compact comms' range. "JSA Corporal James, this is Captain

Wayne of the British Columbia Coast Guard cutter God's Pocket. We are five mikes out from your position."

"Call me Viper, Captain," Kesa said. "Nice of you to come and wrap up for us. We seized a freezer trawler on behalf of the Alliance and hold twenty-two prisoners, a handful of whom need medical attention or a coroner. The whole mess is about to become yours, so I hope you brought sufficient resources to handle it?"

"Wilco, Viper," said Captain Wayne. "We can take your hand-off. Orders or not, we are pleased to cleanup for the famous Phoenix Fireteam."

"Excellent. I need you to locate JSA General Max Williams and link him up to me via a secure channel," Kesa asked.

"Viper, I hear congratulations are in order. Is your team OK?" Max asked over her comms two minutes later.

"Nothing more than cracked ribs, bruises, and a grazed shoulder," Kesa said. "I have a couple of special requests for you to wrap this situation up, sir."

"I'm glad your team is near intact. Loop me in if you need any treatment requirements expedited," Max said. "What are the requests?" he asked apprehensively.

"Mitsuitoda Corporation holds the crew and guards' families as hostages to force their labor," Kesa said. "If we publicize that the crew and guards resisted our seizure and refuse to cooperate, we will protect their families from the corporation. It may encourage the crew to offer useful information."

"Off the cuff, that sounds like a wise move. I'll advocate for it to the leadership. The other request?"

"One of the crew claims to be a Sea Shepherd operative. She says she initiated the true transceiver signal and I believe her. Can you verify Arakayo Cutknife is one of theirs? We're holding her with the other prisoners for now, so I want to cut her loose ASAP if she's legit."

"Well, we can't condone private organizations performing operations like this, but if her claim is true, she broke this whole thing wide open. We'll dig into it and work out a solution. Did you find evidence showing how far up the chain this goes at Mitsuitoda?"

"We're just about to sweep for intel. My gut says anything we find is going to trace back to lower-level managers. Whoever is really in charge of this is at the level where they lay a paper trail to sacrificial lambs. Maybe we'll get lucky with some HUMINT if we can manage our incident reporting to protect the crew's families."

"Contact me ASAP if you acquire useful intel. The JSA analysts are dissecting the digital existence of the Furaingu Datchiman and the Nisshin Maru 2. They'll uncover any links to anyone soon enough. Whoever's operation this was is going to be pissed, scared or both. We need to find out who it is to be prepared for retaliation and to hunt them down with AsiaPac friendlies' help, stat."

"Wilco. Viper out," Kesa said.

CHAPTER FORTY-ONE – 13:00 June 7, 2070 –
Meanwhile, Back at the Office

With power comes the abuse of power. And where there are bosses, there are crazy bosses.
It's nothing new.
Judd Rose

"They WHAT?" screamed Hideki Gao Yang, the infamously volatile CEO of Mitsuitoda Corporation.

Jun Aruita cringed. She was the fifth executive assistant to the CEO in the last year. The corporation expected up and coming junior managers to serve as long as they could as the CEO's EA as a combination of learning experience and trial by fire. "Sir, Phoenix Fireteam of the Alliance seized the Nisshin Maru 2. Our allies in AsiaPac leadership advise that the majority have opted to cooperate with the Alliance in bringing us to justice. They don't want to spend political capital defending what is being called the 'nightmare floating slaughterhouse' in the news. We stand alone in this matter."

"Gutless traitors. How much do we pay them to protect our interests in AsiaPac governance?" Hideki raged on, now hurling the latest batch of fragile and expensive desktop ornaments around his office overlooking Tokyo downtown.

Fortunately, none of the projectiles flew at her head. Jun didn't answer the CEO's rhetorical questions; she made that mistake only once. Silence was always the safest course of action, especially when objects were being thrown.

Destruction of the ornaments providing the needed catharsis, Hideki's jaw unclenched and the fiery red faded from his face. His expression shifted to his usual cold cunning. "The Nisshin Maru 2 operated for decades without detection. How did the Alliance find it?"

Jun had quickly learned the art of differentiating the questions needing answers versus the rhetorical. This question required an answer. "The Sea Shepherds recruited a sympathizer in our human resources department to add an operative to the Nisshin Maru 2 crew for this sailing. Our spies in the Alliance report someone activated the ship's real transceiver in Alliance waters. The Alliance hunted for this ship for a long time, so were eager for the catch. They moved on it with JSA assets before our spies even became aware of an operation. Media stories state the crew and guards resisted the seizure, suffering injuries and one death, and are not cooperating."

"Hmmm," Hideki said, "no doubt the crew and guards are keeping their families' safety top of mind. Is the sympathizer, their family, or the operative's family in our custody?"

Sour news was always best delivered direct, and the more dreadful the more direct. Jun tried to soften the blow once and suffered a half hour tirade about the EA's role. "They are all long gone, since the Sea Shepherds arranged for emigration to the Alliance weeks ago."

Hideki didn't even blink at this. Jun had observed that he assumed his adversaries were intelligent, and he didn't waste rage on the expected.

"Direct the head of security to formulate options to strike the Sea Shepherds in a manner that will not trace back to us," Hideki said. "We cannot risk striking the JSA, AsiaPac will serve us up on a platter if there is any whiff of our involvement. Who executed the recent Alliance police station bombing?"

Jun prided herself on being prepared for Hideki's questions, but this one was unexpected. Fortunately, as an avid news surfer, she recalled this Alliance incident as it was a top story even in AsiaPac. "The Birthers. A terrorist group fighting the half child rule in the Alliance."

"The Alliance is weak, coddling their lunatic fringe and allowing terrorists to spawn from herds of shallow thinkers. AsiaPac squashed half child protest decades ago. Well, their weakness is our opportunity." Hideki paused, narrowing his eyes before continuing. "Arrange a conversation between the Birther leadership and one of our off-book facilitators. They must pose as a wealthy Alliance benefactor needing anonymity to protect their reputation. Our facilitator shall not mention the corporation. Let's find out what might help the Birthers with their struggle against their oppressors, especially the JSA." Hideki smiled deviously as he issued the order.

"Yes, sir," Jun said. She maintained her outward composure only long enough to answer and leave the office. Out of Hideki's sight, she crumbled. *What have I gotten into? I wanted to be an important executive battling other corporations for profit and market share, not consorting with terrorists. Mother and father cautioned me about what went on in the secretive elite. Now our lives are forfeit unless I am complicit with Hideki's machinations. Damned if I do, dead if I don't. How do I fix this?*

[End Book One Utopia]

DEAN WHITFORD

ALMOST THE END

Did you enjoy Crossroads 2070? Please log into your Amazon and Goodreads accounts and leave a review!

If you didn't enjoy it, go to the contact page at deanwhitford.com and tell me why not.

THE END

About the Author

Dean Whitford is a senior program manager / software development manager with experience in a variety of engineering related realms. Nothing makes him happier than an elegantly designed and built application supported by efficient work processes. Dean writes for business by day, following up with articles and creative writing at night. To enable Dean's off-hours writing, his son Damon keeps the vehicles running and his wife Cheryl keeps the household functioning. Kona does her best to ensure that everyone has her needs top of mind. She's a bit of a bully.

Deanwhitford.com

About the Authors